CONFESSIONS OF A FAILED ENVIRONMENTALIST

Also by the Author

CONFESSIONS OF A FAILED ENVIRONMENTALIST

A NOVEL

Jennifer Ellis

MOONBIRD
PRESS

Cover Design by: Design for Writers
Editing by: David Gatewood

Moonbird Press

To make sure you get the latest information and offers from Jennifer Ellis, be sure to sign up for her email list. As a subscriber, you'll receive the latest updates, information on promotions, Advance Review Copies (ARCs) of Jennifer's books and bonus novellas, for free! So make sure you are subscribed. **Sign up on her website: www.jenniferellis.ca**

Book Layout © 2015 BookDesignTemplates.com

Confessions of a Failed Environmentalist/ Jennifer Ellis. -- 1st ed.
ISBN-13: (ebook) 978-0-9921538-8-5
ISBN-13: (print) 978-0-9921538-9-2

For everyone who has taught me to think more deeply about the earth...

CHAPTER ONE

The Bet

Alana Matheson drew daisies on her recycled paper while trying to concentrate on the voices on the speakerphone on her desk. The mid-afternoon sun cut a brilliant swath of white on the floor of her office, and she could see the edges of the glorious blue sky through the window. She stretched her toes out until they were bathed in light and warmth and stared at her seed packets laid out and organized on the floor. She wanted more than anything to be out in the garden turning over the soil, breathing in the peaty sweet scents of spring and letting the cool earth fall through her fingers.

Rita's voice came over the speakerphone. "We really have to think of the optics of using that much paper. We should talk to other people in town about innovative ways to message out. *Greg Wilson* has some good ideas on how to get information out there."

The undercurrent in Rita's voice, and her emphasis on "Greg Wilson," suggested that she thought Alana *never* had good ideas. Greg Wilson was the new, and apparently hot—but not in the attractive sense, although she had never met him, so knowing her luck, he was an Adonis as well—sustainability expert in town. Greg had the balls to call himself an expert, whereas Alana merely billed herself as a consultant.

Alana rubbed her sweaty palms on her bamboo skirt. The clock read 2:26. Still time to walk to the school to pick up Katie and Duncan. Well, time to awkwardly run-walk to the school anyway. It was already far too late to stroll with her face tipped to the sun, to feel some glimmer of connection with the natural world that she was apparently working to protect. But the monthly Regional Environmental Board conference call showed no signs of ending. The board members were now engaged in a circuitous debate about whether or not it was ecologically appropriate to print their already graphically designed and written newsletter, rather than just maintain a web presence.

That was what happened when people crossed the line into uber-environmental consciousness; when they *knew* the world was caught in a shit cloud of human destruction. They got panicky and lost perspective and started to overthink every little thing—although the ones who smoked a lot of weed managed to keep it under control better. Alana decided it would be unproductive to mention that, for all the money and time they'd already wasted discussing the issue, they could have dug a well in Kenya and bought a few goats to boot.

She was the coordinator of the board, which basically meant that she had to execute on every half-baked plan they decided was a good idea. When she took the job, she had hoped it would involve steering the board to the best decisions possible, but the board made decisions by consensus minus one, and she was the minus one. Although she could make "suggestions," the board members didn't usually like her suggestions. They didn't like each other's suggestions either, except, occasionally, the ones Alana considered exceptionally bad, so generally everyone was unhappy.

She slid her cork sandals out from under her desk and slipped them on as silently as possible while someone noodled about the importance of doing the right thing. The call was supposed to have ended at two. She considered slipping out, getting the kids, and returning to the call without telling them. But knowing her luck, this call would be the one time when they actually decided to ask her opinion on something.

To Alana, it seemed that the board often spent more time wringing their hands about sustainability than they did doing anything to actually *achieve* sustainability. She just wanted to *do* things—ban plastic bags in town, garden, buy solar panels, build bike trails—without so much discussion. Even if half the things they did were the wrong things, those actions would better prepare the region for the end of the world than would perfecting the words on their website splash page. Last week the board had spent two hours—two hours!—discussing why only twelve people had showed up to the invasive weed pull last fall. They felt it had something to do with inadequate advertising or messaging. Alana felt it had something to do with the fact that few people wanted to spend a gorgeous Saturday pulling invasive weeds. But what did she know? She only had a Masters degree in Geography. Greg Wilson and Fiona Granger, her other local competition, had professional degrees and a multitude of more relevant-seeming acronyms behind their names, like R.P.Bio., P.Ag., C.I.P. and M.B.A.E.S. She should just start making some up and adding them to hers, like H.T.J.D.S. for "hoping to just do something."

In a desperate attempt to steer the meeting to a close, she interrupted the noodler, who generally didn't like being interrupted. "Look, guys, we agreed we have to communicate," Alana said. "It's unfortunate that it uses some paper, but you get upset when people don't know what the board is doing. Why don't we just proceed?"

An ominous silence ensued.

The noodler resumed talking. "As I was saying. We have to find other ways to really get people excited about sustainability, like a potluck or community meeting. We should really consider bringing in some experts."

Alana clenched her fingers around her pen and drew another daisy, pressing the pen so deeply into the paper that it almost ripped. For some reason, the board members always thought the experts could save them. She was tempted to make an observation regarding the utility of experts—and in particular, of Greg Wilson, with his collection of flashy degrees and his apparent bamboozling of everyone into thinking he was the environmental Messiah—but she was saved from that likely relationship-ending remark by the chair suggesting that the matter be referred to a subcommittee.

Great, another meeting. At least it ended this one.

Alana checked the clock. 2:36. Too late to even run. She grabbed the keys to the SUV. On the drive to the school, she tried to erase the horrifying vision of herself attempting to attract uninterested seniors to a sustainability potluck. In her imaginings, this event somehow involved a lot of unidentified bean dishes, accordion players, Greg Wilson leading the group in "blue sky" thinking, and her sticking out like a throbbing anti-environmental thumb due to her use of mascara.

Katie and Duncan stood on the edge of the playground clutching their backpacks, their expressions solemn, like they had been abandoned for weeks and had made the best of it by eating melting snow and the rotting contents of their Planet Box lunch containers.

"Where were you?" Katie said.

"Meeting," Alana said, swinging Katie into her arms and dropping a kiss on top of Duncan's toque. "How was kindergarten, sweetie?"

Duncan interrupted. "You always have meetings. Can I have a play date?"

Alana ran an inventory of the fridge contents. "No, we need to go get groceries. I'll buy you a snack." She wished this meant organic carrots or blueberries, not sushi and sugary yogurt drinks. Greg Wilson's future children would probably gorge on organic carrots. Who was she kidding—carrots? They'd probably skip over carrots and go straight to kale.

She hustled the kids into the back seat while Katie expostulated regarding their grade two reading buddies and how she didn't want to be matched up with Duncan because he was her brother. Alana made sympathetic noises in the appropriate places, then froze when she spotted Therese, the chair of one of the Regional Environmental Board subcommittees, strolling past.

"Driving again?" Therese said with a smile. "I thought you lived within walking distance."

Alana's smile turned weak and unreliable, and her relief at being out of the meeting evaporated. Somehow as an "environmentalist" in a small town, she was always either in a meeting or on trial—and she wasn't actually sure which was preferable. Alana fought the urge to show Therese the SUV odometer, to highlight the lack of kilometers on the vehicle, while mumbling something about usually walking, and wanting to buy a Prius but not being able to afford one.

She coughed out a semblance of a laugh. "Yes, I know it's terrible. But I had to work up until the last two minutes before school got out." It was her pat line that probably convinced nobody and made her feel like a fraud.

Therese cocked her head to the side and offered a quizzical toothless smile. Therese was an environmentalist; she wouldn't be on one of the board subcommittees if she weren't. And Alana realized that she was beginning to live in fear of environmentalists—which was kind of funny, because until recently she had hoped she *was* an environmentalist. But *real* environmentalists would manage their meetings better and arrive at school on foot early, bearing zucchini chia seed muffins. At least she no longer had to apologize for Blaine and his suit-wearing, Audi-driving ways, now that she and Blaine were no longer married. But even so, the glaring SUV and decided lack of muffins threatened to out her at every turn. The SUV was actually an ancient GMC Jimmy, but she had so internalized its size and supposed frivolous function as a "sports" utility vehicle that she just called it the SUV. She had considered spending money she didn't have on a Prius just for driving to and from the school, but given the emissions and waste associated with making and transporting anything, especially a car, she wasn't sure that would be a better choice for the planet—even though it *would* dramatically improve her personal optics.

She smiled and gave some sort of bobbing half bow to Therese like they spoke a different language or something, then hopped in the SUV. She looked once again at the odometer. Only 90,000 kilometers in seven years, which was less than 15,000 kilometers a year and way under the Canadian average. She suspected, however, that posting this information on the side of the vehicle would be viewed as strange and desperate.

She took the most efficient route to the grocery store and then rummaged through the cloth grocery bags in the back of the car, trying to find one or two that hadn't been used to wipe the back windshield or somebody's sticky hands.

"Why can't I ever have a play date?" Duncan said. His earnest blue eyes met hers over the back seat. His woolen dog hat perched askew on his head.

Out of the corner of her eye, Alana spotted an older couple, Sharon and Mark, from a climate change committee she had worked for on another contract. They had walked to the store, of course, and were the visual epitome of environmentalism: old Gortex jackets, backpacks, sensible shoes, and short grey hair. Alana huddled against the back of the SUV, feeling conspicuous in her sleek new raincoat, which had been an impulse purchase from a reputable local store and was made by a company that supported philanthropic causes. Sharon and Mark passed by without acknowledging her. She hoped this was because they didn't see her, and not because they were offended by her, were disgusted by the SUV, or perhaps the raincoat, or had seen through the façade and knew that, now that she had a job and two kids, she only playacted at environmentalism.

Or perhaps Alana had always playacted at environmentalism. Tabitha Greene, Alana's best friend—and the executive director of the Rainforest Coalition in Vancouver—was the real environmentalist. Her and her entire family.

The Greenes had practically adopted Alana into her home after the death of Alana's mother. For two years, Alana had slept there almost every night while her father dealt with his grief. And Alana had been gobsmacked by the differences in the Greenes' lifestyle and her own. The Greenes took short showers, watched public television, made their own granola, quoted *Silent Spring*, regularly attended environmental protests, cried when birds were extirpated from local marshes, and went to drumming camps in the summer. Tabitha's mother, Margaret, washed out plastic bags, gone to Greenpeace rallies, and made carob chip cookies long before it was fashionable to do so. Even now Margaret continued to spearhead local environmental causes—that is, when she wasn't traveling around Guatemala in her Volkswagen van with her birdwatching husband, John, helping to dig wells and provide medical services in remote villages. Their name was even Greene, which Alana found somehow funny, although the Greenes never seemed to get the joke.

The Greenes were part of the reason Alana went into environmental studies, gave up wearing eyeshadow, and tried her damnedest to toe the environmental line. When faced with a decision that had environmental implications—which was pretty much every decision, as far as Alana was concerned—"What would the Greenes think?" inevitably ran through her mind.

The Greenes had also been convinced that Alana's mother's bladder cancer had been caused by the textile mill upriver. It had spewed chemicals into the soil and water when her mother was a child, before environmental regulations had been developed, before most of the dirty industries of the world had all been moved to India or China to poison people who had less capacity to stand in protest.

"Mom," Duncan yelled. "You didn't answer my question."

Alana jolted her attention back to the present. "I know, sweetie," she said. "It's hard for Mommy to work all day and then have a bunch of kids in the house. I just want to hang out with you guys."

"Why don't you just quit your job," Duncan said.

Alana suppressed the small swell of hope that this suggestion always generated. If she didn't have to work, she could get her garden going again, wash out plastic bags, make fresh herb salads with edible flowers, bake quinoa muffins, hang her laundry to dry, walk to school consistently, and have whole packs of kids digging holes and making mud pies in her back yard. But she was divorced. She had to work, or there wouldn't *be* any quinoa, or plastic bags for that matter. And their ancient farmhouse stove always burned muffins anyway. So she spent every day at her desk, while the weeds and grass in her yard flourished, and her garden beds sat empty and cold, and the "North Star Farm" sign that she and Duncan had painted and hung on the gate four years ago seemed like more of a joke every day.

"Because I can't," Alana said, hustling the kids into the grocery store. "We need the money so we can eat." Every time she said this, she felt a twinge in her forehead. She wondered if there was some way she could do it, if she gardened, sold some of her harvest, repurposed, and scrimped—if she became a true environmentalist. But she had tried it before—when she and Blaine had still been married, when she had convinced him to move to Silver Peak and buy the old farmhouse and two acres of land, when she had packed her mesclun mix, carrots, and other produce down to the farmer's market every Thursday only to discover, after a year, that farmers—at least small-plot farmers—couldn't generally make a living.

Besides, the kids would want more expensive, stylish clothes soon, and trips—they were both already obsessed with skiing—and they would need money for education. Alana didn't want Blaine to be the source of all things good, while she offered only thrift store clothes and fresh grown peas.

And she hoped, someday, to meet someone new. How attractive would she be in second hand clothes, no makeup, and frizzy hair?

She spent the next ten minutes dodging Sharon and Mark and picking out organic produce and grocery items. The sandwich ham was a compromise because the kids couldn't take peanut butter to school and wouldn't eat anything else. The organic milk at double the price was too expensive, but everything else in the cart was solidly eco-friendly, except the ground beef and the chicken, which she covered with the organic Kamut cereal.

When they were married, Blaine had informed her pointedly on several occasions—often following some particularly disastrous vegetarian offering—that he was a meat eater. He even gesticulated at his canines as if to emphasize the rightness of his decree. Now that Blaine had moved out, Alana tried to cook vegetarian three nights a week. Tonight was pinto bean, tomato, and butternut squash soup. Despite the fact that this was clearly good for the earth, it wasn't perfect, because she didn't have time to soak dried beans, and the kids would probably hate the soup.

"Canned beans are okay. Canned beans are okay," she repeated to herself as she marched down the grocery aisle. Maybe *she* needed to take up smoking weed.

She rounded the corner to grab a loaf of the local organic sourdough bread and nearly crashed her cart into a dark-haired man with spiky hair and eyes as turquoise as his sneakers.

"Sorry," she stammered, veering the other direction with the cart.

"No problem," he said with a roguish smile. She eyeballed him again. Who was this guy? He wore a grey T-shirt with a saxophone on it and almost skinny jeans. But unlike most men, he looked good—outright hot actually—in the skinny jeans. He was about her age, but he definitely was not one of the playground dads, or at least not one that she had ever seen.

He must have noticed her staring, because he winked, grabbed a loaf of organic bread, and sauntered off down the aisle, a white motorcycle helmet tucked under his arm. She watched him go, then shook her head. Even if he was single and lived in Silver Peak, which he probably wasn't and didn't, she wasn't going down that road again. She had gone the clean-cut, totally attractive route with Blaine, and look where that had gotten her. This time she was going for a man with a beard and dreadlocks, canvas pants, and Birkenstocks—a true blue environmentalist. The only problem was that in Silver Peak, unemployed ski bums often *resembled* environmentalists, and they generally didn't have jobs or an overly environmental outlook.

She arrived at the checkout, the kids compliant after being bribed with the promise of fruit popsicles. She just had to plant a garden again this year, despite her job. Sharon and Mark grew most of their own food, and they had been friends with Alana in her farmer's market days. Now they probably trembled in horror as they strolled past her weed-strewn beds.

As she waited for the items to be rung up, Alana occupied herself with visions of spending the summer with her fingers in the rich brown earth, surrounded by heaps of potatoes, bush beans, and carrots, Katie and Duncan bounding through the sprinkler eating pea pods. The grocery total brought her back to her sharp-edged reality: $146.78 for three days' groceries. Eating healthy organic food was beginning to be out of her price range.

When Blaine used to make rumblings about reducing grocery costs, Alana had always reminded him that they ate well, and she questioned whether he really wanted her to serve more processed food. Then again, whenever she had gone away for work, he and the kids had subsisted on Pop-Tarts, frozen pizza, and hot dogs, and he did leave her in favor of a woman who could barely run a microwave, so maybe he *had* wanted her to start serving more processed food.

"Mommy," Duncan said as they wheeled toward the exit. "Why didn't you buy anything for Larry?"

Larry Lund was a local homeless man with a cloud of white hair who sat in the town square near the grocery store in the afternoons, sort of panhandling and sort of just hanging out; Alana was never clear which, but lots of people gave him food. The story was that he lived in the woods—hiking, prospecting, and panning for gold—and had past drug addiction problems, which he had apparently mostly kicked, although if his breath was any indication, he had some lapses. He seemed friendly enough, and he took great pleasure in telling Alana in his soft-spoken voice about his most recently staked claims and how they were going to make him millions as soon as he got the mine into production. Most recently Larry had informed her, in a whisper, that he had discovered uranium. She had hoped he was joking or mistaken—he *had* to be mistaken, right?—and wondered if she should call the authorities. Except who would she call?

Alana usually bought him a can of tuna—dolphin friendly, of course—and Duncan always took great joy in handing over the small offering. Larry always said thank you by way of a famous quote or saying. Recently he had taken to quoting Chinese proverbs about luck, courage, and rats fleeing sinking ships. But Larry hadn't been in his spot for the past few weeks. Alana knew that he sometimes spent stints in some of the local group homes when he needed some time away from the bush. Hopefully that was where he was, not lying somewhere dead from radiation.

"Larry isn't around, honey," she said. "I'm sure he'll be back soon."

Alana ran up and down the street outside the house while the kids watched their video. It was not an ideal exercise scenario, but she checked in on the kids after every lap and watched for strange cars and undercover child services workers in the neighborhood. And she was certain that if she didn't spend at least fifteen minutes outside every day, she would spontaneously combust.

She inhaled the fresh mountain air and raised her face to the brilliant blue sky and rugged mountains of Silver Peak, for which the town had gotten its name; on most days, this made everything better. This connection to the fragile and yet enormous beauty of the earth drove her; and fear regarding the kind of messed-up, bereft-of-resources planet her children were going to inherit was the clincher.

The personal is political. Be the change. I have to be the change.

The kids had completed their homework and the soup was bubbling on the stove when Blaine walked in the front door, carrying a six-pack.

The kids ran to him and threw themselves into his arms with exclamations of "Daddy!"

"Aren't you supposed to knock first?" Alana said, crushing the lurch her heart still felt obligated to execute when she saw her ex-husband.

Blaine shrugged, his handsome features sheepish. "It was open. It's a small town. You tell other people not to knock."

Alana tried to contain her sneer reflex. "Other people haven't left me for their assistant."

Blaine had the decency to glance at his feet. "I know. I'm sorry. I'll knock in the future. I was hoping I could hang out with the kids for a bit again tonight. You said it was okay. I miss them."

Blaine had been doing this for the last month, dropping in around dinnertime for an hour or so to hang out with the kids and have dinner with them a couple nights a week. She had said yes initially because Blaine had let her have full custody of the kids, which was what she had wanted, so it was understandable that he missed them, and she didn't want him to start messing with the arrangement that he had agreed to.

She had also said yes because at first she had thought that maybe he wanted to get back together. Too many subsequent Heather-filled conversations had since disabused her of that notion, although she did learn that Heather couldn't cook and taught Pilates three nights a week. But Alana had decided to let him continue to show up because it made the kids so happy to see him. And, realistically, she was lonely. A small part of her still hoped he would change his mind about Heather, and about her.

But the not knocking—that was too much.

Blaine opened a beer and sniffed at the pot on the stove.

"It's only soup," she said.

"Smells great," he said. His voice contained a hopeful but uncertain undertone. This was code for "I really want a steak." Alana scowled. She should start giving him a bill for his weeknight dinners, but he was being generous on the child-support payments, which he provided without quibble, and he helped with the dishes and some of the male-oriented household tasks. As far as exes went, Blaine was pretty much a model student.

And if she was honest with herself, she really wanted steak too.

How could she make any headway on being an environmentalist if her stomach remained firmly entrenched in its carnivorous ways?

After Blaine made his usual noises about only needing a small bowl and eating with them just to keep them company, she ladled out the soup with more vigor than necessary. Duncan consumed a few half-hearted spoonfuls of the soup before devouring his bread and carrots. The soup was tasty as far as soup went, but now Alana was focused on a steak, and she blamed Blaine for not being more enthusiastic about the soup. Perhaps if she had a partner who was a bigger environmentalist than she was, she would be carried by the righteousness of his beliefs and would love the soup. Or maybe she wouldn't. Maybe she would become a closet steak eater, wolfing down chunks of rare meat in her office and hiding out by the beef fondue at dinner parties in her hemp dress.

But Blaine would never be the source of her righteousness, or steer her in the direction of good clean environmental living. She should have known that right from the beginning, when he drove up in a Corvette waving a car phone the size of a loaf of bread. Actually, she *did* know that right from the beginning—but evidently she ignored it in favor of the potential to finally own a pair of good leather boots and a nice house, which none of her patchouli-loving, Birkenstock-clad ex-boyfriends had ever seemed inclined to sanction.

"I've been thinking of getting chickens," she said to Blaine after the children had been excused. "That way we can eat meat without feeling guilty. They provide manure for the garden and eggs. And they're like pets."

Blaine's features widened and separated fractionally. "Chickens? They stink, and they'll attract bears. Are you going to shovel manure?"

Alana contained her irritation. He wasn't completely out of line in his response. He had been the traditional handler of animal excrement in their household, at least until Duncan's gerbil, Squealer, had run away because someone had left the cage door open. Alana tried not to harbor any suspicions on this front, even though she knew Blaine had never been overly fond of Squealer, because, well, he had squealed rather a lot.

"And what if you go away?" Blaine asked. "Who's going to look after them?"

"I don't know," she said.

He gave her his squinty-eyed look, which strongly implied that he was not inclined to look after the chickens for her. "I have one word for you: worms."

She had insisted on getting a worm composter, but due to its unfortunate odor and pernicious tendency to attract fruit flies and maggots, it was down in the freezing basement and difficult to access. It was an expensive, special, layered composter, in which the worms were supposed to migrate down to the next floor after creating a rich compost on the top floor. But the worms had not only remained stubbornly entrenched on the upper floor, they had turned out to have rather dainty appetites, and barely put a dent in the pile of fruit and vegetable waste Alana's family produced on a daily basis.

And because of the swarm of insect life that had emerged from the composter every time the lid was opened, Blaine had become the official worm feeder until he moved out, a duty he had not embraced with enthusiasm.

Alana felt her excitement sag a little. "I don't think I'll ever become a real environmentalist."

Blaine laughed. "You think chickens are going to make you an environmentalist?"

"Well, they're a first step," she said. "And I should probably get goats too, but I don't really have enough land."

"That is not the way to become an environmentalist," he said.

"What is, then?"

"You garden, you walk the kids to school, you spend a billion dollars on your groceries, and you don't buy things. I think you're doing pretty good."

A flash of ferocious anger swept over her—at her lack of environmentalism, at Blaine for thinking she was an environmentalist (which in fact showed *his* complete lack of environmentalism), at Blaine for leaving her and for now having the audacity to sit in her kitchen with her like they were still married, and at Heather for being younger and, apparently, cuter than she was, although Alana kind of thought Heather was a bit insipid-looking.

"That's not good enough," she hissed.

Blaine's eyes went buggy, like they did when he was afraid a fight was coming.

"I'm not an environmentalist because you were never really committed to it," she continued. "If you had your way, you'd burn thousands of pounds of jet fuel touring the world, golfing, water skiing, and living a life of leisure. If you had been committed to it, then we would live totally differently." *And we might still be married*, she thought.

One corner of Blaine's mouth curled up and he raised the opposite eyebrow, his eyes still bulging out of their sockets. "Not committed to it? I spend an hour a day on a crappy bus with freak shows. It's like a driving mental asylum. Not committed to it? I helped dig your garden beds and fed your worms and ate chickpeas. I spent twelve years freezing because you wouldn't turn on the heat. My shoes have holes and my scalp still itches from that vegan shampoo. What more did you want me to do? Wear baggy pants and tie-dyed shirts and sing 'Kumbaya' around the campfire?"

His tone was a combination of exasperated and aggressive, as if he really had no idea what to do with her. Maybe she *was* completely exasperating. That was probably why he left.

"I don't know. I just wanted us to do better. I wanted *you* to do better. I wanted you to advocate, or take on a cause, and garden more and act like you liked it, not like it was akin to torture," Alana said. "We should have always been trying to see how environmental we could be."

Blaine remained silent for a few seconds, his face tight with disdain, then he shook his head and shifted his lips into a terrible smile. "Fine. I'll show you how environmental I can be. But I want to put a wager on it."

"On what?"

"On who can be more environmental: you or me. If at the end of a year, you win, I will toe the environmental line for the rest of my life."

"And if you win?" she said, feeling rather faint. Blaine was highly competitive, and the last time he'd tried to prove a point they'd ended up in a Volkswagen van deep in rural Mexico eating mustard and stone-wheat thins and evading the Federales.

"We move to Los Angeles," he replied evenly. "Heather wants to try her hand at acting, and I need a real job."

A sharp pain cut through Alana's chest. It was no secret that Blaine hated living in Silver Peak. Leaving his job as CFO of a small electronics company and moving from Vancouver to a small town had been her idea, and he had reluctantly agreed to support her. Now he stayed at a job he hated—teaching economics at the local college—to be near the kids. Was this challenge just a means of forcing her to move? To Los Angeles, the epitome of anti-environmentalism? She'd disintegrate completely.

"No way," she said. "I'm not moving."

Blaine rolled his sky-blue eyes—eyes that she used to melt in. "What about Vancouver, then? Just think about it. I can't live in this one-horse town for much longer. And we need to think about the educational opportunities for the kids. It's fine for now, but I really think they should try private school when they're older."

Vancouver, where she could be close to Tabitha, who was her best friend, even if Tabitha made her own organic yogurt and outdid Alana on every environmental front there was. At least in Vancouver she might have the prospect of meeting a man. But she would have to abandon her dream of farming and being self-sufficient.

"I am not moving based on a bet," she declared.

"'Kay, fine. How about this? If I win the bet, you promise to at least be willing to sit down with Heather and me to discuss moving. If you win, I'll look after the chickens and whatever other farm vermin you acquire, except cows and horses, whenever you travel for work."

Alana envisioned the conversation with Heather, with her straight silky blond hair and little freckled nose. Somehow the conversation involved Alana having her hands wrapped around the other woman's throat, but she decided not to mention this.

And it would never come to that anyway. Blaine didn't have an environmental bone in his body. He would do something stupid like buy a powerboat or clear-cut the piece of property he and Heather had purchased on the edge of town for their dream house. There was no way he could win this challenge.

"And hand water the vegetable garden," she said.

"And hand water the vegetable garden," Blaine replied.

"Fine," she said. "It's a bet."

CHAPTER TWO

The Best-Laid Plans

"**O**kay, so I think we need to set up a point system and some rules," Blaine said on the phone over the high-pitched squeals and thumps of the kids wrestling.

Alana set down her egg-laden fork. Blaine knew the rule, or she thought he did. No communication regarding anything important before eight a.m. Exceptions were made if he had just severed an artery or had one of the children's school agendas. But he was definitely not to introduce any new plans, ideas, or proposals this early.

"I'll type it up and email it to you," he said. She could hear him moving around collecting his stuff, no doubt about to head off to work. She imagined Heather, the wanna-be actress, drifting about their condo in filmy lingerie, while she, the aged hippie granola-cruncher, was eating eggs in her sweats. She hung up and imagined pinning pretty little lingerie-clad Heather to the ground in hand-to-hand combat.

Blaine sounded too chipper, too sure of himself. What had she agreed to?

Visions of stone-wheat thins skittered through her mind.

On the way to school, Duncan and Katie dawdled and chased each other over the melting mountains of snow on the side of the road. They had been twelve feet tall at the height of winter, but they had now been reduced to dirty mounds of gravel, leaves, and ice crystals that sometimes didn't disappear until the end of May. The edges of Katie's pink skirt were already damp and muddy.

"Please, you two," Alana said. "We're going to be late." She hated having to hustle them along, to rush them from this glorious nippy sunlit morning, into the shadowy halls of the school. It seemed unnatural somehow—this constant hurry of modern life. She wondered again why she wasn't homeschooling. If she homeschooled, there would be no hurry. They could jump around on the snow banks all morning collecting buds, sticks, woodlice, and robin eggshells for science projects. Then they would spend a cozy afternoon reading and working on math and spelling sheets at the dining room table with mugs of hot cocoa.

But then reality pushed its way into her fantasy. She would get cabin fever, they would be broker than they already were, and the children, who weren't extroverts to begin with, would become loners and outcasts, sitting home alone on Friday nights in their teens.

"Duncan and Katie. *Now*, please. We have to go." The ominous undercurrent in her voice snapped them to attention, and they clambered down from the bank and trudged obediently the rest of the way to school.

She covered their faces with goodbye kisses and walked home. The wind raked across her face and through her damp hair. She tried not to blow dry due to the energy cost, but weather like this tended to make her curly hair frizz up like Bobo the clown's. She caught sight of her wild hair and red nose in a car window and cringed. Some people were just not cut out to be environmental hippies. She might have to take up wearing a toque indoors—or better yet, a balaclava. Maybe there was a market for ninja hippies.

She spent the day editing a climate change research paper, coordinating a report for one of the more dysfunctional board subcommittees, and answering endless emails. After starting dinner in the slow cooker, she sprinted around the block before picking the kids up from school.

She showered maniacally while the kids were at their piano lessons, then dragged out the soil, plastic pots, and seed packets. If she was going to have a garden, she had to get some seeds started.

The kids helped for a while, marveling at the tininess of the carrot and lettuce seeds and spilling most of them on the floor. But they wandered off partway through the process and then dogged her to let them watch TV. She relented an hour before dinner and tried not to cringe at the sounds of SpongeBob while she plunged pumpkin and cucumber seeds into the soil and frantically labeled each of the pots. Her theory that SpongeBob was reducing the IQ and motivation of children had not been well received at the last Parent Advisory Committee meeting. Evidently none of the other mothers had experienced a brief and terrifying phase in which their child was determined to grow up to be

Patrick the starfish.

She still had to unload the dishwasher, serve dinner, and clean up before Blaine arrived to babysit so she could go to the PAC meeting at the school. *PAC meetings are another thing I could give up if I home-schooled.* She returned to the vision of engaging in hours of productive learning with the children, but it was quickly overtaken by images of her lying in bed until nine in the morning and then lounging around the house in her pyjamas. Maybe her obsession with homeschooling was just a big smokescreen for wanting to sleep in.

Duncan wandered back into the living room as she vacuumed up the last of the spilled soil.

"It's jersey day at school tomorrow, and my jersey has ketchup on it," he said.

Alana swore, less internally than she would have liked. Duncan had only one jersey due to her firm policy of not supporting overpaid athletes. Even this one precious Vancouver Canucks jersey had only been purchased after the kids made fun of him last year for hand-making his own jersey with paper cutouts glue-gunned into place on an old soccer uniform. Alana had thought it was creative and cute, but clearly the other six-year-olds at Silver Peak Elementary had stricter standards.

She scrambled through the pile of dirty laundry to find the appropriate items to make a full load, then launched them into the washer with a capful of eco-friendly soap. Her washing machine was old and beat up and voraciously consumed gallons of water. But chucking old appliances and making and shipping new ones actually consumed more energy than continuing to use the old ones. All of which was beside the point, really, since she couldn't afford a new one anyway. She knew she should also hang the clothes to dry, but that experiment had gone awry far too many times, with rain and windstorms leading to yanking sodden clothes off the line, or out of her neighbour Rick's yard, and flinging them into the basket while agonizing about the wasted time spent hanging them out earlier that morning.

Jersey day. It could lead to an entire cascade of environmental shoulds, apparently.

Alana returned to the kitchen and poured herself a large glass of wine. Did her mother experience this kind of stress? No, she just thrust their polyester and rayon clothes into her Kenmore dryer with a sheet of Bounce, all while smoking a Camel cigarette, without the slightest twinge of guilt.

Blaine's email blipped up while she was adding some of the final in-gredients to the slow cooker. At first she assumed that the document labeled "Point System" was something to do with their still-shared Alaska Airlines account, which he had always pestered her about, wanting to fly here or there, mostly places with golf resorts and moun-tain biking trails. She had always meant to do more research on carbon offsets to figure out which ones were worth buying so she could make some of the trips happen, but she had never had the time. Blaine still pestered her about the account, but now it was mostly about her figur-ing out a way to sign the points over to Heather.

She opened the email, and quickly realized that the Point System had nothing to do with traveling.

Taking the bus: five points. Well, there was an easy five points for him every day. She had no place to take a bus *to*. There was no bus that went to the school or grocery store. It got worse. Cycling to the gro-cery store: five points. Great, except that she didn't own a bike. Showering only once a day: two points. She usually showered twice a day because she worked out. The second shower was a quick rinsing affair, but still. Blaine, who did not have children to walk to school, usually worked out before going to work in the morning. Hanging the clothes to dry: two points. But she was the one who had to do all of the kids' laundry. No new clothes in a month: five points. No personal care products in a month: five points. Production of three pounds of vege-tables: two points. Keeping the heat at eighteen degrees: five points. Easy for him to say. He spent his day in a positively sultry office build-ing. One vegetarian meal a week: five points. Taking an eco-friendly vacation: ten points.

She closed the document. Clearly Blaine planned to play hardball. She was going to have to get in front of this or she would lose the bet and end up moving to Vancouver—and that's only if she didn't first go to prison for strangling Heather... *and* Blaine.

After dinner, she dragged the kids through piano practice, spelling re-view, and a craft using food coloring, dish soap, and milk, wondering if there would be minus points for wasting the milk.

Blaine arrived for his babysitting gig, whistling, as she finished the last of the dishes. When she failed to make eye contact, he realized there was something wrong.

"Are you upset about something that happened at work?" he said, all chipper-like, as if he only lived to help her.

She shook her head and glared at the sink.

"Something that happened with the kids?"

She continued to glare.

"Me?"

She turned at this point. "Where are you going on vacation?"

Blaine's smile faltered a bit. "A meditation retreat in San Diego. It's ranked as one of the most eco-friendly resorts in North America. They use grey water on their gardens, bamboo linens, and source only Marine Stewardship Council-certified seafood."

"Right, and are you cycling there?"

"No, we're flying, but I'm going to buy offsets."

"I think you're co-opting my thing and turning it into *your* thing. *And* into a game," she said. "And it's not a game. It's very serious. We're destroying the world."

"I'm not co-opting your thing. I think we should do this. We can even blog about it and make money."

"We're not blogging about it. I don't want to make money off my environmental efforts. I'm trying to live more sustainably, and you're the Corvette-driving, car phone-wielding business guy who leaves the lights on and buys Sunlight detergent."

Blaine rolled his eyes. "Alana, in case you haven't noticed, I haven't owned a Corvette since the early nineties. I take a bus to work. It's big and foul-smelling, and it doesn't resemble a Corvette in the slightest."

"Yeah, well you still leave the lights on."

"Okay, so I'm not perfect. Shoot me."

"You don't like chickens."

"You can get chickens. I don't even live here anymore. I just made the observation that shoveling excrement hasn't traditionally been your thing. I'm just trying to show you that there's more than one way to be environmental."

"Right, and you prefer the five-star-resort way."

A knock on the door interrupted them. Alana plastered a smile on her face as her friend Suzanne poked her head in the door to return some skates she had borrowed, her long blond hair in a plait and her car still idling in the driveway. Alana offered an enthusiastic greeting and Suzanne came in, closed the door behind her, and started chatting about her week. Suzanne wore her usual sweats that emphasized her tall, broad, athletic body. Alana blinked and tried to focus on what Suzanne was saying, expecting her to leave, because after all her car was idling. But Suzanne kept talking, asking about the kids and saying hi to Blaine, who was smiling and chatting back in response.

At the three-minute mark, Alana realized that she had no idea what Suzanne and Blaine were talking about, and she wondered if Suzanne knew that Silver Peak had anti-idling bylaws, and even if they didn't, that idling, unless you lived in the frigid north, was bad, and that she was sending more and more carbon dioxide into the air with each second she let that car run. Alana started thinking about all the people driving or walking past her house and seeing a car idling in her driveway. What must they be thinking?

At the ten-minute mark, Alana began to get panicky, but at that point it was too late to say anything without seeming weird. Suzanne was telling some story about the new computer inventory system at the bookstore she co-owned in town, and Alana tried to insert the appropriate responses in the right places, but she was so focused on the car that she was probably talking gibberish. She excused herself, saying that she had to go check on the kids' homework, and Suzanne and Blaine continued to talk for five more minutes before Suzanne finally slipped out into the night and drove away.

Alana emerged from the dining room, her eyes wide. "Did you see that? She idled. She idled for almost fifteen minutes. I have a friend who's an idler."

Blaine shrugged. "Well, at least I know better than to idle."

"Yeah, but you don't compost, and you *golf*," she shot back.

Blaine just laughed, and Alana felt bad about her comment and about her freakout over the idling. After all, she wore makeup and tumble-dried her clothes. Maybe that was worse than idling or golfing. She should stop wearing makeup, but a quick glance in the mirror confirmed that this was likely a bad choice. She suspected most successful environmentalists were naturally cute, like Tabitha.

At the PAC meeting, there was the usual talk of fundraisers and curricula. The moms who ran the PAC bubbled with enthusiasm and life. Alana felt like her usual dark plague beside them, wringing her hands silently and alone about plastics and wireless Internet waves blasting the children. She tried to get excited about cake bingo. A true environmentalist would take over cake bingo and have everyone make carrot pumpkin cakes and ensure that the money was donated to save gorillas in Africa. Alana internally writhed about the value of organizing yet another fun, sugar-filled event for children who had everything. But these events helped build community, and she was all about community. Wasn't she? Or was she a misanthropic hermit who colored her ill will toward the world in a cloak of environmentalism?

She had plunged so mentally deep into the ethics of cake bingo that she almost missed it when Lisa read out the letter from the City of Silver Peak seeking parent input on the sustainability plan for the city. Alana felt a small surge of hope. Zander, the city planner, had spent over a year developing the plan, and Alana had been paid to help him with several sections. They had developed a really cool plan, she thought, with as much focus on economic development, which Silver Peak desperately needed, as on environmental protection. She roused herself to a more upright position in her chair, thinking that the other PAC members would probably want to ask her questions about the plan.

But the other women were focused on the fact that the plan proposed removing a third of the parent parking spaces at the school in order to construct a natural playground, and they didn't seem aware that Alana had been involved in the development of the plan at all.

"I don't know where they think people are going to park," Gillian said.

"You know they're also removing half the parking downtown," Lisa said. "And they're going to make all the parking parallel parking."

"Think of the disruption to local businesses," Gillian said. "And the expense. I can't believe they spent money on this when we need a better recreation center." She waved the document in the air.

Alana felt frozen in her chair. She should be stepping up to defend the plan, but she was afraid of these women—and worse, she was afraid they were right. She and Zander had included some bold recommendations that were supported by the people who had come to the open houses. But maybe only environmentalists came to sustainability plan open houses.

Claudia rolled her eyes. "The whole plan is crazy. You should see the proposed development cost charges. If this goes through, nobody will be able to afford to build a house in Silver Peak. Ryan says it will kill the town for sure."

Ryan Roberts, Claudia's husband, was one of the biggest developers in town, and the developers, with their tanned faces, aggressive tactics, and swaggering attitudes, scared Alana more than anyone else. But it was just a plan. Alana didn't even really believe in plans. Half of it, including the development cost charges, would probably never be implemented anyway. But they were a small start, a guiding vision. If people couldn't even buy into the vision, they were in serious trouble.

"There are a lot of important things in that plan," she finally said over the melee. "I really think you should give it a read."

Eight sets of eyes swiveled in her direction. "Do you know something about it?" Gillian asked.

"Well, a little. I helped with certain sections. I know some things like the parking and the development cost charges might not seem ideal, but it's all about moving us toward sustainability. If new developments don't foot the bill for connecting to the city water and sewer lines, then the rest of us taxpayers have to."

Claudia sniffed. "Well, if the city makes it too expensive to build, everyone will move away. Ryan and I will certainly be leaving. You just can't go killing people's jobs."

Alana swallowed. Gillian looked from Claudia to Alana. "We don't have to make a decision until next month," Gillian said. "Why don't we discuss it again then?"

Everyone nodded, and Alana rose and slunk out of the building, her palms damp. She got into the SUV for the short drive home. She should walk, but then she wouldn't have time to help the kids with their reading, and Blaine always did a perfunctory job. She needed to make sure they could read, or they would never get jobs, and she would have two Patrick the starfishes on her hands.

Why couldn't any of these things be easy?

The main floor of the house was lit up like an amphitheater, and Alana could hear Blaine reading to the children upstairs. She went from room to room, flicking off lights.

She washed her face in the bathroom after Blaine left. Her eyelashes drifted down the drain and stuck to the sides of the sink. Tube lash mascara. The greatest thing in the world for people who were follicularly challenged. Probably environmentally unfriendly, but she didn't wear many cosmetics—surely wanting longer lashes was okay.

But wasn't that how anti-environmentalism started? A slippery slope of justification after justification, until next thing you know you're driving a Hummer in high-heeled boots, eating ribeye steak, and insisting on angle parking with your back seat full of Bloomingdale's bags and house knickknacks.

The lashes collected in the bottom of the sink, slowing the draining process and dirtying the water. They contributed to a gradually forming clog that required Drano once every two weeks. Another demerit in the environmental marathon.

But she believed in the sustainability plan. It was a good plan, and she was proud of it.

She kissed the kids goodnight and read for a few minutes before retreating to the soundness of sleep. In sleep, she couldn't do any more environmental harm.

At least, she didn't think so.

CHAPTER THREE

Environmental Dementors

It was possible, she decided, that she was in love with Jonah, one of the clerks at the nursery, in a theoretical, environmental kind of way. He was terribly cute and smiled at her as he wheeled her purchases to the SUV. Manure, bedding soil, blueberry and raspberry plants. It didn't matter what other people did. Today was the first day of the rest of her environmental life. She would *be* the change.

She studied Jonah's retreating back. Visions of a tabouleh-filled lifestyle with a greenhouse and tons of compost flitted through her mind whenever she saw him. She was clearly under the influence of his gorgeous brown eyes and firm ass. But looking amazing in overalls, working at a nursery, and having dirty fingernails did not make him an environmentalist. For all she knew, Jonah could eat Kraft Dinner every night and go mud-bogging on weekends. And he was twenty-seven, or maybe thirty, but definitely younger than her.

The manure and plants came to $167.45. She sighed and passed over her MasterCard. She wondered whether all her efforts in the garden even remotely paid for themselves. If she had chickens, at least she wouldn't have to buy manure.

She should be working on a grant application for one of her non-profit clients. But if she hurried, perhaps she could compost and manure the garden, dig the holes for the blueberry and raspberry plants, and still be at her desk by eleven.

It was a glorious day to be out working in the garden. The apple and cherry trees were in bud, and soon the side yard would be filled with the delicate white and pink blooms. Crocuses littered the grass, forming a carpet of blue, yellow, and white, and jays darted in and out of the hazelnut tree gathering the previous year's leftovers. Turning over the first furrows of rich, dark, pungent soil in the garden made her borderline gleeful; too few people appreciated the fulfilling nature of digging in the dirt.

There was not much arable land left in rocky, mountainous Silver Peak—just her property, and Rick's next door, and a couple of small hobby farms on the other side of town. Most of the farmland had been gobbled up, bit by bit, by monster houses and the relentless creep of suburbia. Even the plot of farmland where North Star Farm now stood used to be part of a larger farm, but it, too, had been carved up over time, with a row of townhouses to the right and a few massive show homes on manicured half-acre properties at the back. Luckily the couple who owned the land before Alana had wanted to keep part of the original property undeveloped, so when Alana and Blaine bought the place, two whole acres of flat land with a battered old chicken coop and small goat shed remained.

She was pretty sure she could grow enough on two acres to support a family and still have some produce to sell. Researching climate change for one of her clients had made her hyperaware of food security and the expected decline of existing agricultural areas in the US and Canada. California was already in drought. How long would it be before grocery store shelves sat empty and North Americans had to rouse themselves from their *Breaking Bad* and *The Bachelor* stupor to try to figure out where it was their food came from again? Of course it might never happen. Probably would never happen. Blaine thought she was nutso. But just in case, she had wanted to have a little piece of land, and Silver Peak, which was expected to have longer growing seasons and more rainfall in the future, seemed like the perfect place, much to Blaine's horror.

And so what if she was a crazy prepper? She loved her two acres and wanted to live more sustainably, so it was a win-win, even if paying for them was going to give her an ulcer.

She paused and wiped her forehead on her shirt. It was best to avoid thinking about her financial situation too often. Most people in the world were in far direr straits than her. She pictured those fierce single mothers in developing countries who fended off land-hungry corporations, mothered seven children under ten, and still managed to run a profitable farm—wearing a skirt no less. Her situation was laughably cozy in comparison.

Maybe her plan to become a full-time farmer had been overkill and not very realistic, but buying North Star Farm had not been a mistake, even if Blaine thought it was riotous that the farm name acronym was NSF—*Non-Sufficient Funds*. But North Star Farm had won out as a name over Duncan's preferred name of Leaping Frog Farm because Blaine had taken to calling it Limping Frog Farm almost immediately.

Blaine. He just couldn't help himself. If there was a joke to be made, he made it.

Now she had a farm with a name that reminded her of her empty bank account every time she looked at the sign.

She just needed chickens—and a very good-looking farmhand. Or at least a willing farmhand, but good-looking wouldn't hurt. That probably made her terribly unenvironmental and shallow.

By 11:40, sweat trickled down between her breasts and a thin veneer of manure and compost covered her jeans. The manure had wended its way into the spaces between her clothes and skin, and another shower would now be necessary because she was not sufficiently environmentally developed to want to wear shit, or sleep in it, even fermented shit. She had decided to place the blueberry and raspberry plants on the edge of the property so as not to take up any of the existing beds, but she'd hit a layer of hand-sized rocks and was forced to resort to the pickaxe. The blank pages of her undone grant application swam before her eyes every few seconds. She had only a few hours before she had to collect the kids at school.

She decided to dislodge one more rock before calling it a day. She swung the heavy pickaxe with as much energy as she could muster and then started to work her fingers around the edges of the rock. The wail and grind of an ATV punctuated the calm before the stench of fuel pierced the air. Her recently retired neighbour Rick rode his ATV around his two-acre property and often stopped in for chats. Sure enough, he pulled up to the fence and cut the engine, studying her tank top and dirty jeans with interest. At least he wasn't idling. She gagged slightly on the exhaust fumes that always accompanied the ATV.

"Whatcha up to?"

"Oh, just trying to dig some holes to plant some blueberry and raspberry bushes," she replied.

Rick's rather small and deep-set eyes somehow shrunk to half their usual size beneath his Budweiser cap. "What for?"

"To eat," she replied, jamming her fingers on the stubbornly entrenched stone.

"Bears'll get 'em before you do. Bears love blueberries. With blueberry bushes and your plum tree, you'll have a swarm of 'em."

Alana paused, picturing her yard teeming with bears. Her property already became a bear highway in the fall, the lumbering beasts casually snacking on fallen plums and compost en route to the downtown dumpsters. Could she get a dog? She really didn't have time for one, and Blaine would blow a gasket—not that he should have any say, because after all, he got a girlfriend. She could get a gun, but that would be too risky with the kids, and realistically, would she shoot a bear? She couldn't imagine. A sprinkler deterrent system, like the kind used on deer, would probably just make bears mad. What would do the trick was a six-foot-high, barbed-wire fence—but that would be too expensive, not to mention hideous.

Rick pulled a package out of his pocket and unwrapped a Ding Dong. She couldn't believe that they still made Ding Dongs, or that people bought them. Rick settled in to eat his snack, watching her while she continued to struggle with the rock, as if she was the morning entertainment. She dislodged the stone and, having arrived at no satisfactory solution regarding the bears, stood and fluttered her hand at Rick in a gesture of goodbye.

"Seems like a lot of effort for a couple quarts of berries." Rick's voice emerged muffled through the last bite of the cake, a spray of brown bits falling from his lips.

Alana nodded slowly. He was right. If she factored in her time, buying the berries in the store would probably cost less, at least in the short-term.

"I know," she said, and shot him the jovial "I know I'm a nutter" smile she wore with non-environmentalists. "I just really like the idea of growing my own food."

She returned the pickaxe to the garage and headed inside, trying not to picture the bears already beginning to gather at the fence line. The ATV started up again outside.

She rinsed off in the shower, hoping there was no manure in her hair. The steam made her hair stand on end, and she resisted the urge to rewet it and flat iron it.

She raced through the grant application, impressing herself with her efficiency, but wishing she didn't feel the bile of haste in her throat as the clock ticked closer to pick-up time. She needed to spend more time working, or she would *have* no work, but the work often made her sick with despair. The causes were worthy, the pay was okay if she stood her ground on not doing extra hours, which she didn't always, and at least she could work from home. But her clients were often bitter, grumpy, and impatient from a lifetime of waving the sustainability flag while everyone else on the planet exuberantly hopped on board the party bus of environmental doom, clutching their knockoff Louis Vuitton handbags and shaking their Justin Bieber maracas. True environmentalists, except the ones who smoked a lot of weed, or weren't very bright, or were practicing Buddhists, often had a peculiar look of tightness around the lips and eyes, as if their faces were so accustomed to flipping into a sneer of derision or judgment that their features never fully returned to their relaxed and happy state. Nothing was ever good enough: no sustainability plan went far enough, no rally had enough attendees, too many ATV drivers ignored carefully worded signs regarding sensitive areas, everyone still drove to work and school, the fast fashion market fueled by child labor was booming, no campaign sufficiently stopped corporations from gutting global ecosystems... the list of failures went on and on.

And no matter how hard she tried, she couldn't change most of these things, and she couldn't make most people care about the environment, at least not enough to actually do enough. She could barely make *herself* do half the things she should. Even she owned fast fashion items and drove to school. She might as well take up the maracas and belly up to the appetizer table on the party bus.

She wondered what it would be like to work for the entertainment industry, or a big oil and gas company. Did an air of celebratory self-congratulation pervade the office? Did they engage in backslaps and high fives every few hours, sporting cheery unlined expressions, as the millions accumulated in their bank accounts and lucky employees jetted off to swanky retreats wearing cones of denial? They probably actually believed they were saving the world through the trickle-down effect. Maybe they were.

At two in the afternoon, she chopped onions like a maniac, cooked spices until they released their flavors, and tossed chicken and coconut milk into the slow cooker. Then she watered her seedlings, collected Duncan's soccer stuff, and drove to the school.

Adrian, one of the few single playground dads, sidled up to her as she scanned the schoolyard for Duncan and Katie. "Day off today?" he asked. He asked this all the time, and while she had explained many times that she was a consultant and worked school hours from home, he never seemed to get it. She considered just telling him she was a stripper.

"No. I worked today," she said. "And I gardened. I'm really trying to grow more of our food this year."

"So, you basically hung out in the sun? I'm on to you now." He smiled with what she suspected he thought was a charming, flirtatious smile. "Don't you know you can get your vegetables pre-cut and frozen?" he continued with a wink.

"Food is important to me," she said with a tight smile, eyeballing his shin and thinking about how much she would like to kick it. Clearly she was still not party bus material.

Duncan and Katie flung their backpacks in her direction and darted off for one last frolic on the playground. Suzanne wedged her way in between Alana and Adrian, giving Alana a total up and down.

"What happened to your hair?"

"Don't ask," Alana said.

"It looks fine. It's just different."

"No it doesn't. It looks ridiculous. I'm trying to use less energy these days."

"Tell me about it. I think that is really important. Good for you."

Alana had to stop herself from muttering something about idling, like someone with environmental Tourette's. Suzanne volunteered at a shelter for battered women and went with women for protection when they had to go back to their houses to pick things up. Keeping the car idling was probably a habit. An important habit. For all she knew, Suzanne lived a more sustainable lifestyle than she did. And even if she didn't, Alana could certainly point her fingers at far bigger environmental offenders. Like Gillian, who had just appeared at Alana's elbow looking like a bedazzled Beelzebub, her white teeth gleaming and streaked hair fluffed into a perfect, product-enhanced, inverted bob. Suzanne, who avoided members of the PAC like they were a pack of enraged fire ants, slunk off into the crowd.

"So, have you decided if you can help out with the hot lunch?" Gillian pressed.

"I'm not sure," Alana said. "I think I have to work that day." The hot lunch consisted of highly processed pre-cooked meatballs, likely containing bits of a thousand cows, tomato sauce, and white Catelli pasta. Things she would prefer not to serve in her household, much less promulgate to all the children at the Silver Peak Elementary like a gateway drug to further dietary disasters of high glycemic index carbs and salted chemical soup proteins. She couldn't believe the meatballs passed the Healthy Eating Guidelines for Schools for the province. But then again so did hot dogs, as long as they were all meat. It was like Ronald McDonald, Oscar Mayer, and Jack in the Box had collaborated on the guidelines. But her own kids would scarf those meatballs down in seconds, making ecstatic chortles of delight, so she was probably just being a hard-ass for trying to get out of participating.

"Puh-lease, Alana. We really need your help."

"Fine," she said. What were a couple of chemical meatballs once a year?

Alana whisked Duncan off to soccer then ran and got the mail and a few groceries with Katie during the practice, arriving back in time to watch the short game. One of the coaches gave out Jolly Ranchers to all the kids at the end of the game, and Katie somehow managed to sneak into the line. As Alana hustled them back to the SUV, their lips stained pink and the fruity smell of candy on their breath, she tried not to imagine their teeth as blackened slimy stumps, red dye 40 circulating in their veins.

She allowed the kids to watch a video while she finished off the grant application. It seemed like a necessary evil, and it was within the guidelines set by the Canadian Academy of Pediatrics. While Phineas and Ferb were perhaps not ideal role models, and it was odd that Ferb did not speak, she rather liked Perry the Platypus, and no amount of Googling could turn up any peer-reviewed academic evidence, or even fringe claims, regarding the negative aspirational influences of children's TV—though she still harbored deep-abiding suspicions. The nature documentaries she had attempted to get the kids into had not been well received.

She had just hit send on the rough draft of the application when an email from Blaine popped up on her screen: his scorecard for the day. The bastard had already given himself twenty-five points in advance for busing to work this week, and six points for remembering his lunch. She annotated his list, subtracting two points from his total for forgetting to turn off the lights the other night, then started to add up her own points. She decided to give herself three points each for manuring the garden, buying the blueberry and raspberry bushes, cooking a meat-free meal, not blow-drying her hair, and not wearing makeup. Then she reduced his bus score from twenty-five to fifteen. It should be three points for everything. Busing was not that much more environmentally friendly than manuring. Clearly they were going to need an independent arbiter.

She was about to remove the children from their video appendage when another email appeared. The all-caps title—"HAVE YOU SEEN THIS?"—caught her attention. It was from Maude, one of the members of the Regional Environmental Board. It was to Alana, but all the other members of the board had been cc'ed. Inside was a link to the City of Silver Peak's council agenda.

Alana opened the attachment with shaking hands. What had she missed? It was her job to track all municipal environmental initiatives in the region. But the city agendas were often two hundred pages long, and it was impossible to read them all every two weeks. Technically the municipal staff were supposed to update her, but some of them were not as forthcoming as others, and the City of Silver Peak, whose staff must have recently attended a weeklong workshop on "Loose Lips Sink Ships," was the least forthcoming of all. And Alana had spent the morning manuring, when apparently she should have been reading.

On page one hundred and twenty-six of the city agenda, after a lengthy report regarding the plans and winning bid for the repaving and refurbishing of the two main streets in Silver Peak by DKP Construction, Inc., was a letter from a company called Mountain Magnesium Resources proposing to put a magnesium mine in the Silver Peak community watershed. A twinge pinched Alana's right eyebrow. A mine in the community watershed? What impact would a mine have on their water supply? Probably a negative one. Yet there would undoubtedly be a lot of people who would support the jobs it might bring. It could end up being an all-out war, and the board might expect her to be in the middle of it... that's if she didn't get fired for missing the letter in the first place.

The letter indicated that the formal proposal would be submitted to the city in three weeks. She sent an email to the board apologizing effusively and promising to get more details on the mine the next day.

The phone rang as she threw the last few ingredients in the crock pot for dinner. She snatched it up.

"How did today go?" Her dad always led with this, as if her breakdown were imminent.

"Fine," she said.

"I met a guy on the chairlift today," he said.

"Mm-hmm," she said with what she hoped was a sufficient amount of interest.

"I think I got you a job."

A jolt of fear shot through her gut. What had her dad gotten her into?

"I gave him your card. Told him you were an environmental consultant and a whiz with media relations. He seemed very interested."

"I see. And who is *he* exactly?"

"The CEO of the new magnesium mine."

The jolt of fear became a wave of horror. Her dad thought she would be interested in working for a mining company? Where had the lines of communication broken down?

"Right. I'm not sure if I'm actually in favor of the mine, Dad."

Duncan flipped a playing card at Katie. Alana gave him a bulgy-eyed look, but he ignored her.

"Oh, don't worry about that. Just talk to him. He'll be calling you."

She considered explaining that ethically she would not be interested in working for a mining company, but then stopped herself. Her dad would just brush this off as stupid. Actually, it wouldn't even register as stupid on his radar; it would be so outside of his worldview that he would take it as the inane rambling of some slightly unhinged person who could not be his daughter, and he'd carry on stalking the CEO on the chairlift and show up at the company Christmas party because he was certain his daughter was a company employee.

Blaine called next. The kids were now engaged in an all-out card war.

"That was fun, Mommy! Can we do it again?" Duncan called out.

"Sure, but can you do it in the living room please, and you have to clean up."

"Why did you take points off my score?" Blaine said.

"Because there's no reason riding the bus should count for more than gardening."

"Okay, but you actually deducted points."

"That was for leaving the lights on."

"I don't think we should do minus points."

"Why not? Do you have some behaviors that you should be concerned about?" she replied. She wasn't above recording anything he confessed to and deducting the points later.

"No. I am going to become environmental Super Blaine."

"Shouldn't that be Super Environmental Blaine?"

"Maybe."

"Either way, I'll believe it when I see it."

"That's not very nice. You should nurture and coach people to turn over environmental leafs instead of zotting them like an environmental dementor." Blaine punctuated his comment with strange hissing noises, as if he were an actual dementor.

"That's leaves, Blaine, not leafs, and dementors don't zot. They suck all the happy memories out of you."

CHAPTER FOUR

Temptations

A lana hated waking up scared. Scared about the choices she would make that would affect the world and her children's lives. Scared about the choices that other people would make that would affect the world and her children's lives. Scared that there really was no hope for them from an environmental perspective. That humans had ravaged the earth of primary resources, established unsustainable, consumption-based economies, and allowed the global population to expand beyond the earth's carrying capacity if all people wanted to attain first-world living standards, which by rights they should.

She actually preferred it when she could find a way to forget for a while and live like a normal North American watching *Dancing with the Stars* and *Doctor Who*, buying clothes, furniture, and other household items, partying with her friends, and enjoying an afternoon at the spa reading celebrity magazines. This of course was further evidence that she was not a true environmentalist. But the worry would always come back. She spent so much time reading about sustainability for her clients—or rather current levels of *un*sustainability—that fear was an occupational hazard. Maybe she should do something else, like become a dog groomer or a street sweeper.

Blaine had always had faith that science and technology would save them. Someone would invent a perpetual motion machine, better solar panels, nuclear fusion, or garbage-eating bacteria, or perhaps already had. They would learn to colonize other planets or other dimensions. The necessary medical advances would happen before they got old or sick. Blaine was always confident in the future.

She and Blaine had met while teaching at community college in Vernon twelve years ago. He had taught commerce. She had taught environmental studies. They had not really seen eye to eye. Blaine used to call her his environmental zealot. But the sex had been good and they had appreciated each other's wit.

Perhaps she should have taken the zealot nickname as a warning.

And now she had graduated to environmental dementor, apparently.

The dementor outlook was not uncommon in the environmental field. Three of the professors of environmental studies she'd been taught by at UBC were nicknamed Dr. Doom, Dr. Dark, and Dr. Dismal. They had brooding, world-weary airs, as if fatigued by the notion of having to convert yet another naïve set of undergraduates. There was just no easy way to put a positive spin on the material they had to deliver about devastated landscapes, mountains of garbage, a changing climate, and millions of the world's people living in abject poverty. Most of Alana's classes were outright depression-fests, and she and the other students would gather in the dim recesses of the university pub to drink the cloud of pessimism away. Many of her friends lapsed into strange hedonistic behaviors—drugs and sex and dropping out— because what was the point if the world was ending?

Other profs seemed to be able to detach themselves from the material they spent their lives immersed in. They lived relatively normal, chipper lives, with children and mortgages and parties, coming to work with a bounce in their step. Good anti-depressants, maybe. Or a talent for cognitive dissonance.

She knew of some environmentalists who had quit abruptly, taking jobs with the industries they had long fought against and announcing that things had changed, or that things were not actually that bad after all.

The idea that things had changed made her laugh. As far as she could tell, society was more focused on superficiality and consumption than ever. It was just that now that they recycled and bought organic carrots, and the economy was in the dumpster, they didn't make any apologies for it anymore. Because consumption made the world go round.

Maybe Blaine was right. She *was* an environmental dementor. Except that sometimes she really wanted to be sipping freshly squeezed orange juice in the sun on a yacht, while her personal chef whipped up breakfast.

Maude pounded the tom-toms on email and Facebook all morning rounding up everyone in the community who was expected to oppose the mine. A meeting of concerned citizens was already scheduled at her house on Tuesday. Alana decided early on to let go of the reins, and now she just watched the emails fly past. A hasty search that morning had turned up little information regarding the environmental impacts of magnesium mining and even less about the company Mountain Magnesium Resources. Magnesium was a low-toxicity metal, but who knew what chemicals were used in extracting it? Not to mention the likely sedimentation from digging holes and having big trucks in the watershed.

Alana glanced out her office window. Jonah was digging holes shirtless out in the yard, the muscles in his back flexing and compressing with each stroke. He had agreed to come and work in the yard every Friday for a few months. Just knowing someone was out working in the yard restoring the farm was incredibly therapeutic, even if it was costing her an arm and a leg.

She sped through the edits on a flagship document on climate change for the provincial government. Another underfunded contract, which required that she hurtle through everything. All environmental government agencies were forced to do everything on a shoestring these days. Thus she was always working at a breakneck pace, trying to save the environment with words and plans—the secret little sweatshop of attempted environmental salvation.

She snatched up the phone when it rang, scarcely glancing at the caller ID. Most clients emailed her so it was probably a friend.

"Alana Matheson?" a man's voice said.

"Yes." She moved quickly from her casual friend tone to her professional tone.

"My name is Nate Steeves. I'm the CEO of Mountain Magnesium Resources. We're looking for a local public relations person with an environmental background, and we understand you do that kind of work."

"I do," she managed to stutter, searching for the words to nicely say no before this went any further.

"Would you be willing to send us your CV and come in and meet this week to talk about the position?"

She hesitated, looking for some sort of excuse. "I appreciate your interest, Nate, but I'm not sure if I'm the right person for the job. I only work part-time, and I just don't know if I could bring the level of commitment to the job that you would need." Why was she always so nice? She should just tell him she was an environmentalist. Who liked yachts.

"That's not a problem. We're only looking for someone part-time at this point, and I've seen some of the work you've done for the SREB."

"How part-time? I already have a lot of commitments," Alana said, hoping to find an out.

"We've budgeted twenty hours a week at fifty thousand dollars a year, with four weeks holidays to start."

Her heart sped up a little. That would be fewer hours than she currently worked and a substantial increase in pay. It would allow her to start paying off her monstrous line of credit and pay her property taxes. But she couldn't do this. She wouldn't do this.

"I'm afraid the whole thing might be a little controversial in the community for me."

"I understand your concerns. We plan to do this whole thing right and take the concerns of the community into consideration. It is going to be a small mine for starters, and we're going to use a bunch of innovative methods to minimize impacts and make it as sustainable as possible. Some of the board of directors of the company are planning to live here with their families, and we don't want anything that wrecks the watershed."

He sounded very sincere, but people who worked for industry were probably used to lying and deluding themselves. Sustainable mining was an oxymoron.

Another email popped up on Alana's screen. Something from Maude about the travesty about to unfold in the watershed.

Alana took a deep breath. "Yeah. I appreciate that. But I'm concerned that there just *is* no way to do it right. It's our watershed. It's where we get our water. Water is the most important thing. No matter what, you can't mess with a community watershed."

"You do know that the city has additional watershed reserves, right?"

"Where?"

"On Booker Mountain."

"So are you saying you *do* expect to ruin the current watershed?"

"No, of course not. But in the highly unlikely scenario that there was a problem, the Williston intake could be shut off and water could be piped from Booker."

"Who would pay for that? And does Booker provide the same quality and quantity of water?"

"When they originally selected the city watershed, both Williston and Booker were up for consideration. Williston was chosen because it's slightly closer, but Booker Creek had higher flow volumes. We've been in to talk to Stewart Kepper, the city CAO, and he indicated that the city was looking at developing a reservoir at the base of Booker anyway. Something about climate change and ensuring water security."

Alana looked out the window to check and see if she had just arrived in the twilight zone. *Her* sustainability plan had recommended expanding the city water storage capacity, although she had only suggested cisterns on individual properties, and swales and wetlands in city parks, not a whole new reservoir. Even so, she and Zander had placed bets on what percentage of their sustainability plan Stewart Kepper would reject outright and what percent he would just ignore. Stewart didn't even live in Silver Peak, so he had limited personal stake in its future—and he was pretty much the environmental Antichrist and ran the city like a personal fiefdom, with a management style that was a cross between Edgar J. Hoover and Don Draper.

"Look, none of this is a done deal," Nate said. "It's just in the proposal stage for the purposes of investment. We want to establish a mine that will provide jobs for the community and help make Silver Peak more sustainable. We could really use your insights."

Rick had arrived on his ATV to watch Jonah dig. Three more emails from Maude had made their way into Alana's inbox.

"So you'll send me your CV and come in and talk to us?" Nate said.

"Okay," she heard herself say. They arranged to meet on Tuesday—the same day as Maude's "save the watershed" meeting.

Alana hung up and wandered over to watch Jonah talking to Rick. What had she just done? Was she completely incapable of saying no? Maybe if she went in there and seemed sufficiently uninterested, Nate would decide he wanted someone else. She had done that before when a power company tried to woo her. Perhaps she could even gather information to help Maude with the cause at the same time. So she would be doing her environmental duty.

Blaine was ecstatic. "Fifty thousand dollars! Congratulations! That's awesome. Now we can go to France and Australia next year and still buy new skis."

"What do you mean by 'we'? You mean you and Heather?"

"Well, I was thinking you could come too. That way the kids can come."

"And what, I'd be like the nanny?" Sometimes she just wanted to slam her fist right into Blaine's perfect jaw.

"No. It's just that I think the kids should travel, and I know you won't take them alone, and Heather can only take the kids in small doses. We'd have separate rooms of course. Maybe even separate hotels. You'd love Paris."

It occurred to Alana that Heather's absence of concern about Blaine coming over for dinner, calling Alana on the phone all the time, and now inviting Alana on a trip to France was a clear sign of Alana's complete lack of sex appeal. The thought was almost as gut-wrenchingly awful as the state of the environment, and it reinforced her desire to take Heather out for a long walk in the woods and see if the Pilates princess could find her own way home.

"You know how I feel about flying."

"Yeah, well, we'll worry about that when the time comes."

"What do you mean by that? You mean like when our flight is leaving, or when you're proposing booking the tickets and I say no?"

"I don't know. One of those times. Maybe we can just drug you."

"It's not just fear of flying, Blaine. It's the whole environmental impact thing and whether we in the first world have a right to add huge amounts of carbon dioxide to the atmosphere just so we can enjoy ourselves, while the people living in low-lying coastal areas and impoverished nations will bear the cost of climate change and will never have the opportunity to set foot on a plane." She rescued Katie's glass of milk from the edge of the counter and threw some chopped dill into the salad.

"I don't understand why they can't just develop a filter for that or something."

"A filter? For carbon dioxide." Alana pictured a plane wearing something that resembled a big white diaper.

"Sure. I'm sure I just read an article recently about carbon dioxide-eating bacteria. By the time our trip rolls around, maybe the whole issue of carbon dioxide will be solved."

"Maybe. But will you please stop calling it 'our trip'? I'm not taking the job. That's if they even offer it to me. And I'm not coming with you and Heather to France."

"Not offer it to you?" Blaine's voice rose a decibel. "He called you. That's practically offering it on a silver platter. Do you need him to skywrite it?"

"He just asked for my CV. Stop putting the cart in front of the horse. Like I said, I'm not even taking the job."

"This is your chance to change things from inside. That's where the real change happens."

"Or the real selling out happens," she said, hanging up.

She was reading about carbon dioxide-eating bacteria while guzzling a glass of red wine when Maude called. Carbon dioxide-eating bacteria were not expected to be commercially viable or able to do anything on a large scale any time soon, and there were concerns about the potential for them to unbalance the carbon dioxide in the atmosphere in the other direction. This did not bode well for a trip to France, or a yacht.

"I'm just calling to make sure you're coming to the meeting on Tuesday, Alana. We're going to need your skills to fight this. We're asking that you bring at least three of your friends to the meeting. Since you're the only person involved so far that's under forty, we need you to be the person to connect with all the other parents at the school."

Alana did a quick scan of her friends and came up blank as to whom she could invite to an environmental activist meeting. She generally tried to keep her politics and friendships separate; she didn't need *everyone* to think she was an environmental dementor. And she wasn't even sure she was attending the meeting on Tuesday. Maude's fanaticism scared her. But this *was* the community watershed. Alana should go to this meeting. She should be involved in this fight.

"I'm not sure if I can make it, Maude. Katie has Sparks on Tuesdays and I'm a leader." It was not her day to lead, though, so she could easily get out of Sparks if she needed to. "But I'll see if I can get someone to fill in for me."

"We were hoping you could set up and maintain the website for us."

"I don't know. I could set it up, but I don't know if I can commit to maintaining it. I have to work." This was weak.

Maude blew air out through her nose. "Well, we all have to do our part, you know." This was not said unkindly, but rather, with the resignation of someone who was always trying to rally people to causes.

"I know. I'll see what I can do. I could show someone how to maintain it. Hey, did you know the city has an alternate watershed area?" Alana debated telling Maude about the interview with Nate, spinning it that she was going in to get intel for Maude, for the cause; but before she could, Maude cut in.

"Where did you hear that? Did Zander tell you that?" There was a layer of suspicion in Maude's voice that alarmed Alana. Maude could so easily flip on her. Alana knew that in Maude's eyes, she was only a few good environmental intentions and actions away from being the enemy, the pariah. She couldn't tell Maude she was even talking to Nate Steeves, much less that she was meeting with him.

And why *was* she meeting with him? And why had she mentioned the alternate watershed? What would the Greenes think? She needed to call Tabitha.

"I can't remember," Alana said. "I just heard it somewhere. I was just curious."

Maude's tone turned patronizing. "Even if it's true, you don't wreck one watershed and then move on to the next one."

"I'm not suggesting that. I was just surprised because I've never heard about it."

Maude acted as though she hadn't heard Alana. "These millionaires always thinking they can move in and take advantage of little communities, extract their resources, ruin their watersheds, and then move on." Her voice cracked, and Alana wondered if she was crying. "I have to go."

Tabitha picked up on the third ring. "Hey, sis, how's it going?" she said in her low growly voice. Alana wondered if it was from the pot smoking.

"Okay, Tabbie. You?" Alana said.

"Well, the usual excitement. I have three protesters in jail right now and have to arrange for bail. The Steveston Valley, you know."

"I heard." The Rainforest Coalition always had active protests in the once-pristine forests of Vancouver Island that were now being logged. "Listen, I've been offered a job by a mining company that plans to set up a magnesium mine in the watershed here. Blaine thinks I should take it and try to change things from within. I don't know if it's a good idea."

Tabitha let out a disgusted snort. "You can't change mining companies. They're a bunch of pirates, worse than forest companies, and the free entry system makes them think they own the entire province. Did you read the latest WELA paper on the free entry system?"

Alana always had to take a moment to transcribe the acronyms that rolled so easily off Tabitha's tongue. Western Environmental Law Association. She hadn't read the paper, of course. "No. It's in my to-read pile, but I've been so busy with climate change that I haven't kept up on mining."

"Read it. I gotta get down to the police station. Talk soon, hon."

CHAPTER FIVE

Alternatives

Monday morning dawned glorious and warm, and Alana decided to spend a few hours in the garden, not being involved in the mine or the watershed. Jonah had done a lovely job with the blueberry bush holes; they were deep, and he had loosened up the soil on the bottom and worked in a bit of manure. She eased the blueberry bushes out of their burlap wrap and placed them gently in the ground, working the soil up and around the edges. April in Silver Peak was too cold for vegetables outside, even in cold frames, but she decided to plant a couple of trial rows of lettuce and spinach in the greenhouse.

She was planting out the raspberry canes when Rick arrived to take up his usual post on the opposite side of the fence. She wiped her hair out of her eyes with a dirty, gloved hand, smearing soil across her forehead. She hadn't showered yet and probably looked dreadful with her filthy jeans, wild hair, and unmade-up face.

"So, you decided to take the risk, eh?" Rick laughed. "Well, don't come crying to me when some big fat bruin has his arse sticking out of your bushes."

Alana smiled weakly and continued planting. Rick watched. Maybe she should start selling popcorn.

"You've heard about the new mine?" she said when she was almost done planting the canes.

Rick nodded. "It's great news. I just hope our greenie-green city council don't scare them off with a bunch of crazy demands."

The fact that he considered the mostly conservative city council "green" was almost breathtaking.

"You're not worried about our water?"

Rick snorted. "Our water's clean as clean and it always will be. Comes from a pristine mountain stream. You take a look around at where other people's water comes from. Besides, you can eat magnesium. I take it every morning. Add a little to our water and we'll all be better for it."

"But what about runoff and chemicals?"

"They can deal with all those things now. We need the jobs and the money. The mill's shut. The tourism development boom is done. Fewer people ski these days. What else are we going to do?"

"Agriculture?" Alana said.

Rick eyeballed her as if she had just proposed establishing a zoo or a strip joint. "Agriculture is hard work and it doesn't pay shit. You ain't gonna convince anyone to bust their ass tilling the land for ten bucks an hour. Most farmers have day jobs just to make ends meet. Mines bring union jobs and union pay."

"Value-added farm products," Alana said.

"What are those?" Rick cracked a grin, his bulbous belly pressing against the fence post and his arms resting on the slat. He clearly enjoyed these discussions, even though she was sure he thought she was cracked.

"You know, like jams and jellies, and sun-dried tomatoes," she said. "There's a growing market in small-batch organic products with the hundred-mile diet and all."

Rick rolled his eyes dramatically. "We were all a lot healthier before we started overthinking every damn thing we put in our mouths."

For some reason this statement made Alana start craving a McDonald's McChicken, and she decided it was time to call it a day in the garden. She started collecting her tools and made as if to sidle back toward the house.

Rick leaned farther over the fence. "You do know it's all a farce, right?"

"What?"

"All this environment stuff. It was invented by a bunch of hysterical city folks with too much time and money on their hands."

Alana's knees felt slightly soft. What was Rick going to do if she joined Maude's environmental coalition? Although she had no idea why losing Rick's strange friendship meant anything to her. Surely she viewed him as more of a pest than a friend.

"You think?" she said.

"I know," he said, and he gave her a big wink.

She returned to the house and showered. After staring at her reflection in the mirror for a few minutes, she decided to screw it and blow-dry her hair. She was not going to look like Bobo the Clown for another day. Maybe her track record of not eating McChickens had earned her that right. Then she applied a small amount of makeup and pulled on a swishy black hemp skirt. Feeling pathetically relieved to be looking moderately attractive again, she drove down to City Hall. She parked a block away, as she was always worried who might be watching her through the frosted glass windows and tut-tutting that the coordinator for the Regional Environmental Board couldn't find a more sustainable means of transportation. Her armpits were damp as she turned the SUV off, but she did a sniff test and decided that they were okay. She reserved antiperspirant for important events, such as public presentations, wine and cheese parties, and exercise class, where she knew she would be doing a lot of arm-waving. At any other time she could feel the carcinogens eating away at her skin.

As soon as Alana walked in, she saw that Maude had Zander pinned against a wall at the back of the reception area. The crease between Zander's eyebrows pinched together slightly when he saw Alana. She and Zander had a vague alliance, but he was often too busy toeing the strange and unpredictable City Hall line to be completely reliable.

She darted around the corner to the part-time building inspector's office before Maude saw her. Charlie was an old-time Silver Peak resident and one of Alana's few solid allies at City Hall.

"What is going on out there?" she said.

"I dunno. Maude came in all fired up about seeing the maps showing the boundaries for the alternate watershed."

"Do we have an alternate watershed?"

Charlie flipped Alana a half smile and the ends of his white moustache twitched. "Sure. On Booker. There's a report in the files somewhere from like 1950, but as I understand it there were problems with Booker and who knows if they actually used flow meters to determine volumes back then. And building a new reservoir and piping for the water would not be cheap."

"I heard that it's under consideration," Alana said. "For water security purposes."

Charlie gave her a squint over his half-moon glasses. "News to me. Then again, a lot of things around here are news to me," he said, shooting a look in the direction of Stewart's closed office door. "I just stick with houses. It's safer that way."

"Can I get a copy of the report?" Alana said.

Charlie snorted. "Have you seen the city file room? That was before the digital age. You'd have to dig for years to find that sucker. And that's assuming someone hasn't burned it or filed it in the garbage."

Alana had heard stories about the city file room. Apparently, despite having a reasonable-sized staff, file management didn't fall under anyone's purview. Either that or the person whose purview it fell under did not feel obligated to do their job.

"How does Zander think Maude found out about the other watershed?" She really hoped Maude hadn't mentioned her name. She might have to take up antiperspirant use until the mine issue was resolved.

"I didn't hear that part of the conversation. She came in here and took a few strips out of him for withholding information. She's demanding maps, flow monitoring, use rates, all the water quality tests that have been run on Mur Creek in the last year, the mine proposal, Stewart's jock strap size, and pretty much anything else that could be even remotely relevant. The photocopier's going to be running for days. She's also indicated she's going to FOI any permits the city issued for prospecting in the reserve. Like there were any. Apparently she doesn't know that that's under provincial jurisdiction."

"Does the city have the proposal yet?"

"Not that I know of."

"And what do *you* think of the mine?"

Charlie winked. "*I* have learned that in this town, you keep your head down and your opinions to yourself. But the bottom line is, mining is under provincial government jurisdiction. The provincial government is *supposed* to consult with us, but I'll believe that when I see it. Unless the city mounts a massive protest, the province could approve it without us having any say at all."

Alana stared at him. Was he saying the mine was as good as a done deal?

He pressed a finger to his lips and fluttered his fingers as if telling her to move along, that he had already said too much, and he lowered his eyes to his desk.

Alana lurked uncertainly in the hall. She had come in to drop some things off with Zander, mostly as an excuse to find out what he knew, but she didn't want to interrupt him now. She left the items, now slightly rippled from the sweat of her palms, on Zander's desk and slipped out the fire exit like a criminal.

She would return home and edit her climate change document. She would garden and look after the kids. She would *not* get involved in this.

She spent the rest of the afternoon researching how mines got approved in community watersheds in British Columbia, and she read the WELA paper that Tabitha had referenced. As far as she could tell, given that the Crown owned the subsurface rights in almost all of BC, even on private property, it appeared that as long as the mine passed an environmental assessment—assuming it had a high enough expected production rate to even trigger the BC Environmental Assessment Act—and met provincial regulations, there was nothing a community could do to prevent a mine from being established in its watershed.

Then she read a depressing report on how disrespectfully community watersheds had been treated by the province in the past. She ended feeling rather ill about the prospects of keeping the mine out of their watershed.

Maude's cohort, now mobilized, spent the afternoon exchanging protest strategy emails and scathing commentary regarding Zander's competency and morals. Alana sent a polite and carefully worded little note indicating that she'd mostly had positive experiences with Zander and hinting that maybe Zander didn't have as much influence at City Hall as they thought. She didn't want to say outright via email that she thought Stewart might be a lunatic. Her note was met with a barrage of patronizing emails citing Zander's frequent failure to answer emails and questions.

Alana chewed on her thumbnail. She didn't know what to do. Communication wasn't Zander's forte, but Alana was fairly certain that it was because he was often hard at work on reports and grant applications, not because he was singlehandedly orchestrating the corporate takeover of Silver Peak by Monsanto, Walmart, and ExxonMobil.

She had wanted to send an email confirming her understanding of the mine approval process, but she felt dumb asking, like she was the only person who couldn't comprehend the provincial Mines Act. And after the response to her email about Zander, she wasn't sure if she wanted to say anything more at all. There was an undercurrent of mania to their emails that she found a little disconcerting.

She scurried down to the school feeling foolish for having wasted an afternoon on something she was *not* going to get involved in. Outside the school, the other parents milled about as normal, discussing play dates, their exercise regimens, and weekend plans, evidently unconcerned about the looming threat in their watershed, their city planner's work habits, or the coming environmental apocalypse, for that matter.

Maude's orders to bring three people to the meeting on Tuesday lingered heavy in Alana's mind, and she started scanning the playground for even remotely viable options. She wasn't even sure if *she* was going to the meeting, and yet she felt obligated to produce attendees because she had been told to.

Sometimes her sense of duty was over the top.

Therese stood talking to Lou, one of the resident grandfathers who picked up his grandchildren once or twice a week. She sidled over to them. Lou had to be part of the local environmental faction. He gardened, wore his white hair long, and often sported dirty hippie-type clothes. And he was talking to Therese.

"So, have you two decided who you're going to hit up to invite to the meeting on Tuesday?" Alana said.

Therese recoiled as if Alana had forgotten the secret handshake. She twitched her head violently like she had a tic, and then beamed brightly. "Alana. You know Lou, right?"

"Of course." Alana offered the older man a tentative smile. He was Lou. He was on the playground every afternoon just like her. But then she realized she didn't know a thing about the man. She searched frantically for reference points—write-ups in the *Silver Peak News*, introductions at parties or events—but came up blank. Lou smiled at her with a similar absentness.

Therese's eyes bored into Alana, but whatever message Therese was sending, Alana wasn't getting it. Alana shifted her eyes from one to the other with a stricken grin.

Therese turned to Lou. "Lou, I'm sure you know Alana's dad, George Matheson."

Lights flicked on in Lou's eyes, and he looked Alana over. She stood there looking, no doubt, like a dull-witted goat.

"Oh, of course, I know your dad. We golf."

Alana nodded back. "Yup. That's my dad. He loves golf." She gave a bit of a thumbs-up to Lou. In difficult social situations, the general rule was that she became colossally idiotic. "I better go. I see my kids. Great talking to you."

She grabbed Suzanne on her way to collect the children. "I just made a total ass out of myself. Who is Lou?"

Suzanne shook her head and laughed. "Louis Steeves, the richest man in town. Father of Leonard and Nate Steeves, the two cutest guys that went to Reedmont High, except for Nate of course who was a genius and left in grade ten to go to boarding school. I made out with Leonard at a dance once. He was the only guy taller than me back then. It's so unfortunate what's happened to him."

Alana reviewed the unfortunate things that might have happened to Leonard, the unremarkable balding and portly father of the two boys that Lou picked up every day—and then realized that Suzanne was referring to Leonard's decline in appearance, not some ghastly disease or loss of a child. Alana racked her brain for some recollection of Leonard and Nate in high school and came up blank. Of course, she had gone to the smaller Silver Peak High School, not Reedmont, and Suzanne was a few years older than her.

Alana realized dimly that Nate Steeves, the owner of Mountain Magnesium Resources, whom she was meeting with tomorrow, could be the Nate Steeves that Suzanne was talking about. And she had been about to inform his father of Maude's meeting tomorrow, which would explain Therese's reaction. Not that Maude's meeting was secret—at least, she didn't *think* it was secret. Maude *had* asked her to invite people. But maybe it was secret. Which would make it difficult to invite people.

Suzanne was now staring at her, and Alana drew the conclusion that there was some conversational space that she was expected to fill.

"Are you okay?" Suzanne asked. "Your hair looks nice."

"I'm fine," Alana said. "I think I might be meeting with Nate tomorrow. Don't tell anyone. I think he's offering me a job, to help with the public consultation on the proposed mine." When Suzanne's face remained impassive, she added, "In the watershed."

"Oh, you'll love Nate. He's so nice, and super hot. And I'm sure he's better now. A mine in the watershed? Is that a good idea?"

"I don't really know. I don't think so. There are too many risks of chemical runoff, increased sedimentation, and other disturbance. Do you want to come to a meeting about it tomorrow night?" Duncan was now butting up against Alana with his book bag and Katie leaned against her thigh.

Suzanne moved into a full bolt at the mention of the word "meeting." "Oh, no. I don't do meetings." She waved her hand at Alana and slipped into the crowd before Alana could say anything more, or ask what Suzanne had meant when she'd said she was sure Nate was "better now." Better from what?

Katie and Duncan hopped in puddles and kicked at the last remaining skiffs of snow in the playground while Alana stalked potential people to invite to the meeting. She approached a quiet member of the PAC who had always been very friendly on the playground, who walked everywhere and who had talked about environmental issues before. But the woman's brush-off was efficient and practiced, as if she knew all too well the way Silver Peak environmental meetings went. "Thanks for the invite. But we're moving."

Alana raced after another friend, Sabrina, whose husband ran a ski shop in town. Sabrina's eyebrows shot over her glasses. "Oh, no, I'm not getting involved. We were at a dinner party on Sunday and the guests got into a fight about the mine, and now some of the people aren't speaking to each other. I don't really have an opinion and can't afford to pick sides or Tim's business might be affected."

Alana nodded her understanding and walked away.

Her neighbor, Marie, smiled at the invitation. "Oh, I know I should, Alana. But I just don't like those kinds of things."

Alana arrived home utterly defeated and demoralized. She had hoped to get a sense of how other people were feeling about the mine, so she could get a sense how *she* was feeling. She had also hoped to find some like-minded people to take with her to Maude's meeting tomorrow night.

Instead she would have to face Nate Steeves—whom she had now painted in her head as a callow and wealthy pretty boy with great abs and a motorboat—with no sense of how other people were feeling, other than that they evidently equated environmental meetings with having a root canal. The abs and motorboat would at least make it much easier to say no—although she doubted he parked his boat at the office.

Then she would have to go to Maude's meeting utterly alone.

CHAPTER SIX

Needs

Blaine knocked on the front door just as Alana stepped out of the shower. He had agreed to take the kids to Duncan's soccer game so she could go to her meeting with Nate. She flew down the stairs in a towel to find him fully outfitted in his red, white, and blue spandex road biking gear. He didn't teach on Tuesday afternoons, and she had some vague notion that he usually went biking.

"I said 2:20," she said, pulling the towel more tightly around her breasts.

"I know. I wanted to go through the workbench downstairs. I'm still missing some of my bike tools."

"Fine," she said. "You're not going biking while Duncan is at soccer, are you?"

"I thought I'd go out for a little one."

"What about Katie?"

Blaine shrugged. "There are plenty of parents there. She'll just hang out with her own friends and watch like she usually does."

"So you're a free rider?"

Blaine, with his degrees in economics, knew perfectly well that she was not referring to his biking. He offered a tight smile. "Yes, Alana. I, Blaine, am a free rider."

She shook her head, repressed the urge to wrap his tight little red shorts around his neck, and marched back up the stairs.

She blew her hair dry quickly, trying not to stare at the few grey strands that mingled with the deep brown of her natural color. She might have to start dying it soon. A bigger person—or a bigger environmentalist—would just let her hair go grey. Then again, she always wondered about Tabitha's hair. There was no way she could get that lush auburn color unless she had horseshoes up her ass.

Beauty was challenging to surrender, even for environmentalists.

She selected a black hemp skirt that fell just below her knees, black leather boots, and a tailored white shirt. It didn't scream environmentalist, but it sent a message that she wasn't a corporate lackey either. Was it okay to want to look environmentally sexy?

She went downstairs to the workshop to suggest to Blaine that he not leave Katie alone at the soccer field. All three lights in the workshop were on, and the blinds on the two windows were closed, blocking out all signs of the glorious sunlit day outside. The lights would also no doubt be on when she arrived home in two hours. Blaine was bent over one of the big plastic bins he had always chucked his tools into, his perfectly shaped red spandexed ass sticking up into the air. One really could only pull off red spandex with a perfect ass. She snapped open the blinds and flicked off the lights. She didn't get it. Who would want to do anything in a bunker when one could be in the warm glow of the sun?

"You know," she said, "it's light out. You'd save energy if you opened the blinds."

Blaine regarded her blankly. He didn't get angry at her constant reminders; they went right past him. The expected and inconsequential nattering of some sort of environmental conscience perched on his shoulder. "I must have forgotten to open them. I'm only going to be in here for a few minutes."

"Blaine, 'forgetting' is when you do it most of the time and then have a lapse. Not when you never do it."

Blaine made the environmental dementor hissing noise again.

As she climbed into the SUV and pulled out of the garage, Blaine, who had emerged from the basement, gave her two thumbs up. She closed the garage door to shut out his grinning face. He wanted her to get this job. She had no idea why she was even going for the interview. What was she doing? What would the Greenes think?

She drove downtown and parked a block away so the dilapidated, dirty SUV couldn't be associated with her. The Mountain Magnesium Resources offices shared the back of a converted brick warehouse with a small coffee shop and a yoga studio. She opened the funky turquoise door, as Nate had instructed, and stepped inside the foyer.

Sunlight flooded the room and small triangles of red and blue fell from a stained glass window onto the creamy wooden floor. A formal-looking chartreuse settee sat against a brick outer wall with a square glass coffee table in front of it. Windowed offices lined the hall that led away from the empty foyer.

A tall, nicely built man with medium-brown spiky hair emerged from one of the offices, wearing dark jeans, turquoise sneakers, and a blue and white checked shirt. The attractive man from the grocery store. His striking blue-green eyes seemed to catch and hold her somehow.

"Alana Matheson," he said, his voice gentler than she had expected.

"Yes," she managed.

"I'm Nate Steeves."

Suzanne had been right. He *was* hot. Supremely hot. What *had* happened to his brother, Leonard? But there was a spareness to his expression that didn't jibe with the friendliness he exuded on the phone. Tired lines were etched under his eyes.

"Pleased to meet you," she said, extending her hand. A hand textured with strange calluses took hers.

"Why don't you come into my office and we'll talk." He turned, and she followed him uncertainly. She hadn't been nervous before, when she thought he was a slick corporate guy and she was planning to make it clear that she was unsuited for the job. But now she was speechless and jittery. And curious. Environmentalists did not evaluate people based on their looks, she reminded herself. She was uninterested in good-looking men. Or at least her brain was. Other parts of her body evidently harbored less earth-focused intentions.

A large burnished cherry desk occupied the center of the room. Papers stood in neat stacks on top of it, and a white motorcycle helmet was perched on the front right corner. Nate gestured to a leather couch and settled into the office chair behind his desk. Alana perched on the edge of the couch and set her briefcase on the floor.

Nate offered a faint smile. "Why don't I give you a little background, and then you can tell us whether you think you might be a fit here. Not surprisingly, there is going to be some opposition in town to the development of a mine in the watershed. We need to try to get the word out to the public that we're not trying to wreck the watershed. But we also need to run a public consultation to determine what people's concerns are and figure out how to address them. It's our goal to do everything on the up and up and be as open and transparent as possible."

He glanced down at his desk occasionally while he spoke, waiting for an email maybe, or just uninterested in her. Maybe he had only called her in as a favor to her crazy dad, who had no doubt applied significant pressure. Or perhaps she was staring.

She shifted her eyes away from him. A large framed MBA from Queen's University hung on the wall beside his desk, flanked on either side by black and white photos of black jazz musicians she didn't recognize. Three teardrop-shaped blue lights dangled over his desk, illuminating his work area, and eight squares of sun from the old paned windows of the warehouse brightened the floor. It was a gorgeous office, precisely to her tastes—or the tastes that she *would* have if she allowed herself to care about decorating, which she didn't, because she was an environmentalist.

"I've heard you have a talent for framing things, Alana, so we were hoping you would consider coming and working with us. Part-time."

"You aren't just going by what my dad said, are you?" she said.

His smile looked vaguely pained. "No. I called your references. I'm not just going by what your dad said."

"Don't you want to ask me some questions?"

He pursed his lips in a secretive, sexy sort of smile. "Sure, we can do that, and you should ask me questions. This isn't exactly an interview. It's more of a conversation. Why don't you tell me what you know about magnesium?"

Those eyes. Those eyes could pretty much kill someone, she decided, but she managed to shift to her professional interview tone and thoughts. "Well, I know it's used as a structural metal to reduce the weight of things, like cars and airplanes, to reduce their fuel consumption. So that's a positive. I know it's also used in a lot of electronics and medications."

"What do you think would be your biggest challenges if you took the job?"

"I would be concerned about the runoff from access roads and a mine in the watershed. I know magnesium itself is considered fairly harmless. But if I learned something bad was going to happen, I don't know if I could lie about it for you. So I don't know if I'm the best choice for this."

The sexy smile returned, as if he found her amusing. "I understand your concerns, but we don't intend to do anything to harm the watershed."

She leaned back and crossed her arms over her chest. "Well, that's great, but at a certain point your investment will become such that it will be hard to walk away, and your and my levels of risk tolerance might be quite different."

"Okay, I do understand your strong environmental convictions, and that's part of the reason we want you to work here. The board of directors feels confident that this mine can be done with little environmental impact. Mining is changing, and we want to be at the forefront of doing it differently. And we really need to think about the economic benefits for Silver Peak. Economic diversification and small-scale industry can be important for sustainability. But if you don't feel it's the right fit for you, I understand."

Instead of relief, Alana felt a small frisson of panic. He was letting her off in the politest way, which was what she wanted, wasn't it? What sort of voodoo magic had those blue eyes worked on her?

"It's not that I don't want to help you. I would be willing to research it and put out accurate information and help you to understand people's concerns. It's just that at some point, if I decide the environmental impact is too significant, I may have to resign and join the side fighting against the mine. I'm not sure if you would want that."

His mouth twisted in a sort of half smile and he arched an eyebrow. "So, you're sort of sort of in. But you might turn on us at any time."

She smiled back, hoping this was sort of funny to him, or at least that he wasn't angry. "I understand you might not want me based on that."

"Why don't we both think it over and then talk again tomorrow? We have one other person to talk to, and we would require you to sign a nondisclosure agreement, which would mean that you couldn't fight against the mine for at least a year after you resigned. So if you're planning to be on the front lines of protest, you probably should not take the job."

They were talking to someone else. Who else were they considering? If she wanted this job, which she didn't—or did she?—she had said a whole bunch of things she shouldn't have.

Nate rose and gestured to the door.

She rose too, scrambling for her briefcase. "Well... I'm not really sure if I'm going to join the protestors yet. I'm not necessarily planning to at all. I like what you're saying about making it a sustainable mine. I might be interested in the job. I just want you to know I'm pretty environmentally focused."

"And that's exactly why we want you," Nate said, his eyes intently focused on hers. Alana imagined some of the other contexts in which Nate could be saying "want you" to her. "Why don't I call you tomorrow after we've both given it some thought?"

"Sounds great," she said cheerily, her hearty manner at odds with all the arguments she had just put forth regarding taking the job. As she followed him into the hallway, her heart pounded strangely. He smelled of leather.

A woman stood in the reception area, her hair a cloud of spun gold in the sunlight. Fiona Granger, Alana's archenemy, except that Fiona didn't know it, and most of the time Alana half liked her, or at least admired her. Fiona was effortlessly beautiful in a natural way, with glorious hair and perfect skin, even if her eyes were a bit intense. Blaine always gutted himself when Alana compared herself to Fiona, saying that Fiona looked like a cross between a scorpion and a carp. But Blaine said that kind of thing about everybody.

Fiona was also an environmental consultant, except that she charged more, took on bigger projects, spoke four languages, dressed in eco-fashions sourced from Paris, and had degrees from better universities. Fiona was also far more assertive than Alana. Alana figured it was because Fiona had been on the Canadian downhill ski team when she was younger and had gotten pretty comfortable with pushing boundaries. Blaine called Fiona a ball-busting close-talker—she tended to stand very close when talking to people—and even in his least charitable moods during their divorce he continued to maintain that he'd hire Alana over Fiona any day. Then again, very assertive women always had tended to creep Blaine out.

And although Alana and Fiona had tried, they couldn't quite seem to see eye to eye, which Alana chalked up to Fiona being more of... well, pretty much everything than Alana.

Nate was obviously considering her for the job too.

Fiona would be a better choice. She didn't have children, and she was far more dedicated to her work than Alana could be. It was for the best, but something in Alana's heart ached at the prospect.

Fiona greeted Nate with one of her over-the-top hugs, complete with air kisses, some sort of affectation she had adopted after spending a year in France, and Nate good-naturedly returned the hug, saying that it was great to see her.

Clearly, Fiona and Nate knew each other.

Alana bid her goodbyes and slipped out while they were distracted.

She found herself on the other side of the turquoise door inhaling the damp April air. The breeze had edges of warmth to it, and the sky was a vivid swath of blue punctuated by the crisp white tips of the mountains. The skeleton trees all around town lifted their bare brown branches to the pale yellow sun. She made her way down the sidewalk, past the Eternal Bean coffee shop and yoga studio—and the scents of roasted beans and patchouli—and onto the main street of Silver Peak, where she stood in front of the Wise Owl Bookstore, Suzanne's shop. She peeked inside, but only Adrianne, Suzanne's partner, who was childless and always impeccably dressed and behaved, stood behind the counter.

The entire street would be ripped up that summer, the iron-rich red earth exposed, and the ancient water mains, storm sewers, gutters, and pavement replaced as part of a decades-long process of renewing the infrastructure that Silver Peak and other communities across the province had built at the turn of the century. It was renewal that most communities couldn't afford, but they had to undertake it, lest their vital infrastructure crumble beneath them.

At four in the afternoon, the downtown of Silver Peak still drifted of the brink of unconsciousness. A street sweeper made its way toward Alana, taking another pass at the grime of winter, while a logging truck piled with logs charged through the main street from the other direction, leaving curls of dust in its wake. Several cars occupied the grocery store parking lot, always the busiest place in town. The after-school bustle had ended, and the five o'clock crescendo—when working folk stormed the grocery store in search of dinner—had yet to start. Then the street activity would taper off again, leaving Oak Street devoid of anyone but the few bar-goers and teenagers by mid-evening.

The town's quiet had been growing ever since the mill closure and associated layoffs two years ago. The ripple effects continued to wind their way through the fragile little economy of the rural town, and empty storefronts now lined the main street, gradually but perniciously edging out the remaining businesses.

She knew the local merchants had a hard time making a go of it. Tourism was now Silver Peak's biggest economic generator, but restaurant and hotel jobs didn't pay mortgages, and the ski hill already hung on the edge with unreliable snowfall and rising energy costs. And travelers were a notoriously fickle lot, whose continued spending hinged on their own comfortable incomes. Global pressures and economic downturns could eliminate the tourists' wealth, and then what would happen to Silver Peak? The town was hanging on for now, but barely, and even the most rabid of local environmentalists, at least the rational ones, knew that economic diversification was necessary.

Maybe Silver Peak needed the mine.

But did Alana really want to be involved? She used to come to the Eternal Bean a lot. She and the other moms would cluster around the tables, clutching white mugs and sharing stories about the front lines of motherhood, while the kids guzzled steamers and picked dandelions in the empty lot next to the warehouse. She missed the simplicity of her mandate back then: get through the day, ensure the house was clean-ish, cook dinner, garden a bit, and most importantly, keep the children loved, fed, and alive. Four years ago, cooking, shopping, and walking everywhere were her biggest political acts. But that was when she and Blaine were married—when she believed that she could change the world through motherhood. Now she knew it was far more complicated.

She spied Maude lumbering along the sidewalk on the other side of the street. She slipped around the corner of the warehouse, heading to her vehicle to collect Duncan and Katie. Tonight would be soon enough to see Maude.

CHAPTER SEVEN

Choices

Maude's purple house glowed in the hazy setting sun. Alana lurked a block away, watching people with grey hair arrive on foot. Wasn't anyone under forty an environmentalist these days?

Alana had never been to Maude's house before and wasn't sure what she expected—a shanty built entirely of driftwood, a yurt, a tiny duplex? Instead, Maude's house was a sumptuous modernist '60s rancher with floor-to-ceiling windows and an immaculate yard filled with small river rocks, birdbaths, and low-maintenance shrubbery.

Maude, the uber-environmentalist, didn't garden. Alana breathed a small puff of relief. There was a small chink in Maude's eco-armor that Alana could clutch when she was deep in a pit of self-loathing over her own planet-despoiling ways.

She was still working up her courage to enter when Fiona sauntered up the street, wearing some sort of snood over her lush locks.

"Playing both sides," Fiona said in greeting. A slight tone of laughter undergirded her words, but it was more bemused laughter, as if she didn't quite get Alana.

"I could say the same for you," Alana said.

Fiona swept the snood from one shoulder to the other. "Nate called me in to ask for some high-level advice on some issues," she said, as if the idea of taking a mere job with Nate would be beneath her.

"Well I was just there telling him I wouldn't do a very good job for him because I don't really believe in the mine."

"Hmm. That's too bad. He needs someone like you."

"Aren't you opposed to the mine?" Alana asked, flipping her hand in the direction of Maude's house.

"Yes. But I'm objecting more on process. I think the province needs to include communities in decision-making relating to mine development. Or Mountain Magnesium does. You could change all that around."

Or find myself directly in your "process" crosshairs, Alana thought grimly. "Change provincial or corporate policy? That's a pretty tall order. I doubt Nate will hire me after what I said today, anyway. We should go in."

The interior of Maude's house matched the exterior. Slanted wood paneling covered one wall, and colorful, dated, geometric furniture filled the living room. A sea of grey heads occupied the sectional sofa and the chairs scattered on the creamy shag carpet. Everything was old, but retro-stylish and immaculate.

Fiona proceeded to do her hug, greet, and air kiss with practically everyone in the room, and Alana slid into a dining room chair in the back. Maude swanned about at the front in nondescript, ill-fitting khakis and a large green t-shirt with a row of trees silkscreened on the front. After finishing her rounds of the room, Fiona joined Maude and clapped her hands to get everyone's attention.

Alana felt a twinge in her stomach. She had not expected that Fiona would be at the helm of this. Alana should be doing this kind of thing—running grassroots environmental campaigns was what real environmentalists did—but she didn't have the stomach, or perhaps the balls, for it. She offered silent, half-hearted smiles to the people in the chairs around her and then sat unspeaking in their midst, her hands folded on her lap, feeling somehow as though she had stumbled into the very wrong meeting and would have to endure until it was over. She shouldn't feel that way. These were her peeps. These were the people who believed in the same things she did.

When she'd collected the kids from Blaine earlier, she had casually suggested to Blaine that perhaps he should go to the meeting too. "Sure, I'll go," he'd said. "Do you think they're ready for Super Environmental Blaine? What views do you want me to put forth? No magnesium mine in our watershed ever? All the little old ladies will be so excited to have an environmental superhero in their midst."

Alana looked around at the gathered crowd. These were not little old ladies. They were seasoned environmentalists, and they would have eaten Blaine alive.

Super Environmental Blaine, however, was not present.

Fiona introduced herself, and then had everyone in the room do the same, which took a long time because several people felt they had to go into great detail regarding their environmental pedigree: the campaigns they had fought, their time in the environmental trenches cozying up to national environmental leaders, their love of the wild, their hiking and birding. Alana could only fall back on her education and work, which sounded lame next to the bird and tree love in full bloom all around her.

"So the main purpose of tonight is to discuss principles," Fiona announced at last. "Principles of communication and how we expect City Hall and Mountain Magnesium to deal with this. And how we will deal with them." Alana's eyes widened, and she could feel her contacts air-drying. She blinked hastily and tried to compose her expression. She had expected that someone would speak about the risks of a magnesium mine in the watershed, and was hoping that Maude had managed to round up a mining expert who could provide some background on the geology of the watershed and how magnesium was extracted. Talking about principles seemed right out of left field. Yet everyone else was smiling. Hands were raised as Fiona solicited suggestions. Honesty, integrity, transparency, and collaboration were put forth and scrawled in Fiona's illegible handwriting on the flipchart that Maude had placed at the front.

After fifteen minutes, Alana tuned out, still trying to understand what vague principles had to do with the situation. She found herself thinking about Nate and his undeniably perfect jaw and cheekbones, and whether she wanted to work for him or not. Then she tried to figure out how long it would be before Maude called a bathroom break and she could slip away. She wanted to be snuggled under the covers with Duncan and Katie reading about the land of Oz. A grey tabby cat patrolled the living room, and, apparently having decided that Alana was the one, leapt into her lap, settled himself, and started purring.

"And Alana, what do you think the most important principle for communicating with Mountain Magnesium would be?" Fiona wore the look of utter euphoria that she got when she was facilitating. Everyone turned to stare at Alana. She quickly focused back on the flipchart. At least thirty options were printed, in every conceivable location.

"Knowing what we're talking about," she said flatly.

"We're prioritizing now," Fiona said as if speaking to a small child, the snood swinging perilously over her right shoulder. "The time for adding new principles has passed. That one isn't on the list. Do you have a suggestion for the most important principle—from the list?" she clarified.

Alana tried to keep her grimace neutral. "Um, transparency, I guess."

"Perfect," Fiona trilled, adding a checkmark to that word. "I think we have our list of principles. We're going to move into breakout groups now."

Alana almost recoiled, and the grey tabby dug his claws into her lap to stabilize himself. She hated breakout groups. She considered them the worst invention since... well, since something. But Fiona was already moving through the room, assigning people to groups. Alana hoped she'd be grouped with the cat, but instead she was placed in a group with two older men and a squat middle-aged couple.

Her group eyed her with undisguised superciliousness. She was used to this in environmental settings. It was the mascara and use of hair products... or maybe her expression of undisguised fear. She put the cat down, not certain he was contributing to her credibility. Cats killed songbirds after all.

The rest of her group all seemed to know each other, so the introductions focused on Alana. Her name did not twig with any of them and they continued to regard her with patronizing expressions. Not unusual, but the plus side was that she would likely be able to depart in complete anonymity. The middle-aged woman, Kathy, wore no makeup, had unstyled greying hair and seemed to have adopted the Maude dress code, except her t-shirt had cows on the front. Where did they get these clothes? Alana understood that environmental living required sacrifices, and that one's appearance technically shouldn't matter, but even the thrift store offered more stylish choices.

"Your group will be reviewing the watershed maps," Fiona said, thrusting a map tube into the midst of the group and wandering away. Kathy pulled out the maps and unfurled them. As the group leaned in to study them, Kathy pointed to features with authority: Mur Marsh, which sat in the center of the watershed; the watershed access road; Baynes and Silver Mountains, which framed the watershed area; the Williston reservoir; and Mur and Orrington Creeks, which met at the reservoir and provided the community's water. Kathy traced the course of Mur and Orrington Creeks carefully with her finger, glancing at Alana every few seconds to ensure she was following.

"So, what exactly are we supposed to be doing?" Alana said. *Review the maps for what?*

"This is the city watershed," Kathy said, enunciating each word carefully as if Alana might be too slow to follow, and emphasizing the word "city," as if Alana might have thought they were looking at a map of Arkansas.

"I know," Alana said. "But are we supposed to be looking for anything in particular on the maps?"

Kathy made an irritated wheezy sound at the back of her throat. "It's important that you know where the creeks are and have an understanding of the watershed. Do you need me to explain the features on the map?"

The rest of the group eyed Alana with patient but condescending expressions. They had pulled their chairs into a tight circle, preventing the possibility of bolting. Alana pondered how it was that, despite taking cartography in university, she came across as being completely unknowledgeable about maps. Perhaps it was the eye makeup and she would do better with a snood or a balaclava.

"No. I'm good," she mumbled, dutifully shifting her gaze to the contour lines, feeling like she was in a prayer group. The other group members regarded the map profoundly, every so often pointing to items and murmuring, "Look at this," like they had spotted something particularly gruesome in the watershed, or as if the mine entrails were already splashed all over the map.

Fiona clapped her hands at the front. "Shall we have a reporting out of the groups, or move directly into the break?"

Alana's jaw tightened. The only thing she hated more than breakout groups was the reporting out of breakout groups. At that moment, Maude appeared at the entrance of the living room with a tray of baked goods. Amidst the oohs and ahs about Maude's baking, Alana noted two youngish people standing in the kitchen holding beers. She slipped away from her group, almost tipping over her chair in her haste, and joined the man and woman in the kitchen. The man glanced at her, picked up another bottle of beer from the counter, popped the lid, and handed it to her.

Alana took the beer gratefully and extended her hand. Max and Laney introduced themselves as newcomers to Silver Peak. They looked about thirty and outdoorsy in a non-threatening kind of way, with stylish jeans and t-shirts, good haircuts, and clear evidence of regular grooming. Laney even wore eyeliner and blush.

"We're not really sure what to make of all this," Max said in a hushed voice while the breakout groups started their reporting out in the other room. "Maude's our neighbor, so she roped us into serving drinks tonight. Of course we don't want a mine in the watershed, but Maude's already talking about occupying City Hall and getting some planner guy fired for withholding public information."

"Hmm," Alana said noncommittally after taking a generous slug of beer and letting the hoppy bitterness erase some of the strain of the day. It helped that there were no snoods in sight. Get some planner guy fired? Why was Zander bearing the brunt of this? She took another large swallow of beer.

"Don't you think the city council will just listen to the public if we say we don't want the mine?" Laney said.

"I think the public is going to be divided," Alana replied. "It's not a city responsibility. The province will make the decision, and Silver Peak might not have a lot of say. Based on its track record, I think the province will approve the mine. Magnesium mines aren't as bad for the environment as other kinds of mines."

"Maude says it'll destroy the watershed," Laney breathed, glancing over her shoulder as if Maude might bear down on them at any second wielding a hiking pole.

"I'm not sure about that," Alana said. "I think there's the possibility that they could do it right. I'm not sure about that, but I think it's at least worth hearing what the mining company has to say." She heard these words coming out of her mouth with a sense of horror. What was she saying? She was at an environmental meeting. It was the beer. It sometimes made her think that it was okay to allow the thoughts that ran around inside her head to exit via her mouth, which was definitely *not* okay.

"You sound like you already know a lot about it," Max said. "You should talk to the group."

An icy frisson of fear shot down Alana's legs. "No, these people don't want to hear from me, and I don't know anything at all. There's no way that some people here would be receptive to the notion that maybe a mine in their watershed might, possibly be okay. And like I said, I really don't know what I'm talking about."

A couple of other people came into the kitchen—the breakout groups had clearly finished their reporting out—and Max offered them beers. Alana smiled weakly at them, polished off her beer, edged the bottle onto the counter, and slipped out of the kitchen while Max and Laney talked to the new arrivals. She darted through the hall past the entrance to the living room, which was now a melee of chattering bodies, her palms sweaty. She had her shoes on in an instant and escaped out into the night.

The mountains cut deep and silent shadows into the starry sky. Silver Peak had a desperate, desolate beauty about it. A hidden gem. An escape from the crowds. Unspoiled nature. That was how Silver Peak was marketed to the world. But its remoteness made the cornice upon which its economy hung all the more delicate. She worried that the baby boomers at Maude's had their minds entrenched in the past, back when government and mill jobs were plentiful. Most of them were financially stable and retired. They saw no reason to create jobs, other than the service jobs at the tourist operations in town that they liked to frequent. But communities and countries couldn't be built on service jobs.

Alana sank onto the cement steps of the high school for a few seconds while the sweet, cool mountain air found its way through the folds of her clothes to find skin. Was she really advocating, even if only in her mind, for a mine in the watershed that her children drank from? If there was ever a pivot point for ceasing to be an environmentalist, surely this was it.

Back at the farmhouse, she sent her dad home and pressed her lips against the smooth plump skin of Duncan's and Katie's cheeks, so perfect that sometimes she wanted to pull them back inside herself just so she could have them again and always. She had never imagined motherhood would be so deliciously fraught with wonder and horror.

Blaine's daily score sheet sat in her inbox. Blaine had added points for his daily bus ride and vegetarian lunch—"disgusting," he had noted in brackets—beneath the demerits she had given him for leaving the lights on.

She started recording her own demerits for the day. Two showers. Using the SUV to get groceries. Tossing a milk carton that could have been toted several kilometers to the local recycler. Wearing Gap clothes to Maude's. Wearing eyeliner. Putting clothes in the dryer. It was like an environmental confessional.

Once one started down the slippery slope of engaging in acts against the environment, rationalization became practiced and eventually second nature, until one lived in a cocoon of cognitive dissonance. She could not let that happen.

She vowed to spend the next week in a toque with dirty hair, visiting the library and grocery store on foot, and recording the arrival of songbirds. She would decline the job at Mountain Magnesium and call Maude and volunteer to help. That's what a true environmentalist would do. But somehow Nate's warm and cozy office building seemed a safer place than Maude's oddly glitzy turquoise and cream living room packed with people Alana was sure she agreed with.

So why was it that people she was sure she agreed with scared her so much?

Nate called the next morning while she sat on the front stoop in the thin shafts of morning sunlight, watching for her chickens, or rather her eggs.

In a fit of environmental fervor or penance for the previous night, she had finally broken down and decided that she would more seriously consider getting chickens. One of the local farmers, whom she knew from the local farmer's market, had always indicated that he would sell her fertilized eggs and loan her his egg incubator whenever she was ready to get started. When she'd called that morning to ask if he had any eggs available, just so she knew whether it was an option or not, Edgar had been overjoyed and announced he'd be at her house within the half hour before she could find a way to back out of it.

She was now so rattled by the imminent egg arrival, and by the fact that she wouldn't be able to hide the decision from Blaine, that she snatched up the phone without even thinking about it when Nate called, almost as if he were a friend with whom she needed to share her chicken angst. She and Nate exchanged pleasantries while she gawked at the driveway, expecting to see the tail end of a blue farm truck wedged against her front door at any second; Edgar's eyesight wasn't so good, but he continued to believe that his driving skills compensated for a lack of clarity around the edges of his vision.

"I understand that you may not want the job, but if you're interested, we'd like to have you. Fiona spoke very highly of your skills," Nate said.

Alana raised her eyebrows. She wondered if Fiona had also indicated that she was a deranged flight risk who wasn't sure what side of the environmental fence she was on. Then again, Fiona obviously played both sides of the fence herself. Alana walked in a slow circle on her porch. She had to give Nate an answer. She wanted to see him again. But did she want to work for a mining company?

She sighed and closed her eyes, imagining him standing on the porch with her, and she felt a little concerned by the degree to which that thought caused her heart to flutter. "I'll do my best to help you find out what the people here think of the proposed mine, and I'll help make the research understandable for the public, but if I reach a point where I'm convinced the mine is a bad idea, I'll have to step down. And I only want to work until two in the afternoon unless there's a meeting or something."

"We can live with that," Nate said.

Alana felt a jolt. She hadn't expected him to be so amenable.

"Can you start next week?" he said.

She heard the roar of Edgar's pickup wheeling around the bend in the driveway. "Yes, I'll come in Monday morning. I'm afraid I have to go. My chickens are here."

"Did you say chickens?"

"Yes." Was Nate going to think the chickens would interfere with her work? Edgar's tailgate grazed her camellia bush, and she braced for impact, but he righted himself and coasted to a stop a foot from her front door.

Nate's voice seemed almost wistful. "I've always wanted chickens. See you Monday."

She hung up the phone and went out to greet Edgar. What had she just done?

CHAPTER EIGHT

Vermin

"Chickens?" Blaine said, staring at the incubator as if it teemed with germs and poultry lice. He sniffed the air. Alana rolled her eyes. She had carefully washed—several times, with vinegar water—the surprisingly modern electric incubator that Edgar had provided. There should be nothing to detect in the smell department.

Blaine went and stood over the eggs.

"Hello, future vermin," he said. "I just can't wait until you're filthy chickens wandering and shitting all over my old yard. We're going to be such good friends."

He turned away with a shudder, as if the presence of the eggs in his former living room might just send him over the edge. Alana decided not to tell him that she had caught Duncan and Katie rubbing the eggs against their cheeks earlier to keep them warm.

"So I agreed to take the job at the mining company," she said.

Blaine gave her a big thumbs-up. "Whoo hoo! Congratulations! A real job with a real employer. That's awesome."

Alana tried to extinguish her flare of fury. Blaine wasn't worth the emotional energy she put into being irritated with him. "What exactly do you call the work I've been doing for the last two years?"

"Hmm, yeah, you're right. That probably wasn't my most supportive statement, was it?"

"Don't worry, I'm used to it."

"I'm just thinking it'll be nice for you to be able to start spending more money and getting yourself some new furniture." He cast his hand around the living room, which, after he had removed his share of stuff, was somewhat bereft of accoutrements. "And you won't have to work with those environmental bozos anymore."

"They're not bozos, Blaine. The Regional Environmental Board was nice enough to let me take a leave of absence for six months. I'm still working for them." The board had, rather too gleefully she felt, accepted her request for a leave, and had hired Greg Wilson to fill in for her while she was gone. "Of course, when they find out why, or when Greg Wilson blows their minds with his graphic facilitation skills, I'm sure they won't want me back. And I'll probably get fired from Mountain Magnesium or quit within a couple weeks."

"That's the spirit. Once they see how good you are they'll want you full-time."

"Right, and if I work full-time, who's going to look after the kids?" She checked on the stuffed chicken breasts in the oven, which almost felt cannibalistic given the eggs nestled in soft blankets in the living room.

"Me!" Blaine declared.

"You? Remember when you tried that a few years ago? How long was it that you lasted again? Let's see..." Alana stroked her chin and looked at the ceiling, even though she and Blaine both knew perfectly well that Blaine had lasted three months before announcing that he couldn't handle it anymore and had taken a job. And she hadn't even been working full-time then.

"Yeah, but the kids were younger then. And if I look after them, I can start my own business."

"No," she said.

Duncan burst into the kitchen clutching the camera. "Look, Dad. The chickens are going to have a little house with a ladder thing. Jonah's building it. I'm going to do an Earth Day presentation on it. Mom says I can even take some of the chicks into class to show everyone."

"That's great, Duncan," Blaine said, ruffling his hair. "That isn't the camera I just bought last year, is it?"

Alana rolled her eyes at Blaine again. He knew it was. They only had one camera. "Duncan is being very careful with it."

Duncan gave his best gap-toothed grin before skipping off to the living room to add egg shots to his photojournalistic efforts.

"Of course he is. It's great that you have a handyman in your employ."

"He's just fixing up the old chicken coop and helping me out a bit, Blaine."

"Well, when I start my new business I'm going to hire my own handyman."

"Right. 'Cause you know, having a handyman is all the rage these days. Just remember, you do have children to support."

She felt bad for saying this. After all, they were her children too, and she had just as much obligation to support them. But she did feel he had an obligation not to do anything too risky while they were still young. Blaine had been making suggestions that he was planning to quit his job and start a business for years, except he wouldn't tell her his new business idea... possibly because she made fun of his last idea, which *had been* completely stupid. She couldn't tell how serious he was this time, but it was always a worry.

"So I have something new to add to my list of pro-environmental actions this week," Blaine said. "I ordered new flat screen TV. It's twice as efficient as our old one, so I'll be using less energy."

"But I didn't think you even watched TV. You didn't used to..." She trailed off, realizing that the new Blaine, *Heather's* Blaine, might have the TV on all day.

"That's because our TV was the size of a postage stamp. I'll also save on gas costs driving to the theater."

"Blaine, you also have to consider the energy costs of making and transporting the new TV and getting rid of the old one. Sometimes buying something energy-efficient is only a positive environmental action if you absolutely need the thing you're buying." She tried to keep her voice upbeat and encouraging.

Blaine's face dropped into his haggard dog expression. "So I can't claim any points for that? Maybe I should cancel the order."

Had he seen his former life as an endless string of sacrifices to the environmental dementor? Was that why he had left?

"You can get the TV if you want it."

"Really?"

"Yes, really. I'm not the environmental police, Blaine."

"Good, because I sort of ordered a sound system to go with it."

"Of course you did. Just make sure you don't record it on your environmental plus list."

"Roger dodger. What's for dinner?"

She shook her head at him. "*We* are having chicken. *You* are having whatever you and Heather are making."

She offered Jonah a bowl of chicken stew, which he accepted gratefully, although he insisted on sitting outside since he was dirty. He was a man of few words it seemed, or he thought she was a strange older woman. Either way, it was a bit of a relief after Blaine's ceaseless chatter.

He sat on the deck, alone, staring out at the backyard for several minutes after finishing his stew. She went out to retrieve the bowl and inquire if he wanted more. The heavy rays of the setting sun filled the yard with golden dappled sunlight and glinted off the tiny flashes of green on the trees, little jewels of life about to unfurl.

Jonah declined another serving of stew, and she paused for a second to listen to the trill of the crickets.

"I was just thinking about the goat shed," Jonah said. "Goats really like decks. It would be great to put a platform above the shed porch so they could hang out up there, and the rabbit hutch is in pretty good shape. It just needs to be reinforced."

She smiled. "Yeah. I know. But I'm not sure if I'll ever get goats. I've heard they're pretty hard on the land, so I'd really need another acre."

"Right. Well, it's still a beautiful piece of land. You sure lucked out, Mrs. Matheson."

"Please call me Alana, Jonah. And yes, thanks. I know."

"The cherry and apple trees really need to be pruned."

"Can you do that?"

Jonah shook his head. "Not my specialty, and it has to be done just right. But I can find you someone. Larry Lund used to be a master gardener and a tree pruner by trade, before things went sideways on him. He was even married, if you can believe it. I've heard he's the best, especially with old trees that need some serious restoration. He still prunes sometimes."

"Is Larry even around anymore? I haven't seen him in a few weeks."

Jonah shook his head. "I dunno. But I can ask around."

"Is he safe to have on the property? With the children, I mean. I've heard he had a drug problem."

"I think he's fine, but if you like, I could ask him to work only on the days that I'm here."

Alana nodded. "Okay, great."

Jonah rose and placed his ball cap back on his head. "Thanks very much for the food, Mrs. Matheson. See you next week."

On Thursday morning, Alana got the kids off to school, fussed over the eggs a bit, and then retreated to her desk. She had a few projects to finish off for the board before she started work for Mountain Magnesium on Monday. She hadn't been axed from Maude's email list overnight, and judging from the exchanges, they had formulated a plan. They were going to start with a letter campaign, presentations at the city council meetings, media releases, and a website. They spent the day dividing up research assignments, and Alana prayed that nobody would notice that she hadn't raised her hand.

In a move that surprised her, they selected a man, Tom LeDrew, as their leader. She would have thought they would have chosen Maude. But maybe Maude preferred to have a figurehead to take the heat. Tom was a property manager and so convinced of his own brilliance that he couldn't see beyond his own moderately adequate ideas, and the puffed flattery that accompanied his selection and acceptance bordered on nauseating. Maude had better keep him on a tight leash.

Everyone seemed geared up and gung ho. They oozed environmental goodwill and volunteerism as they thanked each other and gave virtual backslaps. The cynical part of Alana, which these days felt like it occupied too large a portion of her black little heart, wondered if maybe they shouldn't extract themselves from their "save the world" haze long enough to check on the true pulse of the town. Of course, she had no idea what the true pulse of the town was either.

She was also starting to feel like a spy. She should tell Maude that she was going to be working for Mountain Magnesium Resources and should be taken off the list. Except she was afraid to.

Maude called after nine p.m., clearly not understanding that Alana preferred to operate in a communication blackout after eight. And Maude's voice was chuffier than it had been the other night. She had backing now. "What happened to you on Tuesday night?"

"Duncan was feeling sick. I had to go." The lie sounded too rushed, and she almost felt like she was pleading with Maude to forgive her for leaving her dumb meeting.

"Hmm." Maude's tone suggested she didn't believe Alana. "I just wanted to follow up on the website."

"Right. I'd be happy to set it up for you this week." That wouldn't be a conflict of interest, she didn't think. She hadn't signed a contract at Mountain Magnesium yet. It was all still theoretical.

"Oh, that's okay. We have two other people who want to do it. We just wanted to get your recommendation on WordPress versus

Squarespace."

"They're both great," Alana said, feeling a bit put out that she'd been so easily replaced. She would have done a great job on the website. Did they not *want* her helping out? Maybe they didn't think she was committed enough to the cause. Which might have been true, but she didn't want people to know that.

"So no preference?"

"No. If you need me to do anything just let me know."

"We have it all under control. Goodnight," Maude said. There was a frigid layer to her voice. Fiona must have told Maude that Alana went for an interview at Mountain Magnesium Resources. So—it had started. She was going to become an environmental pariah. She would be ostracized and outcast. She would have to move and drag Katie and Duncan from a community they loved. Blaine would be overjoyed, of course.

Maybe she should just tell Nate she couldn't do it. She was less afraid of him than she was of Maude and the environmental army. Which was a bit whacked, and should probably tell her something if she believed in all that mumbo jumbo about the messages your body gives you. Which she didn't. So it probably told her nothing other than that she thought Nate was nice and already considered her a flight risk so he wouldn't be too disappointed.

On Saturday afternoon, she set the kids to paint the fence with watercolor paints while she cleaned up the left-over wood from the chicken coop and stacked it against the house. She was going to plant out some garlic since she'd missed planting it in the fall. She figured it might be ready by September. "Better late than never" was usually her gardening mantra, and sometimes it worked out. Other times she ended up harvesting underdeveloped carrots and beets, elevating her squash so the rotting vines didn't ruin the fruit, and trying to coax little green tomatoes to turn red before the frost.

Rick startled her as she was pulling apart the garlic bulbs for planting.

"New playhouse for the kids? It's a little small." He occupied his usual position against the fence. He was ATV-less today, and he must have crept through the grass from his house with deliberate stealth. She wondered how long he'd been standing there.

She laughed. He *was* joking, right? "No. It's for chickens. We have a dozen eggs. They'll hatch in the next three weeks."

Rick gutted himself laughing for several seconds, but then he realized *she* wasn't laughing, and he wiped the tears from his eyes. "What's next, a cow?"

"I was thinking rabbits. They're easier to manage."

"You know, you could just relax."

She turned and scrunched her eyebrows together. Normally she would take this kind of statement as an insult. A commentary on her uptight nature, which in her mind was not really uptight but rather orderly, efficient, and precise. She was a lot of fun when the work was all done and she had six shots of tequila under her belt.

But Rick wore a massive grin and looked hopeful, like he was actually trying to help her. "You know, drink a beer or two, get a bucket of KFC. You don't have to do all this all the time. You need to take a load off. Just hang out. It'll all be all right. You'll see."

Duncan peeked over the fence at Rick.

"Thanks, Rick," Alana said, "but I like doing this kind of thing. I'm not all that good at hanging out."

"That's because you don't practice."

"That's because I don't have time."

"That's because you're afraid."

"Afraid of what?" She was afraid of a lot of things. But she tried to keep that hidden, and she wasn't sure what he was getting at.

"Afraid of just letting go."

Great. Now she was being psychoanalyzed by her neighbor. Her redneck, down-home neighbor with a Ding Dong habit and a mullet. If she let go, her entire household would crash down around her, not to mention the fact that she would not be doing her part as a global citizen.

"I'm not afraid of letting go. I just don't have time to let go." She wasn't even sure what he was talking about her letting go *of*. Her hands felt itchy and sweaty in her gardening gloves, and she had to get inside and get dinner started.

"Suit yourself. Just letting you know that there's a cool frosty waiting for you at my place anytime you want it. I got a real nice view from my deck."

She wondered what Mrs. Rick would make of this invitation. Then she realized she didn't even know if there was a Mrs. Rick. She had glimpsed a female form on Rick's property and porch before, but that could have just been a neighbor or a friend. She smiled her thanks at Rick for the advice and then turned her back to finish planting the garlic.

"Mommy, that weird man is gone," Duncan said after a few minutes.

"Sweetie, please don't call him weird."

"Why?"

"Because we don't call people weird. It's not nice."

"Daddy calls him a redneck."

Alana noted that Katie had started painting her skirt and legs rather than the fence. "I know, but he shouldn't. We don't actually know that much about Rick, and we shouldn't jump to conclusions. He may have different views than us, and we can disagree with his views. But we shouldn't call him names."

"What does redneck mean?" Duncan popped up under her digging arm, knocking a clump of dirt from the spade into his brown hair. Showers for both kids would be required this afternoon. She thought again about the possibility of rigging up rain barrels that fed into a solar heating system. Maybe Jonah could help with that.

"It used to refer to someone who burned the back of their neck because they were always out working in the fields. Now we use it to describe someone who is uneducated and has kind of backwards attitudes."

"Like you mean they got to play soccer all day?" Duncan asked.

Alana found it ironic that her child could only equate the word "field" to a soccer field.

"No, I mean they were out farming in the fields, where you grow crops like wheat and corn."

Duncan cocked his head, still not quite getting it.

Alana opened her mouth to start her "people used to have to farm to get the food that they ate" sermon, but Katie interrupted.

"Are we really going to get bunnies, Mommy?" She had walked through the other recently dug garden bed, and dirt now clung to her freshly painted legs. "Can I bring one to school?"

Alana dropped a kiss onto Katie's soft, plump cheek. "We'll see how the chickens go, and then, yes, we might get bunnies. But Katie, they aren't going to be pets. We're going to eat them."

CHAPTER NINE

The Dark Side

She walked to Mountain Magnesium Resources after dropping the kids at school on Monday. If she was going to sell her soul to the corporate world, at least she would do it on foot. She and Blaine were neck and neck in the "who can be more environmental" competition—mostly because she recorded so many demerits for herself last Tuesday night—but there was no way she was going to let Super Environmental Blaine win.

Once the turquoise door of Mountain Magnesium Resources was in sight, she looked around to make sure nobody was watching, then made a run for the door, hoping to slip in without being seen.

She was so focused on her stealth optics that she didn't notice Zander exiting the building until she slammed into him. Her lip gloss left two faint pink marks on his white shirt.

Zander didn't say anything. He just stepped back and surveyed her as if she catapulted out of nowhere and crashed into him on a regular basis.

"Sorry. I wasn't watching where I was going."

Zander grunted as if this was to be expected, and he patted his hair and shirt back into alignment. He looked almost ruffled and twitchy, trying to sidestep her and continue on his way.

"What are you doing here?" Alana asked.

"Meeting," Zander said over his shoulder.

"I wanted to talk to you about a few things," she called. She figured she should tip Zander off that Maude and the army were for some reason out for blood. Zander's blood. "When's good for you?"

Zander didn't appear to have heard her—at least he didn't respond. Instead he crossed the street, got behind the wheel of his black Ford Escape, and drove off.

Alana stepped into the foyer of Mountain Magnesium Resources just as Nate came walking down the hall with Lou. Both men wore suits. Expensive, well-cut, navy suits. On Lou, whom she was used to seeing in shleppy gardening gear, the effect was jarring, and panic swept over her. Was this the Mountain Magnesium dress code? She was wearing a casual, sleeveless, red hemp dress, her usual business-hippie attire.

A broad smile appeared on Nate's face, and for a millisecond, he seemed to sweep her body with his eyes before resuming his professional affect. "Ah Alana," Nate said. "Have you met my dad yet?"

"We know each other from the playground, sort of." She extended her hand to Lou.

He took it, placed his other hand on top, and gave her a wink. "Glad to have you on board, Alana. I hope you can keep my son out of trouble."

Alana flicked her eyes to Nate. What did Lou mean by that?

Nate's pleasant grin had hardened a bit. "My dad is on the board of directors," he said. "We just had a board meeting, which is why we're dressed like this. Jim, Lawrence, and Roger skyped in from Vancouver. They're a little more formal there than we are in Silver Peak. You'll get to know them soon."

"Is Zander on the board of directors?"

"Zander?"

"Zander Peters."

"No."

"He was just here," she said.

"Well, we were in the boardroom. We didn't hear anyone come in. Anyway, my dad was just leaving. Let me show you to your office."

After Lou ambled out, Nate escorted Alana to an office one door down from his. She ignored the surge of electricity that ran down her spine at his proximity. He was her boss, and clearly, as the CEO of a mining company with an MBA, he was on the other side of the environmental fence. Shafts of morning light painted the desk in slats of creamy warmth. The office was a bit smaller than Nate's and lacked a couch. Black and white photos of a piano, trumpet, and guitar hung on the wall behind the desk.

Nick gestured at the photos. "You're welcome to take those down if you want to personalize the office a bit."

"Oh, no. They're fine. I love music."

Something pained flitted across Nate's face, and he paused for a second as if waiting for her to say something before smiling. "I have some calls to make. Feel free to settle in. Copies of all the files are in the central directory. Get up to speed. The outside consultants are still working on the formal proposal, and we won't have it until next week. I need you to start planning the open house for the residents."

"Will do."

"I'm here if you need me. Curtis and Len, our geologists, should be in from the field by mid-afternoon. You can meet them then. Other than them and our board of directors, we're it for now, till we start operations." Nate gave her a flash of his wicked smile, and she only managed to prevent her legs from turning to rubber this time by running through her list of reminders as to why she and Nate would never date. He was her boss. He was an anti-environmentalist—although she really shouldn't call him that. Maybe he was just a capitalist—but most capitalists were de facto anti-environmentalists. The reality was, she really didn't know what he was, and he was now regarding her a bit strangely.

"Thanks," she managed to stutter.

"Welcome aboard, Alana," he said, and he departed her office.

Alana had worked steadily for a couple of hours when Suzanne called her cell phone.

"How's your first day going?"

"Fine," Alana said cautiously. "But I can't really talk."

"I just want to know, is he as cute as he was in high school?"

Alana snorted. Suzanne was nothing if not consistent. "Since I didn't know him in high school, I can't say. However he is definitely not lacking in the cute department."

"Well, keep me posted. I can't wait to hear all about it. He's single, you know. It's been so long since I've seen him in person."

Suzanne hung up, and it occurred to Alana that this was an odd statement. When had Suzanne seen him *not* in person? Maybe they were Facebook friends. Maybe Suzanne, newly divorced herself, was after Nate, which wouldn't be surprising, as the number of available, and desirable, and employed men in Silver Peak could probably be counted on the fingers of one hand. The prospect of Suzanne dating Nate sent a shot of envy through Alana's soul.

At noon, she proceeded to the tiny staff room in search of a coffee maker. She found a small espresso machine and a bag of organic fair trade coffee in the freezer. Since growing the beans for a single cup of coffee required about sixteen liters of water, coffee consumption was one of Alana's biggest black marks in the environmental department. However, most environmentalists swilled coffee like junkies, so she rationalized it. Maybe she should just go home for coffee and lunch. Nate hadn't explained whether there was a coffee pool or free access. Perhaps this coffee was his.

She was also feeling a bit twitchy about leaving the eggs at home alone. If she had driven, she could whip home and check them, and get something started in the slow cooker for dinner. She had always struggled with the North American custom of spending an entire day at a desk. If everyone reduced their work hours, more people could share jobs and have a living wage, and everyone could spend more time cooking, looking after their children, volunteering in the community, and gardening, which would all be good things—essential things—for sustainability. The idea of working half-time didn't seem to be gaining any traction in North America though.

She was standing there holding the bag of coffee when she heard a rustle behind her. Nate had changed into his sneakers and a navy t-shirt and cords.

"Sorry," she said. "I wasn't sure if the coffee is for everyone."

"You and I can start a coffee pool," he said. "You wouldn't want the rubbish that Curtis and Len drink. Do you know how to use the machine?"

She shook her head and he stepped over, pressed the switch on the coffee maker, and removed the bag of coffee from her hand, his fingers barely touching hers. "I'll make you a cup. Americano good?"

"Sure," she said, and then blurted, "You changed."

Nate shrugged. "I'm not good with suits." A dusting of blue underscored his eyes, and the rims were reddish. He looked like he hadn't slept well the previous night.

"Where did you work before?" She had assumed he had been in big business, probably in a city, and was used to wearing suits.

"Here and there in Vancouver. They were more creative ventures, so I never had to wear a suit." He was regarding her oddly again, and she had a funny sense there was something she was missing.

While he ground the coffee beans, she pulled her couscous salad out of the fridge and sank into one of the leather seats in the corner of the staff room.

"How do you like being back in Silver Peak? You grew up here, right?"

"I like the recreation opportunities here, but I miss Vancouver sometimes. It can seem a bit claustrophobic living here sometimes."

She nodded in response. It always felt like everyone in Silver Peak knew—and cared—a bit too much about everyone's business. "How do you think the city council feels about the mine?" she said.

Nate shook his head as he scooped the coffee into the round thing with a handle. "I'm not sure. Stewart is supportive, but I expect they're waiting for the actual proposal. My dad and the mayor are golf buddies. I think the mayor's in favor of the mine, but that doesn't mean the rest of council is. It doesn't matter of course, but it would be nice to have council on board."

"Do you golf?" Alana asked.

Nate's white teeth flashed as he collected two cups from the top of the machine. "No. I hate golf. I hate rules and all the competitive asshattery that goes with group sports. I prefer to ski, hike, and run. Sorry, I guess I shouldn't say that. Do you golf? 'Cause if you do, that's great." He offered a toothy smile.

Alana laughed. "No. I despise golfing. I like to run, too."

Espresso streamed from two spouts on the machine, filling the room with an intoxicating, bitter chocolate aroma. She knew that dandelion root coffee was a more sustainable alternative, but if even real environmentalists didn't bother getting off the coffee train, she wasn't going to either. Maybe the whole world would end as a result of coffee. And professional athletes, and the fashion industry, and Monsanto...

She jerked herself out of her end-of-the-world environmental rat hole when Nate extended a cup of steaming liquid with a perfect froth of crema on top. His mood appeared to have shifted again, and the tiredness she had glimpsed earlier had returned to his eyes. Or maybe it was sadness.

"Here's your coffee. I better get back to work."

Alana sat in her office, hedging on hitting send on the news release announcing the open house. Nate had checked it over and given it the thumbs-up with no changes. But as soon as she sent it out with her name as the contact on the bottom, Maude and the rest of her environmental associates would know that she had gone over to the dark side. The email chatter of the Mountain Stewardship Society, or MSS as they had dubbed themselves, had been frenetic all day, and given their level of fervor, Alana wouldn't be surprised if they surrounded her house as soon as they learned she had defected.

She decided to hold off on the email for now and continue working on the plan for the open house instead.

By two in the afternoon, she had most of the event plan sketched out, but she'd gotten a bit sidelined reading about watershed reserves. Although watershed reserves were originally intended to be protected from resource development, the province started to ignore its own rules in the '60s and quietly allowed logging in watershed reserves without referring the matter to the municipalities affected. Now resource development, including mining in watershed reserves, was business as usual. And most municipalities hadn't even tried to object. According to some reports, the majority of municipalities didn't even *know* that their watersheds were reserves, or that they were supposed to be protected, which made Alana wonder what the hell happened in municipal filing rooms. To top it off, the provincial government had been allowing global corporations to bottle and sell BC groundwater for free for years, although apparently they now planned to start charging the corporations a nominal fee.

The whole thing was such a bureaucratic clusterfuck that she had to wonder if there was any hope they would ever even get to the sustainability starting line. It seemed like they would remain forever tangled in their own shoelaces with their shorts on backwards guzzling urn after urn of coffee and going on salmon-fishing junkets with industry, while expecting clean, abundant water to magically appear in perpetuity.

She looked at the clock. She had to get to school; she couldn't avoid sending out the news release any longer. She had kept it simple: it announced that the mine proposal would be available in a week, stated the general location of the proposed mine, noted the possibility of a provincial environmental assessment if it was called for, and invited the public to the open house to learn more and provide their feedback.

Alana sucked in her breath and hit send, then grabbed her stuff and departed the office for the school. It was only a matter of time before she received the flaming emails. She was used to being the white hat in these processes—or at least the off-white or cream hat. Being the black hat was terrifying.

She slunk up side streets like a criminal to the school and then tried to look inconspicuous while Katie and Duncan frolicked around the playground with no clear intention of departing. Parents darted looks at her, and she felt a sheen of sweat on her forehead. The news release had only gone to the media outlets and several key organizations in town, including the Stewardship Society. Alana had decided—probably out of terror—not to spam everyone on her normal distribution list. She had been hoping this would buy her time to go home and design some sort of disguise to wear on the playground and around town for the next month, before everyone knew of her new status as destroyer of the watershed. Shaving her head and getting tattoos had crossed her mind. Maybe if she looked sufficiently scary and unstable, people would stay out of her way. Then again, she probably already looked scary and unstable.

She nearly yelped when she realized that Gillian had approached from behind and stood beside her, a look of consternation on her carefully constructed face. Surely she didn't care about the mine.

"Kara canceled for popcorn duty on Friday," Gillian announced. "I don't know what we're going to do."

Alana forced her mouth into a smile. The PAC raised money by selling yellow death popcorn to the kids. It took several volunteers several hours to make every Friday morning, and the proceeds were used to pay for a bouncy castle for the kids at the end-of-the-year party. Alana didn't understand why they didn't just charge admission to the bouncy castle, or better yet, use the money raised to support a foster child in South America. Or even better, have the kids go for a hike in nature instead of catapulting around in a bouncy castle. But those killjoy thoughts were what made her an environmental dementor. The kids loved the popcorn and the bouncy castle.

"I can fill in for Kara, if you need me," she heard herself say. Evidently, according to her subconscious, popcorn-making was one of the twelve steps to dementor recovery.

Gillian's face brightened. "You can? Thanks so much!"

Gillian traipsed off to talk to some of the other mothers, no doubt to tell them about the popcorn debacle.

Alana collected Katie and Duncan and escaped the playground.

CHAPTER TEN

Warnings

Katie and Duncan groused and plodded the last several blocks home and largely ignored Alana's valiant attempts to entertain them with bright talk about their day and the opportunity to search for four-leaf clovers on the side of the road.

She should arrange more play dates for them, but Katie's and Duncan's friends generally arrived expecting to watch TV or play videogames. As the play date host, Alana assumed it was her obligation to ensure that other people's children did not spend two hours glued to a screen. She was sure that's what the other mothers did. Didn't they? But saying no resulted in bewildered expressions on the part of some of the children—which made her wonder what actually happened in other households. And then, instead of finding something creative to do outside, or with their well-stocked art supply closet, the children usually wandered around like stunned zombies for the next two hours asking what they could do. If the zombie apocalypse were to ever happen, Alana was certain it would be led by seven-year-olds.

The whole thing was excruciatingly stressful and caused Alana to ricochet among the conclusions that Katie and Duncan were boring, she had no idea how to run a play date, or humanity was doomed.

There had, of course, been a few times when she'd given in to a half hour of playing videos. But when the half hour was up, she hadn't been able to get the zombie kids away from the TV. Several of them just ignored her request to turn it off until she actually cut the power. And when she tried to delay the videogame playing until the last half hour of the play date so the arrival of the children's parents would be a logical stop point, the whole play date consisted of them watching the clock and pestering her until the magical half hour arrived.

She longed for the good old days when kids played outside in their own neighborhood and play dates didn't have to be arranged. Then again, she herself had seen every episode of *Gilligan's Island*, *Little*

House on the Prairie, Three's Company and *The Flintstones* three times. So her memories of the good old days were probably a crock of crap.

After arriving home and giving Katie and Duncan a snack, she checked her email. There were no new messages, not even from the Stewardship Society, and knowing their usual level of email traffic, she should have received at least a couple of emails while she was picking up the kids. So. She had been excised. She had known it would happen. But two hours ago she'd had a whole circle of environmental friends, or at least colleagues. Well, okay, people who emailed her and who might acknowledge her in the street. Now she had Nate, and Len and Curtis she supposed, but they hadn't yet returned from the field while she was in the office, so they were still pretty theoretical. She would just have to make some non-environmental friends, like Suzanne, or Gillian, who were good people, even if they didn't worry about water.

She sorted recycling while Duncan and Katie rode their scooters in the driveway. Silver Peak offered curbside pick-up for hard plastics, glass, and paper, but wine bottles, soft plastics, tetra packs, corrugated cardboard, and milk cartons all needed to be returned to the recycling depot. It was stinky, sticky work, and she often wondered if recycling actually helped anything, or if the stuff she so carefully sorted ended up on a ship to a Chinese landfill.

She returned to the kitchen and started chopping vegetables for a curry. When it was simmering, she trolled through her email, Facebook, and Twitter, looking for any sign that anyone cared about her. At 4:23, she called Suzanne.

"Hey, how are you doing? Just calling to say hi," Alana said.

"I'm good. How are you?"

"Oh, okay I guess. I don't think some of the enviros are super happy that I'm working for Mountain Magnesium."

"Aren't they all wackjobs anyway?"

"No. Not necessarily. I don't know."

"Well I don't like that Maude woman. Why can't she get a decent haircut?"

"I guess it's not important to her."

"Hmm, well the rest of us probably worry too much about our hair. But she would look so much better if she just cared a little. So what was Nate like?"

"He seems nice. Kind of somber though."

"Well, that's not surprising, is it?"

Alana furrowed her brow. "What do you mean?"

"Alana, do you know anything about Nate?"

"Well no, not really. He has an MBA. His father is Lou. He grew up here. He seems smart. He likes good coffee and running." She searched her mind for any other relevant facts, because what she had come up with sounded a bit lame.

"Hmm, yeah. You might want to ask him what he's been doing for the last twenty years."

"Why? Was he incarcerated or something?"

Suzanne laughed. "Alana, have you been living under a rock?"

"Possibly." *Was being an environmentalist sort of like living under a rock?*

"Nate was a famous jazz musician in Vancouver. Well, semi-famous. He had a breakdown last year. Drugs, I heard. Lou got him on at the company as part of his rehab, and so he could try something new. I hear he's not going back to music."

"Really? Nate?" This was the last thing she'd expected. Well, not quite the last. Stand-up comic and professional wrestler were lower on the list than jazz musician, but only marginally.

"That's what I heard. Just Google him. You need to stop reading so many scientific reports and watching The Knowledge Network."

"Well, that's entirely possible. It's just... drugs? That doesn't seem like him." Although Alana had to admit, she really didn't know Nate in the slightest. Nor did she have her finger on the pulse of designer drug users.

"It's always the quiet ones," Suzanne said, as if she worked in a drug rehab center and had profiled the clients extensively.

Alana Googled Nate Steeves as soon as she got off the phone. He had no official website, but she found enough reviews of his musical career to know that at least part of what Suzanne had said was true. He had been a well-respected and major player in the Vancouver jazz scene up until two years ago, and then all the articles and references to performances stopped. Alana stared at a photo of him hunched over a piano. His eyes were closed and the light shining on his hair made him look almost ethereal. She looked for more photos. There were a few pictures of him playing the saxophone and a publicity shot in which he looked much younger. But she kept flipping back to the first photo. The image haunted her, like he was completely absorbed in his music, like it was everything to him. Like it had been to her mother.

She shivered. How could someone who clearly cared so much about their music just give it up?

But it didn't matter, because he was just her boss. And he was clearly a capitalist, and potentially a drug addict. And hotter than hell.

She played the piano that night after she put Katie and Duncan to bed. First scales and then a Rachmaninoff piece she had been trying to master. But she missed the F sharp again and again. She tried to fit piano in around all the other pieces of her life, when the mood struck and she didn't feel completely overwhelmed by everything else. But the Rachmaninoff did not conform well to being fit in around the edges, and she tossed it aside in frustration, switching to a flowy canon she knew well. The feel of the keys and the rhythm of the music in the dark carried her.

Alana had once thought to make her living off of music too, but her mother had informed her flatly, unequivocally, that she wasn't good enough. And her mother knew what she was talking about. She had been training to be a concert pianist when she met Alana's dad and got pregnant, and she became a piano teacher instead of a performer. She taught piano for twenty years before she died. Every afternoon, kids trooped through their rec room and played for her mother. Some good, but most bad, playing halting, uncounted nonsense because their parents made them, while Alana and her brother tried to do their homework.

When the students all left for the day, Alana's mother would sit down at the piano and play. Every evening for an hour, she would summon some kind of magic, filling the house with music. She always only played for herself, never once responding to Alana's dad's urging, pleas, and eventually jibes that she play for guests.

Alana's clumsy fingers had never flown across the keys like her mother's did—every sixteenth note perfectly placed and counted—but at night in bed, she had composed symphonies in her mind.

When her mother was done playing for the day, she would close the piano resolutely and go to the kitchen and start dinner. "Go into science," she would order. "This world is no place for artists."

So Alana went into science and the symphonies stopped. But sometimes she still chased them around in her dreams, and she always wept at piano recitals and Christmas concerts. The children in angel outfits, their chipmunk voices lifted to the sky. Her mother at the piano, a curl of cigarette smoke rising into the air.

Alana's mother died when Alana was fifteen. Cigarettes, the doctors said, but Alana had never believed them. The Greenes had presented a compelling case regarding the water contamination from the textile mill upriver.

For a while in school, Alana had become an expert in environmental toxins, the most depressing and isolating of all environmental fields. Nobody liked a grim reaper at their parties. They especially didn't like to know that their moisturizer, couch, bacon, and hair dye were all sources of carcinogens. So instead Alana became an environmentalist for the sake of the environment, which allowed her to hug trees, smoke a little weed, and spend lots of time in provincial parks instead of obsessing over the slew of toxins that insinuated themselves into everyone's bodies every day. The tree-hugging segment of the environmental movement was a jolly bunch of devil-may-care skylarkers compared to the environmental folks that focused on chemicals and cancers. The animal rights enviros could be downers too, but at least they usually had cute pets.

The textile mill that had potentially caused her mother's cancer had closed more than forty years ago, but the blackened waste pipes still stuck out of the cement retaining walls and hung over the river, a reminder of how things had once been done in North America. Before people were environmentally aware; before there were regulations.

Was Alana now paving the way for metaphorical pipes in Silver Peak? No. She couldn't let herself think so. Corporations no longer ravaged the environment as badly as they once had, did they? It was possible to mine sustainably.

Alana played the last notes of a hymn and let the notes of the amen hang in the air before lifting her foot from the pedal.

Tabitha called just before ten—her usual time slot. Saving the environment was a twelve-hour-a-day job. The other parents on the playground may not have seen the news release indicating that Alana was now working at the mine, but Tabitha had.

"You need to see your lawyer," Tabitha's gravelly voice announced.

"What?" Alana said.

"Well I'm assuming that that dickhead Blaine isn't paying you enough child support. I'm so sorry, honey. You should have told me. I could have gotten you on here at the coalition. We always need media support."

"What? Tabbie, Blaine pays enough child support. Are you talking about my new job?"

"Of course. I'm assuming things got desperate around there. That's why women should never have children." Tabitha almost ended her sentence in a whimper.

Alana barked out a nervous laugh and decided not to point out that it was *only* women who could have children. Was her new job really enough to drive Tabitha to tears?

"Things are not desperate, or not super desperate," Alana said. "I took the job to ensure that the company stays on the up and up and listens to the perspectives of the people who live here. I'll stay on the environmental straight and narrow, I promise. I'm sure I'll end up quitting before too long."

Tabitha was ominously silent for a few seconds. "Are you sure? I could get David to set you up with something better next week. Things are still going strong in the Steveston Valley. I'm heading up there to sleep on the tree platform next week, so we'll need someone to backfill my job."

"I appreciate it, but I'm going to give this a go. Don't worry."

"But you can't possibly support a mine in the watershed. Mom is going to go around the bend when she hears. I haven't been able to reach her. She and Dad are on a trek in the Andes."

And hopefully they'll stay there for a bit, thought Alana. As freaked as Tabitha was about the mine and Alana's new job, Margaret Greene was going to wig right out. "I don't support the mine, but I think it's important that all the information gets out."

"Well, just be careful. They could be just using you because you have a good reputation in the community, and you're not an outsider. Remember what happened to Daniel."

Everyone knew what had happened to Daniel, a high-profile environmental leader, who in his forties had turned his back on the environmental movement that he had supported for years and had joined forces with the forest industry. "Don't pull a Daniel" served as an ominous warning in all quadrants of the environmental sector and was trotted out whenever someone even blinked in a friendly manner at the opposition.

"I'll be careful, I promise."

Alana checked her email once more before going to bed. Nothing. She had checked it pretty much every fifteen minutes throughout the evening like a deranged whackadoon, looking for any signs of anything, an olive branch, a snotogram, a link to a newspaper article highlighting how stupid, ill-intentioned, or incompetent she was. But her inbox remained terrifyingly empty. She checked her service provider's website for any notice of a file server meltdown, but all seemed well in the land of email. There was no way that Maude had not received or heard about the open house announcement.

Blaine called the next morning. "I just enrolled the college into the Cross Canada Energy Conservation Corporate Challenge. We're going head to head with other organizations across the country to cut our energy use by ten percent over the next month."

"You did tell the president of the college, right?"

Blaine snorted. "Of course. He's super excited. We're going to win and get the college's name plastered all over the media. And as the college environmental coordinator, yours truly, Super Environmental Blaine, will also have his name plastered all over the media."

"Since when were you the college environmental coordinator?"

"Since yesterday."

"Did you get a pay raise?" Alana felt a brief surge of hope that she could quit her job and grow heirloom tomatoes and keep donkeys.

"No. But I should ask for one."

"Hmph," she said. "You know those kinds of challenges don't really make much difference. People just revert to their old ways once the challenge is over."

"You are a real piece of work, Alana." Blaine made the environmental dementor sound again, except at least he switched to sucking instead of hissing.

She interrupted his performance. "Are you doing it for the sake of the environment? Or to get your name in the news and win our environmental challenge so you can make me move to Vancouver?"

Blaine's response was chipper. "Both. Real environmental benefits happen when it's win-win for everyone. And I'm not making you move. I'm asking you to consider it."

"Great," she mumbled. "I don't believe in that, you know."

"You don't believe in anything. You're not going to save the environment through martyrdom. People just don't work that way."

"I'm not moving to Vancouver."

"Just keep an open mind."

She hung up on him and then felt guilty. She had agreed to the challenge, and she shouldn't discourage Blaine's nascent environmental endeavors, even if he did have questionable motivations.

Owen Jackson, the local newspaper reporter, called her at home just as she arrived in the door from walking the kids to school. She had dealt with him lots before on Regional Environmental Board issues, and they were friendly on a social level. He was definitely the safer of the two local reporters and worked for the more mainstream *Silver Peak News*. Ramona Lockey, the reporter for the online *Silver Peak Scoop*, who was known to devise entire articles based on hearsay, was the one Alana had to watch out for.

"Hey Alana, can we do an interview on the upcoming Mountain Magnesium Resources open house?"

"Sure."

Owen's questions, expressed in his laconic ski bum drawl, were predictable. The usual media schlock, confirming the timing of the event, walking through what the open house would look like, and talking about why it's important for people to attend the event.

She deferred the question regarding the environmental impacts of the mine, indicating that if the province deemed it large enough, a complete environmental assessment would likely be done, and noting that people should come to the open house to outline their environmental concerns.

"And when will we see the proposal?"

"Soon, I promise. The consultants are just putting the finishing touches on it."

The fact that she hadn't yet seen even a preliminary draft of the proposal made her a bit twitchy.

They finished the interview and she was about to hang up when Owen said, "Off the record, do you think the mine is a good idea or not?"

"Off the record, I can't answer that, Owen. I really don't know. I'm just working for Mountain Magnesium to help them understand the perspectives of Silver Peak residents and make sure they undertake good communication and consultation approaches. I'm neutral."

"Kind of hard to be neutral when you're in the employ of the company, isn't it?"

"No, I don't think so. It's important that industry have neutral people working for them."

She hung up the phone and pressed it to her sternum. She *was* neutral. She did not necessarily support the mine. Nate was her boss, a capitalist, and a drug addict. She would repeat this mantra as often as necessary.

CHAPTER ELEVEN

Heat

S he drove to work on Wednesday so she could hurry home at eleven to turn the eggs and then go see Duncan's class sing at the local Senior's Hall. A light blue Vespa pulled into the parking spot next to her, and Nate got off. She did a double take. Blaine would rather eat his Bostonians and ride the smelly bus than drive a Vespa.

Nate looked windblown but sexy in a black leather jacket and jeans, and Alana snapped her mouth shut when he saw her staring. He fell into step with her, carrying his white helmet.

"It's good on gas and it's fun to drive. It was useful in Vancouver, especially when I had to find parking," he said.

"Oh, no, I think the scooter is great," she said. "It's so…" She trailed off when she realized saying it was "so cute" was probably a bad idea. "I'd love a scooter, except my hair would get messed up, and I have bad hair." She contemplated this. Did she really burn way more fossil fuels than she needed to for the sake of her hair?

Nate scrunched up his eyes at her as he held the door open for her to enter the building. "You could always wear it in a ponytail."

"My ex said I looked stupid in a ponytail," she said, and then froze. She was giving too much information as usual. "Well, he didn't say that exactly, but he preferred it when I wore my hair down."

"Hmm," Nate replied noncommittally. He probably thought she was a superficial bonehead now. She considered launching into an explanation about how men expect women to look, even if they didn't realize it, and that she would be penalized financially and socially if she didn't manage her hair into some sort of appealing style.

"For the record, I think you would look amazing in a ponytail, so don't let that stop you from getting a scooter," Nate said. Then he turned and entered his office.

Boss, capitalist, jazz musician, drug addict, she repeated. Who drove a Vespa.

She heard voices from Len and Curtis's shared office. She skulked toward their door on tiptoe and went to scurry by, but glanced in on her way past. The two men inside jumped to their feet. A tall, tanned, white-haired man in wranglers and work boots reached her first and took her hand in his with a broad smile. Freckles and white patches covered his hands.

"I'm Len. You must be Alana. Welcome. It's about time we had a pretty face around here. I get tired of looking at Curt's old mug."

Even though she suspected she should be raising some feminist alarm, she found herself wildly pleased that he would refer to her this way.

Curtis elbowed in front of Len. He came to Len's shoulder and wore a forest green almost-ranger-uniform-looking outfit, his dark hair styled in an elaborate comb-over. "Ignore him. He likes to think he's still a charmer. I'm the one to come to when you need anything," Curtis announced.

Len feigned a hurt look. "Course we spend most of our time out in the field anyway, so it'll be good to have someone here in the office. Can't have Nate rattling around here all on his own. He said you might need some stuff for the open house. Maps or something."

"It's nice to meet you both," Alana said. "Yes, I'll need maps of the watershed and the proposed mine site. I'll send you a detailed list of what I need them to show. Do either of you have any experience speaking in public? Could you be on hand to provide some background on the site at the open house?"

"We don't usually get involved in that part of the business. We're the dirt and rock guys," Len said.

"But Len here is a certified toastmaster and auctioneer. He's done weddings and funerals all over the province," Curtis said.

"Yup, when I get going, I'm kind of hard to shut up," Len said, leaning against his desk. "You say the word, young lady, and I'll have my wedding and funeral suit pressed and ready to go. I also have a stand-up comedy routine. I only use that at the weddings, so I can throw some jokes in there too."

Alana blinked her suddenly very dry eyes at the image of Len managing the open house. "Let's just keep that one in the hopper for now," she said. "I'll let you know if I need you. It was great to meet you. I'll send you that list." She started to sidle toward her own office.

They watched her back out, as if they were unused to having their coffee klatches end so abruptly. "Anything we can do to help," Len called after her. "Just let us know."

As soon as she'd settled into her office, Alana opened her email. Thirty-five new messages popped up. She started to click them open with sweaty palms. Indignant declarations and blistering accusations regarding the plan to destroy the watershed filled her screen. She writhed with each statement of shock and absolute opposition. She knew these people. They knew her.

She flipped to the *Silver Peak News* website. Owen had posted his article. Mostly just the facts about the open house. No innuendo about the mine destroying the watershed... yet.

She scrolled down to the comments section of Owen's article, her heart thudding.

Fiona's name flashed up as the first commenter. The coffee Alana guzzled that morning started to rove around in her gut with ill intent. Fiona dressed down Mountain Magnesium Resources for their communications strategy and "legacy of secrecy," as if Mountain Magnesium had been covertly operating in the community for a decade. She then proceeded to say that as an "environmental professional," she wanted to point out the multiple flaws in the Mountain Magnesium Resources website. No maps of the mine location, no description of the extraction methods, no indication of the size or commercial value of the ore body, no outline of the approval process.

She was right. They had to get that information out, and the news release had clearly indicated it was coming soon, but *Alana* didn't even have it yet. Now thanks to Fiona's comment, Alana, as the communications manager for Mountain Magnesium, looked like a fool.

Perfect. Fiona had recommended Alana for the job, and yet she could not resist the opportunity to score points when the opportunity arose.

Maude's comment was next. Not surprisingly, it referred to the looming travesty in the watershed, outlined the importance of drinking water for health, denigrated the city council for being a bunch of yes men and women, referenced the "out-of-towners" at Mountain Magnesium Resources who didn't care about Silver Peak, and provided facts on the impacts of mining in watersheds. The facts were not specific to magnesium mining though. Her comment ended with a rallying call to arms for the Silver Peak townspeople and provided a link to the Stewardship Society's website. Maude certainly had the ability to craft a damning message. She kept the hyperbole in check and avoided the use of all caps, which had gotten her into trouble in the past.

Alana clicked on the link to the Stewardship Society's website. It was still mostly under development. A map and photos of the watershed had been posted. The main page showed the moonscape of a massive open pit mine with the caption: "Do you really want this to be your watershed?"

It was effective, if inaccurate.

Maude and her environmental army had come out of the gates full throttle. It was only going to get more intense from here.

How was she going to stay on top of this?

Alana grabbed a notepad and stuck her head in Nate's office door. He wore headphones and had his eyes closed. She received no response when she said his name, and she had just started to edge back out of his office when his eyes flicked open. He removed the headphones and gestured for her to come in. As she approached, he held the headphones out.

"Do you mind listening to this?"

She hesitated, then circled around to his side of the desk. Putting the headphones on brought her into very close proximity to Nate, and once again she caught the faint scent of leather. A slow, sad saxophone song played. She listened for a few seconds and then removed the headphones so she wouldn't tear up.

Nate regarded her through his shocking blue eyes. "Do you like it?"

She nodded yes, wordlessly, worried it might be a test. She didn't know enough about jazz to know who it was. It might have been Nate playing, and now she was standing so close to him that it was getting challenging to breathe. Apparently the boss, capitalist, drug addict mantra didn't work at the thirty-centimeter mark.

She lurched back and shifted her gaze to his computer. His email was open and several emails from Zander Peters sat in his inbox.

"You wanted to talk to me?" he said with a lazy, cat-like smile.

"I just want to know our overall strategy. This is already starting to get ugly. How do you want me to respond to things? Because I could respond to everything or just let our official literature be the main source of information."

"What do you think we should do?"

"People are going to want transparency. But responding to everything could absorb a huge amount of resources. And I really need the details of the proposal as soon as possible. Otherwise I'm basically saying nothing."

"The proposal's coming," he said. "I don't have it yet either. Everyone needs to just settle down a bit. We've barely stuck a shovel in the ground, and they're acting like we've set off an atomic bomb."

Alana cocked her head and squinted at him. His smile, while appealing, seemed strained, and he wore an overall expression of resignation. She wondered if he was cut out for this, if he even wanted to be doing this. Of course, she wondered if *she* was cut out for this. If *she* wanted to be doing this.

She nodded and tried to offer what she hoped was a reassuring smile. "Okay. I'll try to put out some of the fires until we get the proposal. What are we doing in terms of communications with the city? Are you the official liaison or am I?"

Nate shrugged. "What do you suggest?"

"I think you should send them a letter outlining the proposed consultation process and say that you hope to work collaboratively with them every step of the way."

"Okay, but it's not their final decision. Of course we should keep them informed and try to address their concerns, but doesn't saying 'work with them collaboratively every step of the way' seem a little over the top? I've already met with Stewart, and he seemed supportive."

Alana put her hands on her hips. "It's Zander you really have to talk to. Stewart is..." She paused. She had almost said crazy. "Stewart doesn't always know what's going on in Silver Peak. Would you proceed with developing the mine if city council isn't supportive?"

Nate gave her a thoughtful look. "The board of directors would be the one making that call, and in my experience, city councils don't always make decisions that are in the best interests of their communities."

Alana flicked through Silver Peak's seven council members in her mind. A retired car salesman, a golf pro, the owner of the ski shop, a librarian, a teacher, an engineer, and a realtor. How many times had she lambasted them to Blaine over swigs of wine for their idiocy, short-sightedness, and inability to read and/or remember anything longer than two pages without garbling it beyond recognition?

They weren't all bad, of course, on all issues. Madeline Geller, the librarian, and Jane Dewey, the teacher, generally tried to support environmental initiatives. But due to the outrageous reading load and Stewart's obtuse methods of communication—deliberate or otherwise—the whole council often got confused or misled and made bad decisions.

Alana always felt guilty about badmouthing them. It wasn't like *she* had ever volunteered for the thankless council job, where the biggest perks included trips to provincial conferences and the opportunity to dress up as lumberjacks for the annual Silver Peak Loggerhead Festival. And several of the council members were capable of making the right decisions with a lot of coaching. Alana had tried that once or twice on Regional Environmental Board issues. But the amount of coaching required to get them there was mind-blowing, and they could flip to the other side at any second depending on whom they had just talked to in the grocery store. As a result, the city rarely did anything really progressive.

Alana realized that Nate's expression had grown more quizzical than usual during the long gap in which she reviewed the voting habits and IQs of the council members and essentially stared into his electric blue eyes. But the arch of his lips suggested a faint amusement, and he held her gaze. *Damn.* She was attracted to him. Not useful, although she shifted a fraction of an inch closer to him just to feel the air between them compress before snapping out of it and drawing herself back into her professional, authoritative stance.

"No, they don't always make the right decisions, but we still have to live in this town, both of us, and if we exclude the council, which represents the residents, it will have negative repercussions for our lives here and for Mountain Magnesium's future operations. This is a small town, and trust me, you don't want everyone to hate you. They will not hesitate to let you know exactly how they feel by the cauliflower in the grocery store, and you will no longer get invited to potlucks and children's birthdays."

Nate shook his head solemnly. "And just at the start of the birthday season too."

"Nate!"

His lips crinkled into a smile. "Set up a meeting with Stewart and Zander. My schedule's on the intranet. We can go talk about what we plan to do and scope out their concerns."

Alana had just finished firing off a meeting request to Stewart when Nate appeared at her door holding a stack of papers.

"So, it seems that the newspaper article has generated a fair bit of interest," he said.

Alana felt a riff of alarm. "What are those? Death threats?"

Nate snorted. "No, Alana, they're resumes. People started dropping them off half an hour ago. Listen, Len and Curtis have to head back into the field, and I have to do the phone interviews for the receptionist. I know it's not in your job description, but do you mind manning the front door and accepting the resumes? Just tell them we aren't hiring until the mine is approved, in about a year, but we'll put their resume on file."

The next five hours brought men and a few women of all ages in all states of formal and casual attire, clutching file folders and glossy Duo-Tangs containing their resumes. She recognized some of them from the soccer field, from the playground, from the grocery store. She'd had no idea so many people in Silver Peak were unemployed. Some of them talked about how excited they were about the mine and bumbled something about really needing a job. Others were sheepish, embarrassed that she now knew their secret. Yet others were stoic and made small talk about soccer and the ski season.

She accepted and filed resumes and passed on the same message to each. They would be hiring in a year, if the mine was approved.

The crestfallen expressions and anxiety on some of their faces in response to this statement almost felled her.

CHAPTER TWELVE

A Many-Faceted Thing

The stereo was blaring with disambiguated alternative music when she arrived home with the groceries. It was Blaine's one afternoon to look after the kids, and it was easier for him to do so at the house instead of in his tiny condo, where Heather, who "found children stressful," had decided to decorate everything in white.

Blaine greeted her in shorts and a t-shirt, obviously fresh from the gym or a run. A jumble of shoes, hoodies, water bottles, music bags, and backpacks littered the hall. She suppressed her usual wave of irritation. It wasn't Blaine's house anymore. He couldn't be expected to pick up.

She dropped the first of the heavy grocery bags in the hall. "Can you please turn that down? I can't even hear myself think."

He obediently turned down the stereo and then stood typing on his iPhone while she lugged grocery bag after grocery bag in from the car.

"You know, you could help me carry the food for your children," she said on her final trip.

"Oh, you are just always so feisty," Blaine chirped.

She pushed past him and started to put away the groceries. She glanced over at the egg incubator. The light was off. Her chickens. Her babies. They would freeze to death and die. May have *already* frozen to death and died, their fluffy little bodies motionless in their chilled tombs.

She wracked her brain for the fit of absentmindedness that would have led her to flip the switch this morning after she'd carefully turned them all.

She whirled to Blaine, who was busy tying up his shoelaces to leave.

"Did *you* turn off the incubator?" Her voice emerged as a hiss, and she was sure that with her windblown frizzy hair and black work dress she looked like the possessed offspring of the Wicked Witch of the West and an environmental dementor.

Blaine peered around the corner. "Oh, whoops. Maybe. I was just going around turning things off. I just now did it though."

She raced over, flicked the light back on, and reached her hand into the incubator. Still warm. Her little chickies might still be alive. If she was this attached to them now, how would she possibly kill and eat them in the future? Maybe she could hire someone to do it. But if you're not willing to kill and dress your own meat then you really shouldn't be eating meat.

Maybe they would just be egg chickens.

The echo of *Scooby-Doo* drifted up the stairs from the basement. Of course Blaine let them use their half hour of video time on his watch. She hated how Katie and Duncan raced immediately for their allotted video time the second they arrived home, like they had been deprived all day and must return immediately to plug in to the hive. She cursed her inability to get them excited about other things, like reading, or crafts, or chores, the way good environmental homesteading children—the ones in her mind—lived.

"What other possible things could there have been to turn off?" She was sure the subtext of chick murderer was evident in her voice.

"There were things on, okay?" The defensive "don't push this" tone had crept into Blaine's voice.

"I never leave things on."

"Well, you did today."

"Like what?" She felt faintly close to tears. She never left things on.

"I don't know. You're not really asking for examples, are you? I'll cut you some slack and not deduct it from your environmental points for today." The words *like you did to me* hung ominously.

Was this what had killed their marriage? She pulled a Post-it note out of the junk drawer, wrote "Do Not Turn Off" on it in all caps, and stuck it to the incubator.

"So just so you know..." he started.

She froze. This was how Blaine introduced something she wasn't going to like. That and "Don't be mad but..."

"What?"

"I started the talk with the lawyer about reducing the child maintenance payments now that you're working more." He held up his hands. "Just a little bit, I promise. Things are really tight and I want to get a new car. I found a secondhand one at a really good price." Blaine smiled and nodded the way he did when he was willing her to agree with him.

"What kind of car?"

"It's really good on gas."

"What kind of car, Blaine?"

"It's a Miata. Blue. Greg's selling his for cheap."

"Miatas only have two seats."

"I know. That's why they're so good on gas."

"But it won't be very practical for driving the kids around and stuff."

"Well, yeah, no."

"But that means I'll still be stuck driving them around to everything."

Blaine rolled his eyes dramatically. He found her so-called "feminist" rants painful. In his cheerful and sunny Blaine-centered mind, they split things totally equally and any suggestion to the contrary was some female mental aberration.

"I can borrow Heather's car sometimes," he said.

"Why don't you get a Vespa? Then you don't have to take money away from your children."

"I don't think a Vespa would send the leadership quality message to my colleagues that I want to inculcate."

"It would reinforce the Super Environmental Blaine image. Look, I was thinking, if I *am* going to work more, which means more money for both of us, I was hoping you could start looking after the kids more, like maybe two set afternoons and evenings a week, instead of just when I ask you to fill in."

Blaine's face contracted and sharpened. For all the sacrifices she'd thought she'd made by being the one to stay home in the early years and then ease back into work—which included leaving early so the kids didn't have to be at daycare, moving meetings and deadlines around when they were sick, and shuttling them from appointments to activities to birthday parties—Blaine thought he had made equal sacrifices, staying at a job he didn't like, doing dishes, making lunches, and looking after them on the evenings she had work meetings.

"I can't," he said. "I'll help out when I can. Like I have all along. You know my work isn't as flexible as yours is, Alana."

"I just need more help."

"Then maybe it's time to hire someone. Like everyone else in the world. You wanted this custody agreement, remember?" Blaine flapped his hands at her as if she was being unreasonable and marched out the door.

"You can't claim points for the Miata!" she shouted after him.

It had always been like this. She had resisted daycare and had wanted the household and childcare tasks to be split fifty-fifty, or at least sixty-forty. But it always came down to that nebulous problem of tracking who had done what, and they each had their own accounting systems. Blaine had counted his higher income as part of his contribution. She had argued that the unequal sharing of household and childcare tasks was part of the reason her income was lower. Blaine had contended that she *wanted* to be the person looking after the kids, which boxed her into a corner, because he was right. But she had also wanted help.

Now they had this bet, which established a whole new and equally nebulous system of accounting.

Had this move been worth it? If they still lived in Vancouver, maybe she and Blaine would have worked things out. They certainly wouldn't have had the Heather complication. Blaine's assistant in Vancouver had been an efficient sixty-year-old named Vero who kept Blaine in place and always reminded him when it was Alana's birthday.

Alana washed the lettuce, cut up vegetables, and started the rice— white rice. Katie and Duncan would not eat brown rice, despite years of coaxing. She checked her watch; she would have to get the kids off the video in five minutes.

She pressed her face against the window and stared out at the yard. It was a stew of unraked leaves that blustered across in brown swirls. Blaine had mowed them every spring—*the lazy man's way of raking leaves*, he had always declared jubilantly, as if he was proud of his ability to outsmart the leaves. If lawnmowers were supposed to be used in that way, everyone would do it, Alana had thought. But he had threatened to buy a leaf blower any time she objected.

Now somebody would have to rake them. When Blaine had groused, she had always claimed that manual labor was good for the soul.

That was easier to say when it wasn't her doing the labor.

She checked the comments section of the *Silver Peak News* again after dinner. More comments had been added of course. Most in abject horror at the notion of a mine in the watershed. A few brave souls had dared to comment on the potential economic value of the mine and the medical uses of magnesium, but they had been soundly berated by the anti-mine side. Alana debated creating an anonymous account and adding in some comments to correct Maude's claims, but stopped herself. She was working for Mountain Magnesium to ensure that the process was as fair as possible, not to ensure that the mine was established. The community should be able to have its say in whatever manner it wished.

She closed the *Silver Peak News* tab on her browser. Then, her heart beating just a little bit too fast, she downloaded a few of Nate's songs to her phone.

Mud spattered Alana's legs as she ran up the Mur Creek trail. She had managed to get Suzanne to agree to a childcare exchange for an hour and a half before dinner three days a week so they could each spend forty-five minutes exercising. Streams of water from the melting snow on either side of the trail coursed down gullies carved into the wide path. The Mur Creek thundered past on her right, almost overflowing the banks with the spring freshet. She gulped the clean air of the valley that was part of the city watershed. Birds flitted in and out of the budding trees, and a cool mist hung over the creek. In a few weeks, when the leaves came out, the trail would be gloriously beautiful.

Even if the mine didn't impact the city water, would it impact the narrow little valley in which she ran? And how much did these places matter to communities? But if there were no jobs, would anybody care? Lots of people in Silver Peak, especially the environmentalists, talked big about economic diversification involving alternative energy plants, tech start-ups, or cottage industries, but few of those ideas ever came to fruition.

Alana heard the distinct sound of feet splashing in the mud behind her. She turned automatically. The trail was well enough traveled that she didn't feel threatened, not by humans anyway—bears were another story—but she liked to allow faster runners to pass.

Nate came running up in a sleeveless t-shirt and long grey sweat shorts, his slender arms and legs cut and muscled. She whirled back around to avoid gaping at his body, and she tried to remember the mantra. Something about Nate being a drug addict, although she had a hard time believing a drug addict could run quite so effortlessly, unless he used athletic performance-enhancing drugs of some sort.

When he caught up, she slowed down and ran along the edge of the trail so he could pass, although this part was wide enough for two people to run side by side. "Go ahead," she said. "I'm slower than you."

Nate shot her his grin, which was all the more wicked and sexy thanks to his lack of sleeves. She quickly turned her gaze to the muddy wet trail.

"I do intervals," he said. "I just finished my sprint. I'll run with you for a bit, if you don't mind."

She shrugged and picked up her pace again. "Do you run often?"

"I try to run every day. I used to be on the road a lot, and running was about the only thing that kept me sane. You?"

"Not as much as I would like. It's hard with the kids."

"I understand. My brother Leo never seems to be able to find the time. I think his kids are about the same age as yours. I suppose I should enjoy my freedom now."

"Before you have kids, you mean?" Her lips curled in a smile.

"Yeah. Or meet someone with kids, or end up having to look after my dad in his dotage or something. I always try to remember to appreciate my freedom now." He paused. "Not that I think kids or aging parents are akin to going to jail. They just make life different. I'm sure kids make life better."

Alana snorted. "They do. But they definitely make it different too."

She had listened to some of his music the previous night after the kids had gone to bed, and now she was more confused than ever. He was clearly talented. Why had he given up something that was evidently his passion—and to be the CEO of a mining company? Maybe it was just too hard to make a living as a musician. Maybe his drug problems had forced him to quit. She tried to check out his pupils. She should probably be doing that on a regular basis. She surreptitiously shifted her glance to his arms and legs, looking for needle tracks, but saw only healthy-looking, and very nicely shaped, limbs.

She searched for something to talk about. She didn't want to ask him about his music in case he had been forced out or was upset by the fact that he was no longer doing it.

"So do you play the piano too?" he said.

She shook her head. Too? What did he mean by that?

"You said you had to take your kids to piano when you left the other day," he said. "I just wondered if you played too."

"Oh. Yes. Not really. I did. But not well enough for anything. I only went to grade six. My mother said I wasn't good enough to make a living at it." Alana wanted to pull the words back into her mouth immediately. The statement was so automatic that it had slipped out, and there was no need for it. She had never planned to make her living playing the piano.

"Hmm. Well, it *is* pretty tough to make a living at it. Your mother always told me that too."

"What?"

"She was my piano teacher," Nate said.

Alana tried to stop her eyes from automatically filling with tears, as they always did when someone else mentioned her mother.

Nate must have been her mother's star student. Alana wouldn't have known, since her mother had kept her separate from the other students. Alana never performed in or attended her mother's piano recitals. Alana had always thought it was because her mother wasn't proud of her playing and didn't want her teaching ability or her own talent evaluated on the basis of her ability to pass it on to Alana.

"Oh," she said. "I didn't know that."

"She was a great teacher."

"She was pretty demanding."

"She was passionate," Nate said.

Alana flipped a sideways look at him. Was he defending her mother? Had he thought she was attacking her mother? She blinked back another wave of tears.

"Not with me," Alana said. "It was like she wanted to keep that part of her life separate from us, since we were the reason she had to quit and didn't ever get to live her dream. And then she died."

Nate didn't respond, and Alana concentrated on the rhythm of their breaths and the slap of their shoes in the mud, trying to get her emotions under control.

"I don't think that's true," Nate said softly. "In my later years, when it looked like I really might make a career out of music, and I started getting stage fright, she started telling me stories of her anxieties on stage, and how debilitating they were. She coached me on how to just focus on the music and forget about the audience, but she used to laugh that she hadn't been able to take her own advice. I don't think she quit because of you and your brother at all."

"Oh," Alana said. That throaty dry cigaretty laugh of her mother's. She could barely remember how it sounded, but how she missed it. Nate had only known a part of her mother. But then, Alana supposed, so had she. She wanted to ask what had made *him* quit being a musician, what he knew of anxiety. "This is a great trail for running," she said instead.

"Yes, it is," Nate replied.

They ran in silence for a few more minutes before Alana realized she was at the twenty-five minute mark and would have to turn back.

"I have to go," she said. "My friend and I do an exercise exchange and my turn's up."

"All right, well, I'll see you tomorrow. We could go running at lunch if you're interested."

"Oh, you're way faster than me."

"Not really," he said. "Why don't we give it a go? I could use the company."

The mantra seemed to have ceased to work, and the words "Sounds great" exited Alana's mouth.

She raked leaves for several hours after dinner while Katie and Duncan ran circular laps of the trampoline, whooping like lunatics. Nate had insisted on running with Alana not only back to the parking lot, but all the way back to Suzanne's, where his muddy form was greeted with a lot of eyebrow wiggling and wide-eyed secret smiles in Alana's direction, all of which Alana tried to ignore. On the way, he regaled her with hilarious stories about his mother, Eve, who was a fashion designer and lived in France with an architect named Grant. From his commentary, she discerned that he didn't think a lot of the fashion industry. So they had that in common at least, not that it mattered. The boss, capitalist, drug addict mantra was far more effective when she was not in his presence. And now she could even add "son of a fashion designer" to the list.

Rick's ATV thundered up to the fence in a blaze of dust.

"So, you got a new job?" he said, cracking an enormous grin.

She bent down to examine her raspberry canes. The buds were still intact, so they were obviously still alive. "Looks that way."

"It's always the quiet ones."

"What?"

"Just you over here pretending to be the all-American environmental hippie chick."

"I *am* very environmental. I don't know about hippie chick, and I'm not American."

"How does that jibe with your new job?"

"What, not being American?"

Rick let out a wild guffaw, apparently delighted with her new approach to life. He took a sip of the Pilsner he had in the ATV's cup holder.

She sighed. Despite the fact that it was obvious they were complete opposites, she sort of liked Rick. "I took the job to see if I could do environmental good from the inside. Environmentalists are always complaining about the decisions that corporations make. I wanted to see if I could influence things from inside, if I could be part of a corporation with more of a green conscience. If it doesn't work out, I'll just quit."

"They paying you well?"

"Well enough."

"That guy, what's his name, Nate, treating you well?"

She faltered a bit until she realized that Rick was definitely talking about Nate in the boss context. "Yes."

Rick took another swig of the Pilsner, and she made a mental note to not let the children play too close to the fence line in the evenings. "Don't quit then," Rick said.

"Pardon me?"

"You got a job that pays well and they treat you well. This mine is important to this community. People need jobs. Why would you quit?"

"The principle of the matter."

"Look, I'm not even sure what principle you're talking about, but if you quit, someone else is going to come along behind you and take the job. You quitting ain't gonna make one whit of difference in terms of whether the mine goes in or not."

"I know, but I don't want to be associated with something I don't believe in."

Rick threw his arms into the air. "Your generation, always spouting a bunch of pie-in-the-sky causes and believing you have to follow your bliss. My generation, we showed up and did whatever shitty job we were asked to do and hoped we went home with both our hands and our dignity at the end of the day."

She didn't even know how to respond to this.

"I'm just saying be sure you have your principles straight in your own mind before you let them interfere with a perfectly good job."

"The environment is pretty important to me."

"Get on a plane to China or India then. That's where the real environmental damage is happening. All them folks trying to live the way we live. That'll be the end of the world as we know it. This little mine here? It's nothing but a drop in the bucket compared to all the shit that's going down over there."

Alana knelt by the small artesian spring that spouted a tiny trickle of water between their two properties in the early spring. She let the water flow between her fingers. The water looked so clear and crisp, but she dared not drink it, for fear of some contaminant or giardia. She'd seen Rick slurp it by the handful, but who knew what kind of intestinal parasites occupied his gut. Maybe Hostess cupcakes provided some protection against bugs.

Rick's eyes widened and he extended his index finger over her shoulder. "Looks like you've got some visitors. And they don't look happy. I think they have their principles in a bonnet."

He winked and cranked the ATV engine.

Alana turned to see Maude marching up the driveway with Tom LeDrew in tow.

CHAPTER THIRTEEN

Principles

Alana leapt to her feet and glanced at her sprouting garlic, turned and manured garden beds, raspberry canes, apple tree, strawberry patch, and greenhouse. She had a fleeting hope that these and the North Star Farm sign would redeem her. But judging from the expression on Maude's face, this was unlikely. Perhaps these things would at least prevent her lynching, or perhaps Maude would just lock her in her own greenhouse in front of Katie and Duncan, who still squalled like unhinged orangutans on the trampoline.

Maude's face was a study of fury behind glasses that darkened in the sun and always seemed a hint too grey. Tom trailed behind her wearing a look of patent fear. Maude ignored everything in the garden and arrived in front of Alana with her arms folded under her generous breasts, her feet planted apart.

"So..." she said.

"Nice evening for a walk," Alana said. She nodded at Tom, who stood a foot behind Maude. Tom nodded back.

"You sold out," Maude said, breaking into a big smile. A big, scary smile.

Alana drew back a couple of inches. The woman didn't beat around the bush. Maude didn't even bring bushes into the equation, which was unfortunate, because if there were a bush right now Alana might go hide behind it.

A ridiculous torrent of words emerged from Alana's mouth. Clearly, if she were ever in an interrogation situation she would cave immediately. "I haven't, Maude, I swear. I'm just helping Nate with process, so it's as fair as possible. If I find out anything that makes me concerned about having the mine in the watershed, or if I feel like they aren't doing things by the book, I'll quit immediately. I figured it's better to be working on the inside than trying to fight them on the outside."

"So, you're opposed to the mine?" Maude asked.

She did have a way of getting right to the nub of the matter. Out of the corner of Alana's eye, she could see that Katie and Duncan had stopped jumping and stood with their faces pressed against the protective mesh netting of the trampoline.

"Probably, but I don't want to prejudge it. I think it's possible that a magnesium mine could be done properly in a way that doesn't harm the watershed, and it could create a lot of jobs."

"So you want to feed the industrial engine at the expense of our health and local ecosystems?" Maude was still smiling, which was unnerving.

"No, not necessarily. Like I said, I'm only doing it to ensure that the consultation process is fair, and I'm waiting to see the data just like you are."

"And if Mr. Steeves asked you to cover something up, or whitewash it, what would you do?"

"Do you really think I would do that?"

"Well, if you'd asked me yesterday if you'd be willing to work for Mountain Magnesium Resources, I'd have said no, but here we are."

Maybe she *had* sold out, Alana thought. The worst part was that she hadn't even been that expensive.

"I'm not selling out, really."

"All right, get us a copy of the mine proposal then." Maude folded her thick arms under her breasts.

Alana let her mouth fall open at Maude's sheer audacity. Part of her wanted to rush into the house, log on to her Mountain Magnesium account, print off the proposal, and hand it to Maude. Then she would be the environmental savior and they would all love her. If she actually had a copy of the proposal. But she reminded herself that she was a professional and that professionals didn't just leak documents at their first opportunity. And she didn't have a copy of the proposal.

"It's not quite finished. We're just doing some fact checking on some of the proposed containment methods. It'll be out before the open house, I promise."

Maude rolled her eyes right in Alana's face. Alana heard Tom's voice. It seemed faint after Maude's thundering oratory. "The open house is in a week and a half. We need to be able to prepare. Releasing the proposal just before the event is not good process."

Alana's mind flashed to Nate saying the proposal wasn't ready because they were waiting on the results from some core samples and a certain map. He wouldn't delay just for the sake of preventing the Stewardship Society from getting the proposal early enough to prepare for the open house, would he?

"At least tell us the proposed location," Tom said. "Is it Sanderman's Bluffs or Orrington Creek?"

Alana shook her head automatically. Truth-telling was so ingrained in her that she couldn't *not* shake her head.

"It's Mur Marsh then."

Alana nodded slowly.

Maude lit up. She had a cause, a grapple hold, and she puffed up with the glory and righteousness of it. "But Mur Marsh is a wetland of provincial significance. Wetlands are natural filters. They clean the atmosphere and the water. They provide essential habitat. Mur Marsh is home to the sage thrasher and the white-headed woodpecker, both of which are red-listed."

"Maude, we don't have a provincial significant wetlands policy, and on the scale of provincial wetlands, Mur Marsh is a small one, and the mine isn't in the marsh. We're calling it the Mur Marsh location because that's the closest landmark. The mine won't touch the marsh, and Mountain Magnesium plans to build a trail around the marsh and along Orrington Creek."

"Listen to what you're saying!" Maude's eyes bulged at Alana behind her smoky glasses. "You're advocating for the wholesale destruction of a provincially significant wetland. You're already arguing around the edges like a corporate apologist." Maude threw her arms into the air. "It's not official, it's a small wetland, the mine isn't in the wetland," she mimicked Alana. "How can you live with yourself?"

Alana squinted and blinked back the tears. Maude used to be a lobbyist and campaigner for a big environmental organization in Vancouver. Now she worked for a local ecological society. Her causes were white hat and she cloaked herself in that intimidating sheen of goodness, but it seemed like she used black hat methods. She made her living—and a pretty decent one too by the look of her house—advocating that places remain forever untouched. Protecting places was important, but Alana wasn't sure how Maude expected *other* people to make a living.

And at this moment, Alana just wanted the whole mine and Maude and Silver Peak to go away and leave her with her garlic and raspberries and eggs that would soon be chickens. She wanted her environmentalism to be a simple matter of growing her own grains, putting up solar panels, and using grey water on her garden—not choosing between economic development and environmental conservation.

She was about to launch into a long apology and reiteration of her plans to quit, when the sound of an ATV engine being gunned ripped through the yard. Rick sailed past the fence on his ATV and then pelted by again and again in a cloud of exhaust and dust, spinning donuts. He had removed his helmet, and his longish dark hockey hair streamed out behind him, the crack of his ass all too apparent in his ill-fitting jeans. The noise made it impossible to continue talking. Normally Alana would be outraged that he was doing this so close to the children; right now, though, she had an odd compulsion to laugh.

Maude blinked in shock, but she quickly recomposed herself and replaced one moral indignation with another. "Quite the neighbors you have here," she said over the scream of the ATV as if Alana were clearly tainted by association.

"Yup. Rick is one of a kind. I have to put my kids to bed, Maude." Alana sidestepped the older woman, nodded at Tom, and went to retrieve Katie and Duncan from the trampoline.

"Who was that woman, Mommy?" Katie said. Alana snuggled beside her in the bed, feeling her warmth, the silk of her skin, and the angles of her bones. Duncan pressed against Alana on the other side. They smelled so young and hopeful, and Alana felt herself crushed with the privilege and joy of being able to love and hold them, and the grief and fear of knowing the kind of world they might inherit.

"That was Maude, a woman I work with."

"Why was she yelling so much?"

"Because that's what some people do, sweetie, when issues are important to them. Maude cares about the marsh and the plants and animals that live in it, and she thinks I don't."

"Don't you?"

"Of course I do. But different people go about taking care of the plants and animals differently. Maude believes that leaving everything totally alone is the only way. But maybe it isn't the only way."

Duncan head-butted her arm gently.

"Read," he said.

"Okay," she said. It was probably better to focus on *The Velveteen Rabbit*, as she wasn't really sure how she would explain how she was planning to take care of the plants and animals by supporting the development of a mine. As she read, her brain conjured up vision after vision of Mur Marsh looking like the obliterated Truffula tree forest from *The Lorax*, complete with choking, gasping birds and bloated dead fish under dark, smoke-filled skies while Nate shuttled around in a limo, in a sleek black suit designed by his mother, listening to Duke Ellington.

But even if everyone gave up their industrial twenty-first century lifestyles and lived a pioneer life off the land, would the amount of environmental destruction and degradation be any less? As much as she might yearn for a little homestead, there was the argument that the protection of ecosystems was best accomplished in countries that could afford it, places where people didn't depend directly on the land for their survival. And that was possible only because they leaned on the ecosystems of countries that couldn't afford environmental protection. In short, the ecological footprint of North Americans far exceeded the North American land base. Perhaps it was time that communities like Silver Peak started experiencing some of the environmental impacts they usually foisted on other countries.

Alana had heard once that raising one North American child consumed the resources of thirty children in developing countries. Thirty. She looked down at the perfect, soft, unruly-haired heads of her children as she read about the rabbit who was loved so much that he became real, and she tried not to see the specters of sixty other children in the room with them. She loved Katie and Duncan so, so much. They were real. They were her primary responsibility.

She really didn't know what the answers were. She just hoped Maude and Tom weren't camped out in the driveway.

Alana was updating the Mountain Magnesium website when Nate came in and slapped the paper version of the *Silver Peak News* onto her desk.

A grainy photo of Mur Marsh occupied the front page. "Mountain Magnesium Resources Plans to Defile Provincially Significant Wetland," the headline read.

"Seems they know where we plan to put the mine," Nate said. Alana wanted to slide off her chair and hide in the darkness under her desk. She scanned the article for any mention of her name. She should start gathering her stuff in anticipation of her imminent firing.

"I'm so sorry. I didn't mean to."

Nate cocked his head. "What are you talking about? They probably went up to the site and saw the activity by the marsh. It wouldn't take a genius to figure out that's the preferred site, and it's not like it's a major secret."

"Maude Kinney and Tom LeDrew showed up at my house last night. They were making guesses about the location. I gave it away." She offered Nate a weak smile while the words "loose lips sink ships, loose lips sink ships" ran in her mind. Her inability to keep her mouth shut had always been a professional liability.

Nate raised his perfect eyebrow. "This was probably printed yesterday. How could it have been you if whoever they were, Tim and Maude?"—Nate paused as if to inquire if he got the names right; Alana couldn't believe he didn't know who Maude was yet—"were at your house last night? I'm sure it's not your fault, but we do need to do some damage control. Can you call Owen?"

"Of course," she said. "What's our official position? That the mine will be next to the marsh."

"The *proposed* mine," Nate said. "And emphasize that it won't harm the marsh."

"Right," she said.

Nate looked back over his shoulder as he left her office, as if uncertain whether the matter was best left in her hands. She smiled and nodded encouragingly, her hand resting on the phone, hopefully communicating that she was poised to dial.

Instead, she wrote half a page of notes, confirmed that the province had no provincially significant wetlands, used the ladies room, chatted weakly with Len and Curtis, checked the online comments section of the *Silver Peak News* for the new article, and then, finally, worked up the courage to call.

Owen picked up his cell phone on the sixth ring.

"Owen, it's Alana. I'm calling about today's article about the mine."

"What about it?" His voice already had that defensive edge.

"Don't you think it was a bit one-sided?"

"Well, in an information vacuum, things do end up one-sided. People want to see Mountain Magnesium's proposal, and until you release it, this is what you're going to get."

"You could have called me for comment. There is no provincially significant wetlands policy in BC."

"Who says there has to be a provincial policy for something to be considered significant? Aren't all wetlands significant? Isn't the whole labeling system just a scheme to allow for the destruction of ecosystems deemed less valuable?"

He had a point. "Well, that's just usually how the term is used. Anyway, the mine is not going to be in the wetland. It is going to be in that area, but not anywhere where there's water."

"The littoral zone varies quite dramatically from year to year depending on the snowpack and annual precipitation."

Littoral zone. Christ. Either Owen was a closet environmentalist or Tom and Maude had been coaching him.

"I know. But the mine will be well back." She didn't add "I think" to this statement. "I would just really appreciate it if, as we move forward on this, if Maude or Tom call you with information, call me so I can at least provide our thoughts too."

"Fine. But just to be clear, Alana. I don't have to reveal my sources, and you shouldn't assume it was Maude and Tom who called me. There are a lot of people with real concerns about this mine and a lot of questions about the intentions of the board of directors."

Not Maude and Tom? *Who then?* she wondered. And what was he talking about? What were people saying about the board of directors? "Can you print a follow-up story clarifying some of the points?"

"Send me the proposal and sure."

She heard the click of Owen hanging up.

Nate sat at his desk, his head bent over some papers and his fingers pressed against his temples. He blinked as he looked up, like the light was hurting him. Pink circles underscored his eyes. If we were in a dim bar and writing a song, he would look just right, and she would want to sit with him with her feet entwined with his. But in front of his computer with a silky blue tie pulled tight around his neck, he seemed like a man out of place. Somehow she wanted to protect him, but she had no idea who he really was, or what he stood for.

"I'd really like to see the proposed mine site," she said. "Today."

CHAPTER FOURTEEN

Details

They all crammed into Len's red crew cab, which was occupied by all sorts of tools foreign to Alana. Grime and dust had wedged their way into every conceivable cranny in the truck, and Alana had to hold her breath so as not to start sneezing violently. Curtis sat in the one small remaining space in the back and everyone else had to fit in the front. Alana was pressed between Nate and Andre, Len's dog, a shepherd husky mix with one blue eye. Country tunes blared over the radio as Len drove slowly through town, headed up the old highway, and turned off onto the Orrington Creek logging road.

Once on the logging road, Len picked up speed significantly and practically tore around the corners, making Alana lean into first Nate and then Andre. She tried not to clutch anything, although Nate's thigh seemed rather inviting, and prayed that the dusty red twin cab wouldn't sail off the gravel road precariously carved in the side of the mountain and into the treetops below. The sign warning that they were on an active logging road and that logging trucks had the right of way was emblazoned on her mind. At this speed, she wasn't sure how Len would even see a logging truck coming, never mind stop. Andre licked her neck helpfully every few minutes.

Nate had seemed almost delighted at the prospect of leaving the office, and he had exchanged his tie and dress pants for jeans and a t-shirt with a silkscreen of some jazz musician Alana didn't recognize. Alana had been forced to don work overalls and steel-toed boots, which were oddly the correct size, that Len had procured from a storage room. Now Nate sat staring out the window contentedly, apparently not concerned that they could catapult to their death at any moment.

"So, why do you have a pair of women's work boots?" she asked, trying to take her mind off the careening truck.

"Those were for Fiona," Len said.

"Fiona?" Alana said. "Was she working for Mountain Magnesium?"

"She was supposed to work for us. We bought a bunch of equipment in Spokane in the fall, and the boots were a good price," Nate said, turning his head to stare out the window.

"What job was she supposed to do?"

"Yours."

"And what happened?"

"She decided it wasn't a good fit. She wanted to take advantage of some other opportunities. She suggested you." Nate continued to focus out the window.

Len slapped his knee and guffawed. Alana wished he would keep his hands at ten and two. There were so many potential projectiles in the truck. "What Nate doesn't mention," Len said, "is that there was a lover's quarrel involved."

"You and Fiona were... together?" Alana said weakly. Fiona's air of ownership and the elaborate hug made more sense now, and the knowledge made a little knife in Alana's heart turn sharply.

"No," Nate said, evidently not interested in talking about it.

"Here we are," Len said with a flourish, pulling off the road into a small clearing in a spray of gravel. They unfolded themselves from the vehicle as Andre bounded up and down the road in excitement, sniffing and wagging.

Alana looked around. Spruce and cedar trees covered the mountain slope that rose up behind them. The other side of the road dropped off into a steep bank studded with sharp shale fragments and boulders. She walked to the edge of the bank and oriented herself by tracing the line of deciduous trees that lined Mur Creek snaking up the valley below them. She was pretty sure Mur Marsh lay north of the flat area at the bottom of the shale slope, behind a thicket of evergreens. The air carried a hint of the murky, earthy scent of the marsh, and a group of geese dropped from the sky into the area beyond the evergreens with a wild cacophony of honks. She scoured every inch of the shale slope and the forest floor beneath it, but she couldn't see anything that looked like a mine.

"Where is it?" she asked as Len and Curtis loaded backpacks and tightened bootlaces.

"Well, we have to hike for a bit, my dear," Len said. "Mineral deposits don't generally cooperate and locate themselves right next to roads. The trail is right down here. It's a bit of a scree slope. Pick your way down carefully."

Alana tried to locate the trail on the steep slope of angular rocks.

"Just follow me. Curtis will go behind you so he can grab you if you slip."

Alana was about to say something tart about being an accomplished hiker but thought better of it. She followed Len as he descended slowly through the rock fragments, clenching her toes in Fiona's boots, certain that each footfall was going to jostle the rest of the slope out of place, sweeping them all away in an avalanche of pointed rocks.

Nate brought up the rear, almost distracted, his footfalls certain and lazily graceful. Alana tried to picture Fiona and Nate together, but could only imagine Fiona consuming Nate like a vampire with her sloe-eyed smile.

"Is this the best way down?" she said, scanning the rest of the bank for a gentler trail and finding only cliffs and rock outcrops. The rocks threw off waves of morning heat, and sweat trickled down her back.

"Well, we could go all the way around, but it's an hour hike in through the marsh," Curtis said from behind her.

At the bottom, Len led them through the trees, following the path of the road above. After about ten minutes, they reached a flattish bench next to a sheer cliff. The stench of the marsh was stronger here, and Alana could still see where the conifers gave way to the low shrubby deciduous trees and grasses of the wetland. A hawk circled overhead and frogs mounted tenuous calls against the hum of insects. She shaded her eyes against the sun, wishing she had a hat like Len and Curtis, and work clothes instead of a moderately itchy and not very stretchy hemp tank.

"And voila," Len said.

There wasn't much to see at the site, just a series of small holes next to a rock outcrop, a few core samples, metal bins that she assumed contained more tools, and an old canvas tent with a stack of pots and the charred remains of a campfire out front. It looked like some trees and bushes had been stripped from the ground, which was flattened. Instead of the peaty soil of the marsh, the dirt was dry and dusty, with a pale chalky undertone. Already it looked like a moonscape compared to the cool and shady forest they had just hiked through.

"Why's that tent here?" Nate said.

"It's Larry's. He used to spend the night, and he didn't bother to come up and collect his stuff when he headed out of town," Len replied.

"Are you talking about Larry Lund?" Alana said.

Nate looked at her. "Yeah. Larry prospects and pans for gold. This was his claim. He found the magnesium deposits and then he sold the claim to my dad. I'm sure you've seen him around town. Older fellow. Always carries a backpack and wears that yellow jacket."

Alana nodded. "I know Larry. Where'd he go?"

Len and Curtis looked at each other, and Len shrugged. "Who knows? Probably off hiking around in the mountains somewhere else, looking for the mother lode."

"Just make sure he isn't hanging out around here," Nate said. "We can't have a non-employee camping on the job site, especially when the real work begins." He turned his attention to Alana expectantly. "Okay, Alana, what did you want to come up here for?"

"I wanted to get a sense of the site. How far it is from the marsh? Where will the road access be? Where will the trails be? What will be the dimensions of the pit? What are your plans for reclamation since the water table is obviously high?" *And Fiona,* she thought. *I want to know how long you dated Fiona, and whether you liked her—or worse, loved her.* She clamped her teeth together and plastered a broad and foolish grin on her face to prevent her lips from forming those words.

Curtis lit a cigarette. "That's a lot of questions. You don't need to worry your pretty little head about those things. It's all under control. Len and I got it covered."

Alana shook her head and folded her arms over her chest. "If I'm going to be able to effectively provide information to the public, and understand their views, I need to know those things."

Nate stepped in front of Curtis. "It's going to be an artisanal mine. Small scale. The pits will be twenty-four feet deep and sixty feet in diameter. We've got three sites right in this area that will be in the first wave. Len and Curtis are still prospecting. There are deposits all through the area. It's just a matter of figuring out which ones are viable and make sense from an environmental perspective, and then adding them to the development list."

"And reclamation?" Alana asked.

Andre, apparently finished with his exploration of the site, lay down next to Len, his tongue lolling. The hum of crickets and insects echoed all around them, and the air around them seemed misty with movement. Alana resisted the urge to wave her hands around her neck and ankles to check for bugs.

"At this point, we plan to flood the pits and re-vegetate around them. We're just doing some acid-based accounting tests to make sure that the waste rock and surrounding material aren't going to generate too much acid. Depending on the results of the tests, we'll switch gears and go with a different plan," Nate said. His blue eyes regarded her intently, earnestly. What had he found appealing about Fiona? The boots pinched at Alana's heels.

"The road?"

Len pointed into the trees beyond them. "The road'll drop off the logging road about three clicks up, where the slope is more gradual. That way it'll also have easier potential access to the other sites."

"Have you measured out the distance to the marsh?"

Nate cocked his head to the side. "I'm sure the consultants preparing the proposal have, but we can do that ourselves if you want. Len, you got a GPS app on your phone, right?"

Len pulled his phone out of his pocket and turned to head off the plateau. "Yup. I hope you also packed mosquito repellent, young lady, because as we get closer to the marsh, them buggers become the size of birds."

Alana marched after Len into the trees in the direction of the marsh. Curtis and Nate trailed behind, the poison smell of Curtis's cigarette cutting through the peaty freshness of the marsh.

Back in the shade of the woods, Alana's eyes readjusted to the light, and the cool air was almost intoxicating. The trees seemed almost solemn and insulated them from the sounds of the marsh. Only squirrels scattered and scolded from the trees where slants of sunlight penetrated the canopy above. Andre raced from tree to tree in chase, barking in frustration at their bases. The soil grew darker and softer, almost springy underfoot.

But as suddenly as they had entered the woods, they emerged into the deciduous tree zone of alder and willow around the marsh, the air thick with bird calls. Sedge grasses, skunk cabbage, and cattails ringed the marsh, giving way to lily pads and other floating vegetation in the middle. A loon with two fluffy babies on its back made its way across the small section of open water.

Mosquitos descended in a frenzy, concentrating their efforts on Alana and Nate. Len and Curtis must have been wearing Deet. Alana bolted back to the trees, swatting and slapping, and she could hear Len and Curtis chuckling in the distance. Nate went the other direction around the marsh, pushing his way through the grasses, looking up at the hill from which they'd just come. The mosquitos followed Alana though, and she half jogged back through the forest to outrun them. Andre skipped along beside her, clearly excited at the prospect of a faster walk.

She stopped several times to look back at the marsh, thinking she had outrun the mosquitos, but they trailed her relentlessly until she emerged back out into the brilliant sun on the plateau. She was alone at the proposed mine site when Len and Curtis swaggered back up the trail wearing shit-eating grins. Nate wasn't with them.

"So," she said.

Len punched a few buttons on his GPS. "A hundred and eighty-six meters, give or take. Well beyond the riparian setback requirements."

"What are the setback requirements?" she asked. She should know these things. A good environmentalist would, but provincial guidelines around resource development were often too complex for any layperson to understand or remember. Half the time she wondered if the provincial officials responsible for developing and enforcing them had any idea either.

"For a wetland, less than five hectares, twenty meters."

Twenty meters. That was all that was required to be between a wetland writhing with life and an open pit full of machinery?

Nate strode up the path, his face crinkled with thought. "Did Larry actually stake the ground here? Or did he file electronically? Do you know?"

Len scratched his head. "Larry's old school, and I highly doubt he has Internet access. He staked it with posts. Why?"

"Can you show me the posts?"

"Sure."

Nate followed Len into the trees. They looked like they were bushwhacking, and Alana just remembered it was tick season. She decided to stay where she was, surreptitiously checking her ankles for the small disk-like creatures. She was definitely not cut out for fieldwork.

Curtis lit another cigarette. The crickets clicked and chirped in the afternoon heat in the grasses that surrounded the site.

"They don't know what they're talking about, you know," Curtis said.

"Who?"

"The enviros. They get their knickers in a knot every time a pine-cone is overturned. Most of them haven't ever left their warm little houses or yards. Their understanding of wilderness is from the Internet, documentaries, and David Suzuki. I don't think they even look out the windows when they fly over it, jetting from one urban area to another." Curtis paused to flick his cigarette ash onto the ground. The slight breeze lifted the edge of his comb-over.

"When they hike, they go to provincial parks and protected areas and they get a distorted idea of what the woods are like. When you spend as much time as I do outside, you realize how endless the woods and trees are, how abundant the wildlife. They chain themselves to bulldozers for the sake of a little twig, but they don't consider the families, the people, who rely on these resources for a living, people who make it possible for them to be doctors and shopkeepers and policy analysts, and whatever other desk jobs they seem to flock to. Have you seen the number of for sale signs in this town? People are hurting. This place needs some local jobs. Without them, Silver Peak will die just like all the other rural ghost towns in this province that used to have a mill or a mine. But ecosystems repair themselves. Trees regrow. Animals come back. We even have a name for it: succession. A hundred years ago, fires obliterated these forests on a regular basis. Now they're sacred cows."

Alana thought of some of the denuded landscapes she had seen over her years as an environmentalist. But she realized she had only ever seen them in pictures. She'd never visited a damn one and had never seen any follow-up photos.

Curtis wasn't completely correct. Some environmentalists—researchers, conservation area managers, outdoorsmen—spent a lot of time on the land. But he did have a point. There *were* a lot of desk environmentalists... like her. Maybe they didn't really know what was going on out on the land.

"But what about things like water quality?" she said. "Even if things do grow back, don't you think there can be long-term impacts on water quality from sedimentation?"

"We already chlorinate and filter our water."

"I know, but if the water quality drops too much then it's more expensive to treat and may become unusable." She paused again as she was uncertain about the threshold where water became unusable.

"We're nowhere near our water supply creeks right now."

Alana looked down to where Mur Creek wound up through the valley. She could only vaguely hear the whoosh of moving water through the trees.

"But what about runoff and sedimentation and leaching into groundwater?"

"That can all be controlled. And you think there isn't natural leaching and sedimentation? We act like Mother Nature is all benign and warm and fuzzy, but she can dish some pretty nasty things into our watersheds too. I'm not saying we shouldn't do things right and respect nature. But that doesn't mean we shouldn't do things at all. This province is run on natural resources. We can't all be doctors and lawyers, or there'd be nobody with money to put in their pockets."

"But what about the runoff from the marsh? Doesn't that creek run just below this plateau?"

"Yes, but it's a minor feeder stream. Just think about the Mur Creek trail at the lower elevations. A thousand dogs shit beside that trail every day and nobody bats an eye about that."

He was right. Everyone walked their dogs along the portion of the Mur Creek trail closer to the city. And nobody picked up. A hundred dogs a day probably trampled through that creek, drinking, splashing, and peeing in the water.

Nate and Len returned over the edge of the embankment. Nate was shaking his head, staring at Len's phone in his hands, and then headed off into the trees on the other side of the site with Len scurrying behind.

"What is that all about?" she asked Curtis.

"Dunno," Curtis said.

But when Len and Nate returned, neither seemed inclined to share, and they drove back with Carrie Underwood blaring on the radio. Nate stared out the window wearing a scowl.

They rounded a corner when Len suddenly slammed on the brakes and yelled, "Shit!" Andre lurched forward and smacked into the dash. The tools in the back whacked the seat and fell to the floor with a resounding clank of metal on metal, and Alana let out a scream. The truck fishtailed to the right and skidded to a stop a few feet from the bank.

A small white Toyota Corolla sat in the middle of the road. Maude and Tom sat in the front seat, looking over the edge of a large map wearing floppy sunhats and expressions of shock. Andre scrambled back up onto the seat and started to bark at the Corolla.

"What the hell are they doing up here in that thing in the middle of the road? Don't they know it's four-wheel drive only?" Len laid on the horn and gave them the finger as Tom pulled over to the right and resumed his slow drive up the hill, the whiteness and tightness of his knuckles apparent even from where Alana sat.

Len gunned the engine, sending a shower of gravel at the Corolla, and headed back down the mountain, blessedly at a slower pace and with his liver-spotted hands more carefully placed on the wheel.

"That was Maude and Tom," Alana said to Nate. "The Mountain Stewardship Society folks I told you about. They're on their way to the site I bet."

"They better not touch anything," Len said.

CHAPTER FIFTEEN

Colonizations

When they arrived back at the office, Nate, Len, and Curtis spent half an hour in the boardroom reviewing maps, and Alana could hear sharp snippets of conversation through the walls. Then Nate appeared in her office, where she sat at her desk running Internet searches on standard open-pit mine production levels, sizes, and environmental impacts. He shut the door and plunked down in one of the leather chairs in front of her desk.

"I'm wondering if we should delay the open house."

She squinted at him. As painful as publicizing an open house was, unpublicizing one was worse. "We've put out publicity. People are expecting an open house. We can't cancel. They'll go berserk. Have you read the *Silver Peak News* and Facebook lately? You need to get the proposal out there."

Nate's face contracted and tightened fractionally. "I said delay, not cancel. Some new information has come to light today on the site visit. We have to redo some of the maps and site plans."

"Talk to me, Nate."

Nate sighed and pulled his hands through his thick hair. "There was a mistake in some of the coordinates Larry gave us. Well, more accurately, the coordinates don't match the claim posts. They were just a bit off. Larry had two claims in the area, and he didn't use a GPS when he placed the posts. Len and Curtis just assumed the claim posts were right and based some of their core sample analysis on spots within the posts, but when we were out at the marsh and I looked up at the mountain, I could tell from the topography there was a problem. Len and Curtis aren't from Silver Peak, so they wouldn't have noticed. That's why I had to see the claim posts. So two of the proposed sites will push us into Larry's second claim. It's no big deal. We own both. I just wanted to make sure there weren't any other mistakes." Nate's eyes still seemed strained.

"If it's not a big deal, why are you looking at me like that?"

Nate pursed his lips and didn't respond for a few seconds. "The second claim is within the city boundaries. The good news, for us I suppose, is that it's still not up to the city. Mining is exempt from municipal zoning, so the city doesn't have a say as to whether the province issues us our permits or not."

The city *didn't* have a say, even though resource development in the watershed was totally counter to the sustainability plan. Alana pondered the absolute lunacy of not giving a municipality influence over land within their boundaries within their own watershed. She also pondered the fact that she was working for the type of company willing to take advantage of this. Could she really have a more positive impact on decisions from the inside, or was she just deluding herself on that front? Was her attraction to Nate muddling her thinking? Should she quit?

"The sustainability plan doesn't support mining or any resource development in the watershed within city boundaries," Alana said. "As a courtesy, I think you need to call Stewart immediately and let him know. I also think you have to get that proposal out there as soon as possible. I wouldn't delay the open house. You might have to just be honest about the mistake. You gave the city the original coordinates. If *they* decide to tell people about the screw-up, you're going to look like a liar, which isn't going to make you any friends in this community."

"Fine. I'll call Stewart now, then let's go for a run," he said, rising.

She ducked her head into Nate's office just as he was hanging up the phone.

"Did you call Stewart?"

"Yes."

"And?"

"He said he would let council know, and he asked me to send the proposal with the correct coordinates."

"Did you point out the sustainability plan problem?"

"He didn't think it was going to be an issue. He said the sustainability plan was more of an advisory document than a plan, that council could take it under advisement but didn't need to follow it, as long as the sustainability vision was achieved, and that council can decide new visions are more reflective of the wishes of the community. It didn't make a lot of sense, but I think he was saying it isn't an issue."

Alana made a mental note to remember that plans clearly had about as much longevity in Silver Peak as a fugitive with an untraceable platinum Visa in a train station. The sustainability plan hadn't even been approved yet, and apparently already it was out of date, able to be replaced by a "new vision."

"So, we don't have to delay the open house?" she said, trying to ignore the twang she felt at the prospect of completely undermining a plan she and Zander had worked so hard to develop.

Nate closed his eyes and pressed his forehead against his steepled fingers. "I guess not."

"It's just that the more discussion that happens in informal settings, the more this thing seems to be going supernova. We need to get in front of people and answer questions."

Nate's lips twitched into a wry smile. "Believe me, I know about discussion in informal settings. The consultant is sending a copy of the proposal late this afternoon. I assume you still want to see it."

"I'll review it tonight," Alana said in a cheery voice. Finally she would get to see what the hell she was buying into. Or the reason for her resignation.

Nate was silent for a few seconds.

"There's something else?" Alana said.

Nate shook his head. "No. There's nothing else. It's all good. Let's go for our run." He rose energetically and beamed at her. But there was something sort of weak and half-hearted about it, and he was less chatty on their run than usual.

After lunch, she checked the number of comments on the most recent *Silver Peak News* article, the one about the mine being in Mur Marsh. Forty-two. Christ. She scrolled through them frantically. About a third of the commenters were in support of the mine; the rest were appalled. The ratio wasn't necessarily relevant since the pro-environment faction tended to be more articulate and likely to comment. Still, the level of vitriol was a bit alarming. The early replies were lengthy pontifications on development, mining, the economy, wetlands, and the sacredness of water by local know-it-alls. The later comments degenerated into venom-filled insults from both sides about the various people who had their heads up their asses and didn't give a crap about the future of Silver Peak.

Alana switched to the Mountain Stewardship Society page. They had added a Twitter feed. There was a picture of Maude by the marsh, her giant sunhat shading her face and her generous behind in the air as she leaned over to point to a mass of frog eggs. It was accompanied by the text: "This will be destroyed forever." Another picture popped up. Maude by the marsh again—this time standing amid some of the reed grass, next to a small black bird with a red stripe on its head.

Double Christ. They were live-tweeting their visit to the marsh. Pretty soon there would be photos of Mur Marsh sage thrashers and bitterns and ducks shared all over the Internet. If Maude managed to snap a photo of the loon babies, Alana's PR campaign for Mountain Magnesium was pretty much dead in the water.

She flipped to the *Silver Peak Scoop* next. Ramona had been blessedly quiet for the last two weeks. She was probably on one of her month-long vacations in Mexico; that was the only time the *Scoop* went silent. Alana prayed Ramona had decided to take up crocodile farming or iguana conservation—as crocodiles and iguanas were probably the only creatures who could handle the woman—and was planning to stay in Mexico forever.

Unfortunately, it seemed that while the crocodiles and iguanas were safe from Ramona, the people of Silver Peak were not. A new headline had appeared underneath the curling S of the stylized "Scoop." "Liars in City Hall," it read. Alana almost passed out with relief. Ramona was focusing on her usual target. Then she scrolled down and saw the picture of Nate and Zander having a beer together in the dim basement of the Silver City Brew Pub. The story indicated that the city was refusing to release any information about the mine, even though they clearly had it, as evidenced by the photo.

Nate and Zander. Why were they together? She would have to ask Nate. Still, aside from the picture and a single paragraph regarding the mine, the article focused mostly on innuendo regarding other mistakes apparently made by the planning department, such as approving a rezoning that would block existing resident's views—probably Ramona's—and failing to fully identify every line item in the main street redevelopment budget when it was in the proposal stage.

She scrolled down further. "Former Drug Addict Capable of Running Local Company?" read the next headline. Alana blinked at the harsh white on black text. The article was all about Nate: his album deal with a small recording studio, some initial success in Vancouver clubs—complete with a photo of Nate leaving a club, looking totally hot with a leggy brunette—and then an alleged spiral into drugs and alcohol that resulted in him getting dropped by his record label. It insinuated that Nate only got the job with Mountain Magnesium because his dad was on the board of directors, and it concluded with the "general" question of whether failed, and troubled, jazz musicians had the capacity to run mining companies in community watersheds.

Alana felt sick. Trust Ramona to go for the jugular. She scrolled past the next headline—"City Considering New Reservoir Because Council Members Want Swimming Pools"—closed her browser, and dialed Fiona's number.

"Bonjour," Fiona answered. Alana suppressed a twitch.

"Fiona. It's Alana. I need to know if you're working with Maude."

All traces of French departed Fiona's voice. "Why?"

"Because I want to talk to you about a few things, about Nate, and I'm not going to if you're working with Maude."

"I wouldn't exactly say we're working together."

"What does that mean?"

"Look, it doesn't matter. Is Nate okay?"

"He's okay. But that was quite the article Ramona wrote about him."

"I know."

"Are those things true? Do you know?"

Fiona went silent. "You should ask Nate yourself."

"You can't tell me anything?"

"I really can't. Just ask him."

"Do you think I should be doing this job?"

"Why not?"

"Because I might get lynched or guillotined."

Alana heard a forced laugh. She was never quite sure what Fiona made of her theatrics. Fiona probably didn't worry about mobs.

"You'll be fine." This sounded remarkably insincere, like Fiona was helping Maude rig up the guillotine in her back yard. Then again, Alana did have a tendency toward paranoia.

Alana hung up and walked back to Nate's office. He looked up, the white of his computer screen reflecting off the curve of his cheekbone. Her stomach gave a minor hop. *Drug addict*, she reminded herself. She forced her mouth into a wide grin that probably looked scary.

"I've read the article, Alana," Nate said.

"Oh," she managed to mumble.

"Look, it's okay. I was an artist. I'm used to people saying whatever they want about me, as if I'm not even a real person. I did strike out as a jazz musician. I didn't use any more drugs than the average performer—I really didn't use a lot at all—but I did go through a major depression when everything got screwed up, and I lost my label. Being a musician is a tough gig, and maybe I just wasn't good enough, which was a difficult pill to swallow. But it's probably better for my career here at Mountain Magnesium that we don't mention that I'm prone to debilitating melancholy." Nate flipped a faint smile in Alana's direction. "In our society, being a recovering drug addict is more acceptable than being depressed. It's unfortunate that Ramona didn't think that having an undergraduate degree in economics from UBC with a minor in geology and an MBA from Queen's would give me some ability to run a mining company. But evidently, if a person tried and didn't make it in a risky creative venture, they mustn't have anything else to offer."

Alana sank into the chair across from Nate's desk. "Don't listen to Ramona. She's just mean. I'm sorry to hear about your depression. Are you okay now?"

The corners of his lips curled up in an almost playful smile. "Yeah, I'm actually pretty good."

"I'll try and do some communications damage control."

Nate shook his head. "Don't respond. Don't stoop to Ramona's level. I'm fine."

Alana stood, then hesitated. She wanted to ask Nate so much more, about what it felt like to give up on a dream, and whether he really had, but she didn't feel it was her place.

In actual fact, she wanted to walk around the corner of Nate's desk and pull him up into her arms. But even if he wasn't a drug addict, he was her boss, and a capitalist, although calling him that had started to seem a little funny. But what did a single mother—not to mention a failed, but likely still raving, environmentalist, who had been dumped by her husband no less—have to offer a sexy former jazz musician who likely had his pick of women? Even if he did have some issues.

The mine. She had to focus on the mine. That was her job.

"I'm having copies of the proposal printed for the board so it's easier to review," Nate said. "It won't be ready until later this afternoon after you've left. I'll swing a copy by your house tonight if you want it right away."

Alana hesitated. She didn't really need a paper copy. She usually reviewed things on her computer. But she wanted to see Nate. "Sounds great," she said. "I live in the old Fraser farmhouse on Meadow Creek Road. You know it?"

Nate's eyes lit up. "I love that farm. The Frasers used to have Leo and me over every spring to meet the baby goats."

"No goats now, I'm afraid. The farm fell into pretty bad disrepair when Ingrid got sick, but I'm trying to fix it back up." *On my own*, she didn't add.

"That's awesome," he said. "Is six okay?"

She prepared a news release clarifying the provincial policy regarding wetlands and emphasizing that the mine site was over a hundred and fifty meters from the marsh, which, although it was more than nine times the distance required by the province, didn't seem like that much. She added that the critical wetland values in the marsh would be maintained and that a boardwalk around the marsh would be built so that everyone could enjoy the special habitat Silver Peak was lucky enough to have in its back yard. She sent it off and then created a section on the Mountain Magnesium website outlining the credentials of the board and staff, especially Nate. Two of the board members, Jim Price and Lawrence Sutherland, had worked for and owned an impressive number of large mining companies. Alana found it interesting that they were willing to be part of such a small operation relative to some of the international corporations they had worked for in the past.

She ran out of the office at three trying not to be too excited by the prospect of Nate dropping by the farm. He was just dropping off a report. The streets were jammed with parents en route to or from the school. It was the only rush hour Silver Peak ever experienced. The parents who did shift work, or managed somehow to live on one income, were always there early, and their children were now nestled in the backs of SUVs and Subaru Outbacks, munching on bunny crackers and sharing the highlights of their day, or skipping through the sunny streets of Silver Peak with their parents, play dates in tow. Alana tried to ignore these parents' seemingly smug and carefree smiles as they waved at each other, organized dinner parties, and blocked traffic while they sauntered away from the school in clusters.

She parked a block away and wove through the idling vehicles, children, and bikes, praying nobody would run her over.

Duncan's and Katie's backpacks sat together at the usual meet-up zone, but Duncan and Katie were nowhere to be seen. She scanned the playground as scenarios of a bearded man in a van with a kitten ran through her mind. They were probably fine. They were just playing in another part of the schoolyard.

Gillian swooped in while she methodically worked her way, one by one, through the leaping and jostling blur of children who remained on the playground.

"You're helping out next week, right?" she asked. Gillian's bangs cut a sharp line across her upper forehead, and even more pronounced streaks of blond sliced through the dark brown of the rest of her hair.

"What's next week?"

Gillian sighed as if Alana was so removed from reality it was painful. "It's a fundraiser for sports day. The bottle drive at the high school. Remember? Your name's on the sign-up list."

"Right," Alana said. Clearly this was another part of the twelve-step dementor recovery program that her subconscious was forcing her along. But recycling bottles—that was environmentally friendly. She *should* help out, and it would count for points toward the bet.

"So, can you be at the high school at eleven on Saturday?"

"I don't know, Gillian. That's the day after the open house for Mountain Magnesium. I might be recovering, assuming protesters haven't carried me off and tied me to a tree in the marsh to be eaten alive by mosquitos and sage thrashers."

Gillian regarded her blankly as if she had never even heard of Mountain Magnesium.

"You know. The mine in the watershed."

"Oh, I heard something about that. Is it actually going to happen?"

"I have no idea. Have you seen Katie or Duncan?"

"They were here somewhere." She fluttered her hand in the direction of the play structures. Clearly, nobody else was haunted by images of child predators circling the schoolyard.

"Right. Well, I need to go find them."

"It would be really great if you could come," Gillian said. "We really need your help, and it's for the kids."

"I'll do my best," Alana replied. She made her way through the hustle of children, feeling heavy with guilt. Gillian was just trying to make life more fun for the kids and raise money for things the government no longer paid for.

At the back of the school, Katie stood on her own on the cement.

"Where's your brother?" Alana said, more sharply than she intended.

Katie pointed to the roof of the school. Duncan's tufty head appeared over the edge.

"Hi, Mom!"

"What are you doing up there? How did you get up there? Get down," she said in automatic confusing order.

"Our ball went up there," Katie said. As if in response, a red rubber ball sailed off the roof and bounced in front of them.

"Duncan, get down this instant. How did you get up there?"

"Everyone goes up here, Mom. It's fine." He walked across the roof, slipped his tiny body through the gap in an iron fence, climbed onto some silvery exhaust ducts, and reached his leg over the ladder rungs embedded in the wall. He descended carefully, then hooked a toe into the chain link fence that he obviously climbed to get to the ladder.

"What are you doing? Be careful. You might fall." She raced over to catch him, but he executed his final moves like an acrobat and dropped surefooted to the cement beside her.

"Everyone does it. How else are we going to get our balls back?"

"Do the lunch supervisors know?"

Duncan shrugged. "They don't come back here."

"I can't believe they haven't blocked that off," Alana fumed. The school and grounds were fraught with safety issues: broken benches with sharp metal bolts, sheer drop-offs from the roof playground onto cement, skating rinks of ice on the walkways in the winter, a playground that flooded with knee-deep water every spring, and, evidently, easily accessible roofs. The PAC raised these issues often to no avail. The provincial government poured money into the Olympics, TED talks, and things the baby boomers wanted instead.

She drew Duncan to her. "Please don't do that again. It's not safe."

His little arms snaked around her, and the warmth of his cheek pressed against hers. Perhaps her expectations of maintenance and safety were simply out of line with the new economic reality.

"It's fine, Mom. I know what I'm doing."

She tightened her grip on him. Soon he would be too cool to hug his mother and she would have to relinquish him into a world of iPods,

Facebook, videogames, celebrity obsessions, designer drugs, extreme sports, and McJobs. The number of ways in which he could go wrong numbed her.

She tried not to hate the baby boomers. They had inhabited a world with low house prices, high incomes, and appreciating assets, and they continued to hold much of the nation's wealth and power while they drained the healthcare system. But perhaps the Gen Xers and Yers, herself included, who wanted to work cushy executive jobs, own five bedroom houses with ensuites, and vacation in exotic locales every year were part of the problem, too. She pictured the tiny two-bedroom house in which her dad was raised with seven other siblings. Her grandparents were for certain rolling around in their urns, gobsmacked by the excesses of the new world.

She herded the kids into the SUV and drove home. Duncan exchanged his backpack and school clothes for shin pads and soccer cleats while she made them a blueberry smoothie to drink on the way, trying not to think about how Grandma Matheson would have made them get their own lard sandwich and ride their bikes to the field.

Back in the SUV, the kids chattered about their day. "Our lollipop tree bloomed today," Duncan said.

"Your what?"

"Our lollipop tree, like in the book," he said. "We planted a lollipop stick a few weeks ago."

"That must have been really exciting," Alana said, repeating the mantra "do not be a fun-killer" in her head. The kids were smart enough to know that lollipops didn't grow on trees. Weren't they?

Duncan relayed the events surrounding the lollipop bloom, and Alana tried to focus, but an alarming number of "for sale" signs *had* sprung up in front of houses in the last few weeks. It was spring, so more people were going to be listing their houses, but maybe Curtis was right. Maybe Silver Peak was dying because people couldn't get jobs anymore. Real jobs that paid mortgages and supported families, because most manufacturing jobs were in China and India now, where people worked for cents a day so North Americans could buy cheap clothes and electronics. Meanwhile underemployed people in Silver Peak and across the province had to buy overpriced houses as boomers tried to cash in on their investment and the real estate and development companies continued to pretend the great real estate party would never end. Then the cash poor and underemployed people with enormous mortgages cross-border shopped and hunted for online deals, which made the local merchants unsustainable and cost the community more jobs.

Her mind was spiraling. By the time they arrived at soccer, she was practically hyperventilating and had a hard time making smiley eye contact with the other mothers who seemed unperturbed by the coming collapse.

Duncan joined his team, Katie ran off with her friends, and Alana searched the field for someone she knew. Perhaps some rational human contact would return her to reality, or at least place her firmly back in the developed-world bubble of happiness.

Cynthia Wilson stood by the side of the field. Cynthia and Alana had been great friends when the kids were younger, spending many enjoyable days in the trenches of early motherhood where really just surviving the day was the great equalizer. But somewhere along the line, Cynthia had become obsessed with redecorating her house, hosting dinner parties, and ensuring her children were in every activity under the sun, and Alana had quickly established herself as a big stick in the mud.

"Hey," Alana said.

Cynthia eyeballed her appraisingly. "Hi, stranger," she said. "How's it going?"

"Oh, you know me. The usual job stress and life stress. How are you?"

"Good," she said, waving her hand in the air. "Course I've got my dining room table completely covered in goodie bags that I have to stuff for the preschool carnival."

Alana contorted her face into a cheerful expression and tried not to think too much about the goodie bags. After all, she had been guilty of overstuffed goodie bags in the past, trying ridiculously to earn friends for her children and meet the outrageous expectations of the partygoers, which were no doubt formed as a result of some other mom's over-the-top goodie bags, which were in response to Alana's goodie bags the previous year. And carnivals were another rat hole for Alana. They always seemed like crazy-assed make-work projects that took up hundreds of hours, required some dad to dress up in a Gumby suit, created a huge amount of garbage in the form of paper plates and goodie bag contents, and if they were a fundraiser, which they invariably were, they only raised five hundred dollars, which largely came from the parents of the kids involved.

And yet half the time she enjoyed the events as much as the kids who cavorted about from the face-painting station to the dad who could make balloon animals and from there to the cake walk, chortling in orange-pop-moustached ecstasy.

Alana could have fun. She wasn't a complete dementor. But just as the requirements for bigger houses, snazzier wardrobes, and better fancier recreational toys of all kinds had somehow grown out of control the past few years, so, it seemed, had the requirements for fun. Nobody could just hang out in their back yard anymore. They might expire from lack of a balloon animal. Even the balloon animals were out of control. Nobody wanted a dog anymore. They wanted a multi-colored unicorn, or crab, or crocodile. She was pretty sure her mother had never baked fifty cupcakes or blown up a hundred balloons for a carnival. And she knew her dad had never worn a Gumby suit.

Cynthia's eyes were beginning to reflect the suspicion that Alana was a little unstable. Alana smiled widely and grasped every bit of sincerity she could eke out of her repertoire of facial expressions. "You do so much for the community," Alana said. "What is that preschool going to do when Isabella graduates?"

Ahhh. Preschool graduation. Another rat hole. In Silver Peak, there was kindergarten graduation, grade seven graduation, and grade twelve graduation. It all made for a lot of congratulating their children for going through the generally required motions of life, which may be why so many of them ended up on *American Idol* thinking they could sing.

So. Many. Rat. Holes. Alana's smile felt tight and forced.

Cynthia waved her statement away. "Oh, well, someone has to do it. What have you been up to lately?"

"Just work mostly... with Mountain Magnesium Resources," Alana added when nothing seemed to register on Cynthia's face. Did nobody with children under the age of twelve know what might be about to happen in the watershed? "I'm their communications director, sort of." She said this and then felt stupid, like she was bragging, like in actual fact all she was qualified to do was lick envelopes.

"That's fantastic," Cynthia said. "Congratulations."

"I guess. It's a pretty political position though, so I'm feeling stressed about it."

"What's so political about it?" There was a tinkling quality to her voice. Maybe it was meant to be reassuring, but Alana couldn't help but think it was similar to the way the staff addressed mental patients in an institution.

"You know, whether the mine will proceed or not. Some people are upset about how it could impact our water. Other people really want the mine because it'll provide jobs."

"Well, I wouldn't let myself get too wrapped up in that. You should let your boss handle that kind of thing."

"Well, I *am* pretty involved. I work there, and you know, it's not all on him."

Cynthia smiled. "You're probably overthinking it. It'll be fine."

Alana gritted her teeth. But she did overthink things.

Then she realized that Cynthia wasn't wearing any makeup and her eyes were bloodshot. "Are you okay? You look a bit tired?"

"I have strep throat and shingles," Cynthia said. "I've been staying up late organizing the carnival, and of course Graham's golf tournament is coming up and I have to get all the silent auction items lined up for that and figure out who's going to be paired with who, and it's so hard to find a good caterer in this town. And the contractor is flaking out on our deck renovation so it might not be ready for our end-of-school party, and of course there's all the driving for the kids' activities."

Alana leaned imperceptibly away from Cynthia to reduce the chances of germ transfer. Cynthia continuously organized parties and events while shuttling her kids to a myriad of lessons designed to make them better people: specialized soccer tutoring, violin, French. There was no end to what her children did, and did exceedingly well. They would no doubt be off to Ivy League universities in the States while Duncan and Katie pumped gas at the Esso.

Alana should be more like Cynthia. But there were just so many rat holes.

After soccer and grocery shopping, Alana set the kids to watching their short video and started to prepare dinner: organic New York strip loin with a mango salsa, sautéed spinach, and a quinoa salad. Blaine's favorite. She fixed her makeup and set the table using some old blue glass plates that she had bought before she married Blaine. Then she picked a few wildflowers in the yard and put them in a glass for a centerpiece. The look was hip casual and she was pleased with the effect. She had been letting things go too much since Blaine left. She knew Cynthia put out an enormous spread every night.

Maybe if she had been more like Cynthia, Blaine wouldn't have left. Maybe it was people like Cynthia who did the real work of sustainability, creating a sense of community and keeping families together. It was so hard to know what the real work of sustainability was.

Blaine knocked and entered the house with a flourish, the door slamming behind him and the thunk of his shoes on the tile. He was never silent. Alana looked up and tried to smile.

He raised his eyebrows at the marinating steak and table setting and cracked a big smile.

"Got the hippie plates out, huh? What's the occasion?"

"They're not hippie plates. Why would you call them that?"

Blaine looked a bit taken aback by her snappishness. "Because you bought them at that hippie patchouli store in your hippie days."

"I was never a hippie."

"Sorry, your granola days."

Tears prickled in her eyes. "Blaine, I was so far from a granola. The fact that you even think I was a granola shows your utter lack of understanding of what granolas are and what I was."

"All right, fine. If you weren't a granola, then what were you?"

She had purchased the chunky blue plates, wooden utensils, and tie-dyed placemats, all hand made in Cambodia, at a craft fair back in the days when she was trying to fit in with the *true* granolas in her classes. She had been on the fringes of the group for many years. She went to their rallies, tried to talk their talk, and attended every dinner party she was invited to. They would sit cross-legged on the floor touching each other, eating vegan food and discussing serious issues about the corporation, alternative movies, and protests, until they got high and danced maniacally into the night to tribal music Alana couldn't identify. She would show up in her faux environmental clothes, always just a bit too tight and well cut, with her poorly prepared salad, and try to engage in the discussion, but she was never really one of them with their beaded shirts, wrap-around skirts, and unmade-up tanned faces and wild hair.

Choosing Blaine with his sports car and anti-Birkenstock ways was just the final nail in her granola coffin. Her first dinner party with the plates and Blaine had been an utter failure. She had overcooked the pasta, chosen the wrong music, and failed to provide a pot-smoking atmosphere, and Blaine had looked blankly and derisively at her friends when they talked of ontologies and colonizations.

"I don't know what I was, Blaine," she said quietly. "I'm sorry. You can't stay tonight. I'm expecting someone."

CHAPTER SIXTEEN

Beginnings and Endings

Nate pulled up just after six. She had timed it so that she would just be about to grill the steaks. She wasn't even sure what she was doing. Had she made this meal, set the table, tidied up, to impress Nate? Was she planning to invite him for dinner, or just have him see what she was capable of? Or had she done it to impress Blaine, and show him what he had lost? She wasn't sure.

Nate stood just inside the door wearing an affable grin, his hair askew from his helmet. He spied the table and proffered the envelope. "I'll get out of your hair. Looks like you're entertaining. Don't feel you have to review the proposal tonight."

"Oh, no, not entertaining. Just a regular weeknight meal. Just me and the kids," she said. If she was going to ask him to dinner, now was the time, but she couldn't quite seem to get the words out from behind her frozen smile.

"Your weeknight meals are very impressive," he said.

"Thanks," she said. She leaned toward him and took the envelope. They held each other's eyes for a few seconds. She breathed in and then nodded. She wasn't quite ready for this yet. He let go and stepped back as though to leave, but just then the kids arrived in a whirlwind.

"Katie's snuggling with one of the eggs!" Duncan yelled, running in from the living room as fast as his skinny little legs would take him. "She won't put it back!" He skidded to a stop at the sight of Nate. Katie almost crashed into him, clearly cradling an egg against her skin inside her shirt.

"Katie," Alana said. "What have we talked about with the eggs?"

"Do you have a motorcycle?" Duncan breathed. He was eyeballing Nate's helmet.

"Just a scooter," Nate said. "It's not quite as exciting."

"Who are you?" Katie said, still clutching the egg to her belly.

"Katie, give me that egg at once," Alana said.

Nate extended a hand, which Duncan, surprisingly, accepted. "I'm Nate, your mom's boss."

"Are you planning to poison us?" Duncan asked.

Nate laughed, but Alana noticed a slight stiffness to his movements. "I hope not," he said. "I'd be happy to take you on a tour of the watershed, with your mom, of course, if you're interested."

"Can I go for a ride on your scooter?" Duncan said.

Alana now held the warm egg against her own skin, which she was finding awkward, since it meant she had to lift her shirt in front of Nate. "Duncan, that's enough. Nate probably doesn't want to do that."

Nate's eyes flicked past her exposed midriff. "I don't mind at all," he said. "Whenever you want, buddy."

"Can I go *now*, Mom?" Duncan almost yelled, even though he was standing a foot away from her.

Alana grilled the steaks while Nate gave Duncan and Katie slow rides up and down the driveway wearing their bike helmets. Then he joined them for dinner and made all the appropriate comments about her cooking and the plates and the rustic old farmhouse, while entertaining Duncan with stories of when he rode a real motorcycle. He politely helped with the dishes, sharing tales of the Frasers and their goats and rabbits and asking with seemingly great interest what Alana planned to plant in each garden bed. She could feel the heat from his body and eyes as they moved around each other in the small space of the kitchen, clearing plates, loading the dishwasher, and scrubbing pots, almost but not quite touching. Almost but not quite there.

When she directed the kids to begin their homework, he gathered up his helmet. "I should go, and let you do the night time routine. Dinner was amazing. Thank you."

"Thank you," she said, not quite sure what she was thanking him for.

He turned and paused at the door, and for a breathtaking and nerve-wracking moment it seemed as though he might want to kiss her, but instead he looked at Duncan, who was skipping around the living room chasing Katie with a rubber pterodactyl, and called his goodbyes to the kids.

As he drove away, she realized she had not yet asked him how he knew Zander.

The proposed mine was small, as Nate had promised. At twenty-five thousand tons per annum production, it would not likely trigger a provincial environmental assessment. The proposed pit would be minuscule by mine standards, and the mine was expected to provide forty ongoing jobs and sixty jobs during construction, with the potential for expansion to more deposits in the area in the future.

Alana read the words in the proposal—things like increased potential turbidity in Mur Creek, no threatened species in the area, and no adverse effects from runoff—and realized how little she knew, really, about the local ecosystem and the impacts of mining. She didn't even really know what plants and animals occupied the hills around Silver Peak, aside from the obvious brown bears and white-tailed deer that meandered through the yard on a regular basis. She knew that there was some combination of fir, larch, cedar, and pine in the mountains, but she didn't know the specific species, or what plants comprised the understory or groundcover. And she had no real clue what the impacts of an open pit mine were. She knew they looked like vast yawning moonscapes, and that nothing lived in the area they occupied during the operation of the mine, but she had no idea of the extent of spillover effects into the surrounding ecosystems or the long-term impacts after the mine ceased operation.

She had a degree in environmental studies, so she knew more than the average citizen about the impacts of mining. At least all of the words in the proposal were familiar to her. And yet she still didn't know precisely what they meant. What the long-term cumulative effects of the mine would be. Whether the mine should happen, or not. Perhaps she hadn't spent enough time in the field when she did her degrees. Or perhaps the whole thing was so complex that even the people who purported to know—the wildlife biologists, the geologists, the hydrologists—didn't really know either. They were just better at throwing around the right terms and phrases. Could any of these supposed experts really predict the big picture effects of economic activities on the landscape? And if they couldn't, how could regular people on the street?

She flipped to the *Silver Peak News*. Owen had posted some of Maude and Tom's live-tweeted photos of the mine site and Mur Marsh—the red-striped bird and thrasher photos had predictably made the cut—along with an interview with Maude and some local wildlife biologist guy named Neil Davidoff about the essential biological diversity and ecosystem benefits of the marsh. Davidoff stressed that special places like the marsh were disappearing or under stress all over the province, and that unless they were protected, completely, from development, the landscape, while appearing to still be healthy, would increasingly be comprised of monocultures, invasives, and limited more hardy species.

Blaine was watching TV when she called. She imagined him sitting in his track pants and ubiquitous grey t-shirt in front of his new very large flat screen TV. Maybe the TV had killed their marriage. Whenever he had watched TV, she had always felt like he should be *doing* something, like building a grey water recovery system, turning the compost, or finding an organic way to get rid of the worms that infested their magnificent cherry tree every year. Maybe she had been totally unrealistic in her expectations.

"How did your dinner go?" he said. The question *Are you seeing someone* played around the edges of his words, but he knew better than to ask it. Maybe he didn't want to know.

"Fine," she said. "What do you think about this mine? Should it go ahead or not?"

She heard him snort. "Silver Peak needs the jobs. People are already moving out. The whole region's in a slump. You know college enrollment has been dropping for the last five years. They're laying off instructors. We need the mine."

"Yeah, but aren't all regions going through the same thing? Isn't it just a sign that the party's over and we all need to tighten our belts?"

"Sure, if the belt tightening were evenly distributed and we all took a ten percent pay cut. But that'll never happen. Instead, it just hits the people who lose their jobs, and you get people out of work who can't pay their mortgages, who move, and then local shopkeepers lose customers and it goes on and on."

"Yes, but couldn't we do something more environmentally friendly, like a community energy system or something like that?"

"If it were economically viable someone would have already done it."

"What does Super Environmental Blaine think about the mine?"

"Super Environmental Blaine thinks we should oppose the mine, sell everything, buy adjoining pieces of farmland in the middle of nowhere, and grow potatoes."

"Why don't we do that then?"

"Because Super Environmental Blaine and realistic, lazy Blaine, who likes to golf and water ski, and who has a very cute girlfriend who likes to shop, don't always see eye to eye."

"I see." Alana wondered how much the realistic, lazy Blaines in everyone ruled the world.

"I gotta go," he said. "Heather's home."

"Right. You should probably deduct points for watching TV."

She wrestled with the proposal until midnight, noting the places where she felt it needed more detail and researching the impacts of open pit mines.

A forester she once worked with had told her that everyone stressed too much about the environment in British Columbia. "People who work in the woods," he'd said, "know how vast our land base is. There's masses of forest and land out there that we never touch, that nobody ever sees."

But were they all single-species stands of trees bereft of thrashers and bitterns and loons?

She sent her suggested changes to Nate and went to bed.

Alana arrived at the office the next morning to find a baby grand piano—a Steinway no less—wedged at a precarious angle in the doorway of the building. Two deliverymen were on the outside trying to figure out the right way to slip it inside, while Nate paced about in the office foyer. Apparently, according to the men, the doorway was six inches too narrow or the piano was six inches too long.

"Playing the piano helps me think," Nate said by way of explanation when she looked at him quizzically over the grunts and heaves of the deliverymen, who were tipping the piano to an even higher angle.

"Great," she said. "The back door is blocked by boxes. Is there a window I can climb in?"

"I don't want to leave the piano," he said. "Why don't you go get a coffee on me until the door is clear?"

"Fine. Did you get my comments on the proposal?"

"I haven't had a chance to look at them yet."

She gave him a bulgy-eyed glare intended to convey the urgency of the situation, but since Nate wasn't even looking at her, this succeeded only in drying out her contacts. "We really need to get it out today," she said. "The open house is in a week and we have to meet with Stewart this afternoon."

One of the deliverymen gave the piano a push and the wood edge of the keyboard scraped against the doorframe.

"Stop!" Nate snapped at the deliverymen. "We're going to have to take it apart." His face was darker and grimmer than Alana had ever seen it. He turned back to her. "Don't worry. I'll handle Stewart. I really need to focus on this for a minute." He gestured at the piano.

"Fine. I'll be at the Eternal Bean. Text me when I can actually get into the office."

Alana sat at a table at the Eternal Bean almost fuming. Last night had been great, and now Nate seemed almost cool toward her. Didn't even seem to care that she had stayed up trying to fix the proposal. Maybe he didn't care about the loss of bitterns and thrashers all over the province, never mind the loons.

She was so embroiled in her thoughts that she didn't notice the soft shuffle of Maude's hiking boots until she was at the table with Alana, her grey hair flopping ignominiously over to one side. Alana had to admire Maude. Clearly she did not feel at all subject to the demands of beauty that modern society had imposed on women. Blaine had once described her as a cow with a fuzzy bulldog face, but Blaine had a lot of opinions about how other women looked.

"They're buying them, you know," Maude said.

"Who's buying who?" Alana said.

"Nate and Lou. Meet me tonight at six at this address." Maude slipped a piece of paper across the table as if they were spies and someone across the room could lip-read.

"I don't know if I can, Maude. That's right in the middle of dinner. I have children."

"Just do it," she hissed. "It's important. You need to know who you're working for."

Alana studied the woman's face; she saw only fervor and no signs of guile. She thought of the photo of Zander and Nate, and the emails from Zander in Nate's inbox.

"I'll see if I can get away," Alana said.

She returned to the office to find the front door of the building back in place and the piano sitting inside. The soft light of the foyer shimmered off of the ebony surface and dust particles hung in the air. She approached it slowly, breathing in the scent of wood and felt. She let her fingers touch the smooth surfaces of the keys.

Alana imagined her mother's dark hair falling over her eyes as she leaned over the piano, her fingers wild, a curl of smoke from her cigarette winding up into the air. What had her mother thought of Nate? Somehow they seemed to have the same streak of melancholy in them, the same need for music. Did they sit in her mother's studio sharing the triumph and deep joy of a perfectly executed piece?

Her mother had never met Blaine.

Nate's head was bent over his desk when she passed his office. She knocked softly and poked her head in.

"Did you have a chance to look at my edits?"

"Yup." The skin under his eyes was a blush of purple and his eyes were squinty like he hadn't slept in days. Yet the previous night, he had looked completely relaxed and comfortable. She entertained the horrifying passing thought that her cooking had made him ill.

"And?"

"They looked fine. I asked the consultant to incorporate most of them. But some of the information you suggested the proposal needed, we're not going to be able to get. The consultants have pretty much gathered as much data as they can for the price we paid them. I just deleted those suggestions."

Alana tried not to contort her face too much. She wondered how much the high-priced consulting firm based out of Vancouver had charged to do a marginal job of information collection. "Did you send the proposal to Stewart?"

"Yes."

"Shall we walk over there together in fifteen minutes?"

He cleared his throat. "I was thinking. You don't necessarily need to come to the meeting."

She felt her back tighten and hunch. Why did he not want her there? Did he not think her an asset, or was he hiding something? Or did he know of her secret rendezvous with Maude?

"I think I should be there," she said.

"Okay. That's fine. I just didn't want you to feel you had to go."

"Just let me do the talking, okay?" Nate said as they stood outside City Hall. He had been standoffish on the walk over, and Alana tried to quell the unease that riffled around in her gut.

She nodded. Stewart's rumored rages, unpredictability, and contemptuous attitude scared her anyway. If Alana had thought the information flow from City Hall had been limited before, it had become pretty much a desert of information under Stewart. During their sustainability plan meetings, Zander had sometimes started to mumble things to her about Stewart, but had then apparently thought better of it and shut up.

Samantha, the city administrative assistant, ushered them into the waiting area outside Stewart's office, cooing over Nate and how long it had been since she'd seen him. Alana focused on a hideous landscape painting on the wall. She had to stop thinking about Nate. He was her boss, and clearly he had mood swing issues. Or she had given him food poisoning.

"Stewart will be with you in a few minutes. He's just in a call. Can I get you anything? Coffee? Water?" Samantha practically glowed as she fluttered her eyes coquettishly at Nate.

She and Nate and both shook their heads to decline the coffee or water, although Alana doubted Samantha would have noticed if she had done an interpretive dance at that point.

Alana and Nate sat side by side in the two cushioned office chairs, their thighs almost touching. This was not conducive to not thinking about him.

"They damaged the Steinway," he said gloomily. "The action on some of the lower keys is off, and the damper pedal is broken."

"Oh no." Maybe she hadn't poisoned him.

"Those two were not professional piano movers. I can't believe someone thought they could be trusted with a Steinway."

"It's absolutely beautiful." She could hear the longing in her own voice. "Can it be fixed?"

"Oh, yeah. Of course. It'll just be expensive. It was a gift, from the board. Give it a go. It's still playable, as long as you don't need any of the lower notes or the pedal."

"That's quite the gift. I'm not really that good. Not good enough for that piano."

Nate snorted. "The piano has no expectations. Music is also about the experience for the performer. Don't waste the opportunity if you can actually get some joy out of it. Life is too short not to play like nobody is listening."

Zander walked down the hallway and waved. Alana blinked. Had a secret look just passed between Nate and Zander? Stewart flung open his door, and she jumped.

An enthusiastic shaking of hands followed. Alana had never seen Stewart so excited to see someone. Although Alana had worked for the Regional Environmental Board for several years, Stewart seldom saw reason to involve himself in any environmental initiatives, so she had almost never spoken to him, and he thought her name was Elena.

"So, you're here to talk about your mine?" Stewart said with a broad and kind of frightening smile.

Nate sounded more direct and assertive than Alana had ever heard him. "Yes. As you know, we sent you a copy of the proposal today, and like I said on the phone, there was an error in the original surveying of the mine site. A portion of two of the open pits will be on city property. As we've outlined previously, and as the proposal highlights, we don't expect the mine to impact the watershed in any negative way. There will be little to no runoff into the creek, and the environmental impacts will be mitigated. We wanted to come in and check and see if you have any questions or concerns before we release the proposal to the public."

Stewart swept his arm through the air with a hint of impatience. "I haven't read it yet. Release it to the public if you want. I don't care. We'll be discussing the matter internally."

"Are there are any improvements you would like to see to the proposal or any additional information you would like?" Alana asked, realizing belatedly that she had promised Nate she would stay silent.

Stewart flicked his watery eyes to her as if she had just apparated into the room wearing an Elena nametag. "We prefer to communicate through official channels," he said.

She smiled. "Sorry. We just want to make sure council has all the information it needs."

Stewart stared over the rim of his fancy heavy-framed spectacles at her and then shifted his gaze to Nate. "This is an economically focused council of course, but we can't make any promises. We have to clearly see the benefits for us. There has to be *mutual* benefit," Stewart said. He put an odd emphasis on the word mutual, and his eyes almost seemed to gleam with a sort of madness. She suspected this was the Stewart to whom Zander often referred.

She nevertheless plunged on, disregarding Nate's rather distinct intake of breath. "We'd be happy to do up a summary of the benefits and how even though it's counter to the sustainability plan in some ways, it's actually consistent with a lot of the economic diversification objectives."

Stewart's eyes flicked to her, and then immediately back to Nate. "If you want."

Nate placed a hand on her forearm. "As Stewart said, the city is doing its own internal review, and I'm sure they'll get back to us with questions, if they have them. Thank you for your time here today, Stewart. We'll look forward to hearing more from you."

Stewart and Nate both stood and shook hands. Alana rose slowly, trying to figure out what had just happened.

As Nate and Stewart exchanged pleasantries about golf and the Blue Jays and behaved as though Alana wasn't there, she stood awkwardly, wishing she had something snappy to say about Tiger Woods or some sort of sports figure, but the closest she could come would be making some sort of observation about David Beckham moving back to Europe, and she only knew that because he was married to Posh Spice and therefore featured in the celebrity magazines that she read furtively in the salon. She slipped out of the room.

Wandering down the hall, she spotted Zander lurking around the corner, his face arched toward Stewart's office. He jumped and scurried away to his own office as soon as he saw her. She followed. Loose papers scattered from the surface of his desk when he plunked himself into his chair, and he swore and bent to pick them up.

"How do *you* think council will feel about the proposal?" Alana asked.

He paused for a second, as if he might actually say something, and then donned a contrived smile. "I haven't seen it. I'm no longer asked to comment on those kinds of things around here."

Before she could ask him what he meant by this he turned away toward his computer screen, muttering something about an urgent subdivision proposal. Seeing that he obviously didn't want to talk, Alana headed back to see if Nate and Stewart were done with their manly sports bonding.

They were not. The discussion had now moved on to something about the PGA versus the European Tour. Alana wanted to lean in and inform them that golf destroyed ecosystems and watercourses, and that the money that went to the ridiculously high-paid players should go to saving endangered species instead, but she didn't think they'd appreciate it.

She decided to leave Nate behind and walk back to the office by herself.

She was in her office when Nate returned. She heard him sit at the piano in the foyer, and then the notes of a flowy piece followed. She listened thunderstruck for half an hour while he turned out piece after piece of stunningly beautiful music that rose into the air and filled the warehouse. How had this man failed as a musician? Why had he failed?

After the piano went silent, Alana started to gather up her things to leave for the day. Nate appeared in her doorway looking pale.

"I'm afraid we're going to have to let you go," he said. "Some of our investors didn't come through. We're going to have to cut back until the mine is approved."

She shook her head in shock. Was she being *fired*?

"I really appreciate everything you've done, and it has nothing to do with the quality of your work. You're amazing, and I'd be happy to give you excellent references anywhere else you apply," Nate continued. He extended his hand with a check in it. "I have four weeks' severance here for you. I'll wait while you pack up your stuff."

"Oh," she said. Tears welled up in her eyes, and she blinked furiously at the blinding, salty, embarrassing existence of them. As horrible as telling everyone she was working for a mining company was, telling them she had been let go would be even worse.

"I'm sorry," Nate said, almost in a whisper.

He reached out his hand to do what, she wasn't sure. Shake hers, squeeze it.

She shook her head at him. "It's okay. I don't really want to work here anyway," she said fiercely. Then she brushed past him, her bag already packed for the day, and raced to the turquoise door.

CHAPTER SEVENTEEN

A Lot

Blaine was mulish about having to look after the kids while Alana met with Maude. He had planned to go to the gym, but they had a standing agreement that unless he was doing something essential, he would help her out at least one night a week.

He stood on the other side of the kitchen island still clad in the tight white shirt and aqua shorts that he wore to the gym, as if she might change her mind. He wore the outfit to give the ladies a thrill, he always quipped. With his buff physique, he probably had a whole cadre of adoring fans. All of them were probably over fifty, but fans were fans.

"I'm sorry. It's work related. I have to go," Alana said, keeping her face down so Blaine wouldn't notice the extra eyeliner she had applied to draw attention away from her puffy red eyes.

Blaine creased his face into a full-blown pout. "Why is it so early? Who meets at six?"

"Environmentalists. Environmentalists meet at six, Blaine."

Maude had emailed earlier to suggest that Alana wear camo. After hunting through her closet of black, red, and turquoise, she had decided that dark brown yoga pants were camo enough. She hoped Maude didn't expect her to arrive with mud on her face and willow fronds woven into her hair.

Alana steered the SUV into the entrance of the curving, majestic, but desolate streets of Greenwild Estates—one of the swanky new subdivisions with two-acre lots that some developer billed as the next great thing in natural living, in one of BC's unspoiled playgrounds, before he went belly up in 2008, because who paid $800,000 for a house in the middle of nowhere during an economic downturn? White survey stakes marked the empty properties, and thrashes of wild grass now covered the cleared sites.

She pulled in and parked at the trailhead. Maude had insisted that stealth was of utmost importance and had instructed her to park and take one of the trails that led through the development. As Alana stepped out of the car, she couldn't help but think she should be at home serving Katie and Duncan roasted yams and frozen, handpicked raspberries, not engaging in environmental espionage. But she plunged on into the trees and hurried down the trail, scanning the woods as she went for any sign of the dark shape of a bear.

She almost screamed when Maude stepped out from behind an aspen near the outlet of the trail, wearing an industrial-sized backpack. Alana wondered if she had missed some vital piece of information and in fact she and Maude and were going camping.

Maude motioned Alana over to the tree and pointed to a faint deer path that hugged the road off to the left. It was overgrown with new bushy deciduous shoots and spider webs.

"We'll go that way," she whispered.

"Where are we going?"

"You'll see," she said, heading down the path.

After fifteen minutes of bushwhacking through maple saplings, ducking under pine boughs, and catching stray gossamer strands of web in her hair, Alana was beginning to wonder if Maude was insane. The path here had become more of a drainage trench that ran beside the road; it was filled with black mud, foul-smelling water plants, and leaping fleas. With only two or three houses in the development, and therefore very little traffic, they could probably have just walked down the road; not a single vehicle had passed on the grey stretch visible through the small breaks in the frenzy of green. But Maude shushed Alana every time she said anything.

Eventually, Maude cut deeper into the woods and they began to skirt a manicured emerald green lawn with a winding driveway. They arrived a few minutes later at a grove of birch trees from which they had a direct view of a stunning brick Tudor house with an arched portico and elaborate manicured gardens dotted with brilliant pink, purple, and yellow tulips and a sea of blue hyacinths. An extravagant rose garden, dotted with tender lime-green leaves, framed a winding stone path through the back yard, and a greenhouse the size of Alana's garage sat at the back of the property.

Despite her determination to live simply and not covet material items, like a good environmentalist, Alana's brain immediately started envisioning the rises in her productivity and happiness that would accompany living in this house, including dinner parties on the stone patio—lit softly with lanterns that sat on the side of the house just past two oversized French doors—and the massive garden she could dig into the soft flat grass. Her brain went on to imagine the large country kitchen, butcher block counters, commercial-size sinks, and a double-wide fridge that must surely occupy the back of the house.

Maude clasped Alana's upper arm in a pincher-like grip.

"Isn't it a travesty?" she said.

Alana blinked herself out of her trance. Of course it was a travesty; it was a testament to modern excess and environmental destruction: acres of monoculture green lawn that required massive amounts of water and choked out natural species, building materials shipped from all over the world, rooms full of new off-gassing furniture, carpets fabricated from countless chemicals, rugs hand-woven by child laborers, drawers full of unnecessary kitchen appliances, pounds of marble quarried and shipped across the country, closets bursting with the latest throwaway fashions made in sweatshops, cupboards stocked with processed GMO foods. It *was* a travesty. And yet part of Alana was so conditioned by modern culture that she wanted it. She wanted to slip into a sunken candlelit tub and roll around in white fluffy towels before sliding into her pillow-top bed with six hundred thread count linens. Instead, she had branch scratches all over her arms, rank mud spatter on her legs, and she was standing in a copse of spider web-covered trees while water fleas pelted her ankles.

Alana blamed Martha Stewart. She was the one who had started this whole "living graciously"—which basically meant living materially—movement. *She* was the one who made all these beautiful things seem attainable and desirable for everyone, leading North Americans to double mortgage their houses, extend their lines of credit, and bankrupt themselves all so they could say "It's a good thing" just like Martha.

"A travesty for sure," Alana murmured. "Whose house is this?"

"Lou Steeves," Maude said, baring her teeth in her big and frightening smile, her body shuddering with suppressed laughter.

"Oh," Alana said weakly. She felt there might be some sort of joke that she should be laughing at, but she wasn't sure what it was, aside from the fact that it was funny that she had assumed that Lou was a vegetable gardener, when clearly he was Brian Minter. She found herself wondering if Nate would inherit this house. Then she pictured Fiona swanning her way through the halls, hosting exquisite vegetarian dinner parties for six, while Nate cavorted around with their beautiful blond children, who played the piano for the guests, something jazzy and up tempo.

She was deep in her imaginings of Nate's future life when a red Ford Expedition pulled into the driveway. Out climbed Stewart, looking puffed and pompous, followed by Bernard Shultze, the retired car salesman on council, and Kailee Bell, the realtor on council. A sleek Audi followed the Expedition, and the tall and portly mayor of Silver Peak, Edward Walters, clambered out.

Alana just about sat backward into the mud in shock. What were they doing? Was this even allowed? Kailee even peered around with her heavily made up face and overly plucked brows—which had the effect of always making her look surprised—as if she thought she might be being watched.

Maude positively quivered with glee and snapped photos with her iPhone.

"See?" she said. "See what kind of organization you're working for."

Alana couldn't even work up the nerve to tell Maude that she had been fired.

Lou answered the door in a button-up Hawaiian shirt and chinos. Maude's iPhone captured photo after photo of Stewart, Bernard, Kailee, and Edward going inside.

"What do you think they're doing?" Alana said.

"Isn't it obvious? They're meeting. About the mine."

Did Nate know about this meeting? Was the Vespa somewhere in the garage? Was Nate a big lying cheat? Alana craned her neck to see if Nate was lurking somewhere behind Lou as he uttered the last of his greetings and closed the door.

Alana pulled out her phone. Knowing whether Nate was inside that house suddenly seemed like the most important thing in the world.

< Hey, do you have time to chat? I just had a quick question. Sorry about before. I was just a bit shocked > she texted.

Maude pulled a small tripod-type seat out of her backpack and trod back and forth through the trees checking out camera angles.

< I'm kind of busy right now. Is it urgent? > Nate texted back.

< Yes > she typed, like a mental patient hitting each letter so hard

that she had to retype the three-letter word three times because her iPhone helpfully suggested "he's" and "Urdu" for what she really meant to say.

< *K call me in 15 minutes* > Nate replied.

Maude settled onto her seat and removed a granola bar and some binoculars from her pack. She seemed to have no intention of leaving.

"Now what are we doing?" Alana said. "Are we expecting more of them?" She didn't bother specifying "council members," as she knew Maude knew what she was talking about. "Or are we going to wait until they leave? 'Cause I have to get home. My ex-husband is babysitting and won't be very happy if I'm out late." It was a complete lie, but she didn't want Maude to know she was calling Nate.

Maude eyed her up and down. "I don't know if we're expecting anyone else. But I really think we should see how long they stay. Don't you understand what's happening here? Are you going to be an apologist for that too?"

"Of course I understand what's happening here. And I'm not going to be an apologist for it in the slightest." Light tones of jazz floated out Lou's living room window. "I just have family responsibilities."

"Right, so watching your local politicians and civil servants potentially selling out to corporate interests, for the company you're working for, isn't important?"

"No, of course it's important. It's just that it's going to be dark soon and I still have to hike back to my vehicle, and I really don't like to piss my ex-husband off too much."

Maude stared at Alana squarely through her dated, clear-framed glasses, her rough hands placed on thighs that strained the edges of her forest green pants. Alana let her eyes drift to the fringe of hairs that lined Maude's upper lip and then to her man-cut hair. Maude had probably never given a crap about any man being pissed off at her. Probably had never given a crap about any woman being pissed off at her, either. And she had done important things. Alana, on the other hand, with her stylish brown wood nymph getup and salon styled hair, designed to look au natural, was worrying about her ex-boss being irritated with her for disturbing his evening, when his dad was clearly trying to buy the votes of council—potentially with Nate's knowledge and assistance—and worrying about her ex-husband being snarky with her for having to put his own children to bed.

Maude had no interest in the flimsy film of excuses Alana always danced in.

"If you take that attitude, your work will never really matter. But I guess that's for you to decide. If your ex-husband can't put the kids to bed occasionally while you're doing important work for the environment, work that is essential for your children's future, I'm not sure what he's good for. And if you're not willing to take a stand against him and explain how important it is, then I'm not sure what *you're* good for. I have two headlamps. You're welcome to borrow one when you make your way back to your vehicle."

Alana wanted to laugh, but it caught in her throat as more of a whimper. She had talked the environment up to Blaine since the day they met. Blaine didn't give a shit about the environment. Well, more accurately, he didn't give *enough* of a shit about the environment if there was inconvenience involved. He had probably left her *because* of the environment. But this conversation wasn't about Blaine really. It was about Nate.

"I have to go call my husband. I'll see how things are going."

Maude gave Alana a dubious look as she walked several meters down the path and dialed Nate's number.

"Hi, Alana," he said.

"Hey," she replied, like they talked on the phone all the time.

"You said you wanted to ask something."

Crap. She hadn't even thought about what she wanted to ask. Nate's voice seemed flat, affectless. "Um, I just wanted to ask a bit about the board members. How well do you know them?"

"Why?"

"I just wanted to make sure they're always on the up and up." Nate didn't say anything, and after a few seconds, Alana rushed on. "Sorry. I didn't mean to suggest anything. I just heard something in town and I wanted to check in."

"Let's talk in person. Can you get away? Do you have the kids?"

"Blaine has the kids right now," she said.

"Okay, come to my condo in fifteen minutes. I live at the mountain—the Cedar Estates, Unit 1352. Park down the street and come to the sliding glass door at the back." He hung up.

Although she should perhaps have been creeped out about being told to go to a man's condo, and to go to the back no less, Alana was shaky with a strange relief. If Nate wanted to meet in fifteen minutes, he couldn't be helping his dad host a dinner party for unscrupulous council members. And she wanted to go to his condo. She wanted to see Nate.

She walked slowly back to Maude, who had trained her binoculars on Lou's living room window.

"I have to go," she said. "I called Nate to find out if he's there, and now he wants to meet and talk."

"You told him where we are?"

"Of course not. I just called him to ask a question, hoping he'd give away his location. He can't be inside. He wants to meet me in fifteen minutes at his place."

"He could still be in there," Maude said.

"Well if he is, you'll see him leave."

"Why does he want to meet you?"

"I don't know." Lights flicked on in the windows of Lou's house, bathing the cream-walled living room in a golden glow. Figures moved around inside holding large tumblers of wine. A man walked around serving appetizers. Lou had a servant? Kailee had a scarf tossed around her neck and appeared to be admiring some art on the wall while she gave her hair surreptitious fluffs. Alana would give anything for a glass of wine right now... and a canapé. Great. Apparently she would throw her environmental ideals over the side of the Rainbow Warrior for prosciutto-wrapped cantaloupe.

"What? Is he going to confess that his father is an unscrupulous lowlife?"

"I don't know."

Maude studied Alana with slitty eyes. But she nodded. "He could be the weak link. See what information you can get out of him. But give me his address. If you don't call me in half an hour, I'm sending someone to check on you."

Alana typed the address into Maude's phone and tried not to imagine Tom LeDrew bursting in on her and Nate.

"Okay. I'm going to head off then. Are you okay here by yourself?"

Maude rolled her eyes and returned to her binoculars. Alana made her way carefully back through the sea of maple twigs and reformed spider webs. By the time she reached the proper trail, she decided it was too dark to proceed into the woods and started to jog around the now darkening loop that formed Greenwild Estates.

She was scurrying along the deserted road when a set of oncoming headlights appeared in front of her. She leapt into the bushes, treating herself to another dusting of webs and spiders, and peered out at the passing vehicle. It was an old taupe Camry, and Zander was unmistakably at the wheel. Zander. On his way to Lou's. Shit Rat Bastard. What a bunch of lying connivers. Even Zander was in on it. What the hell did they think they were doing? Did they operate this way for *all* decisions?

She sprinted the rest of the way around the loop to the trailhead, climbed in the SUV, and headed back down the highway. A few blocks away from Nate's she stopped and checked her appearance. Leaves and bracken stuck in her hair and her pants were spattered with mud. She extracted the leaves from her hair and applied some lip balm.

Nate pulled open his sliding glass door nursing a Switchback beer, and for a brief second he looked at her intently, almost hungrily, before his eyes resumed their usual guardedness.

"So," she said.

"So," he said with a faint smile. He looked like he was going to say more, but then he didn't. He didn't back up when she entered, and now they were standing a bit too close to each other—far too close in fact. If she tipped her head up and leaned in a bit, their lips would touch. "Can I get you a beer?" he said finally.

"Sure."

He turned and headed into the kitchen, and she followed. "Sorry for bugging you at this time of night. I just wanted to ask you some questions." She wanted to tell him the whole thing: spying on his dad, the arrival of Stewart, Kailee, Bernard, and Edward, and then Zander. But she didn't know the best way to get him to talk, if he knew anything. She was also conscious of the clock ticking. Of Maude potentially assembling an environmental SWAT team to extract her with drums and patchouli bombs.

Nate's condo was upscale mountain style, with leather couches and a palette of browns and greens on the walls and floor. A saxophone and guitar sat in stands next to a small upright piano.

"Nice place," she said.

"It's a buddy's. I'm just renting." Nate handed her an open Switchback, their fingers grazing. "What do you want to talk about?"

"Would you describe yourself as an environmentally conscious person?"

Nate laughed, and she got a glimmer of that look again: that heavy-lidded, half-interested look. "Okay, no small talk or jokes about jazz for you. Why don't we sit down then?" He gestured at the couch and continued talking as they settled onto the comfortable black leather. "Um, yes in the sense that I'm aware of a lot of the problems that we're facing on the environmental front. But I'm sure I wouldn't even be on the map in terms of actually undertaking environmental actions."

"And do you care about that?"

"Well, of course, in a small part of my brain. But I also care a lot about other things, like playing my music and hanging out with my friends."

"So you rationalize it?"

"I guess you could say that. What about you?"

"Well, I grow food, and try not to drive, and try not to be a vapid consumer, but I know I'm still not doing half the stuff I should. Realistically, if I really believed half the things I read, I should be planning to hole up somewhere on a small off-grid homestead and raise chickens and stockpile ammo."

Nate laughed. "Do you think?" The usual irony was present in his voice, but his expression was gentler somehow.

"Yes, I think. But like you, I like having friends and all the other trappings of modern society. Like flush toilets, and hotels, and restaurants and pillow-top beds."

"You could probably take your bed with you."

Somehow Nate could make just saying the word "bed" sexy. Alana tried to focus. She only had ten more minutes before Maude roused the special environmental ops. "Maybe, but my ex-husband wants to live in LA, and I want the kids to be close to both of us. I doubt there are any cabins in the woods in California."

Nate took a swig of his beer. "No. Probably not." But he was smiling, and his eyes were engaged. She had caught his interest, even if just a little bit. She had already guzzled half of her own beer and was beginning to feel rather giddy and friendly, a very dangerous state of being at that juncture. Her knees were almost touching Nate's on the couch.

Nate cleared his throat. "So, you said you wanted to talk about the board members. Is this about being laid off? I'm really sorry, Alana. It was my decision though, not the board's. Like I said, the funds just aren't there. We'll have to stumble through without you, and no doubt I'll completely bollix up the open house and Len and Curtis will stage a revolt as soon as I tell them." He had inched fractionally closer to her as if he intended to run his hand up her thigh and lean in and brush her lips with his.

"I'm sure you won't, and Len and Curtis will be fine," she said, trying to stay focused despite his proximity. "And no, that's not what I'm here about at all. How well do you know Mountain Magnesium's board members? Do you have any reason to believe any of them would do anything unethical?"

Nate sat back a bit and his expression sharpened. "I don't know. Can you tell me what's going on? I can't really comment if you don't."

"Would any of them be inclined to entertain city councilors and staff members in the hopes of influencing them?"

Nate's Adam's apple bobbed as he swallowed. "If you saw something, I think you'd better tell me. Perhaps the councilors and staff members approached the board member and suggested they talk. Perhaps the particular board member is just thinking that he or she is being transparent and supporting open communication in agreeing to talk to these people."

"Perhaps. Either way, photos are probably going to be all over the *Silver Peak News* tomorrow morning."

"Okay, Alana, I *really* need you to tell me what's going on."

"Nate, I'm sorry. It's your dad. He has Stewart, Bernard, Kailee, Edward, and Zander over at his house for dinner this very minute, and Maude is out in his yard. Well, not in his yard, she's outside his yard in the trees, taking pictures. I know it doesn't necessarily mean he's doing something wrong, but it doesn't look great."

Nate tipped the bottle of beer into his mouth, swallowed the rest of the contents, and then set the bottle on the coffee table. Then he rose, his lips pulled into a thin, tight line.

"I need to go," he said.

She leapt up too, and wordlessly he escorted her to the sliding glass door, his jaw tight. Any sense of closeness she had felt before had evaporated. She turned and looked back at him as she stepped over the threshold. He leaned against the frame of the door almost haggard, his evening stubble carving shadows into the contours of his cheeks.

"I really like you, Alana. A lot. But stay out of this," he said. "Please." Then he closed the door, picked up his helmet, and walked out the front door, leaving her standing on the patio alone.

He really liked her. A lot. But he was pushing her away.

She called Maude and indicated that Nate hadn't seemed to have known about the meeting at his dad's house, and that he might be on his way.

Maude grunted in response, as if she didn't believe Alana and as if the intel Alana had been able to collect was entirely unsatisfactory.

"I'm heading home, Maude. Keep me posted. Please." Darkness had descended in earnest, and there was no way she was making her way back along the path to Lou's.

Blaine barely looked up from *Mad Men* when she clumped into the house.

While Blaine put his shoes on, she checked for an email or text from Nate or Maude, but there was nothing. She felt like she did in university when there was a major bender going on that she wasn't invited to. Maude hadn't even uploaded her photos in the live Twitter feed on the Stewardship Society website.

"This sure is a nice house," Blaine said. "I kind of miss having all the space."

"It is nice," she said, looking up. What was he getting at?

"I was thinking that since the amount of space one occupies counts toward one's environmental footprint, I should get bonus points for living in a two-bedroom condo, while you live here."

She squinted her eyes and tried not to scowl too much. Lines had started to appear on her forehead from scowling too much, and Botox was definitely not on the pro-environmental action list. "It's not just space, Blaine. First of all, there are three of us here, and it also depends on how intensively you're using the land. Since I own two acres of what is essentially green space that serves as habitat for other species, and the farmhouse hasn't been updated for like ninety years, maybe *I* should be the one who gets the bonus points."

"Hmm. I think we should bring in an arbiter."

"Who would you suggest?"

"I suppose Heather is out of the question?"

"Heather is very definitely out of the question. What about Tabitha?"

Blaine scrunched up his face. "The environmental dementor squared?"

"Suzanne?"

"Too compromised in your favor. How about Rick?"

"No way." She gave Blaine her best smile. "Listen, we can decide this later. There's something going on for my job in the Greenwild subdivision. Some of the councilors are meeting. Would you mind just driving through there on your way home and seeing if their cars are still there?"

Blaine looked as if she had just proposed he backpack across Canada in the winter with burlap sacks tied to his feet in place of boots, when all she'd asked was that he go five minutes out of his way. "Right now?"

"Yes, right now. It's only eight. Please. It's really important."

"Right, and what's in it for me?"

"The satisfaction of knowing that you've totally helped me out."

It was evident that helping her out was not high on his list of satisfactory activities. Either that, or he considered everything he did to be helping her out and couldn't tolerate the addition of one more thing to his terrible burden.

Finally he nodded, wearing an anguished but resigned expression as if he had just been required to clean the toilets with his tongue again. "What exactly am I looking for?"

Her relief and gratitude that he was going was replaced by annoyance that Blaine was making such a big deal out of a little request.

"Forget it. Don't go."

If the original request pained Blaine, the reversal of the request seemed worse. "Do you want me to go or not?"

"Yes, I want you to go. But I want you to go with a good attitude."

Blaine mimed banging his head against a wall. "You want me to go out on some wild goose chase in the middle of the night with a good attitude?"

"Yes, and it's not a wild goose chase. It's important for my work. And it's not the middle of the night."

Blaine squinted one eye and pretended it was twitching—it was his Igor impression, which he pulled out when she was being particularly difficult—and then contorted his face into a beatific smile. "What exactly am I looking for?" He framed his voice in a cooperative tone, but there was an undercurrent of complete exasperation.

"Go to Greenwild Estates. There are only three houses there. Look for the first one on the right-hand side of the road if you took the loop counter-clockwise. It has a portico. If you don't mind parking at the entrance and walking partway in, that would be great. See if there's a red Ford Expedition, a grey Audi, a taupe Camry, or a blue Vespa in the driveway. See if there are any people milling about outside the house. Anywhere."

"Are you going to tell me what exactly is going on?"

"I'd rather not."

"Great, so I'm just the clueless lackey, as usual."

"Don't say that. Just go. I'll explain later. Call me when you get home. Please."

Blaine's eyes narrowed and he huffed through his nose. "Fine." He left the house, and she heard the Miata fire up and peel out of the driveway.

She spent the next twenty minutes pacing and checking her phone. When thirty minutes had elapsed, she texted Blaine. < *Where are you? Who was at the house?* >

His reply came promptly. < *Having a beer with Zander.* >

< *What???* > She didn't even know he knew Zander, although she supposed they must have met on the golf course at some point. < *Where did you meet Zander? Was he at the house?* >

< *I'll explain later.* >

The next messages she sent him, which included a lot of exclamation marks, question marks, and the letters W, T, and F, were marked undeliverable. The bastard had turned off his phone.

She sat there in the dark of the office simmering in cold fury. What was Blaine doing with Zander, who was, at this point in time, practically the enemy? Of course, maybe Blaine was the enemy too.

She checked the *Silver Peak News* expecting to see Maude's photos, but the site instead featured photos of the rolling green fields of a farm with the headline, "Goat Farm Could Be Destroyed By Mine." The story indicated that the farm, just a few kilometers from the marsh and reliant on water from a tributary of Mur Creek, could be decimated by the mine and the runoff from the access road. Two other smaller farms could also be affected. The story went on to talk about the difficulties of farming life, the verdant valley that the farms occupied, and the impacts of corporate greed. She didn't have to scroll far through the comments to see that it contained blistering epistles from the usual suspects: Maude, Fiona, and the rest of the environmental army. How was it that so many of them had so much time on their hands to comment?

Alana swore. Why hadn't she caught this? Why hadn't it been in the environmental impact statement of the proposal? Any decent consultant would have taken a look at a map of the adjacent properties. How many other things had they missed?

And why hadn't Maude posted the photos from Lou's? What was she waiting for?

She texted Nate. < *Just wondering how it went.* > Then she watched her phone like a crazed lunatic while she got ready for bed.

She was reading distractedly when her phone vibrated. It was Nate. < *It was just a meeting for the Art Telethon for the Children's Hospital, which my dad chairs.* >

He was lying, she was sure of it. < *And did you believe them?* > she typed, adding a little happy face on the end to make it seem like a jokey ask.

The dot dot dot of his answer hung in the air for too long, suggesting that he was typing, and then erasing, and then typing again. Finally words popped up on the screen. < *Yes I do. There's nothing going on.* >

The text felt like a gut punch, and tears sprang to her eyes. < *Great. Thanks for checking that out then. See you around.* > She wished she could somehow inject more ice into her text. Maybe there *was* nothing going on.

But before she could stop herself, she texted, < *And thanks so much for telling me about the farms that the mine will destroy.* >

She shut off her phone, turned off her light, and tried not to cry herself to sleep.

CHAPTER EIGHTEEN

The Majority

She checked the *Silver Peak News* as soon as she got up to see if any incriminating photos of Lou's dinner party had been posted. But other than the article about the farms, the photo of the art being created for the Art Telethon for the Children's Hospital still occupied the front page.

She called Blaine. "So, what happened? There was nobody there? You went to the bar and found Zander? You stalked Zander? I didn't even know you knew Zander. Why didn't you get back to me?"

"Is it my turn to talk yet?" Blaine asked. "I went by the house like you told me. There were no vehicles outside, and all the downstairs lights were off. So I continued around the loop and came across Zander talking to that fat, crazy environmental zealot beside a taupe Camry. What's her name? Martha? I sped up, but of course they saw me. Zander waved me over. I rolled down my window to make some joke about meeting in strange places. Anyway, Zander asked if he could grab a ride home. I said sure. He hopped in and Martha sped off in the Camry. Then on the way back into town, Zander asked if I want to have a quick beer at The Cellar."

"Her name's Maude, Blaine, and she's not fat. She's just stocky." Alana dished out two bowls of cereal for the kids, who were now knocking around the kitchen.

"Maude, Martha, whatever. She's a winger that one, and a ball buster. She had little Zander tied up in knots."

Alana let this go. Blaine had never been super receptive to her coaching regarding using appropriate language to talk about women. "So, I don't understand, you know Zander?"

"A bit, from golf. He had a business idea he wanted to talk about. He wanted some marketing advice and he's looking for partners."

"Zander's quitting his job?"

"He didn't say. I think he's just looking at doing this on the side.

Don't say anything to anyone."

"And what is his business idea?"

"It's a secret." Blaine was almost purring with glee.

"A secret? You're not going to tell me?"

"Not until Zander and I finalize our business plan."

"Right, okay." It was too early in the morning to address one of Blaine's get-rich schemes. "Just so you know, Zander might be a liar and a cheat. I wouldn't do business with him." There was silence on the other end of the phone, as if she had started speaking in tongues. "He shouldn't have even been there last night," she continued.

And why was Zander talking to Maude? She had almost started calling her Martha; Blaine's names for people were infuriatingly catching. And when had they become chummy enough to exchange vehicles?

"Anyway, whatever. Do business with Zander if you want." Blaine and Zander's business idea would probably come to nothing anyway. "So I was thinking, I'm going to buy some property in the country."

A strangled noise emerged from the phone. "You already own property in the country. You've got two whole acres of country out there and you can't get much more backwoods than Silver Peak. Where do you want to move? Silverton? Midway? Lytton? How much further into the hinterland do you want to go? Pretty soon you're gonna have to start wearing a tank top and driving a monster truck with a gun rack. Christ, we already get buzzed daily by ATVs and live among the People of Walmart."

"Very funny. I don't want to *move* there. I just want to have a place to go. Silver Peak is still too populated if there was a big economic crash. We'd have raiders on our doorstep within seconds."

"Well, maybe so, but if I have to live in Sperry or Dryden Ridge, I'd be welcoming the raiders with open arms."

"You're really funny, you know. You should have been an actor."

"I keep telling you we need to move to LA."

"Never," she said.

"Just you wait. Zander and I have just the thing to push me over the top in our environmental responsibility contest."

Blaine hung up, singing *California Gurls* by Katie Perry.

The phone rang. She didn't recognize the number, and she snatched it up thinking it might be Nate.

"Alana, it's Dad." As usual, her dad was shouting into the phone. Apparently any time he used a cell phone he thought he was calling from Alabama on a tin can. "I'm just here having coffee with Lou Steeves at the Eternal Bean. Can you come down and join us? He wants to talk to you."

What the hell would Lou want to talk to her about? "Dad, I can't. I have to get Duncan to soccer." She looked at the clock. It was 8:15. Duncan had a game at 9:00 and she still had to shower and run the kids through their entire morning routine.

"Don't worry. We'll wait for you. He has something he wants to tell you. Just be here in half an hour."

Blaine was not understanding regarding her need to have him take Duncan to soccer.

"Sorry," she said. "It's work related." This was a lie, of course. She was technically unemployed, and what the hell could Lou be planning to tell her? She highly doubted he'd be offering a full confession.

"It's Saturday," he said. "How can you have work on Saturday? And why do we have another soccer game? I was hoping to get in a quick round of golf before it gets hot."

"Because. Your son—Duncan, you know, the one you love?— wants to play rep soccer. He eats, dreams, and sleeps soccer. That's why. And Blaine, just a point of clarification, no round of golf is 'quick.'"

"Well, some are quicker than others."

"Just get him to the game. I'll be there in half an hour and then you can go golfing."

"Maybe I could just drop them off. There'll be lots of parents around. Then you could go and pick them up."

"So you're saying you already booked your tee time?"

"Well, sort of. Zander and I were going to meet to discuss our idea."

"You can't just drop them off, Blaine. Katie is only five. Maybe you could postpone your tee time."

"I'm sure you'll be back in time."

"Don't count on it. You might want to give Zander the heads-up."

"Just text me if you don't think you'll make it back in time."

"Fine, whatever. Make sure you pack a lunch."

She drove the Miata down to the Bean while Blaine took the SUV to the soccer field. He had taken the top off and the wind whipped through her wet hair. It would be an uncontrolled pile of frizz by the time she got to the soccer field. Then she'd have to sit through two back-to-back soccer games with all the other moms and dads, looking like hell.

Her dad and Lou were at the back of the Bean, their grey heads bent together. They both looked up as she arrived at the table. Her dad skidded a chair out and motioned for her to sit. "Alana, do you know Lou?"

"Yes, we've met. Hi," she said to Lou, trying not to sound too frosty.

"Lou wants to talk to you about some things," her dad continued. "I have to go. I have a date at ten." Her dad fancied himself as a bit of a ladies' man. On several occasions she had glimpsed him, from a distance, with various female companions, entering and leaving restaurants. But she never got to meet any of them. She wondered whether that was because her dad thought he should still be mourning her mother, or because they were all younger than Alana.

Her dad bustled out, and Alana found herself staring uncomfortably at Lou. She wondered if she was about to get a lecture about her involvement in Maude's surveillance last night, or worse, she was about to be threatened in some way. She glanced around the Bean to see if there were any enforcement-type guys lingering at tables, but it was just the usual old guys, parents, and toddlers.

"Your dad speaks very highly of you," Lou said.

Alana furrowed her brow. Where was this going?

Lou shifted his focus from her to his coffee cup, which he rolled around in his hands while he talked, his white hair a wispy cloud around his shoulders. "I wanted to talk to you about Nate. He respects you, and I need your help. Nate is... well, Nate is, you know, a musician, and an amazing one at that. And I know he's passionate about his music. But it's just not seeming like a career that he can support himself or a family with. He had some difficult times in Vancouver recently, a bad breakup, some drug use, nothing as bad as what the tabloids said, but enough for me to be worried about him. Mountain Magnesium was intended for him to get a fresh start. He's very smart and very capable. I was just hoping that once he experienced another job, one with fewer highs and lows, he'd be happier. Do you understand?"

Lou glanced back up at her. There was an acuity to his gaze that she had never seen before. He might play the befuddled old man in the schoolyard, but Lou Steeves was clearly a player, and she didn't have the remotest clue whether he was genuinely concerned about Nate or was just manipulating her in some way.

Her cheeks felt brittle from forcing an attentive smile. "Sort of."

"Now Nate is suggesting he might quit and go back to Vancouver. I need you to convince him to stay. I just want him to give this a chance. If he doesn't like it in the end, fine. But I want him to give it a chance."

Lou's words cut through her like a chill wind, and she had to grasp the edge of the table to steady herself. Nate was moving back to Vancouver.

"I don't know, Lou. It's not really any of my business. I don't think I have much influence over Nate."

"You work with him, and he likes you, I can tell."

Alana looked at him sharply. Had Nate not told his dad he had let her go? But wouldn't Lou have known about the investors not coming through? Unless Nate had lied about that. "Isn't it important for Nate to do what he wants?"

Lou flicked his wrist impatiently. "Nate's a dreamer and an idealist. Please. He was in terrible shape after his last stint in Vancouver. I don't want him to go through that again."

Alana sighed. "I'll talk to him. But only to better understand his reasons for wanting to leave and to make sure he's thought it through. I'm not going to push him to stay."

"All right, well thanks, and keep working your hardest. This town needs this mine."

"Maybe," she said. "There are lots of people in town who *don't* think we need a mine and are concerned about the environmental impacts."

Lou's fuzzy eyebrows rose, and a hint of wariness scudded across his tanned face. "I'd be careful with that statement. Most of the people I talk to are quite clear that we need the mine. Water and wetlands are sacred cows. But the one thing we have a lot of around here is water. What we don't have a lot of is jobs."

"Well, you're having the open house and doing a survey so the people of Silver Peak can make their opinions known. You should have a sense after that how people feel."

Lou shrugged and rolled his coffee mug around again. "It's only squeaky wheels and rabble-rousers that come to open houses and fill out surveys as far as I can tell. I'm not saying it doesn't have to be done, but I don't think that gives you a true sense of how the silent majority feel."

Of course: the silent majority. They could always be trotted out and said to support whatever the speaker wanted them to support, because they were so damn silent.

"Well, you should strongly encourage the people you talk to to go to the open house if they want their views heard. It's really important to have a real community discussion regarding the mine. You should also know that Nate let me go yesterday. I don't work for Mountain Magnesium anymore."

Lou jerked his head up from his coffee mug. "What? That's ridiculous. You were doing great work. What are you talking about?"

"Nate said some investments didn't come through or something."

Lou shook his head. "I'll talk to him. There must be a mistake. We need your expertise. Just come in on Monday as usual. Convince Nate to stay, and we'll give you a five grand signing bonus."

She blinked at Lou and rose from the table. He couldn't possibly be serious. Why would anyone pay her that much? "I don't know. I'm not sure if I'm interested. I'm not very happy about the fact that the farms weren't mentioned in the proposal."

"Farms?"

"The goat farm, and the other two farms, that are going to potentially lose their water sources."

Lou lofted his eyebrows. "We bought those farms. Gave the owners a good price. The land was marginal anyway. Andrew Webber couldn't wait to sell."

Alana's lips went a bit tingly, and she was sure the blood was draining from her face. "But there was the article in the *Silver Peak News*."

Lou's smile was mild. "You should know as well as I do that the media rarely gets the story right the first time."

Alana closed her eyes. She *did* know this. "Well, thanks for telling me. Can I think about the job? I have to go. I have to get to my son's soccer game."

Lou nodded. "Just come in on Monday if you want the job."

As she left, Lou continued to turn his coffee cup over in his hands, staring at the now empty insides.

Blaine wore a sour expression on the edge of the soccer field. She immediately saw why. Duncan was playing in his Halloween costume from last year, a padded Iron Man suit with a plastic mask. His soccer shin pads were pulled up roughly over the legs. Katie stood next to Blaine in a sparkly Tinker Bell dress and a tiara.

"What are you thinking?" she hissed at Blaine. "He can't wear that."

Blaine flipped his hands up in annoyance. His hair stood in wild spikes, and there were ketchup stains on his white golf shirt. "He insisted."

"Blaine, you don't let a seven-year-old insist."

"I have a tee time." Blaine waved his arms at her and stalked off.

Alana managed to convince Duncan to remove the mask at halftime—to the amused looks of some of the moms and the slightly annoyed expressions of some of the more competitive dads. She tried not to think about Lou and Nate. She should probably just move to Galiano Island and raise goats. She imagined herself walking about in verdant green fields surrounded by her flock.

"Mommy, did you put them in their place?" Duncan said.

"Huh? What?"

"That's what Daddy said you were doing. Going to put some men in their place. He said you were a dog."

"What?"

"A bulldog," Katie corrected.

Alana sighed. "Daddy mistakenly thinks I'm bossy with other people because I'm bossy with him. But I'm really not." She *should* be more bossy with other people. Then maybe she'd have a career that wasn't so messed up.

For most of the kids on Duncan's team, Saturday games were a family affair. The moms had already set up camp with blankets, lunch baskets, and umbrellas. The dads milled about, pointing at the field and miming soccer moves to their cleat-clad kids. Alana had a son in a stuffy Iron Man suit, a no-doubt sunscreenless daughter in a sleeveless Tinker Bell ensemble, no food, and no husband.

When Duncan charged back out onto the field, Alana picked a spot on the outskirts of the blankets next to Gillian and placed her hoodie on the ground to sit on. Cynthia gave her a wave and a smile, and Gillian nodded. Katie skipped off, the light glimmering off her dress, to join some of her friends who were at the game with their older brothers.

"Oh, hey, Alana."

Alana turned in the direction of the voice and saw Katrina, an older woman who Alana used to run with. Katrina stopped and wiped the sweat from her brow. "Wow. That was a good one. My knees are killing me." Alana saw the rest of the triathlon team lingering about with water bottles near the parking lot in their tight little suits with their skinny, sinewy limbs, no doubt discussing how to shave that extra three minutes off their marathon time. "Long time no see. What's new with you?" Katrina said.

"Not much. How are you?" Alana rose to her feet.

"Oh you know, the usual. Training for an Ironman."

Alana glanced wistfully at Katrina's glowing skin and muscled body.

"So, I've been meaning to talk to you because you know about environmental things," Katrina announced.

Alana nodded, wondering what whacked-out question Katrina was going to ask. Her knowledge of "environmental things" often led people to believe that she understood how fog formed, the geological and natural history of the area, and minute details about every species that ever existed.

"I wanted to ask you about the mine. There's going to be this protest. A bunch of us are going to do a sit-in at the Mountain Magnesium offices. I was just wondering if you thought that was a good idea."

Alana stared at her, dumbfounded. Did Katrina know she worked for Mountain Magnesium? Or rather, she used to.

"Well, if you oppose the mine, then sure, why not participate?"

"Oh, I don't really know that much about the mine. But my friend Layla is organizing the protest, and she knows about those kinds of things. If Layla is opposed, then I know it has to be bad. Are you going?"

Alana wondered how many people took this approach to determining their views on public issues. "Um, probably not. I guess the only thing about the protest is that they're generally only effective if you have a large enough turnout. If you don't expect a large turnout, you'd be better off preparing a brief for the open house explaining why you're opposed to the mine and then sending it to the press after the event, or even before."

"Oh, well that sounds like a lot of work. I think my ride's leaving. I'll have to think about it. It sounds like there's going to be a really big turnout at the protest. People are *not* happy." Katrina barked a laugh to emphasize her point. "See you around." Katrina gave a chipper wave and bounced off toward the parking lot.

Alana sank back to the grass, her hands cold in the spring sun. Gillian's husband, Mike, sat on the adjacent blanket.

"Do you really think the open house is going to make any difference?" he said.

"What?" she said.

"These open houses are just window dressing to make us think they're listening. That's how these companies do things. The city'll approve it anyway."

Alana shook her head. "No, I think Mountain Magnesium really wants to hear what the residents of Silver Peak have to say..." she started. But then she stopped. Maybe it had just been *her* who had really wanted to hear what people had to say. Maybe the Mountain Magnesium board didn't care at all. "Besides, it isn't the city that decides whether this mine goes ahead—the province does."

"Oh, well, the province approves everything that could have economic benefits. Look at all their pipeline and natural gas projects. I've seen these kinds of things before. We go in, we tell them what we think, they say thanks very much, and then they ignore it all."

"Well, I would *like* to think that's not how it's going to happen. But you may be right." Alana turned her attention to the field, where the seven-year-olds ran around like a pack of crazed hyenas chasing the ball.

Was Mike right? Maybe nothing they did in their little town so far from the center of British Columbia politics mattered. And now there was a big protest planned too. But it wasn't her problem anymore. She wasn't going to take her job back. She would call Tabitha tonight, and they would have a great time reconnecting and talking about her brief stint on the dark side, and maybe a bit about Nate, but only to reflect on how unfortunate it was that he wasn't an environmentalist.

CHAPTER NINETEEN

Disagreements

She tended her seedlings on Sunday in the lazy warmth of the spring afternoon. She kept them under a blanket for the first four weeks, but she liked to expose them to the sun for a few hours a day when the weather was appropriate. The kids roved the property collecting bugs and leaves for the ant emporium they were apparently building. It was one of those blue sky days that made it impossible not to love being alive. The delicate new leaves on the alder trees lit up the back of the yard in a frenzy of delicate green, and the cherry trees extended their snowy limbs to the sky, sending waves of sweet fragrance rippling on the breeze.

Now that she had been dismissed from Mountain Magnesium, she was officially jobless for a few months until the subcontract on her Regional Environmental Board ran out—presuming the board even wanted her back after the glory of Greg Wilson—so she would need to try to pick up some small contracts in the interim. Tabitha had promised she could find her a few small projects. Municipal taxes were high in Silver Peak, and on a two-acre property, they consumed a significant percentage of Alana's income. All morning, the familiar feeling of fear had started to sink its teeth into her gut, and now, even as she tipped her face to the sunlit sky and reveled in the beauty of her farm, it felt like fear had her stomach in a chokehold and was shaking it and tossing it into the air like a terrier with a rat.

Her line of credit inched up every year, and she had no savings. She had counted on the Mountain Magnesium job to cover her property taxes, which were due in a few weeks. On the upside, given that she was jobless, she might now have the opportunity to win her and Blaine's environmental challenge and be at home when the eggs hatched. On the downside, losing her property and the potential for chickens and gardens kind of rendered the bet meaningless anyway.

While the terrier in her gut launched into the final ecstasy of execution with a frenzy of shaking, an equally aggressive thought started to cycle through her mind. The signing bonus that Lou had offered her to return to work at Mountain Magnesium and convince Nate to stay would almost cover her municipal taxes. But Lou couldn't possibly be serious, and it would be unethical, and besides, she didn't want to work at Mountain Magnesium now with the question of what the councilors were doing at Lou's house. But Maude hadn't posted anything yet. Why would she wait, unless she had discovered it was actually a meeting about the telethon?

Alana had just started to mow the lawn with her manual lawn mower when Rick assumed his usual spot on the other side of the fence.

"Goats," he called out.

"Goats?"

"You need goats. They eat the grass, and then you don't have to mow, and you can get milk and cheese."

"I thought you didn't believe in agriculture," she said.

Rick shrugged. "I don't. I just watched a documentary, and what you're doing looks painful."

"Hmm. Well, it'll take me a while to work up to goats. I think I need a man first, Rick," she said, hoping he wouldn't take this as an invitation. "Full-on farming is pretty hard to do alone."

"You're probably right. Well, if you're looking for a man around here, just a word of advice, you might want to tone down the environmental talk a bit. I mean, you're a good-looking lady and all, but..."

Tone down the environmental talk. Story of her life. "Thanks, Rick. I'll keep that in mind."

"Or you could just do your yard work in a bikini. I'm sure you'd get a date that way. Anyway, I just wanted to let you know that I'm planning to subdivide in the next year. Going to keep my house of course and a bit of land, but Ryan Roberts has indicated an interest in this two-acre parcel."

Alana's bare arms suddenly prickled with the cold of a wind that she couldn't see. "Ryan Roberts the developer? Isn't this area zoned agricultural?" Ryan Roberts specialized in giant multi-family townhouse developments.

"Yeah, but it's inclusionary, meaning that agricultural practices and keeping chickens and the like is accepted here, not exclusionary, meaning that the land is reserved for agriculture or can't be subdivided."

Alana clenched the handle of the mower. "How much are you selling it for?" she said weakly.

"Seven hundred and fifty thousand."

The terrier decided to have another go at her stomach. She tried to imagine getting her garden and vegetable farm up and running next to one of Ryan's monstrosities. She tried to imagine which banks she could rob to purchase the land herself, in her environmental ninja suit with Iron Man in tow.

"Not my preference either," Rick said, echoing Alana's thoughts. "I'm keeping the house. But I need to finance my retirement, and it's the best offer I've had in a while. My realtor says I should jump on it. We're not going to sign the papers for a couple of weeks because Roberts has to sell a few houses to get the financing in place. Hey, you heard that planner guy got fired, huh?"

"What? Are you talking about Zander?" Alana tried to shift from the devastation Ryan Roberts was about to wreak on her farm to this new bit of information.

"It's in the *Scoop*. He was working on non-city projects on city time, apparently."

"That's too bad," Alana said.

Rick shrugged. "Depends what you thought of some of his plans."

After Rick sped off on his ATV, Alana collected the children and went inside, leaving the mower in the middle of the lawn.

The phone was ringing when she reached the kitchen.

"So," said Maude crisply. "Have you resigned yet?"

"I no longer work for Mountain Magnesium," Alana said dully. She flipped open the *Scoop*. Sure enough, the headline "City Planner Dismissed" was splashed across the page, followed by an article entitled "Why Hire a Vancouver Construction Company?" that rambled on about the "heinous" city decision to hire DKP Construction for the road project when there were perfectly qualified local companies.

"Good girl," said Maude. "We could use some help getting the word out about the protest if you're available. It's going to be an amazing event with people from all different sectors of the community. They won't even know what hit them."

Blaine's Miata tore into the driveway and Blaine got out wearing a grim, for Blaine, expression.

"I'll get back to you, Maude," Alana said, interrupting the older woman, who was prattling on about the placard-making station and drummers. "I have to go."

"What are you doing here?" she said without preamble when Blaine stepped in after knocking.

"We need to talk," he said, and he offered watery little smile.

Alana staggered backward a bit. This was how Blaine had prefaced his announcement that he was leaving her. Katie twined her tiny arm around Alana's leg. Alana sank onto the steps and pulled Katie into her lap.

"What's going on?"

"So, good news," he said. "Zander already has investors for our business idea. They're almost ready to sign on. We just have to prove the model."

Because apparently he was working on it on city time, she thought. "What model, Blaine?"

"You're going to love it. It's super environmentally friendly. We're going to turn the old mill into a biofuel facility using wood waste from around the province. Zander has been developing a special patented process. We're going to make jet fuel and diesel, and it's carbon neutral."

Alana narrowed her eyes. "That's great. What's the bad news?"

"In order to get this up and running, I have to move to Vancouver for a couple of years to be near the investors. Zander has already gone. Heather and I are going in two weeks. I've given notice at the college, and I have two months of sabbatical time that I can use, and the term is over, so I can go right away. I'll just need to come back to mark exams." He held up his hand to stop her from talking. "I know you hate Vancouver. But you and the kids could move there. I just want you to keep an open mind. I'm also going to need to ask you for a break on the child support payments. My salary is going to drop almost to zero for the next year or so while Zander and I get this company up and running. Please, Alana, let's just do this without involving the lawyers. We can't afford it."

Alana's lips felt stiff and numb. Only Katie on her lap prevented her from springing to her feet and punching him in the square-cut jaw. "How am I going to support the kids?" she said in a low voice.

"Well, you know... I know you don't want to hear it, but you could sell this place, or subdivide it. Ryan Roberts is interested. I could help you get a good price."

She might have to punch Ryan Roberts in the jaw too. "I'm not selling," she hissed. "How could you do this to us?"

A muscle twitched in Blaine's lips, and his cheeks had gone whitish. "I'm not doing anything to you. I'm the one who's made sacrifices all these years working a job I hated to support you and the kids so you could stay home and pursue your farming dreams. This is a really great opportunity for me, and I'm going to take it. You have just as much capacity to earn money as I do. Maybe it's time you got a real job for once and get paid what you're worth, Alana. It'll be good for you."

Tears started to trickle down Alana's face.

Blaine sighed and pulled his hand through his coarse hair. "Move to Vancouver. We can get places close to each other. I'm sure the environmental dementor squared can get you something."

"I'm not working for Tabbie."

Blaine shook his head. "Look, Alana, these are all your choices. But I'm not living your life anymore. I'll send you some new child support numbers. Please don't take me to court. I really need your support on this. If this business works out, we could all be in the money. Then you could buy a new piece of land in Abbotsford or Chilliwack even. If you want me to talk to Ryan for you, I will, just let me know. But I'm going. This is happening."

He turned and marched out the front door and then sped away in the Miata.

Alana got through the rest of the afternoon with shaky hands and teary eyes. The proposed new payment Blaine had sent by email was a quarter of what he currently paid. There was no way she could make the house payment with that amount unless she got a job that paid more than any previous job she had ever had, immediately. And buying Rick's parcel—which she had entertained for just a second when Rick broke his news—was pretty much out of the question. For that, she would need a job *and* a new husband—one with lots of money.

She put the children to bed and then gazed out the window at the garden beds that she had dug out, framed in, and filled with soil that she had conditioned and nurtured for four years. The beds to the south lay under blankets of white that protected the tiny seedlings that had already started to poke out of the rich earth. The beds to the north were dark mounds ready to be planted in a few weeks when the sun would bathe the valley in reliable warmth; her garden plan was already drawn and on the fridge, the seed packets laid out on the dining room table. Beyond the beds, on the front gate, the blue and gold "North Star Farm" sign, which she and Duncan had painted and hung out front when they had moved in, had come loose on one end and now hung askew. Kind of like her dreams.

She curled her hand into a fist and nearly punched it through the glass of the old farmhouse window.

Blaine picked up on the first ring. He didn't even wait for her to start talking. "I know you're upset, Alana. I know you're on the edge financially, and I'm sorry. But just think of it this way. We're never going to get out of the hole on my piddly college salary combined with your little jobs. I'm having a hard time supporting two households. I need to give this a go, which might mean you have to give up that property now, but maybe it'll give you the chance to buy another, better one down the road. Maybe in an actual farming community."

"Why, Blaine?"

"Why what? I just told you why."

"No, why did you leave? What did I do wrong? Am I just not good-looking enough? Am I not funny enough? Are gardening and parenting just not attractive? Why is Heather better than me? Why?" Her voice was raw and dull.

Blaine gave a nervous laugh. "Alana, you are absolutely stunning, and brilliant, and everything. You're amazing. You're just a lot. You're complex, driven, and focused, and that's a lot. Heather is simple, and I'm just a simple man in a lot of ways, and I like simple, and this farming thing... It's *your* dream. It's not my dream. Wouldn't it be great for you to find someone to support your dream?"

"So I should start hanging out in country bars looking for farmers?"

"Well... I think you might scare farmers."

"Gee, thanks."

Blaine sighed. "I'm sure the right person is out there for you. But I'm pretty sure he has to be as smart as you are, and interested in the environment... and well-off."

The sharpness of this last nearly took her breath away. And yet it wasn't without truth. Environmentalism and farming had both long been a bastion of the very rich and the very poor.

By the time she got off the phone with Blaine, Maude had already filled her inbox with emails regarding the protest—announcements for her to edit, pamphlets for her to distribute, and influencers for her to call.

A LinkedIn request from Zander nestled amongst Maude's environmental calls to action. The message that accompanied it read like a standard professional farewell. "It's been a pleasure working with you. I know you'll do your best to ensure that the sustainability plan gets accepted and implemented. Use the spending habits of those at City Hall as your guide with regard to whom you can trust, especially big expenditures."

Bastard. Nice, environmental, doing-the-right-thing, impossible-to-hate bastard. And that last comment was standard Zander—he had always been a big advocate of evaluating the council based on where they voted to spend money rather than on what they *said* they supported. Still, the message was a little odd. As far as Zander knew, she still worked for Mountain Magnesium and therefore was not a logical champion for the sustainability plan anymore. Unless Zander and Nate were tight, which, given the photos, they might be.

Alana flipped closed the lid of her laptop and went to bed, the North Star Farm sign, retrieved from the front gate, lying on the bedside table, and Lou's words about the job at Mountain Magnesium ringing in her ears.

On Monday morning, she didn't even turn on her computer on. Her inbox would just contain more messages from Maude. After walking the children to school, she dressed and styled her hair. She would go into the office and talk to Nate. That much she knew. She wasn't sure what the rest of her plan was. Yet.

She paused outside the turquoise door. Should she knock, or just go in and go to Nate's office? She elected for the latter, but the door was locked. She stood outside for several minutes. She still had her key, but would it be unethical to go in? Lou had said she could have her job back. But would entering with her key mean she was taking it?

She unlocked the door, went inside, and walked down the main hall, peering into each empty office. The ebony of the piano shimmered white in the morning sun like a mirage. She went and sat on the bench and rested her fingers on the cool white keys.

Maybe it was the piano, or the glorious room in which she played, or the grief over her lost marriage and now her little piece of land, but for once the Rachmaninoff song came easily to her, and she progressed through the piece effortlessly, her eyes half closed. She didn't realize that Nate had arrived until she played the final notes and flicked her eyes up to find him standing just inside the door.

"That was beautiful," he said. "Tough piece. 'Lilacs'?"

She snatched her hands away from the keys. "Yep. One of his easiest. And the only song I know that's mostly in the upper register. Not nearly as beautiful as your playing," she said.

Nate approached the piano. "No. It was. I can't believe your mom didn't encourage you more."

Alana shook her head and pushed away the inevitable sob. "She wanted what was best for me. She knew how hard it was to make it as a musician. I think she worried that if I loved it too much I wouldn't do anything else."

Nate's face tightened and sharpened, but he gave a tired nod. "She tried to do the same with me. But evidently I'm as stubborn as a goat."

"No. You're a genius. You were meant to be a musician."

The corners of Nate's lips turned up slightly in a grim smile. "I wish I could believe that. However, apparently I'm going to give it another go."

"Your dad told me you were leaving. Sorry about the farm text, by the way. Your dad gave me the real story."

"It's okay. Yes, I've tendered my resignation. This business thing isn't for me." He ran his hand through his tufty hair and offered a sheepish smile. "It's hard to keep a musician tied to a desk. They tend to flake out and rebel, and act like goats. I'm not leaving Silver Peak, though. I have a few local gigs in the next month, and there's a record producer, retired from the big time, who lives in town. He and I are discussing working on an indie album, and I'm interviewing some musicians in town, like Zander, to play backup. I might try to find a less corporate job in town, like stocking shelves or pumping gas."

Not leaving. He wasn't leaving. Somehow those words, which shouldn't have changed anything, changed everything. They certainly made the fact that Zander was a musician—which explained why he and Nate knew each other, and would have interested her earlier—much less interesting. She was acutely conscious of how close together and alone they were, and of the fact that he was no longer her boss, or, apparently, a capitalist.

"Your dad wants me to talk you into staying."

"I see."

"And he offered me my job back. That's why I'm here. I wouldn't just break in. I swear."

"So, are you planning to take it?" Nate said. His eyes had narrowed considerably. Did he know that Lou had offered her a bonus if she convinced Nate to stay?

"I kind of need the money. My ex has just resigned from his job, and I don't want to lose my house and property. I know that sounds like a lame reason for taking a job, but that's where I'm at."

Nate grimaced. "It's not particularly lame. It's kind of the story of most people's lives. The only reason I don't have to do the same is that I don't have children, or a house. I just need to find a place to park my motorhome." He drew away from her and turned to look out the sun-dappled window.

"There's a but there," she said, processing the fact that he seemed to have just announced that he planned to take up residence in a motorhome. "What's the but?"

He ignored her question. "Are there other jobs you could take?"

She shook her head. "There are, but none that pay this well. Why don't you want me working here?" He had basically fired her for no reason, and now he didn't want her working here. Did he think she was completely incompetent? She couldn't stop the single tear that escaped her eye and streamed down her cheek. Nate's eyes widened, but he leaned toward her and caught the tear with his knuckle, his hand just barely grazing her face.

He opened his mouth to say something, but there was a jaunty and triumphant knock at the door, and then it flew open. Dozens of people wearing placards reading "stop the mine" and "save our watershed" sprang though the door. Maude was in the lead.

"I knew it," she jeered in Alana's general direction, although her voice was loud enough to be for the benefit of the room. "You're still in bed with the corporation. Literally, even. We're occupying this building until you agree to stop the mine and leave our watershed intact. The photos from Friday night have gone live, and we have half the town out there ready to rip this building down."

Panic skated down Alana's back. More placard-carrying people streamed into the room behind Maude: members of the Regional Environmental Board, Therese, Katrina, Layla, and a few other people she recognized.

Nate stepped decisively away from her. "Alana is no longer employed here, so leave her out of this. And I'm afraid I'm going to have to ask you to leave. You're welcome to take your protest outside, but you're trespassing right now."

Nate's vehement statement that she was no longer employed at Mountain Magnesium hurt somehow, and Alana concentrated her gaze on the door. The flood of people seemed to have ceased. She flicked her eyes to the windows, but no placard-bearing, or pitchfork-carrying, townsfolk gathered out there. Several of the twenty people inside the building had started chanting "save our water."

"No way. We're occupying the building until we're dragged away," Maude declared to Nate.

While Maude and Nate continued to argue, Katrina waved cheerily at Alana. "Oh, hey, Alana. What are you doing here? We're just protesting the mine. I'm going for a run at noon if you want to join me. Are you getting back into running now? I saw you out the other day."

"Um, yeah, sort of," Alana said. "Maude just said you're staying all day."

"Oh, well, I'm not," Katrina said. "I have things I have to do." She looked over her shoulder at the other protesters who had gathered over by the reception desk. "Oh, looks like they need me!" She skipped off in that direction.

Alana walked over to one of the windows and peered out. The parking lot behind the Mountain Magnesium building was empty. Where was everyone?

Her phone vibrated.

< *Are you okay?* > Suzanne had texted. < *Lou just posted a big thing on Facebook saying he'd heard about the protest and that apparently some people in town are willing to lie and go behind people's backs to ruin local businesses. It's caused quite the frenzy.* >

< *You're Facebook friends with Lou?* > Alana texted back. The protesters were now marching in a circle waving their placards, chanting "no mines in marshes."

< *No, Leo.* > Suzanne replied. < *But he's friends with his dad of course. Anyway, Lou said anyone who went to the protest was anti Silver Peak.* >

< *Well apparently there are about 23 people who are anti Silver Peak* >

Alana texted.

< *What?* >

< *Nothing. I'm fine. I should go. Thanks for checking in on me!* > She added a smiley face to the end of the text.

Alana went and rejoined Nate, who stood blocking the hallway to the individual offices with his arms folded across his chest. "What are you going to do?" she said.

"Well technically, since I no longer work here, it's not my problem. And it's definitely not your problem. But I've called Len, Curtis, and my dad."

"You can't be convinced to take your job back?" she said over the din.

Nate's voice had gone flat. "No. I'd get out of here if I were you. I'm going to stick around and make sure they don't hurt the piano or hack into the company files."

"There really isn't anyone outside. Maude's bluffing," Alana said in an undertone. "I can stay with you if you want. Maybe we can talk to these people and try to understand their concerns, use it as an opportunity."

"No, Alana. Go, really." Nate had shifted his gaze to something over her shoulder, and he seemed to be avoiding eye contact.

The dismissal hit her squarely in the chest. For whatever moments she and Nate had shared—at least they had seemed like moments—he certainly seemed to be pushing her away. Then again, she was here trying to talk him into a job so she could collect five thousand dollars.

"And don't believe what my dad says about having your job back. He said he was going to post it."

Alana glared at him. "Thanks a lot. Have fun here today." She turned and swept past the protesters and out into the cool morning air.

Ryan Roberts was standing in her driveway typing something on his phone when she pulled in. He headed toward her with a broad smile and an extended arm.

"How's it going, Alana? Long time no see. Blaine says you'd be open to an offer on the place. I was wondering if I could take a look inside before I send you some numbers."

She scowled at him. "Shitty, Ryan. It's going shitty. And no, you can't come in my house. Please leave my driveway."

She stormed past him, observing his stupefied expression with some small degree of satisfaction.

She stood in her living room staring pointedly at Ryan out the window with her arms crossed until he left. Then she texted Blaine.

< *MY house is not for sale. You and Heather enjoy your new life alone in Vancouver. I hate you.* >

She had updated her LinkedIn page and sent an email to several old clients indicating that she was available for work when Lou called.

"So, no luck, huh?"

"No luck," she said.

"I was wondering if you were interested in Nate's job yourself then, on an interim basis, at least for four months? It's more than twice the salary plus shares, and the dividend package is quite generous. I could post it, but we need someone to take up the reins right away. If you do well in the job, it's yours."

Alana tried to grasp some semblance of sense out of her racing thoughts. *Nate's* job? Nate hadn't even thought her competent enough for her own job. "Um, can I think about that for a few minutes, Lou?"

"Sure, but don't think too long. I need someone in that chair tomorrow morning or we're going to have to cancel the open house."

"Can I work from home after school gets out for the first few weeks while I find childcare?"

"I think we'd be okay with that."

Alana rose and looked out her office window. Ryan had just gone next door and was taking photos of Rick's property, but his camera was all too often pointed at her property as well.

"Isn't there a protest going on at the offices right now?"

"Nah, it's all over. It was a non-event and had pretty much petered out by the time I got there. That Maude woman may think she has the backing of the community, but numbers don't lie."

"I'll take the job," she said.

"Fantastic. Meet me at the offices at four this afternoon and I'll have your contract drawn up for you to sign."

"I'll be there." She hung up the phone and turned her middle finger up in Ryan's general direction, and then for good measure in the direction of both Blaine's and Nate's condos.

CHAPTER TWENTY

Agreements

"It's a standard nondisclosure agreement for executives," Lou said. The office was quiet and blessedly bereft of protesters and Nate, although banter came from Len and Curtis's office. "We just need to make sure that none of our company secrets get shared around town. I can give you a few minutes to read through the contract and the agreement if you like. If you want to postpone the open house until you're able to hire someone new in the marketing position, feel free. As you know, city council is voting tonight with regard to whether to endorse the mine."

Alana eyed him for subterfuge as he said this, but she found nothing readable in his eyes. The council agenda had come out that morning, and Stewart's memo to council regarding the mine was effusively supportive. It indicated that since the sustainability plan was just a guiding document that had yet to be adopted, council was well within its mandate to support the mine, and the mine was entirely consistent with the economic diversification directives of the sustainability plan. Stewart didn't seem to think it was necessary to mention any of the water protection measures in the sustainability plan.

If Alana were on the environmental side—well on the total, protect-everything environmental side—she'd be furious that Stewart was suggesting putting aside a plan she and Zander had just worked on for two years. But maybe the plan didn't really reflect what the people of Silver Peak wanted, or what was best for sustainability.

Or maybe she had become a complete corporate apologist. Wasn't that what corporate apologists did? Rationalized everything. What was she even talking about, 'the total, protect-everything environmental side'? That's exactly what a mealy-mouthed corporate lackey would say.

But Mountain Magnesium was trying to do things right and develop a sustainable mine. She kept repeating that to herself as she reviewed the stack of papers Lou had provided her. She nearly fell out of her chair at the salary figure—$140,000—and the proposed dividend package. Her heart started to accelerate a little. Was this what real jobs paid? If she could convince Rick to sell his land to her half an acre at a time, she might be able to prevent Ryan from getting it. The bank might approve a substantial increase in her mortgage with this new salary.

She checked her watch. She had to get to Suzanne's to grab the kids before too long, since she would have to feed them before taking them to her dad's so she could attend the council meeting that night—there was no way in hell she was asking Blaine to babysit. She reviewed the documents a second time, but couldn't find anything other than the usual standard, alarming legalese.

She removed a photo from her bag—a picture of the kids by the North Star Farm sign—set it on the desk, and then signed both documents with a flourish. She took them to Lou, who sat reading in Nate's old office. It was done. The Greenes would disown her for sure now.

Lou rose from the desk with an outstretched hand. "Fantastic, Alana. We're so glad to have you on the team. I've left all of Nate's passwords on his desk there. Have you decided whether you want to proceed with the open house or not?"

"I think we should go ahead. The intent is to gather information on people's concerns." *And obviously the release of incriminating photos of Lou with city staff and council members didn't cause any real upset*, she thought. She wanted to ask Lou what he had really been doing on Friday night, but she didn't think it would be good form.

Len and Curtis emerged from their office to offer congratulations and indicate that they would try to behave. Unlike Nate, they seemed to think it was perfectly reasonable to have her in the CEO position. Like maybe she *was*, in fact, competent.

"Were the protesters still here when you guys got in?"

Curtis laughed. "That band of crazies. Nah, they dissipated pretty quickly when Andrew Webber, the goat farmer, posted on Facebook that he was very grateful to Mountain Magnesium for buying his property and creating the opportunity for economic development in Silver Peak."

"That's good," Alana said. Her chuckle was a bit thin though, even to her own ears.

Outside in the SUV, she looked up Rick's phone number and dialed.

"Hello," he grunted into the phone.

"Hi, Rick, it's your neighbor, Alana."

"Hi, neighbor! Are you going to come over for those beers?"

"Soon, Rick, I promise. Look, I want to buy your property. Would you be willing to delay selling it to Ryan, or consider selling it to me in pieces, or renting it to me?"

"What are you offering?"

"A hundred and fifty for the first half acre now, and then the rest in a few years." She didn't add the word "maybe."

"I don't know. Roberts is willing to buy the whole thing right now for a higher price."

"I know. Just think about it. Please. What do you want next to you? A big development, or goats? It's one of the few remaining pieces of arable land in Silver Peak. I could give you shares in my farm cooperative."

"Farm cooperative? What, are you going to put an ashram here and have a bunch of hippies living with you?"

"No hippies, I promise, but I *would* like to turn it back into a working farm, somehow."

"So I'd have stinky cows next to me?"

Alana closed her eyes. This was not going well. But Rick was still talking to her, so evidently he wasn't completely dismissing the idea. Or he was stringing her along.

"No cows. They produce methane and require too much land. Just think about it. You could be part of the change."

"I certainly hope you're not talking about the change of life."

"No, Rick. I'm talking about saving the planet."

Alana rubbed the spot between her eyes after she hung up. She had no real plan. The notion of a farming cooperative of sorts had started to blossom in her mind, but she had no idea how she was going to pay for it, or who was going to help her.

Maude regarded Alana balefully through grey-tinted glasses when Alana arrived at the council meeting; news of Alana's new job had likely already traversed all the relevant corridors of Silver Peak. Sharon and Mark kept their eyes averted, and Fiona flounced past with a little supercilious smile and nod, as if part of her enjoyed the drama. Clearly Alana couldn't ask *them* who might be interested in co-owning Rick's land with her.

Alana had settled into a seat next to Lou when she received a text from Tabitha. < *I need to talk to you. It's important.* >

The bile gathered at the back of Alana's throat. Tabitha knew already. She shut off her phone and looked resolutely ahead, ignoring the whispers and dirty looks from the environmental army as they filled the seats around her like a swarm of restless bees.

The council moved through its initial agenda items, including the question of the new reservoir and extending the street construction contract to include the reservoir so the city could save money by not having to retender the project. Stewart spoke eloquently on the importance of water security and how the new reservoir would allow for population growth and economic diversification. He stressed the need for a new, modern facility that could eventually replace the aging Williston one—which, he suggested ominously, could go at any time—and emphasized that more water storage capacity was clearly called for in the sustainability plan. Alana shook her head and tried to form her lips into a neutral smile. This was such an outright lie. Maybe a new reservoir wasn't a bad idea, aside from potentially encouraging residents to become bigger water gluttons than they already were, but to justify it using the sustainability plan was a joke.

Council debated for only a few minutes before voting unanimously in favor of the new reservoir and adding it to the existing contract. Apparently council didn't share Ramona's concerns about letting contracts to the Vancouver-based DKP Construction. Nor did they apparently think that a new reservoir would open the door to a proliferation of backyard swimming pools. Or maybe they were pouring the cement in their back yards as they voted.

Maude expelled a huff of fury when the mayor limited the audience's speaking time regarding the proposed mine agenda item to three minutes per speaker, one speaker per organization. But this was standard council practice, so Alana didn't know what Maude had expected. After a huddle of harsh whispers, Maude selected Fiona to speak on behalf of the Mountain Stewardship Society.

Fiona strode up to the microphone and began a speech about the importance of public participation with lots of allusions to the trustworthiness of the Mountain Magnesium Board and the pictures of the council members that had appeared in the *Silver Peak News*. She spoke well, but it was a grave and almost laughable strategic error. Fiona was, in essence, publicly lambasting the very people she was asking to make a decision to oppose the mine. It would make for splashy news articles, which would no doubt feature gorgeous photos of Fiona with her blond hair and dusky blue eyes flashing righteous outrage, but earned only bland and derisive expressions from the council.

After Fiona was finished, Stewart reiterated what he had said in his memo about the sustainability plan being advisory and the mine being completely consistent with the economic development elements of the plan. He also pointed out that the municipal tax income from the mine would be instrumental in paying for the infrastructure improvements, including the road project and the reservoir, that Silver Peak would need in the coming years. Then the mayor made a motion to send a letter to the province in support of the mine and council proceeded to discuss the matter.

Bernard, Kailee, and Edward were clearly in support of the mine, which meant the motion only needed one more vote to pass.

Madeline Gellar raised her hand. "Permission to address a question to a member of the audience, Your Worship," she said.

The mayor nodded.

Madeline turned and looked directly at Alana. "Alana, you were involved in the development of the sustainability plan. I'm very concerned that we're considering just ignoring a plan that we spent a lot of money and time developing, not to mention the significant public input that went into the plan. Zander is no longer here to advise us. As the co-author of the plan, what do you think?"

Alana's lips felt numb, and her knees wobbled as she rose to her feet. It was one thing to sit silent while Stewart said the plan was advisory. It was quite another to actually speak *against* the plan. But if she didn't, she would be completely fired.

She sucked in a deep breath. "I appreciate your concerns, Madeline. The sustainability plan was developed with a lot of public input, and it is relevant, but it is definitely only advisory. The thing to remember is that the sustainability plan is basically a shopping list of objectives— important objectives, yes, but because it includes environmental, economic, and social objectives, some of those objectives conflict with each other. There are not many actions that you could take that would achieve all of those objectives at the same time. Most things will help in the achievement of some of the plan objectives and hinder in the achievement of others. It's going to be like that for almost every decision you make, I'm afraid, and the mine is no different. It will help with the economic objectives of developing local employers and diversifying the economy, but it does mean some development in the watershed. In short, while the plan is an important touchstone, it just identifies a wide range of things that people in the community want to achieve. Council still has to decide which are most important."

Alana sank back into her chair. Everything she had said was correct, but she was pretty sure she had just betrayed both Zander and the plan she had helped to develop.

Madeline looked over the rims of her red reading glasses. "Thank you."

"Nothing like asking the fox into the henhouse to identify which chickens, or sorry, objectives, go out on a special hike with him," Maude said loudly.

Council discussed the issue further for fifteen minutes, and then voted six to one in favor of endorsing the mine proposal, with only Madeline opposed.

"Great job," Lou said to Alana, as Maude rose and stormed out.

"Thanks," Alana said.

As soon as she felt confident that Maude had cleared the building, Alana excused herself to Lou, then slipped out to retrieve the kids and put them to bed, her heart pounding in her chest.

She worked like a lunatic the next day preparing materials for the open house on Friday night and trying to sort through Nate's files and emails to determine what else, exactly, Nate did on a daily basis. Lou had scheduled a board meeting for Monday after the open house, and Alana wanted to be prepared. At several times during the day she found herself staring longingly out the window at the sky, but she always turned right back to her work. People all across the world spent their days chained to a desk; she was just going to have to suck it up. Maude spent the day filling Alana's inbox with photos of birds from the marsh, and Tabitha sent her several more texts about needing to talk to her.

At the end of the day, Alana opened up the last of Nate's old files; it was labeled "Processing Facility." The file contained some facility schematics and an agreement in principle stating that if the mine were to proceed, the facility would be constructed by Thad Kepper Construction out of Kelowna.

Alana squinted at the agreement in principle. Kepper. It was an un-common name. Odd that it was the same last name as the city administrator for Silver Peak. She closed the file and Googled Thad Kepper Construction. The photo of Thad was inconclusive. The man in it would be the right age to be Stewart's son, but bore only a passing resemblance to the city administrator. Still, Alana felt a small furrow of alarm in her heart.

She ran to the school to collect the kids and tried to spend the rest of the afternoon working on the open house materials amid squeals, out-breaks of hand-to-hand combat, and sticky fingers on her keyboard. She had posted an ad for a nanny and hoped to have someone in place by the following week. She had also asked Jonah to start coming twice a week, so she could be sure the garden got planted and tended despite her new work schedule. The cascade of outsourcing and compromise that dogged all working mothers had begun. She should just be re-lieved that she had avoided it for so long.

After dinner, she recommenced her search for connections be-tween Thad and Stewart. Not surprisingly, Facebook provided the answer. As she scrolled through Thad's photos, she eventually came to a picture of Thad and Stewart arm in arm at Thad's wedding.

So. Thad had the contract to build the processing facility.

Maybe he had offered the best price. Maybe.

The chatter on Facebook had turned somewhat in favor of the mine over the past few days, as the old guard of Silver Peak—friends of the mayor—started trying to dominate the discussion. Maude's cronies were quick to step up in opposition, but they didn't seem to have suffi-cient numbers on Facebook to steer it to any sort of victory. The majority of commenters on the *Silver Peak News* site were still firmly opposed, but the two sides were becoming so vitriolic that anyone who just wanted to ask a question about the mine, or felt neutral, or sup-ported it but had some reservations, got publicly shamed and derided, often by both sides.

The job applications had continued to stream in over the past week, but so too had the emails from people telling Alana that the mine would destroy the watershed and Silver Peak, and that the mine pro-posal sucked and lacked detail—a point with which she agreed.

Redoing sections of the environmental impact statement was at the top of her list of things to propose to the board of directors. Some of the emails also got personal, telling her that she was making a mistake, that she had singlehandedly gutted the sustainability plan, and worse, that a woman had no business trying to run a mining company.

She replied to each email in a friendly and professional manner, inviting the person to come to the open house and informing them that Mountain Magnesium wanted to have a conversation with the community, but twisted representations of her responses soon started to pepper Facebook and the comments on the *Silver Peak News* site.

She slept fitfully and rose early the next morning to answer yet more emails and ponder the Stewart-Thad connection. She would have to review the bid documents on the Kepper contract.

Rick waved at her from the fence as she hurried the kids into the car. "Okay, because I believe in you, I'll sell you the first acre for three fifty," he said. "But I want a contract in place by the end of next week, for my security you know, and I want a covenant or something saying you won't get cows."

Three hundred and fifty thousand dollars. More than he was selling the land to Ryan for, but he was taking a risk only selling half when he had a buyer for the whole piece. How was she going to add $350,000 to her mortgage?

"Okay, I'll go see about the financing at lunch," she said in a voice that she managed to make chipper. "And a no-cow covenant is totally fine."

The bank was more accommodating than she expected. Apparently if you had land to secure the deal, they didn't mind allowing someone to be over their eyeballs in debt. They pre-approved the mortgage increase, conditional on confirming her employment and salary at Mountain Magnesium with Lou, and indicated that the final approval and papers for her to sign would be available the following day. She went to the notary next and asked him to draw up the papers for the sale, for her and Rick to sign.

She was moving on auto-pilot, her feet carrying her from one task to the next, carrying out the logistics of the deal, not thinking too much about the consequences of her actions. It was only after she'd left the notary's office that she got shaky and sweaty with doubt. This *was* the right thing to do, right?

Or was it absolutely crazy stupid?

Ryan accosted her on the sidewalk on her way back to her office, his deeply tanned face dark and dangerous. "Rick tells me he's selling his land to you," he said.

Alana smiled and tried to step around him. "Um, yeah I think so," she said.

"I'm trying to build this community some affordable housing, which is called for in your so-called sustainability plan, and I seem to be blocked every time I turn around. First by your ridiculous development cost charges, which make affordable housing impossible, and now with you stealing the only affordable building site out from underneath me." Anger shimmered off of his hulking form.

Alana's right leg started to shake a bit. "It's not *my* sustainability plan, it's the city sustainability plan, developed by Silver Peak residents."

"Yeah, the ones who don't have to earn a living and have time to show up to all your community meetings."

"Look, building affordable housing is a great idea, and I really do support it, but Rick's property is one of the last pieces of farmland around. It really should be preserved as farmland. Surely there must be other locations for a housing complex."

"Not flat ones, and to be able to build affordably, you need flat. Back off. Nobody farms these days. You're going to put a lot of construction people out of business, and that will not make you very popular in this town." Ryan said this last with slitted eyes and a clenched jaw.

The trembling had spread to Alana's other leg. She felt someone behind her, and she turned to find Nate fixing Ryan with a stony stare.

"Hey, Ryan," Nate said.

"Heard you were back in town, Nate. Big city more than you could handle?"

Alana cringed at the casual hostility in Ryan's words.

"Looks that way. Too many people that'll stick a knife in your back when you're down. Not that much different from here," Nate said evenly. "Listen, I'm curious, is there a market for your new housing complex? I thought population growth was stagnant?"

Ryan let out a nasty laugh. "Look, I'm a builder, you're a musician. So maybe we should all stick to what we know. There's always a market for affordable housing."

"Why not buy and refurbish some of the older run-down housing stock downtown?" Nate asked.

"People want new, not some fixed-up dump. And nobody makes money that way, because we can't keep the unit costs down."

"So if we build on all our farmland, where are we going to get our food?"

Ryan raised a curved finger to his lips and shifted his eyes up and to the left as if deep in thought, but his features were hard and tight. "Hmm. That's a really good question, Nate. Let me think. Oh, wait. Wait for it. I know." He gestured jubilantly at the grocery store across the street. "*That's* where we're going to get our food."

"Right, and if this scenario is playing out in every community across North America, then what?"

"I don't give a shit what's happening in every community across North America. You newcomers think you can just move back into town and play the violin about your precious little causes and destroy the livelihood of everyone who lives here. Back off, or you'll find your life here very unpleasant." Ryan stormed away.

Alana practically leaned against Nate to prevent her knees from going out from under her.

"Asshole," Nate said.

"Maybe he's right, though," Alana said.

"He's not right. He just wants easy and he wants money, and he's used to getting it. Have you seen Ryan's house?"

"No."

Nate pointed at the Vespa, which was parked half a block away. "Let's go for a ride. I'll show you. I wanted to talk to you anyway."

"But I need a helmet."

"I have an extra in one of the compartments."

Alana wondered if the helmet had been Fiona's. As if reading her thoughts, Nate looked directly into her eyes. "It's an old one of mine. It was a little small for me."

With her arms wrapped around Nate's shockingly tight abs and her thighs pressed against his on the back of the Vespa, Alana felt a faint sense of dizzy giddiness. While she would have admitted that she was slightly attracted to Nate, she had not expected touching him to be quite so electrifying. With his warm body up against hers it was all too easy to imagine dropping her hands to his inner thighs and pressing her lips against the small piece of exposed skin on the side of his neck. When he pulled over to a stop in one of the posher neighborhoods of Silver Peak, it was all too soon.

He put a hand over hers when she went to dismount. "Don't get off. Ryan's house is four in on the left. It's blue. You can't miss it. I don't want to stop in front in case he's in the yard. The Vespa is a little conspicuous, so I'm just going to drive by. Then I'm going to head to the Mur Creek trailhead where we can talk for a minute."

"Okay," she managed to mumble, her thoughts still too deep in touching Nate.

Nate set the Vespa in motion again and they cruised past a row of very large, stately houses. It was a new subdivision and the trees lining the street hadn't yet reached house height yet, but with the perfect distinctive houses, winding road, emerald lawns, and lush landscaping, it was already a gorgeous, homey street. Alana's old brown clapboard farmhouse with its thrash of wild grass, brown garden beds, and fruit trees now seemed hopelessly hideous and desperate by comparison. Maybe she *was* crazy to want to farm. She could downsize, buy one of the small houses at the other end of this development, and have a tiny manicured yard. Nate could come over for dinner.

She was so wrapped up in this fantasy that she almost missed Ryan's house when they passed it. Gargantuan even by the standards of the development, it had a palatial air. The finishing was more detailed and the gables and turrets more elaborate than those on the other houses, and she thought she could make out the outlines of a swimming pool behind the hedge. But it was the driveway that nearly made her topple off the Vespa. A beautiful new RV with an ATV compartment sat off to one side, and a flatbed trailer with three snowmobiles was in front of it. Two brand new trucks were parked in the drive and one had four mountain bikes hanging off the back.

She barely had time to process all this before Nate was past the house and around the corner, speeding toward the Mur Creek trailhead. She didn't even know how to feel about Ryan's house. Did it imply that he was doing fine and she shouldn't feel bad, or maybe he was heavily in debt and needed the affordable housing project to pay his bills, or maybe he was doing the affordable housing project out of the goodness of his heart? She had no idea. Still, should anyone live like he lived? She knew there were people all over the world—all over Silver Peak for that matter—who lived extravagant, or at least moderately extravagant, lifestyles, and she tried not to judge. She liked nice things too. She liked nice things a lot. She just believed that people should try to limit the number of nice things they owned. But maybe that was her speaking as a person who had never been able to afford a lot of nice things. Maybe if she could afford them, she would have them too, and would justify it away just as quickly and easily as everyone else.

Without thinking, she had cinched her arms around Nate's waist a bit tighter and leaned into his broad back, her chin almost resting on his shoulder. He smelled nice. Actually, he smelled extraordinarily intoxicating. She lurched upright and tried to draw herself back a bit.

The familiar willow-treed entrance to the Mur Creek trail came into sight. Nate steered into the empty parking lot and stopped the Vespa, and Alana got off reluctantly. Nate turned to her with a funny little smile, but there was an intensity in his turquoise eyes that sent sparks up and down her legs. Before she could step away from the Vespa, he snaked an arm around her, lifted his visor, and pulled her into him, brushing her lips with his gently, and then with more intent, his tongue tasting hers. Alana closed her eyes and let the kiss wash over her, her heart pounding with the absolute insanity and thrill of it. She barely knew this man. He was a musician, and a potentially unstable one, and she had two children, a job, and a farm to think of. And yet she decided that, at this moment, she didn't care. So when he removed her helmet and his own, got off the Vespa, and pulled her into him, kissing her tenderly and ferociously, his hands entwined in her hair, she kissed him back, reveling in all the softness and hardness of his body pressed against hers.

They were both breathing faster when he released her, his hands resting on her hips. "Sorry," he said. "I've wanted to do that since you first walked into my office."

"That's good, I think."

He gave her one of his sexy smiles. "Not so much when you're my employee. I understand you took the CEO job."

"Are you upset by that?"

"At you, no."

"At who then? You don't think I can do the job?"

"I think you can more than do the job. I'm a lunkhead compared to you." He looked over his shoulder at a passing car and dropped another kiss onto her lips. "If anyone sees us," he whispered, "and they will have seen us drive through town, they'll think we're just having a romantic interlude."

"And that isn't what we're having?" she said, trying to surface again from the kiss and sort out what he was saying.

Nate drew back again, but he left his arms wrapped more tightly around her so his blue eyes were close to hers. "We are. And I would like to see you for real soon. But I also need to talk to you about Mountain Magnesium."

She stiffened a bit. "What? So this isn't for real. This is for show?"

"No, this is for real... but it's complicated. I have to leave town for a bit, and there are other reasons we shouldn't see each other right away."

She squinted her eyes at him. "Like what?" What was he talking about? His music career? Drug use? Fiona?

"Your job. I really think you should quit."

"What? The open house is on Friday. I can't quit. I need this job, or I'll lose my house, and I just requested an extension on my mortgage in order to buy a piece of Rick's land. They'll have the papers ready tomorrow afternoon."

"I get it, but surely there must be another job you could get."

"Not that pays this well. And the bank will be calling your dad today or tomorrow to confirm that I have the job. Rick won't wait. Not with Ryan breathing down his back for the property." She pulled away and walked a few feet from the Vespa. "What don't I know?"

Nate ran his fingers through his spiky hair. "I can't tell you. I signed a nondisclosure agreement too. The board has already reminded me that if I say anything, they'll sue."

"Your dad will sue you?"

"He's only one vote on the board, and since I quit, he's pretty pissed at me."

"Nate, please tell me what's going on. Does this have something to do with Thad Kepper?" The crushing disappointment that this was just some sort of game was almost overwhelming, and her voice bordered on shaky.

Nate shook his head. "Look, I don't know anything for sure yet, and

I don't want to put you in a position where you feel you have to break your nondisclosure agreement. Let me try to take care of this. But in case I'm right, please, I think you should quit. Just say you couldn't find childcare or realized it was more work than you expected."

"Are you saying Mountain Magnesium has done something wrong?"

"I'm saying I'm not sure yet. It could all be fine. I checked the bid documents. Kepper's bid was by far the best. He won fair and square. But there are some other things I'm checking into."

"So you want me to quit over something you're not sure about? You have to tell me what you know."

"I can't," he said. He yanked her to him and dropped a light kiss on her cheek. "Laugh at something I said," he instructed.

Alana forced a borderline hysterical giggle out of her throat while Nate nuzzled her neck. An older couple Alana vaguely recognized strolled out from the trailhead and shot them a look. Nate winked and waved. They glanced at him with slight disdain and continued through the parking lot and back toward town.

"There's already a rumor going around town that we're seeing each other, no doubt started by that Maude woman. But my dad thinks I'm a total womanizer, so let's just play on that. He'll think I used you, in my typical screw-up ways, and nobody will question anything."

Alana's arms flew up and she pushed Nate away with force. Tears flew to her eyes and bile gathered in her throat. This was Blaine all over again. The humiliation of being dumped in a small town for someone younger and cuter.

"The last thing I need, Nate Steeves, is a womanizer, and for this whole town to think that someone used me again."

A stricken expression flashed across Nate's face. "Sorry, I didn't think."

"And I'm not quitting and losing my house over something you aren't sure about." She turned and started marching back toward town, back to the office, back to her compromised ethics.

Nate called after her. "I'm heading to Kelowna, this afternoon. I have to check into something. I'll be in touch." Then, more softly: "I like you, really, a lot."

She flipped a look back over her shoulder and saw Nate staring at her with pleading eyes, but she kept walking.

CHAPTER TWENTY-ONE

Waiting

She sat at her desk in turmoil. She couldn't quit, or Ryan would get Rick's land, unless she pleaded with Rick. But Rick was already giving her a deal, and where else, other than this job, was she going to make enough money to pay her existing mortgage, never mind the new one? But what was Nate talking about? Why was he heading to Kelowna? Did it have something to do with Thad Kepper?

She thought about Nate's arms around her and the perfection of his kiss. But what had he meant that they should make it "look" like they were having a romantic interlude?

Her head pounded with the beginnings of a headache, and she was about to leave to go retrieve the kids when an email popped up from Margaret Greene. Her gut sank like it had a boulder and a terrier tied around its ankle.

"We just heard. We're shocked and on our way home just as soon as we finish up at John's Birds of the South conference. Please do what you can in the meantime."

Alana stared at the screen with her mouth partially open. The Greenes knew about her defection and were horrified enough by it to cut their trip short and come home. Her hands started to shake a bit. Or were they horrified by the mine proposed for the watershed and didn't yet know of her involvement? But Tabitha had been texting her for the past several days. Tabitha knew about her new job and must have told her parents.

Alana picked up the kids, dizzy with stress, and made her way home. The kids ran to the trampoline. The yard was alive with birds and spring insects wafting in and out of the burgeoning slips of emerald emerging from the earth and the trees. Did she really need this property enough to risk alienating everyone she cared about? She closed her eyes and felt the pale lazy warmth of the afternoon sun on her arms. She breathed in the sweet peaty scent of spring in the air. The spring freshet had caused a swell in the groundwater and the spring had become a temporary creek, gurgling across the back corner of her property.

She gritted her teeth. She was not giving up this farm.

The Miata peeled into the driveway behind her and Blaine strode up. "Roberts told me what you're doing."

"Yeah, so what? It's none of your business anymore. You're abandoning us and this farm."

"Alana, stop it. Focusing on my own career for a change is not abandoning you. And it's one thing to cling to this godforsaken piece of land in the sticks, but it's quite another to double up and cling to *two* godforsaken pieces of land. Think of what you're doing to the kids. It's great you took the job, and fine if you want to stay here, although I think it's insane, and I have to mention that I think it kind of means I win the bet, but that kind of financial exposure is too much, and who's going to bail you out?"

Alana sucked in a giant flood of tears and snot. "I don't know and I don't care. And you need to piss right off. What's the worst that happens, Blaine? I go bankrupt, and the bank takes the land and sells it to Ryan. So what? Don't you dare tell me what I'm doing to the kids. You left them. I'm buying a farm, not taking up drugs or prostitution. And you have *not* won the bet. Not even in the slightest."

Blaine gave her his tight little angry smile. She'd seen it lots of times, whenever in Blaine's opinion Alana had just gone too far. "That's a low blow. I'm just worried you're getting in over your head, and it's not as if your new boyfriend has a sterling reputation with regard to drugs."

"Right. My new boyfriend. He's a real peach, isn't he?"

"Look, I'm being serious. Is he the kind of guy you want the kids exposed to?"

"Nate is not my boyfriend. Now please leave my property." Alana turned and walked away from Blaine, her heart hammering. She went into the house and shut the door behind her.

Blaine stood in the driveway for several minutes, his face wreathed in frustration, then he went and gave the kids a hug and a kiss before sailing off in his stupid blue Miata.

Alana's phone buzzed with Tabitha's latest text. < *Alana, please. I need to talk to you. I'm driving up tomorrow. I'll be there at about 9:00. I hope that even if you won't text me, you'll let me borrow a bed.* >

It was Thursday afternoon. The day before the open house.

How had this gotten so serious that it warranted a personal intervention?

< *You always have a bed in my home* > Alana texted back. She considered telling Tabitha that she was fine, that Tabitha didn't need to drive up, but suddenly she felt she wanted to see her friend, no matter what kind of dressing-down she was about to receive.

The Facebook chatter about the open house had turned ominous, with friends and neighbors embroiled in caustic exchanges regarding the desirability of the mine and the behavior of Mountain Magnesium and the city, and Maude dropping sinister suggestions into the mix regarding what Mountain Magnesium was really up to. Was Maude just blowing smoke, or did she know something? Did she know about Thad Kepper? Or was there something else? What had Nate been alluding to? Comments were also popping up about the necessity and affordability of the street renewal project. Lots of people wondered why Silver Peak was spending millions of dollars to "beautify" the city. They evidently didn't know that the project was really about replacing the pipes rotting beneath the street.

She was about to close her Facebook feed when Fiona added a new photo—a photo of her and Nate, smiling and standing arm in arm in a fancy hotel bar in Kelowna that Alana recognized. "Good times with good friends," read the caption. *Nate and Fiona.* Was going to an out-of-town hotel for drinks with Fiona part of Nate's "investigation" into Mountain Magnesium? Somehow she doubted it.

Suddenly Alana was too exhausted to care. The people of Silver Peak could go screw themselves. She would facilitate the open house tomorrow, collect her paycheck, hope the bank approved her mortgage increase, endure the humiliation of losing the bet with Blaine, and call it a day. She didn't care.

She went to bed thinking of Nate's lips on hers, his hands on her hips, pulling her against him, the burning intensity of his kiss. No amount of reminding herself that he was a potentially unstable musician who had no obvious ability to contribute to a household, not to mention a self-confessed womanizer, could sway her from the fact that she wanted him, plain and simple.

She dreamed about Nate riding to the open house on his Vespa to save her—from what she wasn't sure. Ryan? Maude? Blaine? Tabitha? Margaret and John? Mountain Magnesium?

Most likely she was dreaming about him saving her from herself.

But Nate would not, and could not, save her.

At midday, Maude made her final calls via email, Facebook and Twitter. She urged all those who cared about the future of Silver Peak to come to the open house and make it clear that a mine in the watershed that would decimate Mur Marsh was absolutely unacceptable. No doubt the environmental phone trees were all activated and the placards would be lined up and ready to go. Alana just hoped Maude didn't intend to bring in guitars, violins, and drummers. It was always hard to speak over music.

Alana met with Len and Curtis to do the final run-through with regard to how they should answer questions at the open house, picked up the open house materials from the printer, made some final changes to her speaking notes, scoured the company files once again for evidence of wrongdoing, and waited for the bank to call indicating her mortgage had been approved. The sickish feeling that had been building all week sat heavy in her stomach. Although it was her job, and she had done over a hundred of them, she hated facilitating public events. And with the degree of controversy associated with the mine and the fact that she was no longer on the comfortable side of environmental righteousness, this one would be worse than usual. Way worse. However, her stomach was no more upset than it would normally be. A sign that everything would be okay? Or a sign that she had completely dissociated herself from reality?

Nate's piano still occupied the Mountain Magnesium offices. She sat at it for a few minutes before leaving to get the kids, her fingers brushing the keys. She wanted to listen to Nate play again, to be wrapped in his music. She pictured the piano in her farmhouse, sleek and shiny against the burnished old wood and dusty air, the music spilling out into the garden while she knelt in the soil nurturing seedlings.

The bank called as she was picking up Katie and Duncan. Her papers were approved and ready.

She drove to the bank slowly. She could still back out. She could still quit her job and sell the farm and move into a small townhouse. She parked and then turned and stared back at Katie and Duncan in the back seat. They had both been silent and withdrawn for the last few days. She and Blaine had scheduled a family meeting for Saturday to break the news to the kids that Blaine was moving to Vancouver for a year or so, but it was as if the kids had sensed something was afoot.

"Hey guys, what do you think about selling North Star and buying one of those townhouses down by where Jackson lives? I could quit my job and we could spend more time together."

"What about the chickens?" Duncan said. Hatching day, which happened to be on Saturday, had been circled on the calendar on the fridge in red felt pen for two weeks.

"We would have to give them away," Alana said.

"And the bunnies," Katie chimed in.

"No bunnies," Alana said. "We were going to have to eat them anyway, Katie, remember? We could get a cat."

Big teardrops had emerged from Duncan's eyes and started to course down his face. "I really wanted the chickens," he whispered.

"I know, love. But chickens can be messy, and a lot of work, and they don't stay cute for very long. They become big stinky birds."

"You said they'd be like pets," Duncan said.

"Well, they would, but all pets are work. That's why Daddy doesn't like them much."

"But Daddy doesn't live with us anymore."

"I know." Alana realized that she was still clutching the steering wheel with sweaty hands. A few environmentalists she recognized passed by on the sidewalk and pointedly ignored her.

"I don't want to move," Katie said. "I just finished building my caterpillar house."

"Do you think that if we got rid of the chickens Daddy would come back and live with us?" Duncan asked tremulously.

"No, honey, you know Daddy loves you very much. It's just me that he doesn't love anymore."

"No, he loves that mean woman!" Katie declared.

"Is she mean?" Alana said. She hadn't known the kids considered Heather mean.

"She's just 'noying. She asks dumb questions or pretends we're not there," Duncan said. "And sometimes she looks mean around the eyes. And she killed Goldie last summer."

"I don't think she intended to kill him. Goldfish aren't the most hardy of creatures."

"She said he stunk," Duncan said.

"Well, thinking something stinks isn't necessarily evidence of murder. If I sold the farm, everything might just be easier."

"I don't want to move!" Katie yelled.

"Why can't you talk really nicely to Daddy and ask him to move back in?" Duncan said. "Ben says daddies leave because mommies aren't very nice to them. Heather just 'grees with everything Daddy says."

"Daddy isn't coming back, guys. It's just going to be me. Sorry. It doesn't matter how nice I am."

She got out of the SUV and slammed the rusty old door behind her. "Because I'm not twenty-six and I don't want to be an actress in Vancouver, which is where your stupid dad is moving," she said under her breath to the closed window that occupied the space between the kids and her. "It's just going to be me."

She could do this on her own. She *would* do this on her own.

Alana helped Katie and Duncan out of the SUV and went in and signed the papers. Her mind was filled with images of Ryan stalking her for the rest of her days as she pushed her shopping cart alone down Hastings after having gone bankrupt and been forced out of town by the placard-waving environmentalists and ATV-driving developers. But Ryan wasn't lurking outside the bank when she emerged, so she risked dashing over to the post office to collect her mail.

A thick white envelope from the Ministry of Energy and Mines was crammed in her small box. She smoothed it out and opened it to find the documents she had requested a few weeks ago when she was still on the right side of the environment. She flipped through them quickly and saw the original claim filed for the mine and some other fairly useless administrative records, including all the other claims in the area. She tucked the package into her purse.

Jonah was hoeing one of the garden beds when she arrived home. He approached as she got out of the SUV.

"I couldn't find Larry anywhere," he said. "I'll try to find someone else, but it'll be more expensive."

She nodded. What choice did she have? The trees had grown wild and unpruned for more than a decade, and now all the fruit grew at the very top of the tree, unreachable even with a ladder, and it attracted bears in hordes in the fall. "Can you start coming three days a week? I really want to plant enough to try to turn a profit this year," she said.

Jonah leaned on the hoe and wiped his forehead with his sleeve. "I'm not sure. I've been meaning to talk to you about that. I'm not sure if I can keep coming. I have a potential other line of business that I've been thinking of getting into. I have to tell the person yes or no tonight, so I'll let you know."

Alana drew back, hurt. She had counted on Jonah to be part of this farm enterprise. Had Zander snapped Jonah up too? Was Zander engaged in some sort of vendetta against her for failing to protect the sustainability plan?

"Oh. Okay. I see. That's fine. It's just that I just bought a portion of Rick's property, so I have a lot of land to get under production. Do you know anyone else that would be interested?"

Jonah leaned on the hoe. "You bought Rick Wyatt's land? I thought Ryan Roberts was buying that."

Alana wondered if she saw fear for her safety in Jonah's eyes, but she forced her voice to be light. "Well, he didn't. I did. Just half of it. But I'm hoping to buy the other half if I can start growing enough to make money. Like I said, if you know anyone at the nursery interested in a side job, that would be great."

She went into the house and poured a large glass of wine and threw some noodles on the stove for the kids. One glass of wine before the open house wouldn't hurt. She should be celebrating the purchase of Rick's land.

While the noodles cooked, she flipped through her work files on her laptop. If she could find the form transferring the mine property from Larry Lund to Mountain Magnesium, she might find a phone number or forwarding address for Larry. She pulled up the file and scanned the claim transfer form. Larry's address was listed as a Silver Peak post box; perhaps she could send him a note.

Then her eyes fell on the signatures at the bottom. The loops in the L's in Larry Lund were large and swooping and the signature largely illegible. She stared at the signature for a few seconds and then reached into her purse to withdraw the original claim form that had come in the mail that day. Larry Lund's name was signed at the bottom in smaller, tighter script with every letter clearly readable. She looked back and forth between the two signatures several times. Even with Larry's potential drinking and drug habits, which might influence his signature, the difference between the two signatures was a little disconcerting.

"Mom!" Duncan yelled, shattering her racing thoughts. "The water is boiling over on the stove."

Alana ran to the kitchen and turned down the burner, then glanced at the time. It was already 5:30. She had to feed the kids, get them to Blaine's, and get down to the hall where the open house was being held.

CHAPTER TWENTY-TWO

Tricks

The venue buzzed with a barricade of protesters holding signs and sitting in front of the front door. She drove past slowly, her hands slick with sweat, parked several blocks away, and sat in the SUV trying to pull herself together. She had several boxes and flipcharts to carry in, and she didn't imagine the bearded and dreadlocked protesters were going to offer any assistance, which meant she'd have to make several trips and endure whatever disapproval they wanted to dispense.

Maybe Blaine had been right. Maybe she couldn't do this. She needed Suzanne for protection, but there was no way Suzanne would come to a meeting like this.

A man knocked on the window, and she let out a scream before she realized it was Len, wearing an affable smile and a white and navy striped golf shirt. "We're here to help if you need us to carry stuff in for you," he said.

She nodded dumbly and got out. Both men had ditched their usual grimy gear; they wore clean blue jeans and pressed shirts and had even combed their hair. They also smelled strongly of beer, but she was nevertheless almost faint with relief to see them.

She distributed the banker's boxes and flipchart paper, locked the vehicle, and followed them across the street, carrying the stack of handouts for the event. At least there had been no complaints from the Mountain Magnesium board regarding the fact that she was using printed materials.

The patchouli-scented protesters in the front gave way to people she recognized from town in the second row, and a flush of shame crept up her neck as she weaved her way through them behind Len and Curtis. Most of the people she knew averted their eyes when she passed, but quiet catcalls of "for shame" followed them into the building. Maude was conspicuously absent.

Once inside, Alana set up her materials, maps, and flipcharts with trembling hands while Len and Curtis held off the hordes.

They opened the doors just before seven, and the protesters started to file in, keyed up and hostile-looking. Some took seats while others gathered in clusters, darting dark looks her direction as they made gratingly hearty conversation among themselves. It took all of Alana's willpower not to duck into the hallway and hide. If she had felt like an outsider in Silver Peak before, now she felt like a complete pariah.

She stood at the front, trying to keep a dazed smile on her face. Mountain Magnesium needed and wanted to hear from these people. Maybe she could convince some of them to support the mine. If not, she at least needed to understand their concerns, although she feared she already knew them—from the perspective of environmentalists, watersheds, wetlands, and mines, no matter how benign, did not mix. At least, they hadn't mixed or coexisted very successfully in the past. A lot of mines in BC had a crappy track record, and the Condor Mine tailings pond rupture last summer hadn't helped. So really, why should the enviros trust mining companies? *She* didn't trust mining companies, and she worked for one. She should probably be totally opposed to the mine too, but right now, as Len and Curtis engaged in some banter next to her regarding the Stanley Cup playoffs, mining companies, or at least their employees, seemed a heck of a lot more friendly than the environmentalists.

Alana tried to imagine herself kibitzing with the environmentalists about her farm plans and environmental ways. She tried to imagine herself belonging in their expansive righteousness. But she never really had. She saw this now, with alarming clarity. No matter how much she'd styled herself as an environmentalist and gone to rallies, recycled, and wore all-natural fibers, she had always failed in some internal environmental way.

Some of the people who had dropped off resumes the week before started to arrive, and she offered them a friendly smile, but although some returned her greetings, they, too, seemed excessively grim.

Ryan Roberts marched into the room and took a seat in the front row, his eyes slitty and his movements abrupt and dangerous.

By the time Lou arrived in his funny little beret and came and squeezed her arm with a smile, she almost wanted to hug him, just for not hating her. It was 7:05, almost time to call the meeting to order, and yet Maude still had not arrived. What was Maude doing?

Lou joined Len and Curtis at the table at the front, and she wanted to ask him about Larry's signature on the mine transfer documents, but there was no time. The pitch of the conversation in the room had risen, and people had started throwing her pointed looks. Owen from the *Silver Peak News* and Ramona from the *Silver Peak Scoop* had arrived with their black cameras slung around their necks. Alana had to get the meeting going.

Almost numb with fear, she raised her voice and announced that the meeting would start in one minute and that everyone should take a seat. A shuffle of bodies in the room commenced, but nobody seemed hurried, conversations continued, and a few people rewarded her with long, disdainful glares as if she were in the wrong room disrupting a party, not trying to start a meeting for which they had apparently all turned up. The cloying scent of patchouli permeated the building, making her want to throw open the hall windows and lean out into the rays of the setting sun.

Her speaking notes were curled and damp by the time everyone was seated, and she started talking with a shaky voice about the important potential economic contribution of the mine to the Silver Peak economy and wanting the operation to be a collaborative affair with lots of buy-in and participation from community members. She stressed that the mine was not a done deal, and that the open house was an opportunity for community members to voice their concerns, so that Mountain Magnesium would have a chance to address them.

Whispers and chatter floated up to the front as she spoke. Some of the protesters had remained outside, and a dissonant drum beat and singing could be heard through the closed hall doors. Several of the protesters who had come inside had nevertheless refused to sit; they lined the back wall still wearing or holding their placards. Alana tried not to let them shake her concentration as she reviewed highlights from the proposal, introduced Lou, Len, and Curtis, and opened the floor to questions and comments, indicating that there would also be the opportunity after the questions for people to circulate to five stations open house style and leave their thoughts on Post-it notes.

At least ten people immediately sprang to their feet and formed a line behind the speaker's microphone. Rick sidled into the room at the back and gave her two thumbs up, which was pretty much the opposite of true right now.

Tom LeDrew reached the microphone first. He withdrew a sheaf of white papers from his coat pocket, and Alana nodded at him to proceed.

"I'm here representing the Mountain Stewardship Society," he said. "We would like to talk about community watersheds and the vital nature of water and watersheds for humans and other species, and the habitual disregard of water and water rights by corporate interests, especially the mining industry, around the world..."

The environmental segment of the room stomped their feet and pounded their hands together in approval. Tom went on and on, describing the travesties that had occurred in other communities and other countries as a result of mining. Then he went into great depth regarding the water cycle and the role of functioning watersheds. The environmental sector thundered their support each time he paused.

Other people—people whom Alana guessed might be on the side of the mine—started to look pained, and demands of "get on with it" started to echo around the room. Alana's lips felt frozen. She should interrupt and put a time limit on the speakers. Tom hadn't even asked a question yet. But stopping him would court censure from around the room. He'd already droned on for almost eighteen minutes. Lou was flipping her the squinty eye and tapping his fingers on the table, and Len and Curtis had already tuned out, probably wishing they were still at the bar downing tequila shooters... or maybe that was just where *she* wanted to be right now. Actually, she wanted to be anywhere but in the center of an environmental filibuster.

She stood and held up her hand. "Sorry, Tom, I'm going to have to interrupt." Boos and applause erupted around the room. "I'm afraid we're going to have to put a three-minute limit on speakers, and we would really appreciate it if you ask a question. There are obviously lots of people who want to speak, and we need to give everyone a chance to be heard."

The pitch of chatter and boos rose and cries of "you don't want to hear from us, eh?" came from the audience, while other folks turned around and snapped something back at them. The chanters and drummers outside, as if on cue, started in on some folk-style version of Twisted Sister's "We're Not Gonna Take It."

"We do want to hear from you. But we want to hear from *everyone*," she said over the melee, the microphone squealing in argument. "Do you have a question, Tom?"

"Yeah, sure. How long do you corporate interests think you can continue controlling the global agenda and destroying communities?"

Loud hoots of approval followed.

Alana flicked her eyes to Lou, but he seemed to have no interest in responding to the question.

"I'm sorry you feel that way, Tom," Alana said. "But as far as corporate interests go, Mountain Magnesium is pretty small in nature and is based in the community of Silver Peak. They have a local board member and local employees, and they are hoping to work with the community as much as possible."

"Perhaps you're not aware of the corporate connections of Mountain Magnesium's board members," Tom replied. "We just happen to have a little handout that summarizes them. I think everyone will find it very educational. I know you'd like to couch this as an artisan mine, but the track records of some of your board members make all your fancy little promises seem pretty empty. 'Cause you know, Jim Price and Lawrence Sutherland are to be commended for the environmental devastation at the Condor mine."

Several of the environmental sector supporters sprang to their feet in rows and started distributing pieces of paper to the audience. A few people waved them away, but others took the paper.

Alana gripped the edges of the podium. Jim Price and Lawrence Sutherland had connections to the Condor mine? Why hadn't she thought to research the backgrounds of the board members? She was an idiot. "Thanks for your thoughts, Tom. Can we give the next speaker the opportunity to speak now?"

Tom gave her a salute, then stepped away from the microphone and went to stand at the back of the speakers' line.

The next two speakers said much the same thing as Tom, with varying degrees of eloquence. They both ignored her when she held up a three-minute-warning sign, continuing amid clapping and foot stomping, until at the five-minute mark, she stood and requested them to finish up and ask their question.

Sharon was up as the fourth speaker, and as she unfolded a thick wad of speaking notes, Ryan managed to edge his way to the microphone in front of her. "These guys have had their turn. I have a question, a really important question, a question I think all of you would like to hear if you'll just give me a minute." The threat and innuendo in his voice caused the room to quiet down suddenly, except for the outside musicians, who kept belting their out-of-tune voices into the sky.

"How is it," Ryan said, "that the construction contract for the processing facility went to a company from Kelowna that just so happens to be run by the son of our city CAO, when there are plenty of local construction firms who would do a great job? Can someone just explain that to me?"

Alana was certain the color had entirely vanished from her face. She had no idea why Kepper had been selected. She turned to Lou. "I think Lou would be the best person to answer that maybe. It was before my time."

Lou shrugged, a hint of frustration that she didn't know how to answer the question in the set of his lips. "Thad offered the best price and has experience with building larger industrial operations. While we appreciate that there are many great construction companies in town, the bid process was fair, and the most appropriate company was selected."

A text flashed up on Alana's phone on the podium. < *Duncan having breakdown. Did you tell him Heather and I are moving? You were supposed to wait. Not impressed. Are you almost done?* >

"And you don't think it's funny that the city council just voted to support the mine on the advice of a CAO whose son stands to benefit significantly from the approval?"

Ryan had the attention of everyone in the room, and the song outside had subsided, leaving the hall deathly silent, save for the crackle of the PA system.

Lou had resumed his finger tapping. He was apparently uninterested in responding to the question.

Alana turned back to her own microphone. "I'm sure the bid process was fair, Ryan, and that the documentation associated with it can be made available to you. As you know, the CAO doesn't have a vote on council, so he really doesn't influence the outcomes of council votes that much. Can you let Sharon speak? She was the next in line."

Ryan threw up his hands. "You know what they say—where there's smoke, there's fire. But I guess you know a little bit about that, Alana, having earned your high-paying job the old-fashioned way, so you can screw everyone else in town out of business deals."

Alana recoiled as if she had been struck. Heads had swiveled from Ryan to her, and a few sniggers rippled across the audience, people no doubt having heard the rumors about her and Nate and seen the photo of Nate and Fiona on Facebook. Alana forced her voice to be steady and frosty. "I don't know what you're talking about, and I don't think that's very appropriate. Sharon, you're up."

Sharon fixed her eyes on Alana and spoke quietly. "Well, I think we all have to be prepared that there are consequences to our actions. And we all know that corporations are not very good at foreseeing or accepting the consequences to their actions, which is why watersheds must be sacrosanct."

"The whole province is a watershed, lady," a voice interrupted. A man had risen to his feet in the front row. "Look, I just want a job. I came so I could ask questions on how and when to apply. Do I really have to sit through all this crap?"

Panic had fractured Alana's thoughts. She needed to get control. She should cut the plenary off, get people circulating to the stations, and hopefully bring the tension down, then reconvene the group for questions later. She opened her mouth to suggest this when the hall door was flung open with a bang. Maude stood silhouetted in the broad entryway, the pounding of drums heralding her arrival.

Larry Lund lingered, almost cowering, behind her, wearing his old and dirty green Gore-Tex jacket and a large framed backpack.

Maude swept into the room, her grey hair windblown and askew, with an air of triumph. Larry clutched his hands together and wrung them, murmuring unintelligibly as he walked, his eyes red-rimmed and bloodshot.

The sea of environmentalists parted to let them through, but instead of proceeding to the speakers' microphone, Maude made her way directly to the front of the room.

"I have Larry," she said to Lou in a low, even voice.

Alana flicked her eyes to Larry. Larry did not appear, at least on initial inspection, to be wearing a placard, or a bomb. Maude's meaning was not immediately obvious, at least to Alana.

As if on cue, the musicians outside launched into "Big Yellow Taxi" with additional, and probably unnecessary, percussion.

"Adjourn this meeting and withdraw your proposal, or I'm going to blow your company sky-high," Maude said in the same low voice.

Lou rose from the table and grabbed the microphone. "We're going to take a ten-minute break. Feel free to look at the maps, ask Curtis and Len here some questions, and have a cookie and some coffee. We'll be right back."

Loud chatter and a rising sea of bodies erupted through the room. Lou pointed at a smaller room that adjoined the hall and eyeballed Alana and Maude. "Everyone except Curtis and Len, in that room right now."

"What is the meaning of this?" Lou demanded once Maude, Larry, and Alana occupied the room and the door had been shut. The hubbub outside had become borderline pandemonium, and Alana feared for Len's and Curtis's lives. Lou's face bristled with fury and indignation at Maude, but beneath his bluster, his eyes had a furtive shiftiness. For Lou to call the meeting to such an abrupt break, Maude had to have something.

Larry found a chair and plunked himself heavily into it. Even from ten feet, Alana could smell the stench of booze and pot coming from him.

"I know Larry didn't transfer ownership of the mineral claim to Mountain Magnesium. I also know that you drove him to Kelowna, hooked him up with a dealer, and gave him a wad of cash, hoping he'd never come back to Silver Peak," Maude declared.

"That is a complete fabrication," Lou said. "We have a signed transfer document on file, don't we, Alana?"

"We do," Alana said slowly. "Did Larry tell you that he didn't transfer the ownership, Maude?"

"As if you could rely on the statement of a man who is clearly an addict and not even close to sober," Lou said. "Look at him." Larry had tilted over to the side in the chair and was resting his backpack and head on the stack of chairs next to him.

"Thanks to you," Maude said. "Larry was pretty much clean until you dropped him off right in the middle of the world he had left."

"That's preposterous. This man has a history of drug and alcohol abuse. And what does 'pretty much clean' mean? He couldn't wait to turn over his claim in exchange for cash. You have absolutely no evidence, and you know it. If you did, you would have gone to the police."

Except that the signatures didn't really match, Alana thought. If Larry *had* been high when he signed the first one, or the second one, or both, he might not be able to sign the same way. Her stomach turned itself into a tighter pretzel knot and the burnished old mahogany floor planks of the hall seemed like they were tilting under her feet. She should say something. But she was trying to decide which person in the room scared her the most. The noise outside the room had spiked, and she wondered if Len and Curtis were being carted off to the guillotine. She needed some air.

Her cell phone rang. It was Blaine. Maude and Lou's argument had devolved into a loud taunting contest as they circled each other like enraged vultures. Alana turned her ringer to vibrate.

"I have to take a leak," Larry murmured.

"I'm taking Larry to the washroom," Alana said loudly to Maude and Lou, who both paused only momentarily to regard her through slitty eyes. Lou looked like he was about to protest. "And I need to check on Len and Curtis," she announced.

She walked over to Larry. "Come on, Larry. I'll show you to the washroom."

Larry rose heavily and shuffled beside her out the door into the hall. Pandemonium reigned. People stood in noisy clumps talking at each other in loud voices. A couple of the drummers had come inside and pounded furiously on their instruments in the corner, so anyone that wanted to be heard had to yell. The environmental faction and the development faction appeared to have chosen opposite sides of the room and darted suspicious and angry looks over their shoulders at the other group while they gesticulated to their own group members. Curtis stood scowling with his arms folded across his chest at the front of the room, his rather large pocketknife hanging ominously from his belt. Len occupied a flipchart and seemed to be trying vainly to explain something to a small cluster of people. Children ran back and forth among the groups, playing tag. What parents would bring their children to a potential lynching?

Alana escorted Larry to the one room bathroom just off the hall, hoping not to be seen. All of the exits to the hall were blocked by swarming clusters of people; she couldn't sneak out even if she wanted to. But CEOs didn't just slip out like criminals. They stood and faced whatever music they had coming. That's what they got paid for.

A life of crime seemed more and more appealing by the minute. Of course, if what Maude was saying was correct, maybe being a CEO and a criminal were not that far apart.

She closed the bathroom door behind Larry and surveyed the room. Her eyes fell on Len's flipchart. It was filled with looping beautiful script—looping script that very much resembled Larry's signature on the mine transfer papers.

Her dinner had turned to acid in her stomach and throat.

She approached the flipchart warily, fighting her way through the horde of arguing bodies to Len's side.

She pulled on his sleeve. "I need to talk to you," she murmured.

He turned quizzically, then capped his pen and excused himself from the people who had gathered around the flipchart. Her eyes raked the room. There was no place to go. She strode off, pushing her way through the crowd back to the bathroom, where she knocked loudly.

"Larry, it's Alana. Are you done? Can we come in?"

There was no answer, at least not one that she could hear over the noise.

"The old souse is probably passed out in there," Len said with a weak smile. His normally ruddy complexion seemed a bit paler than usual and his smile less certain.

She knocked again and repeated herself before opening the door a crack and calling into the bathroom. "Larry! Are you okay?"

When he didn't answer, she pushed the door open and yanked Len inside, shutting the door firmly behind her.

Larry lay on the floor in the corner of the bathroom, his head on his pack. She raced over to him. His eyes were closed, but his chest rose and fell, and when she finally worked up the nerve to grasp his wrist, she found that he had a solid pulse.

She turned and looked at Len helplessly.

"He's just sleeping," Len said, almost defensively, with that same funny smile he had given her a few minutes before.

She regarded the man she had come to consider a potential friend, or at least ally, with his tanned arms and combed-back swoop of white hair. He was old enough to be her father, and she was almost scared of him too. Why was she so damn scared of everyone?

"Did you sign the mine transfer papers?" she said.

Len's affable smile vanished and was replaced by a stony look. "I don't know what you're talking about."

"The papers that transfer ownership of the claim from Larry to Mountain Magnesium. Maude claims Larry never signed them, and the signature doesn't match Larry's on the original claim documents."

Len gestured at Larry. "You think that old coot even knows his own signature? He was happier than a pig in shit to receive the cash we offered him for the mine. Couldn't sign fast enough. Caught a ride to Kelowna with Curtis and me when we went to pick up supplies. Going to celebrate, he claimed. He wasn't even going to develop the mine. He was using his claim as a legitimate means to squat on the property and pan for gold in the creek."

Alana looked from Len's indignant and angry face to Larry's disheveled and moderately grimy form. "Maude isn't going to let this go," she said.

"That old bat's as crazy as Larry is."

"And if she forces the issue and requires a signature analysis? Is that signature going to hold up in court?"

Len crossed his arms over his chest again. "Absolutely."

"You're sure of that?"

"Look, we're the good guys here. We're creating jobs. Larry was living on that property like he owned it, which isn't the intent of mining claims."

"What about Kepper?"

"Don't buy that crap of Roberts. Roberts is a slimeball. Kepper won the bid fair and square and is planning to move here."

The hubbub in the hall escalated, and Alana realized how her disappearance into the bathroom with both Len and Larry must look. Actually, she had no idea how it looked, but however it looked, it probably wasn't good.

She peeked her head out of the bathroom just in time to see Nate, with his helmet in hand, head down the passageway to the room where Lou and Maude presumably still argued... or where one of them was trying to dispose of the other's body. Nate, who had totally humiliated her. Bastard. Fucking bastard. And still her turncoat heart jumped into furious action at the sight of him.

Fiona had appeared as well and lingered at the back of the room talking to some of the environmental faction, her long blond hair glistening in the setting sun. Alana pictured them riding the Vespa back together, Fiona's arms wrapped tightly around Nate's waist.

"Help Larry back to the other room," she hissed at Len before rushing out of the bathroom after Nate.

When Alana opened the door to the side room, Maude pushed past her. "What have you done with Larry?" Maude demanded.

"He's in the bathroom, sleeping," Alana said. "I asked Len to bring him back here."

"I can't believe you're willing to be part of this." Maude spat the words.

Alana looked past Maude to where Nate and Lou were engaged in a discussion, their heads bent together. "I didn't know anything about any of this. And you don't know for sure that they did anything wrong." She was surprised by how automatically these words emerged from her mouth. She *did* know. She *had* known. Perhaps denial and butt covering were fundamental human instincts.

"Look at you," Maude said. "You've become one of... *them*."

Alana blinked back a rush of tears. "I have not."

Maude craned her head over Alana's shoulder. "Where is he then... Larry?"

Alana turned and marched back down the passageway, expecting to see Len dragging Larry's prostrate form in their direction, but the bathroom door swung open and neither Len nor Curtis were anywhere in sight.

She ran back across the hall to the bathroom, sweat pricking in her armpits and behind her knees. The bathroom was empty.

"Where did Len go with Larry?" she said, barging into the group standing closest to the bathroom.

One of the men shrugged. "Old man Lund, you mean? Saw a man helping him out the exit there. He was in pretty bad shape. Someone needs to take him back to his shack in the woods so he can sleep it off."

"Was it Len who was helping him?"

The man shook his head. "I dunno. I didn't recognize the guy." Alana looked around the circle of people. They all shook their heads or wore blank, bored expressions.

"Look, are you going to get this meeting going again? If not, we're going to head out. You're kind of wasting everyone's time here." Shouts had started to break out among some of the groups, with the environmentalists starting to chant "save our water" while a young man in a toque and plaid hunting jacket yelled something about draft dodgers who grew weed and never had real jobs.

"Yes, I'm sorry. Just hang on, please." She ran to the window and saw Len and Curtis standing at the bottom of the exit stairs, talking. She couldn't see Larry anywhere. She heard Maude swearing a blue streak behind her.

She was about to fling open the exit door when Madeline Geller appeared at her side, shaking her white bob and blinking her big blue eyes as if she had something caught in them. "Alana, what's going on? This meeting is a disaster. You need to call things back to order. There's nobody at any of the stations."

Maude opened the side door and barreled out while Alana tried to give Madeline some facsimile of a smile.

"It's fine, Madeline. Everything's under control. We're calling it back to order in just a couple seconds." She flicked her eyes around the room at the protesters. Did they all know about Larry? Or had Maude kept Larry up her sleeve until she had him? Until she could do the big reveal?

"I was just sitting with Greg Wilson, you know. He runs these kinds of meetings, and he said—"

Nate and Lou emerged from the side room and walked purposefully to the front.

Alana cut Madeline off. "I have to go."

She turned and looked back out the window. Maude, Len, and Curtis were engaged in a heated conversation, with flailing arms and pointed fingers being thrust all over the place.

Alana marched to the front. "We need to restart the meeting," she said to Lou. Whatever Lou had done with the signatures, with the contract with Thad Kepper, it would have to wait until they could bring this meeting to a close. She would reemphasize that it was just an informational meeting, that they wanted to hear what people thought, that nothing was a done deal. Then she would confront Lou.

Lou brushed the air in front of him impatiently. "Yes, we do. But I'm going to run it from here," he said. "Nate has agreed to come back as CEO. I'm sorry Alana, I just don't think it's working out. Nate has alerted me to your relationship with Maude, and in particular your role in spying on my house. I don't think that's behavior befitting a CEO, and it's clear that you're a little out of your element here. Just remember you've signed a nondisclosure agreement. Go home and enjoy your two little children. We'll be in touch about a severance package."

The room felt like it was falling away from her. Was she being *fired*? In the middle of a public meeting? By a man who was telling her to keep her mouth shut, while the man who had kissed her so passionately just a few days ago looked on, and had just *taken* her job from her?

Nate's face seemed pale, and his eyes opened wider than usual as he regarded her. He dipped his chin almost imperceptibly when she glanced at him as if he was nodding, encouraging her. She wanted to smack him.

"So if you don't mind gathering your stuff, and leaving, we're going to announce the personnel change and reschedule the meeting. Nate says Greg Wilson and Fiona Granger have some ideas about how to break the group up more to foster discussion and keep the tension down. He's going to bring them in to team facilitate."

"Of course they do," Alana said. "I'm sure Greg Wilson is going to save the world." She snatched up her stack of file folders from the head table. She would just abandon all her facilitation supplies; she wouldn't be facilitating anymore. Maybe Greg and Fiona could use them to run their perfect little meeting in which everyone would hold hands and learn to drum together.

Then she turned and fought her way through the crowd, past the drummers, and out the front door, trying to prevent her lower lip from trembling out of control.

CHAPTER TWENTY-THREE

Goats and Babies

Outside the atmosphere was not much different. Drummers still pounded away and protesters milled up and down the street wearing their placards. A set of scruffy, dreadlocked protesters leaned up against Alana's SUV, drinking beers and passing around a joint.

How was she going to get out of here? After everything, pushing her way through a group of drunk, high hairbags to get to the SUV was just too much. Clearly her usual charitable disposition toward environmentalists had been eroded by the night's events. The tears she'd been holding inside sprang to her eyes.

A spew of diesel fumes hit her nose and the circus of protesters parted as an ATV tore up the street.

Rick stopped in front of Alana. "Need a ride somewhere?" he said.

She was pretty sure he was supposed to be wearing a helmet, and should be offering her one, and that it was illegal to drive an ATV on city streets, but she got on behind him and he tore off into the darkening night, leaving the hall, the protesters, and Nate, Lou, and Maude behind.

A few blocks away, Rick pulled into the city park parking lot, got off the ATV, and withdrew something from his pocket.

"Fireball?" he said, holding out a silver flask. "You look like you could use some."

Whiskey. She *could* use some, she decided. She took the flask, held it to her lips, and ignored the burning as she gulped some of the spicy alcohol down. She felt better almost immediately, and took another large swig.

"'Atta girl," crowed Rick. She wondered how much he had consumed. She didn't care. Apparently she wasn't above drinking in the city park like a teenager.

She let the numbness and warmth of the alcohol settle over her. She was unemployed. She didn't have to worry about the stupid mine anymore. It wasn't her problem.

She looked at Rick. She had just signed a mortgage to buy his property, and she could no longer afford it, even remotely.

She tipped the flask to her lips and took another generous guzzle.

"Whoa," Rick said, looking a little alarmed. "Just remember that stuff is strong. Pace yourself. That was quite the town hall meeting."

She burst into tears.

Rick's eyes went from alarmed to outright buggy. "It's okay. You can have more. Just take however much you want. You look like you can hold your alcohol."

Alana thrust the flask back at Rick and wiped her eyes furiously with her sleeve. "I'm fine. Really. Fine. I just got fired." She started to laugh at the absurdness of it, and the tears on her face combined with snot from her nose and she turned away and lifted her shirt to try to clean up the mess. "I've never been fired before. Never even come close to being fired. I usually overdo every job, so this is a bit new. I'm fine." Her skin burned where the tears and snot had covered it and she was sure her face was a mess of smeared makeup and blotchy skin.

"Fired?" Rick said. "Pfft. You don't want to work for that pompous asshole Steeves anyway. Here, have another drink." He proffered the flask again.

Alana shook her head. The alcohol was already hitting her. "Rick, if I'm fired I can't afford your property. I can't even afford my own. I've messed everything up."

Her phone buzzed. A text from Tabitha. < *I've let myself in. Have to get Mom and Dad from airport early tomorrow morning, so waiting up to talk with you. Need to come up with some options.* >

Alana's stomach fluttered. What was Tabitha talking about? The Greenes were arriving home tomorrow. Were they planning an environmental intervention or something?

The magnitude of her screw-up piled into her like a band of placard-carrying granola crunchers. She had completely alienated her two best clients in Silver Peak—the city and the Regional Environmental Board. She would never work for them again. She had signed a mortgage for a property she couldn't afford and managed to piss off most of the people in Silver Peak, including the developers. She had potentially been involved in criminal dealings at Mountain Magnesium. Blaine was mad at her. Tabitha was disappointed in her, and worse, was waiting in her house for her. She was obviously not appealing to men, and she made seriously bad choices in terms of whom she was attracted to. And she was going to lose North Star Farm, for sure. N.S.F. Non-sufficient fucking ability.

"Well, you could apply for the CAO job at the city. I understand that job has just come up. Or the planner job. You worked for the city before, right? You do the same kind of thing..." Rick trailed off.

"What? What do you mean?"

"Well, I thought you did the same kind of thing."

"No. Why is the CAO job available? Did Stewart get fired?"

"He retired. Didn't you hear? Rumor has it he bought a huge waterfront spread up north by Lincoln Lake." Rick shook his head. "I had no idea CAOs made that much money."

Alana was silent for a few seconds, feeling the waves of whiskey, Stewart's reference to mutual benefit, and Zander's strange message regarding the spending habits of people at City Hall wash over her. "They don't, Rick. Take me back to the meeting," she said, taking one last gulp of the Fireball.

"What? Why would you want to go back to that gong show?"

"Just take me back. Please."

Rick shrugged and got on the ATV, turned around, and sped back in the direction of the hall. Alana jumped off just as he came to a stop a half a block from the hall; she almost fell on her butt. The whiskey was making the road rise and fall a little, and she tried to keep her stride straight as she headed back into the hall.

The drummers were packing up and the front stoop was a mass of swarming people. Lou and Nate, the asshole turncoat, had adjourned the meeting and stood at the front talking to Fiona and a short balding man. The hall was still fairly full as people milled about, putting on jackets and folding chairs.

Alana stepped up to the speaker microphone and flicked it on. Suddenly she was angry—outright livid, actually. N.S.F. It should stand for non-sufficient faith in humanity to find its way out of this environmental rat hole.

"Hey, everyone! I'm back!" She could hear the slippery, not quite yet slurry, tone in her voice as it echoed over the PA system. "As you've no doubt heard, I no longer work for Mountain Magnesium. I just wanted to say a few things. First of all, to all you so-called environmentalists. I just want you to know that your standards are absolutely unreasonable. Maybe a mine in a watershed is wrong, but maybe it isn't. There are ways that mining could be done right, and we do need jobs here in Silver Peak. It would be really nice if you could come to the table for once and discuss things in a reasonable manner. And shower more often, even just three times a week, and remember that not everyone likes drumming." She thrust her arm out to the right to emphasize her point, staggered a bit, and caught herself on the microphone stand. "And you," she said, pointing at Ryan, "are acting like a bully. Don't give me your poor developer routine. I've seen your house. All you're doing is gobbling up the last remaining bits of farm-land in Silver Peak when you could be making this community better and more sustainable by fixing up old houses, building green, and tak-ing lower profit margins. It's really too bad nobody could see past their differences to talk about this in a meaningful way." The room had started to spin a little and she clasped another hand on the microphone for support. "Anyway, that's all moot, because you should know that I don't think everything at Mountain Magnesium is on the up and up."

Until this point, Nate and Lou had been watching her speech with perplexed expressions. However, this statement launched them into action. Nate made a beeline straight for her, his face grim, while Lou cast about for the plug to the PA system, which he pulled just as she said, "You should all be asking questions about Stewart Kepper and Larry Lund" and the last few words were drowned out in the boister-ous chatter from outside.

Nate leaned his face close to hers. "Please stop talking," he whis-pered into her ear. "Please." Nate caught her firmly beneath the arm and started guiding her toward the front door, his other arm around her back.

She tried to shake him off. "Why? So you can be big CEO guy with Fiona the amazing facilitator? Let go of me," she said.

"No. Please, Alana. Trust me. I've got this under control. Just come outside with me for a minute," he murmured into her ear, curving his arm more tightly around her waist. The crowd parted to let them through, and she could see an array of bamboozled smiles—the kind that wedding guests generally sported when Uncle Vince got into the rye and started telling off-color reminiscences about the bride.

As drunk and humiliated and furious as she was with him, his closeness was intoxicating. Then again, she was intoxicated, so proba-bly anyone's closeness would be intoxicating, except Ryan's, as his face was all red and he looked like he wanted to rip her to shreds. Evidently he didn't appreciate the Uncle Vince routine.

"I guess I should have just toilet papered your scooter instead," she said.

"Yes, that would have been preferable. How about I come and park it in your driveway, then you can triple paper it?"

"That would be wasting toilet paper," she said automatically. She flinched away from him. "Let go of me. They deserve to know what your dad is doing."

Nate relaxed his hold, and Alana made as if to spin and return to the microphone.

"Don't," Nate said, catching her arm again and pulling her into the long empty coat closet, his voice angry now and his perfect turquoise eyes slightly unhinged. "Let me handle this. You don't belong here."

"I know about Larry and Stewart," she hissed.

Edward Walters materialized in front of them, his deeply tanned face creased in a frown, his hulking form blocking the hallway as he leaned into the coat closet. "I heard what you said in there, young lady. I just want you to know we won't tolerate that kind of unsubstantiated finger-pointing around here. Go home or you'll never work for the city again." He had leaned in really close to her face and jabbed the air with his own finger while he spoke.

Alana bit back the tears that accompanied her sudden clutch of fear. She had heard from city staff that the mayor could be scary too, but she had never experienced it before. Bile gathered in her throat and the room began to swim a little. She was going to throw up.

"Screw you both," she said, pushing away from Nate. She squeezed under Edward's arm and raced out of the hall, her eyes burning. The street remained filled with people, but Rick's ATV was parked down the road and Rick stood next to it, his arms crossed.

Rick surveyed her with a weary air. "Get on," he said. "I'll take you home."

Her stomach calmed a bit as they drove through the cool night, and she focused on her breathing. In and out. In and out. She had to go get the kids from Blaine's. But how was she going to do that? She was drunk and had no vehicle. She couldn't exactly pick them up on an ATV. Maybe Tabitha could come with her to get the kids.

Rick stopped at the foot of her driveway and she got off. "You okay from here?" he asked.

"Yup," she said. Tabitha's Prius sat silent in her driveway. The kitchen lights glowed in the deepening night.

"Rick, I'm really sorry about your property, but I can't afford it anymore. Is there any way we can undo the deal?"

Rick looked away. "Well you see, after you signed the papers, I went and signed a deal on a little lakeside cottage down at the Pines. If you renege, I'll have to renege, which means I'm going to have to keep your deposit to cover mine. I was going to suggest you swing a deal with Ryan to buy the property from you, but after your little speech in there tonight, I'm not sure if he's going to be interested, and of course he *was* buying it at a lower price. You could always just list it and hope for the best."

"I'm sorry," she mumbled.

She was unemployed. Blaine was unemployed. She had alienated all her potential employers. Her property tax bill was due, and now she had just blown her deposit of twenty thousand bucks, and potentially screwed her neighbor out of a buyer for his land.

Rick shrugged. "Easy come, easy go. Something else will come up. For one of us." He gunned the ATV engine and drove off in a spiral of fumes.

The smell triggered her nausea again and she had to close her eyes and take several deep breaths to dispel it enough to stagger toward the house.

She dialed Blaine's number as she walked down the drive. "How are the kids?" she said breathlessly when he answered.

"Where the hell have you been? I've been calling. Duncan cried himself to sleep."

"I was in a meeting, Blaine. Remember, I have a job too." Or *had* a job, she thought.

"Your voice sounds funny. Are you drunk?"

"No, I'm not fucking drunk."

"Why do you always have to swear so much, Alana?"

"Fuck you, Blaine."

"I don't have to listen to this. How are you going to come and get the kids if you're drunk?"

"You could drop them off."

"Look, it's late. You're obviously in no condition to look after them. They can just stay here for the night. And I've been meaning to talk to you about the custody arrangement. Now that Heather and I are moving, I want to share the kids more equally. And frankly, I don't like the idea of you dating a man with drug problems. I'd rather the kids spent more time with Heather and I. And since you're earning more money than me now, legally I'm entitled to child support."

Alana let this sink in. "You know what, Blaine? I really hate you."

"Very mature, Alana."

"I'll see you and the goldfish killer in court." She jammed her finger on the end button and stopped herself from throwing her phone onto the driveway.

An email popped up on her screen. It was from Lou. "Just to let you know, we may press charges for your violation of the nondisclosure agreement tonight. If I were you, I'd keep my mouth shut. Don't make your case worse."

Great. No job, everyone pissed at her, and she was about to lose her children. No Nate. And she was about to go to jail. She sank onto the porch step in a fresh wave of tears.

The porch light came on. Tabitha's voice floated out into the night. "Alana, is that you?"

Alana rocked back and forth. "Tabbie, not now, please. I can't take a lecture right now. I just got fired, and I'm broke, and Blaine's threatening to take the kids. I don't care if I'm not an environmentalist. I don't even know what being an environmentalist means anymore."

Tabitha emerged from the house and bent down next to Alana. Even in the shadows, Alana could see the heavy swell of her belly. Tabitha Greene was about six months pregnant. Tabitha Greene, who had once claimed that nobody should have children because overpopulation was destroying the earth.

Tabitha placed a soft hand on Alana's shoulder. "Honey, I have no idea what you're talking about, but why don't you come inside and tell me what's going on."

"You're pregnant," Alana said dully.

Tabitha gave a little snort. "Yes, it would seem that I am. And what's worse, it would seem that Jeremy Nichols is the father. My mother is almost apoplectic. That's why they're coming home."

"Jeremy Nichols, the CEO of Island Forest Products? He's a... He's a..." Words failed Alana.

"Rampant capitalist, asshole, and married man?" Tabitha said with a smile. "Yup, he's all that. Unfortunately, he's also wickedly handsome and charming."

Alana rose unsteadily to her feet. "You slept with him?"

"That's usually how pregnancy occurs."

"Oh. Is he..." She trailed off, trying to absorb the earth-shattering nature of this information. Tabitha, the most committed environmentalist in the world, at least as far as Alana was concerned, had slept with someone who was essentially her archenemy. Had Tabitha done it to extract information, to gain the upper hand in some battle over a watershed? These were the only reasons in her mind why Tabitha would possibly do something like this.

Tabitha shook her auburn curls. The pregnancy had darkened the skin of her face, making her freckles and the hollows of her cheeks more defined. "Going to be involved? No. I haven't even told him. Look, I'm exhausted from the drive. Can we go inside and sit on your comfy couches and talk about this and whatever has caused you to be a weeping drunken mess in your own driveway? My parents are arriving tomorrow, and I need to present them with options."

"Options?" Alana apparently had become extremely short of words. Her head had started to throb.

Tabitha looped her arm through Alana's and started steering her toward the house. "I need a place to live, and I want to take at least a year off work. I was hoping I could live here and pay you rent. I don't want to be in Vancouver with a baby, and I don't want to live with my parents. We can share childcare and cooking and stuff. It'll be like a mini hippie commune."

They reached the veranda and Tabitha ushered Alana inside. The single light over the stove was almost blinding, and Alana sank onto one of the living room couches with her eyes closed and let the reality of Tabitha's situation sink in. All the texts Tabitha had sent over the past few weeks had nothing to do with Alana.

"Well, I'm probably going to be living in jail. I'm not sure that's the most hospitable place for a baby, and I'm going to have to sell North Star Farm."

"What?" Tabitha said, setting a glass of water in front of Alana.

Alana told Tabitha about Blaine quitting, her taking Nate's job, the Larry Lund signature debacle, the potential payoff to Stewart, her agreement to purchase Rick's property, the disastrous public meeting, her dismissal, her ill-planned and probably ill-executed speech, Blaine's plan to take the kids, and Lou's email about the nondisclosure agreement.

"He can't go after you on an ND agreement if Mountain Magnesium is doing something illegal," Tabitha announced. "You got screenshots, right?"

"Huh?"

"Of the signatures and anything else relevant."

"No. There *wasn't* anything relevant, or anything much. I have a paper copy of the original claim document. The transfer document is in the files. And there wasn't anything else. The bid process for the processing facility seemed airtight, and there was no evidence of a payment to Stewart. I'm just conjecturing, and maybe the whiskey has made me nuts."

"We need to go look through the files now. Before they lock you out." Tabitha flapped her arms at Alana to move.

Alana stumbled to her office, turned on her laptop, and tried to log in to the Mountain Magnesium site. "Invalid Username" read the return message.

"I'm already locked out," she said.

"Of course you are," Tabitha said, cradling her bump in some sort of yoga pose in the doorway of the office. "Because they're up to no good. You always take screenshots. Nondisclosure agreements are how corporations rule the world. Anyway, they don't have enough evidence to come after you. Let them try. As for Blaine, the man is a first-rate asshole, and I can get you some work through the Rainforest Coalition, if that helps."

"Thanks, Tabbie. But even with you paying me rent, it won't pay enough. I know what the going rate is. I have a huge mortgage, and now if I let Rick's property go, I'm going to be out my deposit." She dropped her forehead into her palm. "I'm so dead, and here I thought all the time that you were coming here to give me a lecture about what an environmental screw-up I am. And now I've screwed *everything* up."

Tabitha drew her eyebrows together. Then she swiveled around the rest of the house, staring first at the egg incubator, then at the rack where the plastic bags Alana had washed out hung drying. She studied the jars of beans on the counter and the seedlings in the bay window seat. "We're all environmental screw-ups, you know," she said. "Even the most hardened of us. To be human is to be a hypocrite in some way when it comes to the environment. It's just that the rest of us don't generally admit it."

A knock at the door reverberated through the house, and Alana let out a low scream. "It's the police. They're here already."

Tabitha went over and peeked through the front door window. "It's Ryan Roberts," she whispered.

Alana contemplated ignoring the knock, but the lights were all on and Ryan pounded on the door again, having likely seen Tabitha pass in front of it. "Be ready to call 911," she said to Tabitha.

Alana walked to the door, put the chain on, and opened it a crack. "Yes?"

"Oh, hi, Alana," Ryan said in a silky tone, as if it was a surprise to see her at her own front door. "I understand you might be in a difficult financial situation. That can happen when people overreach. I might be able to help you out. I'd be happy to offer you the full price that you were going to pay Rick for his property."

Alana squinted at him in the brilliant light of the porch. A tight, unyielding anger bubbled beneath his friendly smile, and goose bumps rose on her arms.

"Of course, since that's way more than I was originally going to buy it for, I'm going to need something from you in return."

"And that would be?" she said.

"I'm so glad you asked. I want your property too. I'll give you five hundred thousand dollars for it."

"But that's less than the assessed value."

"It's more than what you paid, and right now I don't think you can afford to be greedy."

The rigidity of a violent fury gathered in Alana's shoulders and neck. Greedy. *She* was greedy?

"The offer's only good for tonight," Ryan said, "and it drops by five thousand dollars every day you wait."

Alana hesitated. She had been about to slam the door in Ryan's face. But really, what choices did she have? He was offering more than they had paid, and she would walk away with a small profit that she could put into a more affordable townhouse. She could even move to Vancouver. That would make Blaine happy, and maybe he'd give up his stupid custody plans.

"I have the papers right here," Ryan said. "Why don't you just let me in and we can talk about it."

The dangerous smoothness of Ryan's voice made Alana's hair rise. He had wedged his steel-toed brown leather boot into the crack of the door, holding it open.

"I really have to think about it, Ryan. Can you just give me until tomorrow morning at the five-hundred-thousand-dollar price? Please."

Ryan shifted his foot slightly, pushing it farther over the threshold. "Now, Alana. Let's not pretend you're going to be able to get any work in this town after that meeting. I'm helping you out here."

"She said she wanted to think about it, Ryan," Tabitha said loudly from the hallway, the phone in her hand.

Ryan jerked his gaze to Tabitha. "Tabitha Greene, as I live and breathe, with child even. Have you given up your save-the-rainforest crusade to be barefoot and pregnant?"

"Not in the slightest," Tabitha said crisply. "Alana asked for twelve hours to think about your offer, and I think that's reasonable."

"Sure. I have to be on the construction site at five in the morning. Some of us have to work for a living, you know. I can come by at around four in the morning if you'd like to sign then, but it'll be for four ninety-five at that point."

Alana closed her eyes and then nodded. She had to do this.

"Move your foot so I can open the door," she said.

She had reached up to undo the chain lock when a large, beat-up blue truck pulled into the driveway full of goats. Jonah was at the wheel, and a border collie occupied the passenger seat.

Jonah parked the truck and hopped out. He raised an eyebrow at Ryan and then Alana as he approached. "Hey, Alana, sorry it's so late. I just swung a deal with Andrew Webber to buy his goats, and he wanted to have some celebratory beers. You mentioned that you were buying Rick's property, and I was hoping maybe you'd be willing to rent me a portion of it, and the old goat shed. I'll can pay four hundred a month, and I can give you some of the milk. I'll also take you up on that offer to work in the yard more full-time. I plan to open up a goat cheese operation. If you're not keen, it's okay, but I was still wondering if I could keep them here for a few days while I find another place for them."

"Sorry bro, no deal. Alana's selling," Ryan said. "And I don't want goat shit on my property."

Alana stared at Jonah, and then at the truck full of bleating goats, and she felt a small twist of irrational laughter rise in her throat. What on earth was Jonah planning to do with them if she said no? The shift in Jonah's expression in response to Ryan's statement was almost comical, and Alana had a vision of the goats milling around his apartment, chewing on his socks, tea towels, and bedsheets.

She glanced over her shoulder at Tabitha, then back at Jonah and the pathetic North Star Farm sign, and finally at the goats again. They were making a rather beastly racket. Maybe they would be happier in the goat house. Maybe she could learn to love their bleating.

Maybe.

All the resolve she had thrown ineffectually at everything— environmentalism, the bet, her job, keeping the farm, all of it—it now coalesced into one solid thing. She would make a go of this. Somehow. She might be a failed environmentalist by environmentalist standards, but maybe she could be a successful sort of environmentalist by her *own* standards.

She took a deep breath and looked at Jonah. "Don't listen to Ryan. I'm not selling. But I can't pay you much to work in the yard. It would have to be for a share of the farm proceeds. I want to turn North Star Farm into a real farm. Are you good with that?"

Jonah nodded and started to reply, but Ryan cut him off.

"What?" His face had slipped from friendly to enraged. "You'll never make a go of it, and then you'll be *begging* me to buy this dump."

"Well then, you should be able to get it for a good price. But at least I'll have given it a go."

"You little bitch," Ryan said.

"Get off my property or I'll call the police," Alana said. "Now."

"You're making a mistake," Ryan declared, balling his fists, but then he glanced at Jonah and Tabitha and apparently decided there were too many witnesses to anything that he might have been considering doing or saying. He stalked to his pickup, fired up the engine, and tore out of the driveway and across the grass, taking out the North Star Farm sign and sending it flying as he went.

As soon as he rounded the corner, Alana raced across the yard and snatched up the sign. It was in two pieces, but the star Duncan had painted with special glossy gold paint still shone in the moonlight. *Her* farm. *Her* star. She just hoped it was leading her in the right direction.

"Let's get those goats unloaded," she said to Jonah. "Can that dog herd?"

CHAPTER TWENTY-FOUR

Discoveries

At Jonah's direction, Jack the dog leapt out of the truck and started directing the goats with authority, nipping at heels and dashing in circles. However, while he was clearly enthusiastic, he lacked experience. Still, after a few false attempts in which the goats seemed as though they might skitter off into the street or the house, Alana, Jonah, and Jack the dog managed to get them headed toward the back yard. And once the goats were inside the pen, they seemed happier than they had been in the back of the truck, and they settled to explore the decrepit shed and munch on the swales of grass with a low muttering that sounded like a group of grumbling old women.

"It'll hold for the night," Jonah said. "I'll be back in the morning to make improvements to the shed and start working on the fencing and a new pen, if you're good with the arrangement. If you can afford to stay here, I mean. I heard about what happened at the meeting."

Alana wondered how much of a fool she had made of herself in the version that Jonah had heard. "I'm good with the arrangement," she said slowly. She had to be good with it. She had just basically told Ryan to get lost. "I just need a couple more pieces to fall into place."

She didn't mention that they were somewhat big pieces.

They had arrived back at the front of the house, and Tabitha poked her head out. "Just wanted to let you know that I think your eggs are hatching."

"The eggs are hatching?" Alana repeated dumbly, then more excitedly. "The eggs are hatching! I have to get Duncan. I promised he could watch. It's his school project."

She ran back into the house and checked the eggs. Sure enough, all of them had pips, and one little chick was industriously trying to peck its way out of the first egg while another was expanding its pip. She dialed Blaine's number. If she had thought Blaine was pissed before, it wasn't even close to the degree of pissedness that he expressed at the prospect of waking Duncan up and driving him over.

"No way," Blaine said. "He's asleep."

"But he's documenting the hatching for school. If you don't wake him up, he'll miss it. This is really important. I promised."

"It's the middle of the night. Won't a few wait until morning?"

"It's quarter to ten. They all have pips and one has a zip. It could be all over by morning," Alana said. "Tabitha will drive me over," she added, glancing at Tabitha, who looked up from the incubator and nodded. "Duncan will never forgive us if he misses this. It's really important for him to experience this."

"Great, are you going to be a farm animal dementor too?" Blaine said in a sulky tone.

"Just get him up and dressed. We'll be there in seven minutes." She hung up and looked at Jonah. "Can you look after the chicks for a few minutes? Take pictures of anything exciting. We'll be right back."

In the Prius, Tabitha glanced over at Alana. "So is Jonah your boyfriend? He's very cute."

Alana turned in surprise. She had been looking out the cool, dark glass thinking about Nate. About how he had said he wanted chickens. About what a liar he had turned out to be. "No. Jonah is way too young for me," she said.

Tabitha snorted. "Oh Alana, you've always had such crazy ideas."

They collected a sleepy Duncan from a grumpy Blaine and hurried back through the empty streets to the house in time to see Nate pull into the driveway on his Vespa.

"Sorry to be here so late," he said, "but I did a drive-by and all the lights were on." He reached up to remove his helmet, exposing a glimpse of finely cut abs. His hair was twisted into spiky tufts.

"We're just going to watch chickens hatch," Alana said, marveling at the fact that every fiber of her body could want a man who was a liar. Electricity seemed to arc through the air between her and Nate, even though she hated him so much she wanted to sob in fury. Nate hadn't taken his eyes from her, even though Tabitha and Duncan milled around her, and he seemed to be pleading with her in that same way he had at the trailhead.

"How about I take Duncan in to see the chicks," Tabitha said brightly. She thrust out a hand to Duncan. "Come on, Duncan, Auntie Tabbie will take you in. How many chicks do you think are hatched now? Do you want to make bets?"

Duncan extended his arm without hesitation, and Tabitha bent to hear his response as they strolled into the house.

"What are you doing here?" Alana said.

"I've just come from the police station," Nate replied.

"What? You're coming to tell me in person that Mountain Magnesium is pressing charges? Thanks a lot."

Nate's brow furrowed and he raked a hand through his hair. "I thought you'd like to know."

"What, so I can skip town? So you can rub it in? I didn't *do* anything. Nobody heard me say Larry's or Stewart's names. You and your dad are the criminals," she shot back.

Nate started to approach with his arms extended, but then thought better of it. "Alana, I was at the police station giving evidence against the board of directors, including my dad. I was wearing a wire during the meeting."

She had been about to start into a new tirade and almost missed the implications of Nate's statement. "You turned your own dad in?"

Nate's face turned rueful. "Unsuccessfully, at least for now. If I thought I was the black sheep of the family before, I sure will be when this is over."

Alana shook her head, trying to process what Nate was saying. The goats, apparently perturbed by something, let out a chorus of bleats. Nate placed his helmet on the scooter and came to stand closer, careful to remain a safe distance away, his hands thrust deep in his jeans pockets. "I was trying to collect evidence tonight. To get my dad to admit what was going on. That's why I was wearing the wire. The police set it up. That's why I had to get you out of that meeting and convince my dad that I was on his side. Maude and I found Larry trashed out in a disgusting hotel in Kelowna, and he told us how some men approached him on his Mur Marsh claim and asked him to sell it, or they'd report him for squatting, which is illegal. When he refused, they gave him a wad of cash for some of his other claims that he *was* willing to sell, and they dropped him off in Kelowna. I guess they were hoping he'd fall back into his old ways, which he did. But his story is pretty sketchy. He has no idea who the men were, and I didn't get anything from my dad tonight. So either he doesn't know, or he's not talking."

"You were in Kelowna with Maude? What about Fiona?" The words felt impossibly bitter in her mouth.

"Fiona was there for an event. I was just talking to her in a bar. One of her friends recognized me and snapped the photo and then posted it on Facebook. I let them, because I figured it would help throw my dad off the scent as to what I was doing there. I was only at the bar for half an hour. Then I had to hook up with some of my less savory friends in Kelowna in order to find Larry."

"What event? The environmental consultant world domination tour?"

"Actually, she was there for a ballroom dancing competition. She's really into it."

Alana shook her head and looked away, focusing her gaze on the North Star Farm sign, now broken in two. Star Farm. Maybe the farm needed a new name. Black Sheep Farm. Black Star Farm. She ran through the options to avoid looking at Nate.

"Fiona and I are just friends, Alana. She's engaged to Greg Wilson. He was right next to us in the photo. You could even see his arm. They're dance partners. Didn't you see them together at the open house?"

Alana jerked her head up to see Nate standing really close to her now. Her forever-traitorous heart leapt in a giddy spiral. She wasn't going to forgive Nate for the way he had treated her, although she had to admit this was the happiest she'd ever been to hear Greg Wilson's name... and Fiona's for that matter. Ballroom dancing. She couldn't believe it. Still, she managed to keep her lips turned in a scowl. She hadn't seen Greg Wilson at the open house. She didn't even know what Greg Wilson looked like.

Nate tipped his head down so he could look up into her eyes. "I quit because I'd put two and two together about Stewart and Thad, and I got a tip from Zander that some of the board members had been in to see Stewart on their own. Stewart assumed that because Lou is my dad, I was in on it, so he said a bunch of things in that meeting after you left that twigged me that there was something going on. Then I ran into Maude that night outside my dad's, and she asked me if I knew that Larry had left town and nobody knew where he was and that it looked really suspicious. But I didn't have proof until I found Larry." Nate lifted the corners of his lips in a grim sort of smile. "I was afraid to tell you anything until I knew for sure, because it's my dad, and I really didn't want to think he was a criminal, although honestly I still don't know how much he knows about what was going on. I'm still hoping he didn't know much and that he was doing this because he genuinely thought Silver Peak needed the mine. And I didn't want you to be involved. That's why I laid you off in the first place and told you not to take the job. I'm really sorry if it seemed like I jerked you around. I didn't want you to be put in a position where you'd have to get involved. I was panicking. I probably didn't handle it the right way. "

He had tentatively placed his hand on her forearm, and although she stiffened a bit, she didn't move away. "Please don't keep looking at me that way, Alana. I considered telling you, and maybe I should have, but after you took the job, I was afraid if you knew you'd try to handle it all yourself or blow your own nondisclosure agreement, and then I'd turn out to be wrong, or I wouldn't be able to find Larry. For a while there, I was worried they'd had him taken care of."

"Where did Larry go tonight? Why didn't Maude just tell everyone at the meeting?"

Nate plunged his hands back into his pockets and rocked back on his heels. "We were hoping that bringing Larry to the meeting would scare my dad and get him talking. I emailed Len earlier and told him Maude was planning something, and that if she showed up, it was his job to get Larry out of there, which he did, thinking he was helping. Unfortunately, since my dad didn't talk, the case is still pretty weak. Larry isn't a very reliable witness. As for the Stewart situation, Thad's company won the bid fair and square. It was the best bid. I reviewed the file over and over again. It was almost like they had seen the other bids before submitting theirs. But we can't prove anything, and maybe there isn't anything there." He raised his eyes to hers. "The thing I really don't get is why they would pay Stewart off. Stewart just doesn't have that much influence. Even if the city decided not to support the mine, who cares? It's ultimately up to the province. So it just doesn't make sense." His face had taken on a pleading quality again.

Alana relented and nodded. It was a tiny gesture of forgiveness, a signal more to herself than to him. "I definitely don't think Larry signed the transfer papers," she said slowly.

Nate cocked his head. "How do you know that? He says can't remember, which is a problem. But the bigger problem is that the original claim files are missing from the Ministry files, so it's like Larry never filed those claims in the first place, which means he doesn't own them even if the transfer *was* bogus. And unfortunately, like I said, Larry's made so many claims over the years with incorrect coordinates that his paper trail is a nightmare, and they've started to consider him a nuisance. As a result, they might not be as diligent about filing things, or maybe someone on the board has someone on the inside. I don't know. But right now it means there's no case."

"I FOIed the original claim files back when I was going to oppose the mine," Alana said. "I have paper copies."

"Really?"

"Really."

"That's awesome," Nate exclaimed, throwing his arms around her waist, lifting her up, and swinging her around, their bodies pressed together for an exhilarating few seconds. Alana wondered if the grin on her own face looked as stupid and happy as the one on Nate's. She needed to get a grip. His smile was probably related to the fact that she had copies of the claim documents, not because he wanted to move in with her and help her tend goats.

But the curve of his lip when he set her down suggested that maybe it was more than the documents, and there was a brief moment in which it seemed like he planned to kiss her—but Alana stepped back a bit, trying to organize her racing thoughts. She liked Nate, but he was so inherently risky.

"That's so great," Nate repeated. "Can I see the claim documents?"

Alana hesitated, then nodded. "Sure. Come on in. There's a bit of a hatching event going on right now. Tell me... that short, kind of balding guy standing next to Fiona. That wasn't Greg, was it?"

"Sounds like him," Nate said.

Alana felt a tiny smile creep over her face in the darkness. At least he wasn't Adonis. He was probably a very nice person, and evidently he could ballroom dance.

Duncan, Tabitha, and Jonah had formed a semicircle around the incubator, and the kitchen smelled of fresh cocoa. Duncan had the camera clenched in his hands, and Alana had no doubt there would be over a thousand second-by-second photos of the event to be sorted later.

"Mom!" Duncan yelled. "They're zipping. Three have already gone. We can see feathers." He hopped from one little foot to the other as he spoke.

Alana leaned over Duncan to see flashes of the two little chicks industriously trying to work their way out of the eggs. She placed a kiss on top of Duncan's warm head. "Very exciting," she murmured. "Have you named them yet?"

"Jonah suggested Hen Solo and Chewy for these two. But I'm thinking of calling these ones SpongeBob and Patrick," Duncan announced.

"That sounds perfect," Alana said. Suddenly, even though everything was decidedly not perfect, it seemed more perfect.

"Nate and I have to go check some documents in my office. Are you okay here?" she said to Tabitha.

"We're great," Tabitha drawled in her low growl as she narrowed her eyes at Nate. "Do you need help?"

Nate extended his hand. "Nate Steeves, and unless I'm mistaken, you're Tabitha Greene. I've seen you on the news with the Rainforest Coalition."

"That's me. Saver of trees everywhere," Tabitha said, offering her own hand more reluctantly.

Alana pulled Tabitha and Nate away from the incubator and into the kitchen. "Nate is trying to build a case against the board of Mountain Magnesium," she murmured in a low tone.

Tabitha arched an eyebrow and turned to Nate. "Well, that shouldn't be too hard. They're a bunch of crooks, your dad excepted... maybe."

"You know our board members?" Nate said.

Tabitha made a hmph-ing noise. "Not personally. But the business community in Vancouver isn't that large. You get to know the big players, and the players who play dirty, or maybe just a bit dusty, which is a lot of them, coloring outside the lines a bit, believing they're working for the greater good, while also taking the opportunity to ensure their own financial security. Yeah, I know them."

"Go, Patrick!" Duncan yelled from the living room.

"You know Jim Price and Lawrence Sutherland are on the board for Dynasty Metals, which owns the Condor mine up north, right?" Tabitha continued.

Alana shook her head. She knew from the open house that Price and Sutherland were connected to the Condor mine disaster, but she hadn't known they were that closely connected. The Condor mine tailing pond rupture last summer had spilled tons of waste into nearby waterways, killing thousands of fish, contaminating drinking water, and destroying shorelines. "There was no mention of their involvement in the press," she said.

Tabitha toyed with the turtle-shaped hematite necklace she wore around her neck. "With all the massive parent companies and subsidiaries in mining, it's hard to know who has their fingers in what. That's how these guys keep their reputations clean. Anyway, I was surprised when they wanted to get involved in something the size of Mountain Magnesium. It's not their usual gig. The money just isn't there. My gut, as expansive and lively as it is now," she said, gesturing at her rounded belly, "says there's something else going on."

"Why do you think Mountain Magnesium would want to give the Silver Peak city administrator a payoff?" Alana said. "Or at least choose his son's company to build the processing facility. It seems like too much of a coincidence."

Tabitha shook her head. "All I can say is that because our legal system is pretty good at preventing the outright bribes that run rampant in the mining industry in other countries, the Canadian mining industry runs a lot on quiet little exchanges. My question would be, given that Stewart doesn't have a lot of say in whether the mine is approved or not, what *does* he have to offer that's worth a lot of money?"

Alana looked at Nate.

"Contracts," Alana said. "He has infrastructure contracts."

"I can't believe it," Alana said half an hour later as she stared at the screen of her laptop over the chick-related cheers in the living room. She and Nate huddled at her desk, their legs touching, and the current between them was almost electrifying.

DKP Construction, the general contractor for the Silver Peak main street upgrade and new reservoir construction, stood for Davis, Knight, and Price Construction. Evan Price, one of the principals, had owned a building company with Jim Price ten years prior. "A contract for a contract," Nate said. "It makes sense. I bet they're brothers."

"And it was right under our noses the whole time. That's why Stewart has been so crazy about the new reservoir. It was part of the deal."

Nate shook his head. "I just hope it's enough for the police, and I seriously hope my dad didn't know."

Alana thought of Ramona's article on DKP Construction. "I guess we should start reading the *Silver Peak Scoop* more often."

Nate crinkled his face. "What?"

"Ramona wrote an article about how ridiculous it was for a Vancouver company to get the contract, even if they were slightly cheaper, because given their travel and housing costs they would actually spend fewer hours working on the job than a local company. There's usually some little grain of truth in Ramona's articles. Not the one about you, of course," she added hastily, touching his thigh.

Nate snorted, but then he regarded her with his intense stare, his lower lip thrust out in a dangerous and sexy way. "Oh, no, there was a little bit of truth in that one too."

Alana decided not to ask which bits were true. "Do you think Len and Curtis knew about all the backroom deals?" She thought of Len's loopy handwriting and the signature on the transfer papers.

Nate sighed. "Based on the fact that Len and Curtis drove Larry to Kelowna, the police think Len might have signed the papers. They're bringing him in tomorrow. I don't know. I really like Len."

Alana looked at the transfer papers, which she and Nate had printed from the Mountain Magnesium files using Nate's still-functioning password. "The L's in Larry's name on the transfer papers are really nicely done. I don't know about you, but my handwriting, particularly of capital letters that I don't often write, tends to be pretty messed up. These look like the writing of someone who's used to writing capital L's, like... Len. And when I confronted Len about it earlier, he acted pretty suspiciously. If he didn't sign it, I think he at least knew about it." She felt bad saying it. She liked Len too. That was how these guys probably got away with this kind of thing. Maybe they were, for the most part, genuinely nice guys.

"Or maybe it wasn't Len," Nate said, reaching for the mouse and flipping to one of the Dynasty Metals annual reports that they had looked through for connections. "Maybe it was... Lawrence Sutherland!" He triumphantly displayed Lawrence's looping signature on the screen.

Alana nodded. Maybe. She didn't point out that Lou's name also started with an L, and that Lou's actions at the open house had been pretty questionable. It would be better not to be falling in love with the son of an environmental criminal. It would probably count for significant demerits in her and Blaine's bet.

"I guess we have to let the police sort that out," she said.

"At least we have something to give them now." Nate hit print on the page with Lawrence's signature.

Was it enough though? White-collar crime was probably really challenging to prove. As far as she knew, the province could be run by white-collar criminals. She shuffled through the stack of Larry's claims that had come in the mail. "Larry sure had a lot of claims in the area. Most of the rest of them are on Booker Mountain."

"He's pretty messed up. He was barely coherent on the way back from Kelowna. I feel sorry for him. I'm assuming drugs, but…"

"He told me once outside the grocery store—I used to stop and talk to him sometimes—that he had found uranium. I didn't believe him, but maybe it's true. Do you think that might have caused some dementia?" Alana stopped at the look on Nate's face. "What?"

Nate had launched into an upright position in his chair, his finger curved against his lip. "We found a Geiger counter and some radioactive core samples at the mine site that day when we went up there. I'd almost forgotten about it. You wondered why I was so freaked out that day. I didn't want to say anything because that was when I was beginning to wonder what was going on. I was worried they were from the site, but I had Len and Curtis test the samples, and they're not the right rock substrate at all. So I assumed Larry had packed them in from somewhere else."

"But…" Alana said, and paused. "Are you thinking they're from Larry's claims on Booker?" Before Nate could answer, she snatched up her phone and started paging through the phone book.

"Charlie," she said when he picked up on the other end. "It's Alana!"

"I have call display, Alana, and you're just lucky I watch Jimmy Kimmel."

"The report on the watershed reserves. The one that resulted in the decision to go with Mur Creek. Why? What was wrong with the water on Booker?"

"Funny you should ask that. Zander spent a week in the file room trying to dig that report up before he got fired. Never found it as far as I know, and I've only heard rumors of the report. Never saw it. Most of the officials that were around then, that would have read it, are dead and gone, or they suffer somewhat in the marble department. In the world of reports, something written in the 1950s might as well be buried under a pyramid. We don't even consult things from the '90s."

"There's nobody who knows what was in that report?"

Charlie went silent, and she could hear Jimmy Kimmel talking in the background, as well as choruses of egg exclamations from her own living room. "I think there was a committee of citizens," Charlie said. "They liked to have committees in those days. Old Man Wyatt apparently chaired it. He's dead, of course, but I heard he was a hoarder. It's a long shot, but the report might still be rattling around in that old house of his."

Old Man Wyatt. Rick's dad.

"Thanks, Charlie. You're the best."

"Yeah, well, you won't thank me when you're up to your elbows in rat droppings and musty old paper."

"We have to go to my neighbor's house," Alana exclaimed to Nate, who had just returned from an egg check.

Nate flicked his eyes to his watch. "It is getting a little late to show up unannounced, isn't it?"

"I have a standing offer for beers."

Nate drove the Vespa through the cool night air over to Rick's. Lights still shone from Rick's windows, and the TV cast moving blue waves and shadows on the living room wall. Rick answered the door shirtless, his chest almost breathtakingly hairy.

"We need to look through any old files your dad might have had related to any work that he did with the city," Alana said without preamble.

"Oh, hi, Rick, it's nice to see you," Rick said, mimicking Alana's voice. "I thought it was finally time I paid you a visit, being the friendly neighbor that I am. And I brought you a case of beer to make up for the fact that you can't buy that piece of property at the lake anymore."

"Please, Rick."

"That planner guy was here last week. I told him no. What's going on? There a run on old documents on eBay or something?"

"We're trying to prove that Stewart accepted a payout. That's how he could afford his property at the lake," Alana said.

Rick paused for a second, then flung the door open wide. "Well in that case, come on in. No way I'm going to let some civil servant bastard have a lakefront property when I can't."

Rick led them through the house chattering about the evils of civil servants, who apparently didn't work and couldn't be fired, and then started to wax poetic about the managers of civil servants, who were apparently the worst of the lot.

"I won't even start in about corporate managers," Rick said with a chortle, thrusting an elbow in Nate's direction.

The house seemed frozen in the late seventies, with brown, green, and yellow tones, and dark wood finishes throughout. Discolored wallpaper peeled off walls, and a green shag carpet covered the living room floor. A row of Budweiser beer cans lined the marbled Arborite countertop.

At the top of a set of old wooden stairs, Rick flung open a door in a narrow hallway and flagged them in. "My dad's office. I think this is where I say good luck."

Alana stepped over the threshold. The dusty, stale-smelling room was filled from wall to wall with bankers boxes.

"I was planning to have a big bonfire," Rick said.

Alana glanced at her phone. It was already after eleven. She had to get Duncan to bed.

"I'll go through them. I'm used to staying up all night," Nate said. "You go home and go to bed." He turned to Rick. "Did your dad have any sort of filing system? Like by year, or theme?"

"Yeah, he had a system," Rick said. "It's called 'in a box.' Is finding this, whatever it is, going to help me get my lakeside cottage at the Pines? Are you going to give Alana her job back?"

Nate raised his eyebrow at Alana. "A cottage at the Pines, you say? How about I give you my word of honor, Rick, that if you help me, we'll find a way for you to get your lakeside cottage."

"I'll brew the coffee," Rick said. "What are we looking for?"

CHAPTER TWENTY-SIX

Claims

"I still can't believe it was in the *last* box," Nate said, yawning. "And just so you know, in case you're in the market for another roomie, that Rick guy snores and farts like a bastard."

His eyes were bloodshot, like he'd been playing in the bar all night, but he still manage to look gorgeous as they made their way across her property in the tentative mid-morning sun after feeding and milking the goats—an activity in which Nate had participated enthusiastically. Could she possibly date a man who was so beautifully perfect?

It had rained all night, and fog still shrouded the mountaintops and hung in the dips in the fields. The melody of birdsong surrounded them, and the air seemed sweet, fresh, and true. Nate had already been to the police station to deliver the report, which he had unearthed that morning at three, and had indicated that the water on Booker was considered undrinkable due to low levels of radioactivity resulting from uranium deposits in the area.

"The police signature experts are liking Lawrence as the signer of the transfer papers," Nate continued. "They're bringing in Stewart, Jim, Lawrence, and the rest of the board for interviews today, and my dad of course. I just can't believe Stewart would allow a reservoir to be built in an area that he knew had uranium contamination. He's a complete crook."

Alana set the bucket of goat milk on the porch. "Knowing Stewart, he probably figured the report was out of date and potentially wrong. Or he knew they would test the water before allowing it into people's houses, but by then the reservoir would have been built and Stewart long gone to his lakefront property. So no harm, no foul, as far as Stewart's concerned. Speaking of which, I can't believe you promised Rick a cottage at the Pines. What if I have to renege on my deal to buy his property?" Alana said, giving Nate a gentle punch on the shoulder.

Nate chuckled. "Oh, that was a no-brainer. First of all, I have tremendous faith that you, Alana Matheson, are a survivor and will find a way to buy Rick's property no matter what. And second of all, I own a tiny little cottage at the Pines that I never use. I was going to just hand it over to Rick."

"You were going to just *give* him a cottage?"

"The cottages at Pines are mostly shacks, and I was hoping you'd come through with the purchase, which I'm still confident you will. Which means you can potentially be neighbors with Rick at the lake in the future."

"What? What do you mean?"

"I mean when you marry me, someday in the future, my cottage will be your cottage. But we should go on a date first."

Alana's heart did a flip. Nate had delivered this with a wink. He was probably joking.

Alana tried to concentrate, which was challenging given how close Nate was standing to her. "Speaking of cottages, or lakefront properties, I was thinking: Do you think someone actually gave Stewart cash in addition to his son getting the contract? The street renewal and reservoir contracts were definitely worth more than the processing facility contract."

Nate shook his head. "I don't know. I combed the Mountain Magnesium books, and I couldn't find anything. I don't think this is the first time Stewart has done something like this. He probably built up his nest egg a little at a time in municipalities across the province. Maybe the police will chase that down. But if all municipalities do as good a job with filing as Silver Peak, we're hooped."

"Maude called," Alana said. "Believe it or not, she and Larry are talking about setting up an even smaller community-owned mine on the site."

"That's awesome. So maybe this will end well for everyone. Well, almost everyone. I suspect I may have to look for a new family. The police are going to want to talk to you, and to Len and Curtis. I'm not sure how much they knew. But that'll be part of the investigation. I made it clear to them that you knew nothing."

Nothing.

Had she known nothing? She had known some things, or suspected them. Had she ignored them in favor of a paycheck? *Everyone is an environmental screw-up*, Tabitha had said. But where was the boundary between environmental screw-up and environmental criminal?

Jonah had just pulled into the driveway to start refurbishing the goat shed, Tabitha had gone to retrieve her parents from the airport, and Alana had a bottle drive to get to. Duncan hadn't moved away from the brooder since waking up that morning. Katie had joined him in the watch, her reddish-blond curls in a violent tumble of tangles, after Blaine had dropped her off at an alarmingly early hour so she wouldn't wake Heather, who required her beauty sleep. He had indicated he was reconsidering his custody demands, and he would need to find a place in Vancouver in a good neighborhood that could accommodate kids first, which might take a while, apparently.

Alana's eyes fell on the farm sign that Ryan had broken the night before. Tabbie's and Jonah's rent would just about cover her extra mortgage payment, provided she got another one of her regular-paying consulting jobs soon or took Tabitha up on the offer of working for the Rainforest Coalition. She just needed one more piece.

Nate dropped his fingers to her hands and entwined them in his own. "I should head over to Leo's and tell him what's going on. My dad might be more receptive to being bailed out by his preferred and less traitorous son. Listen, I like you, Alana. A lot. I really want to see you, if you'll have me, now, or when this all blows over. I'm not leaving town. I've given my buddy notice on the condo, so I have to move into the motorhome this week. I just need to find a place to set up and then I'm going to do local music gigs. And maybe I'll find another business to set up. Maybe Maude will hire me for her mine. Probably at a substantially reduced rate." Nate gave a wry chuckle. "But whatever happens, please tell me you'll have dinner with me, for real."

Alana took a deep breath and risked looking up into his stunning aquamarine eyes. "I'm not sure how much rent you were thinking of paying to park your motorhome someplace," she said, "but I just happen to have a piece of land available. Provided you like goats... and babies."

Nate drew back a bit, but he didn't release her hands. "Babies? Just to be clear, I'm not opposed to babies." He offered her a careful smile. "But I've never been asked about them so soon."

"Not *my* baby, silly. Tabitha is moving in with me."

Nate cracked his roguish smile and pulled her body closer to his own. "In that case, I can definitely live with goats and babies," he said. "I'll even goat and babysit. Do you think they like piano music?"

Alana took a deep breath. "We'd all like piano music. But just remember, I'm asking if you want to rent a spot on my property, not asking you to move in. And yes, I'll go on a couple dates with you. But we need to take it slow. I have a farm to set up and kids to think of, and I've never dated a musician before. I need to make sure you're not too out there for me, and you should probably make sure that I'm not too much of an environmental dementor for you."

"I think I can live with all that," he murmured. "And for the record, you're absolutely hot when you're environmental."

His lips had dipped precariously close to hers, and she lifted her face to meet them, laughing at the same time. Nate's kiss was thrilling and exquisite, and she felt the weight of Mountain Magnesium and being an environmentalist—ironically, being both *not enough* of an environmentalist, and being *too much* of an environmentalist—lift off of her. She was free to be the change. Or try to be the change. Or fail at being the change. It didn't matter.

Nate's fingers tangled in her hair, and the curve of her body fit into his as he explored her mouth with his tongue. After a few minutes he dropped his lips to her neck, and she let her own rest on his jaw, her heart thundering and her breath a bit ragged.

"And I have a spot for that Steinway if you get to keep it," she murmured.

"The Steinway," Nate said slowly as if almost in a trance.

"You know, the one in your office," she said.

Nate didn't respond for a few seconds, and she could feel his breaths. Then he nipped her ear lightly and placed another kiss on her lips. "Alana, you are not only gorgeous, but a genius. I think I've just figured out how they paid Stewart," he said.

CHAPTER TWENTY-SEVEN

Measurement

Duncan was still riding high on his smash hit presentation at school, complete with three fluffy baby chicks on display. Apparently Patrick and Squidward performed for the class, while SpongeBob had a crisis of confidence and remained in his little house for the entire afternoon. Charlie, and Zander, who was less disgraced now that Stewart had been arrested, had put in a good word for Alana at City Hall, and she was now the part-time city planner. They were also supporting her application to the Canadian Institute of Planners to get her C.I.P. based on relevant experience. C.I.P. Now she would have initials to put behind her name. And maybe H.T.B.H. Hoping to be happy.

The police had arrested Stewart, Jim, and Lawrence, and other arrests were pending, depending on the outcome of the investigation. Nate was convinced that Jim and Lawrence had used the Steinway as a cover for their payment to Stewart. They bought a damaged piano from a dealer who was willing to give them a receipt for more than they paid for it. The extra cash went to Stewart. Jim then filed an insurance claim for the damage, claiming the movers had done it, and split the payout with the Steinway dealer. That was Nate's theory, anyway. The police were still working on it. But they were satisfied that Alana had known nothing. Or not enough. N.S.F. Or in this case, non-sufficient knowledge. N.S.K.

Now Blaine stood in the driveway, the Miata overflowing with boxes and suitcases. He had come to say goodbye, but the kids had lost interest early and were off trying to help Jonah with power tools. Jonah was on Rick's old property, setting postholes for the fence, while the goats frolicked in the back of Alana's yard, eating pretty much everything, and Tabitha made muffins in the kitchen.

"Heather wasn't aware that kids got up at seven, even on weekends," he said. "Or that five-year-olds don't occupy themselves, and they like to ruin lipstick. I was overreacting when I said I wanted custody. It would never work out. I just miss them so damn much."

"Well I guess you shouldn't have left, then," Alana said.

Blaine looked at his feet. "You're right." He lifted his baby blue eyes to hers. "But I don't think we were right for each other anyway. I would have always held you back from the life you wanted. I have no interest in farming, chickens, or goats whatsoever. Even looking at those goats gives me the heebies. I think they're possessed."

"Possessed?"

"Seriously. Look at the eyes. There's a reason they chose the goat to represent the devil. Anyway, any idea why Katie would write G.F.K. in red lipstick on Heather's mirror? Is that a friend at school or something?"

Alana's guffaw threatened to bubble out of her, but she managed to tighten her features into a straight—or straight-ish—face. "I have no idea."

"So I take it we're done with the bet? I'm moving to Vancouver, and you got goats and chickens."

"Looks like we both just did what we wanted anyway."

"And I was hoping that my new super environmentally friendly company would clinch my win," Blaine said.

"It couldn't hold a candle to my amazingly ecological farm."

"Care to put a wager on that?"

The rumble of a large vehicle emerged from down the street. A sleek bus-style Winnebago came into sight and pulled into the drive. The deal had closed on Rick's property that morning, and Nate was planning to begin his rental of the parking spot immediately.

A pained look passed over Blaine's face. He had never been much of one for recreational vehicles, but he didn't seem to be excessively fond of Nate either.

Nate leapt out in grimy work jeans and a plaid shirt, waved hello politely, and headed over to Jonah to get to work. Someone must have said something funny, because Duncan's shrill laughter carried in their direction.

A new sign now occupied the gate. It consisted of four pieces—two new sections hand-carved by Nate, and the star that Alana and Duncan had painted four years ago.

Hope Star Black Goat Farm.

A piece for each of them. Tabitha had chosen hope, Alana kept star, Nate had gone with black, and Jonah, thinking they all were being a bit too flaky, had gone with the more practical goat.

How did one measure the "environmentalness" of one's actions? Alana's comments regarding the city sustainability plan that night at the council meeting hadn't been wrong. Almost every action had environmental and sustainability pros and cons, and who knew which ones were the right ones and which ones were worth more in the challenge to move toward sustainability? She didn't. That was why they had needed an independent arbiter for the bet, and why she had always been so convinced that she was a failure.

But maybe she wasn't.

She smiled at her ex-husband. She would actually miss him. But probably not Heather. "No deal, Blaine. No more rat holes for me. I'm just going to go with being a good-enough environmentalist this time... and hope for the best."

ABOUT THE AUTHOR

Jennifer Ellis writes contemporary literary and action-adventure fiction for both adults and children and tries not to fall into too many environmental rat holes. She lives in a small ski town in Canada with her husband and two boys, where she skis, joins too many book clubs, and works as an environmental researcher. She blogs randomly but regularly at www.jenniferellis.ca and can be found on Twitter occasionally at @jenniferlellis.

A NOTE TO READERS

In this brave new world of writing, readers have a lot of influence over what succeeds and what does not. The most helpful thing you can do for a writer is leave a review and get the word out. A single review carries a lot of weight, so please, if you enjoyed this story and want to read more, go and provide your thoughts on Amazon.com, or Goodreads, or wherever you like to talk about books. I will be ever so grateful.

ALSO BY JENNIFER ELLIS

Derivatives of Displacement Series for kids and adults
A Pair of Docks
A Quill Ladder

Adult Fiction
In the Shadows of the Mosquito Constellation

Novellas in Anthologies
"The River" (published in *Synchronic: 13 Tales of Time Travel*)
"Resistance" (published in *Tales from Pennsylvania*)
"Manufacturing Elvis" (published in *Tales of Tinfoil: Stories of Paranoia and Conspiracy*)

ACKNOWLEDGEMENTS

Writing requires a unique blend of solitude and connection. I spend countless hours alone at my desk with my cat, and it often seems like a lone endeavor, but there are many other people who are part of the process.

My professional team is a dream to work with. David Gatewood, my editor, and Andrew Brown, my cover designer, consistently deliver superior work. It is marvelous to know that I can always rely on them. My writer friends, both near and far, are a never-ending source of support, and I have Chris Pourteau, Michael Bunker, Nick Cole, Hank Garner, Kristene Perron, Rosa Jordan, Jane Theriault, Yolanda Ridge, and many others to thank for their ongoing encouragement and advice. My family consistently sacrifices in order for me to be a writer, and their support and unfailing (well, mostly unfailing) commitment to helping me make my writing a priority is much appreciated.

I also owe all the environmentalists, non-environmentalists, and those in between, with whom I have worked with over the years. Thank you for sharing your perspectives, giving me food for thought. I started this book when I had very young children and was working as a coordinator for a board similar to the Regional Environmental Board (although there were no noodlers and everyone on the board was very nice), and I was very much caught up in a maelstrom of how to do right by the environment in a practical sense—such as walking, growing my own food, hanging my laundry, and recycling—when it seemed that every day the craziness of my job and life required me to do the opposite. Having worked in the environmental field for a long time, I am sometimes struck by how the unwillingness of both sides to recognize the perspectives of others, the complexity of the situation, or their own hypocrisy, can inflame conflicts and prevent us from finding truly sustainable solutions. Add in the very natural desire most of us have to live a comfortable, fun-filled life, and sometimes it seems like we will never win the battle to save the environment. *Confessions of a Failed Environmentalist* was an attempt to poke fun at all the situations, compromises, and emotions that come with trying to live in an environmentally conscious way, while recognizing that many of us fail to live up to our ideals, or the ideals of others. At the same time, it's a call to action, and hopefully a fun story that will make everyone think about the environment and our own place in it. I am a great admirer of those who do manage to live sustainably and hope that you can help all of us to find our way to make different choices as well.

www.ingramcontent.com/pod-product-compliance
Lightning Source LLC
Chambersburg PA
CBHW020555180626
46810CB00007B/2508